YOU'RE

KEISHA ERVIN

COLOR ME PYNK PUBLICATION

D1451032

COLOR ME PYNK PUBLICATIONS

Color Me Pynk Publications is accepting manuscripts from aspiring or experienced fiction, romance, interracial, urban, black woman/white man, alpha male, erotic, supernatural and fantasy authors. The review process can take up to three weeks. We will contact you once a decision has been reached. NO PREVIOUSLY PUBLISHED MANUSCRIPTS WILL BE ACCEPTED.

WHAT WILL SET YOU APART FROM THE REST:

The ultimate alpha male. He's drool worthy, confident, arrogant, strong, great in bed, complicated and flawed. He messes up but is willing to change to better his life and his woman's.

Female leads that are sassy, sweet, loving, ambitious, funny yet beautifully imperfect. She puts up with drama to a certain extent but learns to stick up for herself and what she believes in.

A story that is dramatic, shocking, action packed, sexy, hilarious, romantic and tear jerking.

If you'd like to join the Color Me Pynk fam, dare to be different! There is no story that hasn't already been written so make it fresh and new by adding a new twist to it. We want stories that our readers will read twenty years from now. To be considered please email the first five chapters of your manuscript, synopsis and contact information to colormepynksubmission@gmail.com

Follow us:

IG: ColorMePynkPublications/https://www. instagram.com/colormepynkpublications/

YOU'RE PLAYLIST

Marvin Gaye "Just To Keep You Satisfied"
Karen Clark Sheard "The Will of God"
James Blake "Choose Me"
Jaime Woods "I Got You"
Alex Isley, Jack Dine "Colors"
Syleena Johnson feat Common "Bulls-Eye, (Suddenly)"
Iyla "Juice"
Brandy "Broken Hearted"
Billie Eilish "Hostage"
Meek Mills "Lord Knows"
Beyoncé "Rather Die Young"
Slum Village "Fall In Love"
Nipsey Hussle "Young Nigga"
Summer Walker, Jhene Aiko "I'll Kill You"
Justin Timberlake "Mirrors"
Alex Isley, Jack Dine "Gone"
Tink "Treat Me Like Somebody"
Billie Eilish "Everything I Wanted"
Coldplay "The Scientist"
The Pussycat Dolls "Buttons"
Stevie Wonder "I Never Dream You'd Leave In Summer"
Musiq Soulchild feat Kindred The Family Soul & Cee Lo Green

"Momentinlife"
50 Cent "Many Men"
Donny Hathaway "Jealous Guy (Live Version)"
Tink "I Ain't Got Time Today"
Yo Gotti "H.O.E."
Pop Smoke "Dior"
Jay-Z "Allure"
2 Live Crew "Hoochie Mama"
Jidenna "Sufi Woman"
Omeretta The Great "Pressure"
Kanye West "White Dress"
Jhene Aiko "Pray For You"
Jhene Aiko feat Nas "10k Hours"
Chari' Joy "Fed Up"
Victoria *Monét* "Moment"
Teyana Taylor "How You Want It"
Meek Mills "Dreams and Nightmares"
2 Live Crew "I Wanna Rock (Doo Doo Brown)"
Pink Sweat$ "No Replacing You"
Beyoncé "Love On Top"
King Von "Crazy Story"
Crime Mob "Knuck If You Buck"
Chari' Joy "Porcelain Doll"
Aaliyah "At Your Best"
Chari' Joy "Yours Truly"
Ghostface Killah "Done It Again"
Kim Petras "Heart To Break"
Nicole Wray "I Can't See"
Jhene Aiko "Maniac"
J. Cole "She's Mine Pt.1"
Megan Rochelle feat Fabolous "The One You Need"
Gavin DeGraw "Follow Through"
Emotional Oranges "Motion"
Ari Lennox "Bound"

50 Cent "I'm Supposed To Die Tonight"
Saba "Life"
Odette "Sometimes I Feel Like A Motherless Child"
Coldplay "Yellow"
Yo Gotti "Trapped"

CHAPTER 1

"It's too late for you and me. It's too late for you and I. Much too late for you to cry. Ooh we tried. God knows we tried."- Marvin Gaye, "Just to Keep You Satisfied"

"Where is Cam?" Gray questioned Quan.

"Last time I saw him, he was in the conference room."

Gray didn't even have time to say thank you. Quickly, she raced back inside but as she stepped across the threshold, she bumped right into the man she hoped to avoid. Victor stood there in all his frightening glory with a gold-plated pistol in hand. A silencer was attached to the barrel. The last thing Gray expected was for him to get his hands dirty and kill her his self. Adrenaline flooded her system as they linked eyes. Her body wanted to flee but there was no place for her to go. It was midnight. Time had officially run out. She was so scared she wanted to vomit. Saliva thickened in her mouth as beads of sweat trickled down her spine. Victor raised the gun and aimed it at her forehead. Gray slowly closed her eyes and prayed that her kids wouldn't walk into the winery as her body fell lifeless to the ground.

"Can you please tell Cam and my kids I love them?" She wept.

Victor didn't say a word as he took his gun off safety. Just as he was about to pull the trigger and blow Gray's brains out, the sound of a door opening from across the way caught their attention.

"Gray!" Cam called out her name hoarsely.

Simultaneously, she and Victor looked his way. Cam could barely stand. He stumbled out of the conference room with blood seeping from his mouth and stomach. With great effort, he tried to make his way to her, but all of his strength was gone. The pain in his abdomen burned like fire. A cloud of black swarmed his vision. The only thing he could concentrate on was the sound of his decreasing heartbeat. His breaths had shallowed to virtually nothing.

"Cam!" Gray pushed Victor out of the way to get to him.

Before she could, Cam's body hit the ground with a loud thud. Gently, she took him into her arms.

"Baby, what happened?" She asked, wiping the blood from his mouth away.

"It was . . ." His eyes fluttered then closed.

"It was who baby? Who did this to you?" She held him near as Victor concealed his weapon and called 911.

Cam wanted to tell her it was LaLa who'd set him up, but the sound of Gray's cries grew fainter by the second. She wanted to save him, but it was of no use. It was too late for him . . . too late for them. If it came down to him or her, he'd gladly lay down his burdens and die. Besides, he'd be joining his mother and their baby girl soon. He could die peacefully now. Black filled the edges of his vision as Cam's eyes fluttered again, then closed. His breaths came out in short, ragged gasps as he faintly heard Gray call his name.

"Cam." She shook his face. "You have to wake up . . . Cam!" She cried out and trembled with grief.

She wanted to save him, but it was too late. His time was up. Cam's tired human heartbeat one last time before everything faded to black.

"Cam! No-no-no-no! You can't do this to me!" Gray shook him hard. "Somebody help me!" She screamed as blood soaked into the skin of her hands.

Gray's life might as well have been over. Cam's dying would be her undoing.

"Nah." Quan held his head. "Not my brother!"

"Who the fuck I gotta body?" Stacy bulldozed his way through the growing crowd with his Glock in hand.

He was ready to air the whole crowd out. Priest was right behind him. While Stacy spazzed out, he followed the trail of blood to the conference room, pushed open the door and found Pastor Edris sprawled out on the floor dead. Tons of paperwork from Cam's court case were scattered all around as well. It was apparent that Pastor Edris and Cam had gotten into a physical altercation that resulted in Cam being stabbed and Pastor Edris being strangled. The tie around his neck clued him in on this. For the life of him, he couldn't figure out what had transpired that would make them go at each other. Pastor Edris had been Cam and Gray's marriage counselor for God's sake. All Priest knew was that his cousin had to survive. Their family wouldn't be able to take the blow of another member dying. Grace's death had done unrepairable damage to the Parthens' clan.

"Baby." Gray ran her shaky hand across Cam's face. "You have to wake up! Baby!" She shook him again. "Please Cam! Wake up! PLEASE! You can't do this to me! It's you and me forever, remember? You said you'd never leave me. We're supposed to grow old together. Me and you baby. Me and you." She sobbed uncontrollably. "You said you wouldn't leave me. You said everything would be alright. You promised me. Baby, you promised." She stroked his cheek lovingly.

"We were supposed to have more time. You can't leave me. I won't make it, Cam. I won't."

Cam's beautiful butterscotch skin had turned a sickening shade of blue. Gray's stomach dropped to her toes. His chest was no longer heaving up and down. He'd stopped breathing. Cam had stopped breathing and Gray's whole world had stopped spinning on its axis.

Cam, her husband, her best friend, the father of her kids, her sparring partner, the man that made her heart flutter with just one glance, the man that made her believe in men, in love again, was dead. In disbelief Gray inhaled one loud gasp and held it. Her bottom lip trembled as a stream of tears scorched her foundation covered cheeks. Her entire body turned to stone. She couldn't move a muscle. Gray held her breath so long she almost passed out. Reality had set in. She and Cam's world-wind love affair had come to an abrupt end. Just that quickly they were mortal enemies, then in love, separated, reunited and now torn apart once more but this time by death. There would be no coming back or do overs. It was over, finito, finished.

"CAAAAAAAAAAAAAAAAAAM!" She shrilled at the top of her lungs.

The scream ripped through her like a shard of glass. Eyes wide with dismay, her mouth was rigid and open as she gazed upon his chalky gaunt and immobile face. Gray's pulse quickened as she screamed again. This shriek was just like the last desperate, terrified . . .human. This couldn't be her reality . . . their reality. Gray could feel herself sinking into darkness. If Cam was dead she had no choice but to go with him. There was no living without him. She needed him. Their kids needed him. The triplets had just gotten to know him. If it wasn't for her selfishness they would've gotten to spend the first two-and-half years of their lives with him. Gray would never be able to forgive herself for keeping them apart. She was sure the kids wouldn't either. Where was Victor so he could off her as promised. She wanted to die—no, she needed to die. Living without Cam wasn't an option. Death would not divide them. As Gray looked around the packed winery for him, the sight of several ambulance workers caught her attention. She could barely make them out because her vision was so blurred and bloodshot from crying. Help was finally there but it was too late. Cam was already gone. Gray glanced back down at him. Life had drained from his eyes. He was as pale and limp as a ragdoll. Gray traced his eyebrow with her bloody index when a pair of strong hands pulled her up from the floor.

"No, no, no! Let me go!" She tried to fight the person off of her.

She needed to be next to her husband. He needed her. She needed him. He was all she had left.

"Gray, chill." Quan tried to calm her down.

"No! He needs me!" She kicked and screamed.

"How did this happen?" One of the EMT's questioned.

"I don't know!" Gray wept.

"He was stabbed." Priest spoke up. "The muthafucka that did it and the knife is in there." He pointed towards the conference room.

"He's not breathing." The EMT worker proceeded to give Cam CPR.

"Who did it?" Stacy whipped around.

He needed answers and he needed answers now.

"Man, you ain't gon' believe this." Priest ran his hand down his face, exasperated. "Pastor Edris."

"WHAT?!" Gray clawed at Quan's hands so he would let her go. "No! That can't be true!"

"Gray! Gray! You gotta chill." Quan held her even tighter.

He too was in shock and a wreck, but he had to keep it together for Gray and everyone else's sake. If he broke down things would get even more out of control.

"Why would Pastor Edris do that? Why? None of this makes sense. Why would he kill Cam? He said he was here to help us." Gray wailed, doubling over.

"Stop saying that shit! He ain't dead!"

Quan didn't want to believe that Cam had passed onto the other side. But he'd stopped breathing and not one limb on his body was moving. Gray was racked with grief. He knew that kind of pain. He'd felt it when Diggy was murdered. Gray cried with more violence than any thunderstorm. She didn't break delicately either, it was as if blood vessel in her being screamed in unison, traumatized with the notion she'd have to keep living without Cam by her side. She wailed in such a way that no one could bear the mental strain. She had gone from being in shock to completely losing her mind. Not even Quan could get her to a state of calm.

"We got a pulse and we got him back breathing!" The EMT announced.

Time stood still. Stacy, Priest and Quan all let out a sigh of relief. Gray clutched her chest as she dropped to her knees and thanked God.

"See. That nigga strong. He gon' make it." Quan gripped her shoulder as Cam's body was channeled onto a stretcher and wheeled outdoors to the awaiting ambulance.

Gray swiftly pulled away from Quan's comforting grasp and ran behind them. She would be by Cam's side every step of the way.

"Wait a minute." A female EMT placed her hand on Gray's chest, stopping her.

Gray furrowed her brows incensed.

"Only a family member can ride in the ambulance with the victim. Are you family?"

"I'm his wife." Gray smacked her hand away. "Don't ever put your hand on me. You lost your fuckin' mind?" She ice grilled her and hopped inside.

Seated beside Cam, she took his cold hand into hers. The ambulance had a deathly smell that reminded her of Sulphur and other chemicals that made her want to vomit. It numbed her nose and choked her, but Gray kept it together. None of that mattered. All that mattered was ensuring Cam lived to see another day. It didn't seem like he'd make it with the way the EMT was driving. The ride to the hospital was far more alarming than seeing gushes of blood pour from Cam's abdomen. Every bump and rattle of the bed and IV drip caused Gray's anxiety to skyrocket. It was bad enough she had to witness the love of her life strapped to a stretcher as EMT's worked frantically to stop his bleeding. The blood wouldn't stop coming. It kept coming and coming and coming. His plasma filled one gauze after another.

"Stich him up goddamit! Why are you just letting him bleed?" Gray snapped, holding onto his hand for dear life.

"We can't ma'am. Your husband needs surgery. He's experiencing internal bleeding. His aorta was nicked by the knife."

"Is that bad?"

The EMT looked at Gray with sorrow-filled eyes. Her throat constricted.

"Yes ma'am. It is."

Even when her mother died, Gray had never experienced grief this severe before. It grabbed ahold of her and wouldn't let go. Every memory she and Cam had ever created played like a song in her head, repeating itself. With each second that passed it felt like she was losing the biggest part of her. At first, she thought grief was something that took a person ten-feet under but Gray quickly learned that it was just the price a person paid for loving someone.

Hope filled her chest as they pulled up to the emergency room doors. Like a well-oiled machine, the EMT's wheeled Cam's unresponsive body out of the ambulance and rushed him inside DePaul Hospital. Emergency room physicians were there awaiting his arrival. Gray didn't even get a chance to say goodbye before they wheeled him into a restricted area for surgery. This time, she didn't mind being pulled apart from Cam. The faster he was in surgery the quicker he would be on the road to recovery. That didn't stop Gray from being overwrought with grief. In the middle of the emergency room she stood alone in her ripped and blood covered dress shaking like a leaf. She was sure she looked insane standing there like a statue, but she couldn't will her legs to move. Her body had turned into dried cement. Gray's mind was telling her to go have a seat, but the nearest chair seemed like a million light years away. In the crowded room she was alone. Gray had never felt more deserted in her life. Was this what it would feel like if she became a widower?

The mere thought brought on another onslaught of tears to pour from her eyes. In the past she would've been self-conscious about crying in public, but Gray couldn't help but give into her heartache. She bawled into her blood sodden hands. The tears dripped between her fingers, raining down onto the linoleum floor. Gray cried so hard she started to hyperventilate. All the strength left her legs as her breathing became ragged. Unknowingly, she sank to her knees not caring about how others viewed her. Her wails of despair were so loud that one of the nurses rushed from behind the emergency room check-in to comfort her. Gray was so distraught she didn't even realize she'd been moved to a nearby seat. She cried until no more tears came, but still the emptiness and sorrow remained. Tapping the heel of her stiletto against the floor, she examined her surroundings.

The emergency room passageway was overcrowded, and the air had an undercurrent of bleach. Gray frowned. The walls were a depressing, ugly shade of piss yellow that had been scratched in places from the thousands of stretchers that had bumped into them over the years. The artwork on the walls seemed to be somewhat expensive but did nothing to uplift Gray's somber mood. Repeatedly, her heel tapped. The vibration of her thigh shaking against the seat of the chair soothed the jitters in the pit of her stomach. It seemed like an eternity passed before family and friends started to trickle in. Mo, Boss, Kema, Quan, Stacy, Heidi, Priest, Noon, Aoki and Press all swarmed the emergency room.

"Baby." Noon rushed over to console her.

His long arms wrapped around Gray's torso and squeezed her tight. Gray internally recoiled from his touch. She wanted to tell him to let her go but her lips wouldn't part for her to speak the words.

"Are you alright? You're bleeding." He examined her dress.

"It's not her blood." Quan responded. "It's Cam's."

"Thank God." Noon sighed in relief.

Gray narrowed her stormy blue eyes at him. Her eyes were hard-rimmed and fixed, so much so that it was as if she was no longer able to move her eyeballs. Her vicious glare caused Noon to visibly wilt before her. Without saying a word, her eyes spoke everything he feared. He'd noticed a change in her since he arrived in St. Louis. At first he thought she was just happy to be home and in her element with her friends but soon he realized that it was far deeper than that. He was losing her. All the feelings she claimed were dead and gone for her soon-to-be ex-husband were back and in full effect. He'd witnessed it firsthand when they were on the dance floor. Gray looked at Cam like he was the sun. His light shined down on her, blinding her to the love of anyone else, including him. All she saw was Cam. Noon no longer existed. Now as he stared into her cold eyes and her body went frigid from his touch, it was apparent that his time with her was dwindling down to nothing. Wounded, he pushed his hands into his pants pocket and stepped back. Noon faded into the background as the rest of the clan hugged and comforted Gray. Unlike with him, she seemed at ease.

Everyone crowded around Gray asking questions that she didn't have the strength or energy to answer. Thank God Quan was there. He took over and explained what had transpired to everyone. Gray thought she was a mess. Mo and Press showed out worse than her. Seeing her baby girl in such agony was the only thing that brought Gray out of her trance. Her motherly instincts kicked right in. Lovingly, she wrapped Press in her weary arms and rocked her back-and-forth. Aoki sat next to her with her head on her shoulder. The girls had no idea, but they were Gray's strength. Although she couldn't utter a word to speak, she was finding her resolve each second they were near. All she needed was her little babies, but they'd been taken to Tee-Tee's house. In need of some form of comfort, Gray started to hum. She wasn't the most spiritual person but an old gospel hymn by Karen Clark Sheard titled *The Will of God* came to mind. It was a song that she played often when she fled to Paris.

The safest place in the whole wide world
Is in the will of God;
Though trials be great, and the way seems hard,
It's in the will of God...
It may be on a mountain peak, or in the valley low,
But wherever, wherever, wherever, wherever it may be,
If God says "Go, " oh, go, go...

Instantly recognizing the hymn Aoki held her mother's hand and softly sang the lyrics to the second verse.

The devil's loose in all the world;
There's danger in the land...
The safest place in the whole wide world
Is in the Master's Hand...
It may be on the battlefront, or in, or in, or in the prison walls,
But wherever, wherever, wherever it may be,
If God says "Go, "
If God says "Go, "
You put your trust in Him.

Aoki couldn't sing a lick, but the song resonated deep in her soul. She'd seen her mother at her absolute worst when they were in Paris but when she played that gospel hymn hope was restored in Gray's broken spirit. She prayed to God that this time wasn't any different.

"Where is he?!" Devin raced through the doors in a panic.

Her mere presence caused everyone in the waiting room to roll their eyes and sigh in annoyance. All of sudden all of the air in the room was sucked out. Her presence buzzed around everyone like a gnat no one could swat.

"*HELLO!*" She placed her hands on her hips. "I know damn well y'all hear me talkin'! Where the fuck is my man?"

"*Cam* is in surgery." Quan grimaced. "That nigga ain't yo fuckin' man."

"In surgery? What you mean he in surgery? What are they saying?" Devin continued to yell and carry on.

"We don't know yet and can you stop all that fuckin' yelling?" Stacy barked.

"NO . . . I . . . CAN . . . NOT!" Devin tossed her head from side-to-side while enunciating each word. "It's all over the news that he got stabbed by a fuckin' deacon or some shit! And I know it had something to do with that fat bitch over there!" She pointed her finger towards Gray.

"Oh no bitch! You got my mama fucked up!" Aoki leaped out of her chair ready to fight.

"Aoki, sit down." Gray spoke in a cationic state.

All she had the strength to do was comfort her whimpering child and hum.

"Nah ma! I ain't gon' let this rat bitch talk to you no any kind of way! On God I'll fuck her up!"

"Girl, sit yo' bony ass down and stay in a child's place." Devin waved her off.

"BITCH, don't talk to my muthafuckin' niece like that!" Mo charged towards her only to be stopped by her husband, Boss.

"Yeah, you betta get her." Devin arched her brow.

"Nah, bitch you get me! It ain't nothin' but space and opportunity over here! Run up and get done up!"

"Yeah-yeah-yeah whatever. Ain't you got like 90-million kids you need to be worried about?"

"Yo." Boss interjected. "Real shit. Now ain't the time. Either you gon' sit the fuck down and act like you got some sense or I'ma let my wife run up in your shit. Now which one it's gon' be?"

"Remember what happened at the barbeque." Stacy quipped.

Not wanting a repeat of that horrendous day, Devin decided to fall back. Once again, she was severely outnumbered. Cam wasn't around to save her this time. Pursing her lips, she glared at Mo with contempt and slowly took a seat off to the side.

"That's what I thought." Boss side-eyed her as the emergency room doors opened again.

"Daddy!"

Gray's heart lurched as she glanced up. For some reason, she had hoped it was Cam that was being called, but it wasn't. Mo leaped from her seat and into her daddy's arms. Following behind him was Curtis and Cal in his wheelchair. Gray took notice that Kerry was missing. She would remember that he was M.I.A. when his brother was fighting for his life. Anyone that had ever done Cam wrong would be on her shit list. Gray was gonna go after each and every one of them with a vengeance if he didn't survive. Slowly, she continued to rock and hum.

"What happened to your brother?" Cam Sr. asked.

"He's been stabbed." Mo cried like a li'l baby.

"I knew this street shit was gonna catch up to him one day." Cam Sr. shook his head in disgust.

"Daddy stop."

"No 'cause it's true. That boy don't think about nobody but his self. He has caused this family nothing but grief. Don't make no damn sense. He had all the potential in the world to be something great. Now look. He ain't nothing but a failure and disappointment."

Gray narrowed her eyes on the old man. Every part of her wanted to cuss him out but on the strength that he was Cam and Mo's father, she kept her mouth shut. He, however, had one more time to say something slick at the mouth and she was gonna forget her home training and lose her shit.

Four hours later, Gray hadn't moved a muscle. Everyone around her paced, drank water, went to the restroom and had small talk but she sat humming the same gospel hymn over and over. Quan asked if she wanted something to eat but Gray couldn't stomach the thought of food. It was a hard enough job turning her head from side-to-side to say no. She was so out of it that she didn't even notice the doctor when he entered the emergency room. He was a tall, slender man in scrubs and a white physician's coat.

"I'm Dr. John Waters. Is the next of kin to Cam Parthens here?" He looked around the packed room.

"Yes." The entire family rose to their feet, including Gray.

All of her motor senses came flooding back. She was on high alert with anticipation. Moving quicker than she had since the incident, she pushed her way to the front of the herd and stood next to Mo. Sensing her presence, Mo laced her fingers with Gray's and held on tight. Hands fused they became each other's lifeline.

"Is my brother alright?" Her voice cracked.

"As you may know by now, Mr. Parthens was brutally stabbed in his abdomen. When he arrived, he wasn't responsive and barely breathing on his own. We were informed by the EMT's that the knife he was stabbed with nicked his abdominal aorta and caused an abdominal vascular lesion, which would've been fatal if the knife had fully penetrated the artery. In Mr. Parthens case, because his aorta was only nicked, he didn't die but he suffered profuse internal bleeding. To ensure his aorta didn't fully rupture and send blood into the space around his heart and lungs, we performed aortic surgery and repaired the wounded area—"

"Oh, thank God." Mo let out a sigh of relief.

Stacy gripped Quan's shoulder and brought him in for a one-armed hug. Neither man would've been able to handle another death amongst the crew.

"So, my husband is okay?" Gray questioned wearily.

Until she heard the word yes, she wouldn't be able to function normally. Dr. Waters hung his head low then lifted it back up and stood erect.

"The surgery itself was a success but . . . as we were wrapping things up, Mr. Parthens experienced a stroke."

"No." Mo clutched her chest, fearing the worst.

"I'm sorry to inform you that the disturbance in the brain during the stroke increased intracranial pressure and caused loss of oxygen, and a buildup of toxins, which lead to a stroke-induced coma." Dr. Waters announced regrettably.

"Is he going to survive?" Cam Sr. stepped up.

"To be honest sir, Mr. Parthens is experiencing minimal brain activity and has been placed on a ventilation machine. At this point, things are very touch and go. It could go either way."

Suddenly, Mo couldn't bare the weight of her own legs and she fell to the floor in a heap of tears. Gray almost went down with her but once more her body turned into cement. Wails of hopelessness erupted from the lungs of their family and friends but this time she remained void of all emotion, except determination. Cam was in a coma and fighting for his life. He needed her now more than ever. Gray had sworn before God to fight for him when he couldn't do it for himself. And that's exactly what she planned on doing. She'd take on the devil himself if it meant they'd be able to spend more time together. Fuck crying. She'd done that. It was time to go into survival mode. She and Cam hadn't seen the full scope of where their love could go. It would take more than a stroke and coma for her to give up on what they shared. When she said she'd stick by his side through sickness and health she meant it. Being Cam's wife meant more than wearing his ring or donning his last name. It wasn't something endured but savored. With him she never felt so alive. Without him she was a walking corpse. She needed him there to wipe her tears and tell her everything would be alright. He was the center of her universe. Her world orbited around his. Gray and Cam's marriage was a union of two hearts beating as one. Each of them would sacrifice for the other's happiness and wellbeing. He had to wake up. They couldn't be done. There was still so much more story to tell. They couldn't have reached the until death do us part stage of their union. The thought of death was morbid to Gray. She wanted the fairytale love affair she'd read about as a child. She deserved the "and they lived happily ever after" ending and if it took every breath in her body, she was gonna get it.

CHAPTER 2

"I'd rather you choose me."- *James Blake, "Choose Me"*

DAY 1:

By the time Gray made it back to her Airbnb, streams of sunlight slipped through the trees, filling up space between the branches with golden light. The sky had transitioned from a blush pink to a pristine shade of light blue. Strands of white clouds lined the heavens. They were so thin, they appeared to be brush strokes from Leonardo da Vinci on blue canvas. It was the perfect dawn, one to be treasured instead of squandered. Gray's body was exhausted. She hadn't slept a wink since she and Cam made love until the wee hours of the morning the night before. She needed rest and sustenance, but her mind wouldn't allow her to crash. She had to keep going. Cam needed her. When she'd left the hospital Mo and Cam Sr. was by his side. Gray would've still been there, but she had to get out of the stupid bloody bridesmaid dress she wore. It was starting to feel like Cam's plasma was seeping into her pores.

"Ms. Rose, I heard about the stabbing on the news." Melody her assistant came rushing towards her. "Are the kids' father alright?"

Gray stopped dead in her tracks. Cam slumped on the ground laying lifeless in her arms as blood poured from his abdomen flashed before eyes.

"No, he's not alright. He's in a coma." She swallowed down as much spit as she could to coat her dry throat. It was the first time she'd said the word coma, out loud.

"My God." Melody gasped, clutching her hand over her mouth. "I'm so sorry. Is there anything I can do for you?"

"Umm." Gray replied in a daze.

She couldn't get the visual of Cam out of her brain.

"I need you to book a flight back to Paris and pack up me and the kids things. I need our clothes, underwear, shoes, toiletries, everything shipped immediately. We'll be here for an undetermined amount of time and please handle the sale of the home." Gray rushed past her.

"Oh." She paused midstride. "Also, I need you to get Kilo and Gram from the kennel and personally bring them here."

"Yes, ma'am. I'm right on it."

"Thanks, Mel." Gray resumed walking.

Noon straggled behind her in his tux, as she stepped over Reign's toy fire truck that lay in the middle of the floor. Like a lost puppy, he removed his tuxedo jacket and followed her up the stairs. They had barely spoken two words to each other since he arrived at the hospital. He was trying to be patient and understanding of the situation she'd been placed in. The father of her children might die at any moment but with each second, minute and hour that went by, he lost more and more of his resolve. He needed to know where her head was, where they stood. Gray acted like the sight of him burned her eyes. It broke his heart to see they'd ended up in such an awful space. He used to be the man that made her smile. They were happy in Paris. Now things had changed for the absolute worse.

A million and one thoughts ran through Gray's mind as she scoured the master bedroom. She needed to shower, scrub Cam's blood from underneath her nails, change clothes and prepare bags of clothes and toiletries for each of the children. Until Cam awoke from his coma, Gray would be staying at the hospital with him. She couldn't see herself being anywhere else. There would be no returning to Paris. Cam's hospital room would become her new home. The kids would be taken care of by Kema and Quan. Mo wanted to keep them but eight kids under one roof would be a mad house. The twins and King were heading to camp. Gray wouldn't put that type of stress on her worst enemy. Tee-Tee even offered his assistance, but he traveled a lot for work.

Gray looked down at her ripped blood-stained dress again. The sight of it made her skin crawl. She didn't want the reminder of what Pastor Edris had done to the love of her life on her body. She needed to free herself of the horrific memory. A steaming hot shower was calling her name, but her mind told her to pack the kids bags first, so she made an abrupt turn and headed to the triplets' room. Noon tried to follow her footsteps but found it difficult to keep up. Gray was moving around like a chicken with its head cut off. She hadn't stopped moving since she entered the house. Under her breath she mumbled off a list of things she needed to do as she yanked down the triplets' suitcases frantically one by one. Noon leaned against the door frame with his ankle crossed over the other, watching Gray's every move. A muscle twitched involuntarily at the corner of his left eye; his mouth formed a stern scowl. With arms folded firmly across his broad chest, he angrily watched the woman he'd fallen madly in love with kill herself with worry. It was a sad sight to see her in such a frenzied state. For so long, he'd watched her be everything for every-one. Gray was a giver and a caretaker, but it was his job to make her life as stress free as possible. He'd been killing it as her lover, protector and provider. Their life was perfect. He should've never let her return to Saint Louis alone. As soon as she was back in Cam's presence, she fell under his spell and her life went to shit all over again. Noon wanted to shake some sense into her. For some idiotic reason, Gray thought it was her responsibility to nurse her ex back to health. As far as he was concerned, she didn't owe Cam a damn thing. He'd done this to himself. Now he had to suffer the consequences.

"You need any help?"

"No." Gray answered distractedly.

Her face was rigid with tension. It seemed like she'd aged a million years in just a few hours. Biting her bottom lip, she tried her best to concentrate on the task at hand. There was so much that needed to be done in such a short amount of time. She didn't have time to pacify Noon's sulking in the corner. Cam was stuck in a coma fighting for his life. Every second she wasn't by his side was like dying a slow death of her own. Gray's entire being was riddled with anxiety. She felt like one big ball of stress. If she slowed down, she'd lose her mind. She was sure of it. Gray would have a full blown meltdown and falling into a depression was not on the menu. She had to be strong for Cam, Aoki, Press, Reign, Beaux and Sky. If she succumb to darkness, it would be a domino effect. They're whole family would suffer. They'd suffered enough. Now was the time to fight.

"Why don't you let me do that and you go take a shower." Noon walked over and took one of Sky's nightgowns out of Gray's hand.

"I said I got it!" She snapped, snatching it back.

Gray's entire body shook with grief. She didn't want him touching her baby's things. Not now. Not ever. Noon even being in her babies room was a slap in the face to their father. Stunned by her reaction, he took two steps back and held his hands face up. Gray had a wild, unhinged look in her ocean blue eyes. Her tone was abrupt and cutting. How had they gotten here? She used to adore him. Now he'd become public enemy #1.

"I'm just tryin' to help." He spoke softly.

"I don't want your help." She brushed her hair off her face. "I told you that at the hospital, but you just insisted on driving me home." She rolled her eyes and resumed pulling out the triplets' clothes.

"You've been through a lot. What kind of man would I be if I let you take an Uber home after everything you've been through? I know we're in a precarious predicament right now, but I love you, Gray. It's my job to protect you."

"No, it's not. Not anymore." She quipped harshly.

Noon's heart skipped a beat. His mouth became as dry as the Namib desert. She couldn't possibly be saying what he thought she was saying. It would kill him.

"What does that mean?" His deep voice cracked.

Gray stopped coordinating outfits, closed her eyes and threw her head back in despair. She had to check herself. Noon didn't deserve her wrath, but this was not a conversation she wanted to have. She could barely breathe let alone talk. All she wanted to do was get back to Cam and lay her head upon his lap. If they were skin-to-skin, she was sure he'd awake. Their connection was that strong. Gray was certain of it. She'd bet her life. Cam almost losing his life confirmed what she'd known along. There was no other man on the planet for her. Noon had tried to fill his shoes and Gray had almost tricked herself into believing he had. But she would be lying if she kept on pretending that she was 100% fulfilled in their relationship. Noon was a good guy. He'd come into her life at a time where she wanted to give love another chance. On paper he fit the criteria of what she wanted in a man. He was undeniably handsome, extremely successful, cultured, accepted her children, driven, supportive, affectionate, faithful, and loving. In a short amount of time he'd attempted to give her the world. He wined and dined her like no other but there was always something missing. Noon could never penetrate the part of her heart that Cam left vacant. That should've been a sign that they would never work. It took Gray almost four years and one look into Cam's whiskey brown eyes to realize that she'd never truly stopped loving him. It was then that she accepted that she'd deserted someone who loved her despite her many flaws because of fear. Fear had fucked up plenty of relationships. It was an extremely influential influence. Fear was also a disguised demon. She wouldn't be ruled by it any longer. She wanted her man back. Her family deserved to be whole. There would be no more living a lie. Gray unsealed her eyes and regrettably gazed over at Noon. The sad expression on his face almost crushed her. Her soul broke for him, for what she was about to do he didn't deserve. He'd been nothing but good to her, but the heart wants what the heart wants. Sadly, her heart didn't want him. To be honest, it never did. Swallowing the lump in her throat, she parted her lips to speak. The words she was about to utter would be like sharp blades to Noon's heart. Her actions would appear venomous. Combined it would be a vicious massacre of a loving heart. Noon was a beautiful person. He would make someone a great husband one day but nothing, absolutely nothing compared to Cam.

"I can't do this anymore."

"What?"

"This. Us." She pointed back-and-forth between them.

"What changed in a week?"

"Everything!" She quaked. "I know I told you that I was done with Cam and that I wanted a divorce. I tried to make myself believe that I was done and moving on but none of it was true. I love him. I always have. I always will." She whispered as his stomach contracted.

Gray's words hit Noon hard. Her words were like nails being hammered into his heart. She'd said she loved him, and he'd believed her. She said he was her new beginning. Now under a sunny sky, she announced that she was in love with someone else? A man that disrespected her every chance he got, according to her. Noon balled his fist. It would have been kinder to kill him.

"So, you telling me that the love you had for me just disappeared?"

"I care for you Noon—"

"Care?" He screwed up his face and looked at her like she had two heads instead of one.

"I do but I can't go on pretending like Cam isn't the man I'm . . . in love with. I should've been honest and said this a long time ago and for that I'm sorry. I should've never dragged you into my mess."

Noon's nostrils flared. He wasn't gonna allow her to paint herself as this martyr. She was the one ripping his heart into shreds.

"You so fuckin' full of shit, Gray. You don't know what the fuck you want."

Gray paused before responding. She was trying her hardest to reign in her anger and not spazz out on Noon's ass.

"I know this is hard for you to hear but I've never been as sure of anything in my life."

"So, let me get this straight." Noon scoffed, massaging his forehead. "This nigga cheated on you, lied to you repeatedly, said your kids wasn't his, told you to stick a hanger up your coochie, went to jail for distributing drugs and this is the muthafucka you choose? You sound stupid as hell."

Gray couldn't do anything but chuckle.

"You're right, I do sound stupid."

"I have done everything for you. I was the one there for you and yo' kids when you ain't have nobody."

"And I'll be forever grateful for that."

"Grateful my ass! I would have done anything for you! I was willing to make Paris my permanent home for you! That's how much I loved you. I wanted to be the very best for you. I was the very best for you, but my best wasn't enough to satisfy you, was it? You don't want a man that's gon' treat you like a queen. You just like all these other bird brain bitches out here that want a nigga that's gon' treat 'em bad." Noon shot her a look of disgust.

"Where was that nigga at when you were in Paris raising five kids alone? Behind bars trying not to drop the soap. I was there. Me!" He jabbed his finger into his chest. "I know you got daddy issues but damn. You can't be that fuckin' dumb, Gray. Are you that broken that you would chose a cheating ass nigga with criminal aspirations over an educated man like myself? Do you know who the fuck I am?"

"I know exactly who you are Aubrey Simmons, portfolio manager for the largest venture capitalist company in the world." Gray ambled over and stood toe-to-toe. "You've dated some of the baddest women on the planet from Mariah Carey to Jourdan Dunn. A girl like me should only be so lucky to have you, right?" She smirked.

"You know it's not like that." Noon tried to correct her.

"No. I know exactly how you meant it. But let's be clear. I know

Cam hasn't been the best husband. He has hurt me more times than I care to remember. Sometimes, he doesn't treat me right. He may not work for a fortune 500 company. And if I were sane, I would throw in the towel and forget all about him and be with you. I mean, on paper you're the perfect man. You're what every woman prays for. You're smart, you're funny, you're fine as hell, rich as shit, beyond generous, you spoil me and my kids. Hell, you even got good dick but guess what?" Her eyes turned a shade of molten blue. "Even with all of those great characteristic, you still don't measure up to my husband. He's my soulmate. He brings me back to life when I need resuscitation. When the devil is tempting me on my left shoulder, he's the angel on my right leading me in the right direction. No one is ever gonna love me like him and there ain't a bitch breathing in this world that's gonna love him like me. We were made to love each other. I was made to be his wife. Now I know that's a hard pill for you to swallow—"

"I just don't understand—"

Gray cut him off.

"Maybe it's not for you to understand. When you love somebody the way Cam and I love each other the shit is unexplainable. It can't be boxed in or defined. It just is."

Noon ran his hands down his face. He was depleted of all energy. His mind was telling him to accept defeat and bow out gracefully, but he'd never been the kind of man to give up when he faced a challenge. Gray was a good woman. Any man would be lucky to have her. He'd be damned if he lost her to some common street thug. He loved Gray and he knew deep down she still loved him, too. Emotions were heightened because of the circumstances. Gray wasn't in her right mind. She was stressed out and emotional. When things died down she'd be able to think clearly. She'd see that Cam was still the no good nigga she'd painted him out to be. He'd disappoint her once again and he'd be right there to pick up the pieces like before. Until then, he would fall back and let her do her thing.

"Listen, a lot has transpired over the last twenty-four hours. You're tired. You're not thinking straight. So, what I'm gonna do is give you the time to get some rest and pull yourself together—"

"Noon—"

"Shhh." He held her by each of her arms to quiet her down. "We don't need to make any decisions we might regret later. This is a difficult time for you. I was wrong for putting so much pressure on you. You have a lot going on right now. It's probably best that you focus on the kids and handle the situation with your babies' father. I'm gonna head back to New York and give you the space you obviously need but that in no way means that I have given up on you . . . on us. We're good together, Gray. You just need time to remember that." He placed a soft loving kiss on her forehead.

Gray closed her eyes and let out a long sigh. She wanted to object but she couldn't find the strength to fight another second. Noon could live in whatever fantasy land he wanted to. Her mind wasn't changing. Cam was the man for her, and the quicker she made it back to the hospital, she could start operation loving her soulmate back to life.

CHAPTER 3

*"I'd leave heaven to bat for you, take on the devil. Matter fact, sit back
'cause I got this battle."- Jaime Woods, "I Got You"*

oon's kiss goodbye still lingered on the skin of Gray's
forehead as she held the divorce decree in her hands and
ripped it in half. Yes, Cam had signed it before the attack, but she knew
he'd only agreed to the dissolution of their marriage because that's
what she led him to believe she wanted. When she returned to Saint
Louis she was dead set on ending things but the dance at the reception
changed everything. No matter how much shit she and Cam took each
other through, they were each other's soulmate. Their bond was eternal. Cam was the only man who had enough access to her heart to
break it. Despite his many shortcomings, he was perfectly made for
her. He lifted her heart when the rest of her was down. Nothing could
change the love she had for him. He made her want to be a better
person, to be good enough. She refused to let go of him. Piece by
piece, she ripped the divorce papers into shreds. Once she was

finished, she dumped the bits into the trashcan. She and Cam wouldn't be getting divorced that day or any other day. Letting out a sigh of relief, she picked up each of the kids' suitcases and placed them by the door. Melody would drop them off at Kema and Quan's house before she headed to the airport to board her flight to Paris.

Noon had long gone. After his searing kiss bye, Gray was now dressed and ready to go back to the hospital. Her hair was freshly shampooed, and her voluptuous body smelled of Jo Malone lime basil & mandarin body wash. The blood that marked her arms, nails and legs was washed away. Natural black curls framed her weary face. Casually and comfortably dressed in a black knit cardigan, layered gold coin necklaces, a white cami, blue jean booty shorts, Nike socks and orange, white and black Air Jordan 1 Mid Retro sneakers, she welcomed a warm sympathetic hug goodbye from Melody then stepped outdoors. The bright sun blinded her eyes as she walked down the walkway to her electric blue Mercedes Benz G-Class. The only problem was she wouldn't be able to back out because she'd been blocked in by a blacked out Rolls Royce Phantom. A 6 foot 9, 400 pound, midnight nigga dressed in a two-piece suit and tie stood by the back passenger side door with a scowl on his face. Gray stopped abruptly, turned on her heels and broke out into a run. Whoever was behind Pastor Edris attacking Cam was now after her. She was pretty sure it was Gunz who'd ordered the hit. Gray had never hated a human being more. She normally didn't wish death on anyone, but she wanted him dead . . . ASAP! She didn't even hate Truth as much as she hated Gunz and he'd raped her and tried to kill her. Instead of letting her emotions take control, she should've let Noon stay until she was safely back at the hospital amongst security. And no, Noon wasn't a gangster or a killer, but he was a man that would protect her at all cost. Gray was out here lone wolfing it without Cam. Sure, Quan, Stacy and Priest would have her back, but at that moment, she was prey ready to be eaten alive. Making a run for it, she was halfway back up the walkway when she heard a man shout her name.

"Gray!"

Immediately recognizing the voice, she spun around. Victor sat in back of the Phantom with the window down, reading the morning paper. You would think after she realized it was a familiar face pulling up on her, she'd calm down, but Gray's heart pounded even faster. Nausea overtook her stomach. Her throat felt constricted as if she was being strangled by the air surrounding her.

"Mr. Gonzalez would like to offer you a ride." Victor's goon said more as a statement and not a request.

She hadn't even responded, and he'd already opened the back door. Panic consumed every cell in her body. Gray scanned the area in search of a place to escape but found none. Stuck, she practically felt the rise of her blood pressure, but she knew that this was the least of her worries. Death was knocking at her door. She could either try to make another run for it and get shot in the back or oblige Victor's request. No part of her wanted to be near him. She detested the sight of him, but Gray had to put her ill feelings aside and survive so she could get back to Cam. Inhaling breath into her lungs, she clenched her teeth and begrudgingly headed to the car. The giant chauffer/shooter held the door open for her. Gray threw her purse down onto the plush leather seat and sat as close to the door as possible. Seconds later, the Rolls backed out of the driveway and their ride began. The destination was unknown. Gray said a silent prayer to God that she survived.

No part of her wanted to look at Victor but she needed to ensure that he didn't have any visible weapons on his person. Gazing at him out of the corner of her eye, she peeped that he donned a white and grey checkerboard button up, a grey, slim-fit, three-piece, pinstripe suit and black Christian Louboutin lace-up leather dress shoes. A white rose was pinned to his lapel. His gold commission signet ring shined from his pinky finger. She didn't see any weapon, but Victor was a crafty nigga. He could attack her within a blink of an eye. Despite her disdain for him, Don Victor Gonzalez was undeniably handsome. His low cut Caesar, thick bushy brows, rich brown, almond shaped eyes, full lips and silky beard would make any woman's panties moist. Victor was one fine muthafucka. Notes of Amber, Violet, Mimosa and

Wood from his Gucci *Tears of Iris* cologne filled the interior of the car but not in an overpowering way. The scent let you know that a man of means and power was in your presence. If he wasn't the leader of the Gonzalez Cartel, Gray would've socked his ass in the throat. The cocky bastard hadn't even bothered to look at her once. Legs crossed, he continued reading the St. Louis Post Dispatch as if she wasn't even there. Gray's eyes grew wide when she spotted a picture of Cam being wheeled out of the winery on a stretcher as front page news. Bile rose in her esophagus. She wished this wasn't her life, but it was, and in that moment, she felt powerless to fix it.

"I'll keep this brief." Victor folded the paper back as it was.

His deep voice sent chilling tingles down her spine. With ease, he placed the newspaper in the car seat bag organizer then rested his crossed hands over his lap.

"I know you have pressing matters to attend to, so I'll make this quick." He continued to look ahead. "I got word on Cam's condition. I'm sorry to hear he's in a coma. You must be worried with grief, but I know Cam. He's gonna pull through this. In the meantime, me and my family will keep him in our prayers. If there's anything the kids need, I'm always a phone call away."

He and his family will keep Cam in their prayers. If the kids need anything I'm always a phone call away, Gray repeated in her brain. This muthafucka had balls of steels. Nowhere in his sympathies did he offer any for her. Seething with anger, Gray forgot her place and spat, "My kids don't need shit from you. Considering you were about to kill their mother."

"About to?" Victor arched his brow. "You talking past tense like the shit is over. See that's where you got the game fucked up sweetheart. Murdering you hasn't been taken off the table. You and I still have unfinished business."

Victor's threat was like gasoline being poured over the butterflies in her stomach and being struck with a match. Fire brewed in her belly. It literally felt like her bones had no more strength. She thought that part of the nightmare was over. Did this nigga not have one ounce of a heart? He knew she had the weight of the world on her shoulders. This was the last thing she needed to deal with. The fact that Victor would even drop this shit on her pissed her off to the highest extent.

"You and I don't have shit. I know you have a hard time comprehending inglés, but I told you I didn't do it!" She was sick and tired of him accusing her of snitching and giving the cops the drop info that landed Cam in jail and millions of dollars of cocaine being confiscated.

"Raising your voice won't change the situation. All roads still lead back to you. I still haven't been given concrete evidence that someone else was the snitch that set Cam up and brought unnecessary attention to my organization. Millions of dollars were lost and yes your husband recouped my funds. Since that unfortunate day, the FEDS have not stopped poking their nose in my business. Somebody has to pay but . . . considering the circumstances, I'm gonna do you a favor and you give an extension so you can provide proof on who sabotaged my business. Since you claim it wasn't you."

"And how the fuck am I supposed to do that? My husband is in a fuckin' coma. My kids are suffering! I'm suffering! Every second of the day that he's not awake, I feel like I'm dying! I don't have time to play fuckin' Nancy Drew!" Gray quipped on the verge of tears.

She'd slit her own wrist tho before she shed a tear in front of this heartless muthafucka.

"Well, if you wanna live I suggest you get creative. I would hate to see you in the same position as your husband. I don't think Aoki is ready to be the matriarch of your family."

Gray clutched her chest, unable to breathe. The wind had literally been knocked out of her lungs. The mere thought of her children losing their mother and father was too much for her to bear.

"How much time do I have?" She damn near choked on her words.

"You'll know when your time is up." Victor picked a piece of invisible lint off of his pants.

"How?" She whipped her head in his direction.

"When your ass is dead." Victor tried not to chuckle, but a slight grin graced the corner of his lips.

Gray didn't find a muthafuckin' thing funny. This was her life on the line. She didn't wanna die. Her life was too precious to give up now. The funny thing about life is it pushes you until you break, just to see if you can put yourself back together again. In the past, Gray was able to come out of the corner swinging. There wasn't anything life could throw at her that she wouldn't conquer. She'd gotten through being abandoned by her father, raped, domestic violence, cheated on, losing her mother, losing her baby and heartbreak. This, however, was a whole different demon. Without Cam pieces of her lay scattered about in broken fragments. There wasn't a glue on the market that would piece her back together. To make it through this the sweet, gentle Gray would have to disappear. In order to survive she'd have to morph into Cam; a human with a monster mask. Both of their lives were on the line. Gray would be damned if one of them didn't come out of this nightmare alive. If Victor was gonna have her on a wild goose chase to find the "snitch" then she'd have to put on her big girl panties and tap into her inner Inspector Gadget.

The rest of the ride was met with silence. Victor gazed out of the window completely unmoved by her panicky state. This was part of the game that he'd once hated but became numb to. Over the years, he'd been betrayed more times than he could keep count. Family members and friends instantly turned to foes. Victor couldn't trust anyone. Sometimes, he didn't trust his damn self. If he wasn't who he was, he would be compassionate towards Gray and her situation but when you were a Don of a cartel there was no room for empathy. You had to be morally bankrupt. For all he knew, Gray could really be the op. He had to keep her at arm's length. Being the hand of God came with a lot of pitfalls and this was one of them. In order to make it home alive each night, it was a must his guard stayed up. This was something that civilians like Gray would never understand. Victor could only have a heart for his wife and children. Everyone else was up for grabs.

When the car turned into the hospital, Gray quickly grabbed her purse. The Rolls hadn't even come to a full stop when she pulled the handle and got out. She couldn't get away from Victor fast enough, but like before, her name was called and she halted her steps. This time, she didn't turn around. She'd given Victor enough of her attention.

"Don't even think about running." He spoke cryptically. "You won't make it to the gate at the airport, trust me." He warned and with that being said, he drove off.

A mixture of anger and dread filled every crevice of Gray's tense body. This was not how she envisioned this day going. First she had to deal with ending things with Noon. Then it was mentally accepting she wouldn't see her kids until God knows when. Victor threatening her existence was the straw that broke the camel's back. A crushing pain started to pang on the side of her head. Gray's body was pleading for rest. She hadn't been to sleep in 24 hours. Her eyes stung from exhaustion, but she'd sleep when Cam awake. One foot in front of the other, she walked down the long hallway. The sole of her sneakers squeaked against the shiny pristine tiled floor. Gray took in the hospital décor. The ceiling was made from those polystyrene squares and placed like a grid-like frame. Elegant commercial prints decorated the walls. Above each door that Gray passed was a large plastic sign with black lettering. By the time she reached Cam's room, Gray had a full blown migraine. She just needed to close her eyes for one second but that second would never come. When she walked in, she found Dr. Waters talking to Cam Senior. Mo must've been in the restroom 'cause her seat was empty. The only sign she was still there was the YSL purse left behind. Cam lay unconscious with a tube down his throat. Wires glued to his tattooed chest peeked out from the neck of his hospital gown. The breathing machine he was hooked up to made his torso rise and fall. An IV was stuck in the vein of his right hand. Cam looked as helpless as she felt. No matter how much time passed, Gray would never get used to seeing him in such a vulnerable state.

"Mrs. Parthens, I'm so glad you're back. I was just updating your father-in-law on your husband's condition."

"Has he gotten any better?" She asked with bated breath.

Her heart swelled with hope. She needed good news like a crackhead needed a good hit.

"Regrettably, he hasn't. Things are still how they were when you left."

Gray bit her lip before the tears that threatened to fall could escape. Despite her disappointment, she forced a smile and held her purse close. Her legs felt like they were gonna give out on her at any second, but unlike in the past, Cam wasn't there to catch her. Thank God Mo was there. Behind her Gray could hear her flush the toilet and wash her hands. Gray couldn't wait to leap into her arms for a hug. After the morning she had, she needed a hug like she needed air to breathe.

"M—" She went to speak her name, but her throat closed when she spotted Devin coming out of the restroom, instead of her sister-in-law.

Devin stood in all her wicked glory shooting Gray the evilest grin she could muster. If she had a camera, she would've snapped a picture and framed it. Gray's mouth had literally dropped down to her double chin. The sheer look of shock and horror on her face was priceless. There would never be another moment like it. Pleased with herself, Devin brushed past Gray slightly bumping her shoulder along the way. Gray closed her mouth. If she didn't collect herself immediately there was no telling what she might do. Hate burned in her heart so deep that it was ingrained in the tissue. This bitch was trying Gray's life. She couldn't have seen right. She had to be hallucinating. It was the lack of sleep that had her seeing things. No way was this stank, cunt ho in her husband's hospital room prancing around like she belonged there.

"I know damn well." Gray scoffed on the verge of laughing. It was all she could do; her head throbbed so much. Squeezing her eyes shut, she willed the pain to go away, but after coming face-to-face with Devin, the pounding only increased.

"This ain't happening. I know I'm tripping. This is all a mirage. Any minute I'm gonna wake up and realize that this is all a bad dream. Cause I know DAMN WELL this bitch ain't in my fuckin' husband's hospital room!" She whipped around and threw down her purse.

"You love throwing that husband word around like it mean something." Devin ran her hand across Cam's forehead lovingly. "Number one, this ain't no dream. This is reality." She glared at Gray. "I'm here and I'm not going no fuckin' where. Number two, you and Cam are strictly married on paper. Ain't shit real about that sham of a marriage."

"You know what's gon' be real? When I stick my foot so far up yo' narrow ass these doctors won't be able to get it out!" Gray charged towards her, only to be stopped by Dr. Waters. Collecting herself, she inhaled deep.

"I'm not gon' even get myself hyped up to argue wit' you. Get your shit and get the fuck out!" Gray ordered.

Flipping her 40-inch Peruvian weave over her shoulder, Devin pranced over to the chair where her YSL purse was, picked it up and placed the chain strap on her shoulder. Gray let out a sigh of relief that she was heeding her warning and leaving. Pushing Dr. Waters hands off of her, she pushed her hair from her face and straightened her shirt. Instead of walking out, Devin looked Gray square in the eyes and slowly sat down in the empty seat.

"Make me leave." She cocked her head to the side and arched her perfectly shaped brow.

"Oh, you think this a game?" Gray picked up her purse and threw it at her head like she was a pitcher for the St. Louis Cardinals. Quick on her feet, Devin dipped to the side and dodged the throw. All of Gray's belongings went flying out of her bag and onto the floor.

"Have you lost your cotton picking mind?" Cam Sr. shot indignantly. "Don't you see my son laid up here in a coma? This is not the time nor the place for your Jerry Springer foolishness. Both of you need to act like adults. Now, I don't know this young lady, but I expect more from you Gray. You're somebody's mother for God's sake. Put your emotions to the side and put my son and your family first."

Flabbergasted, Gray drew her head back.

"Old head. Are you dumb? I always put my family first. Unfortunately, I can't say the same for you."

Caught off guard by her swift and savage comeback, Cam Sr. turned back around and situated himself in his seat.

"Uh huh." Gray stalked over to him and placed her lips next to his ear. What she said next was for him and his ears only.

"I know all about you cat daddy so tread lightly. Cause I have had just about enough of you. It's because of me you're even sitting here. Don't forget you're occupying that seat. Your so-called son wouldn't even want you five feet near him."

Standing erect, she focused her attention back on Devin.

"And you. Whatever you and my husband had going on is a wrap. Wifey's home. Your time is up. So, let me explain how this gon' go. You can keep that cheap ass condo he bought you and all the other miscellaneous bullshit that adds up to nothing compared to what he does for me—"

"Gray." Devin yawned. "The only thing that needs to be a wrap is your fat ass body and your horrible eating habits. Diabetes is knocking on your door bitch. I'ma be here forever. I know it hurts but don't get mad 'cause yo' husband." She made air quotes with her fingers. "Chose me."

"BITCH!" Gray tried to get at her again but was held back by Dr. Waters.

"Security!" He yelled.

"He never chose you!" Gray continued on. "You were a warm hole for him to roll over and slide into! None of these niggas ever loved you. Gunz didn't want you and neither does my husband! You were nothin' but Cam's cum bucket. You're pathetic! You like to trap niggas wit' fake babies and orgies! Ain't nobody wifing yo' nasty ass! You a one fuck wonder wit' a Forever 21 nametag! And you can't even hold on to that! Ain't that muthafucka going out of business? Do yourself a favor sis. Stop embarrassing yourself and bow out gracefully. Cause you gon' lose to me every time. Then you gon' lose to my kids and two of 'em ain't even his so what that say about your significance in his life? You have none bitch!" Gray curled her upper lip as two security guards stormed in.

"Security, I need you to escort this deranged, loose pussy, minimum wage making, wide forehead having, Pornhub aspiring, side

BITCH out of my fuckin' husband's room! And make note that she is banned and not to return under *any* circumstances! If I catch this bitch within' twenty feet of this room, I will be pressing charges against this hospital and this rat face ho!"

"She can't do that? Can she?" Devin panicked.

"She's his wife. She has final say. We're gonna have to ask you to leave ma'am." One of the guards grabbed her by the arm.

"You ain't gotta put your hands on me. I can walk by myself." Devin exclaimed, trying to pull away but the guards hold was too tight.

"Hurry up." Gray yelled. "You're moving too slow. Get her dusty ass outta here."

"Fuck you bitch! This shit ain't over! I hope you die from high cholesterol! You fat belly, no neck having ass bitch!"

"This fat bitch got the ring tho." Gray stuck out her tongue and threw up the middle finger. "Retarded ho. You got yo' nerve. Sitting up here shaped liked a Build-a-Bear. Bitch you bad bodied, and you tired!" She closed the door in her face.

Forehead pressed against the cool wood of the door, Gray steadied her breathing. The spike in adrenaline, lack of sleep, headache and no food had her feeling faint. How was she going to make it through all of this sane, let alone alive? It seemed like an impossible fete. The saying goes, *God doesn't put you through anything you can't handle.* Gray wondered how true that was. The devil was busy wreaking havoc. He was working overtime to kill and destroy everything good in her life. He knew she was in a vulnerable position spiritually and mentally, so he took it upon himself to attack every area of her existence. It was only day one and the score was The Devil 1 and Gray 0. With the weight of the world on her shoulders, she pulled her head off the door, turned around and looked at Cam. More than ever, she needed him to awake but this time he wouldn't be there to save her. Gray had to save herself and him, all alone.

CHAPTER 4

"Painting every color for you. Just to show you I still care. Cleared the canvas 'cause that's all you. Let me show you that I still care."- Alex Isley, Jack Dine "Colors"

*L*aLa used her fist and banged on Gunz and Tia's door. After learning the news that Cam had been attacked at Quan's wedding, she immediately knew he was behind the assault. The incident had Gunz written all over it.

"It's open!" She heard Tia say.

LaLa pushed open the door and race walked to the kitchen where Gunz was at the stove cooking breakfast. He was in a cheerful mood. The nigga was actually making eggs and whistling. Tia sat at the kitchen island as their son sat in his highchair eating cereal.

"Hey girl." She smiled, happy to see her aunt.

"Hey." LaLa sat her purse down. "Y'all see the news?"

"Yeah. Gunz got that nigga good didn't he?" Tia smirked, pleased with her man.

"At the wedding tho? Your kids were there Gunz." LaLa stared at him in disbelief.

"Press was there. She'd my child. Aoki chose sides. She don't fuck wit' me no more so I ain't got shit for her."

LaLa always knew Gunz was a petty nigga but she had no idea how far his ignorance went. It was mindboggling how he could just dismiss a child he'd raised since birth. It was then she realized that the man before her had no soul.

"Well, I heard from Aunt Vickie that Cam isn't dead. He's in a coma so your little plan didn't work."

Gunz stopped cooking and threw the skillet filled with eggs across the room. The skillet banged against the wall leaving a dent. Tia and LaLa screamed. Gavin Jr. instantly started to cry. Gunz was furious. He needed Cam dead. Being in a coma wasn't good enough. Gunz wasn't a loser. He always played to win. Once Cam was dead, he'd have Gray right back where he wanted her, under his thumb. She needed reminding that she belonged to him. She would never be free of him.

"Baby." Tia held her chest, mortified. Eggs were dripping from the wall.

"What else Aunt Vickie say?" He ignored Tia's shrills and questioned LaLa.

"Just that things are looking bad. The doctors don't seem to think he'll make it." She answered afraid for her life.

"Okay." Gunz nodded his head. His only choice now was to play the background and see how things played out. If Cam survived, he wouldn't live for long. Gunz was gonna make sure of it.

DAY 3:

Gray lay snuggled close to Cam matching her breaths to his. *Inhale. Exhale. Inhale. Exhale.* Together their chests rose and fell with the calming qualities of a lullaby. Justin Timberlake's song *Mirror* played in the background on repeat. It was one of her all-time favorite songs. She prayed one day she and Cam would get to slow dance to it.

Before the love of her life was stabbed and wound up in a coma fighting for his life, she took breathing for granted. She took it for granted until her ribs became steel traps and she could no longer breathe without him. Cam had literally stolen the air from her lungs. Each night, she woke breathing raggedly as if her body was starved of oxygen. During the day, her breaths came in short shallow bursts. The cozy world Gray once lived in had become a one-way mirror and Cam was on the other side of it. Once again, they were placed in a position where they needed each other but were forced apart.

Gazing up at his sleeping his face, she counted each freckle on his nose and cheeks one by one. There were sixty-four in all. Even though she knew the total, it didn't stop her from recounting them over and over again. *Thirty-two, thirty-three, thirty-four thirty-five, thirty-six . . .* In the past, she never understood his obsession with counting her freckles as they lay watching a movie or resting in bed. Now that she had nothing but time to immerse herself in all things Cam, she fully understood his fascination. His freckles were an extension of him. They were a special feature that many didn't ogle or appreciate but she adored. Gray loved every cinnamon colored spec. If only he'd open those lovely brown eyes and touch her with his soothing large hands and make her feel new again. It was only day three and Gray was hanging on by a thread. Day and night, she lay by Cam's side begging him to wake. Her legs had become numb from laying in the fetal position for hours on end. Her bones ached but Gray refused to leave his side. The only time she moved was to use the restroom. Gray barely slept or ate. She only did enough of both to endure. There were many times she wanted to slip into darkness with him, but the beeping of the machines kept reminding her that Cam was still there fighting.

Sixty-one, sixty-two, sixty-three, sixty-four. . . Gazing at his face, she leaned close, ensuring that she didn't disturb the IV in his hand or the endotracheal tube down his throat and tenderly kissed his cheek. His skin was warm against her lips. Gray wished he'd come to so they could talk and laugh like they once did. He was her medicine. Being in his presence made the pain stop, at least it once did.

The ache in Gray's heart came and went but always returned in quiet moments. Softly she whispered, "*The light of God surrounds me. The love of God enfolds me. The power of God protects me. The presence of God watches over me. Wherever I am God is.*" It was a prayer that she chanted numerous times throughout day. For the first time in her life, she heavily relied on her faith. Nothing or no one, not a doctor or a medicine would be able to pull Cam through; only God. Gray and God had always had a shaky relationship. It was hard for her to trust in an invisible force that allowed her and her mother to live poorly, to be raped by a trusted friend, cheated on and beaten by a man who claimed to love her and her dear mother to be called home to heaven. Gray had always been a decent person. She wasn't a saint by any means, but she was kind, respectful, hardworking, and loving. She didn't do drugs. She wasn't a liar or deceitful. She was good but being good seemed to get her nowhere. Here she was being punished repeatedly while people who lived wickedly lived comfortably and were constantly blessed. She never understood it, so she stayed clear of God. She did her thing and let him do his. The two never crossed paths until now. Even though Pastor Edris turned out to be the scum of the earth, his sessions had changed her life for the better. Gray now had a clear understanding of who God actually was and why he allowed certain things to happen. People had to go through hurt and hardships to grow, to learn, to show us the error of our ways and to bring us closer to him. She fully understood that God didn't allow things to happen to us, sometimes we brought difficulties onto ourselves.

Until their counseling sessions, Gray had no idea that while she was busy going through trials and tribulations God was healing wounds she didn't even know existed. It took for God to bring her and Cam back together before his attack for her to fully know He was real. There was so much anger, mistrust, and resentment between them. Only God could mend all that hurt. Gray now had an unshakable faith. She put all of her trust in our father the creator. For God is love, truth, blessed peace, forgiveness, and joy. Love and fear cannot co-exist, so she chose Him. Gray chose love and laid all of her fears down at God's feet.

That still didn't stop the pain that ebbed and flowed through her veins. Each day Cam lay unresponsive in a coma the ache multiplied. She regretted every horrible thing she'd ever said and done to him when he was well. None of it was ever a reflection of him but her inner demons. For so long, she'd been stuck complaining about everything he didn't do instead of focusing on all the positive attributes he brought to her life. She hated herself for running when he rejected her and punishing him by keeping his kids away. Instead of cussing and fighting, she should've communicated her feelings. The problem was whenever she tried to express her emotions her throat would tighten–and the words she desperately wanted to convey were forced back down to the pit of her belly. So, she eternalized everything instead of speaking up. Dr. Waters told her that talking to Cam may help awaken his unconscious brain. What a better time to tell him all the things she hadn't gotten to say. Weaving her fingers through his, she placed her head on his shoulder and closed her eyes.

"You know the kids keep asking about you. Kema told me that Press cries herself to sleep every night and the triplets keep asking if you went back to work. When you were in jail, I told them that's where you were. *Daddy's working is what I would say.*" She took a deep breath. "Baby, you would be so proud of Aoki. She's stepped up in a big way in my absence. She's so helpful, Cam. I don't know what I would do without my big girl. I miss the kids so much. I know they need me, but I can't fathom tearing myself away from you. You're my heartbeat. Without you, I won't make it." Gray's voice croaked but not one tear fell. She was all cried out.

"I don't even know how I survived the last three years and a half years without you. There were so many nights I wanted to reach out. . . just to hear your voice. But I let my silly pride get in the way. I was so stupid. I should've never let you go. Life is too short to be playing games and holding grudges. If I'm being honest, even though I was fuckin' miserable without you, we needed time apart. I had to learn how to stand alone. My whole life I've been dependent on the people around me. From my mother, to Gunz, to you. I needed to learn how to stand on my own two feet. Doing so made me see that I could survive on my own. It was scary as hell being in a new country by myself with five children, but I did it. I did it and I'm proud of myself for that. Now I know for sure when I say I need you; it isn't because I'm afraid of being alone. It's because falling in love with you was like entering a house and finally realizing I'm home." She ran her thumb across the outside of his hand.

"You know when we first met, I was so lost and confused but you stood quietly by my side supporting me. Yeah, you made fun of me, but you never judged me. Remember you joned on me for wearing that suit to club? You said I looked like a fuckin' Republican." Gray chuckled. "I was so uptight back then. I tried so hard to hate you, but I couldn't. You wouldn't let me. You kept pushing yourself in my life. It didn't hurt that you were so damn fine. Every time I was around you I would become tongue tied. My heart would flutter. My palms began to sweat. You ran circles around me with your quick wit and charm. You were so aggressive and cocky as hell. That shit turned me on. You were always more than just a friend to me. I could talk to you about anything. Remember after the fight at the celebrity basketball game you told me the next time you saw me my mood better reflect my worth? And remember when you gave me that piggyback ride so I wouldn't mess up my shoes? I didn't know it at the time, but I loved yo' ass then. You always made me laugh and gave me tough love and advice. I thought I had my life so figured out, but I didn't. My life was spiraling out of control. Then you came into my world and real love began to take shape in my heart. My universe begins and ends with you, Cam. I could run forever, search forever but I will never find a man that will love me like you. Every path in my life leads back to your soul. We're meant to be together. That's why I need you to come back to me. Our story isn't over. It's just beginning but I can't tell it by myself." Gray raised her head and looked at his expressionless face.

"So, open your eyes baby. Wake up. Come back to me." She begged, hoping he would make some kind of movement, but nothing happened.

Letdown, she placed her head back on his shoulder and willed herself not to break.

"It's okay love. I understand. You're not ready yet. You take care of so many people. You're always on the go. You never get any sleep. So, you rest baby. Take all the time you need. I'll be here when you wake up." She pledged as a light knock on the door caught her attention.

In walked Mo and Quan. Gray lifted her sore body to greet them. She'd completely forgot they were coming. Mo looked as bad as she did. Her mahogany skin was drained of all its color. Quan didn't look any better. He was in need of a haircut and shave. Because of Cam's condition, he'd been promoted to the new lieutenant of the Gonzalez cartel. The extra workload, worrying about Cam and taking care of the kids seemed to be wearing him down.

"How you doing sis?" Mo wrapped Gray up in her embrace.

"I'm here," was all Gray could say. Tears sprang in the brim of Mo's eyes. She wished there was more she could do, besides come and sit and hold Gray's hand. Having six children of her own, a household and husband made it hard for her to do much of anything else. She prayed her presence was enough. She hoped her brother knew she was there pulling for him to come to. Her life wasn't the same without Cam. Out of all her siblings they were the closest. There wasn't a day that went by where she didn't speak to or see her big brother. Not being able to talk to him was killing her softly. If Pastor Edris wasn't already dead, she would've killed him herself. Cam didn't deserve what had happened to him. He'd gone to Pastor Edris seeking spiritual guidance and he'd used his trust to make him vulnerable. It made Mo suspicious of everyone. She didn't know who she could trust. In her mind everyone was the op.

"How has he been today?" Quan questioned, standing at the foot of the bed.

"The same." Gray looked back at Cam.

Nothing on him moved except his chest from the mechanical ventilator pumping air into his lungs.

"Did you bring the file?" She asked.

"Yeah." Quan handed her Cam's court papers. "Like I told him, you're not gonna find anything. The informants name has been blacked out."

That didn't stop Gray from skimming through the paperwork anyway. Victor was on her ass. She needed some kind of information to give him so he wouldn't put two slugs in her dome. Quan hadn't told one lie tho. Whenever the informants name came up it was blacked out. Frustrated, Gray ran her hand through her disheveled hair. Without the informants name she was a dead woman walking. What the hell was she going to do now? She knew much of nothing about Cam's business dealings. What she did know didn't help her any. All she knew for sure was that she wasn't the one who had turned him in. Trying to discover the snitch was an added stress she didn't need. Mentally exhausted, she placed the file down on the nightstand. Noticing the tension on her face, Mo massaged her shoulder and said, "You wanna go home, take a shower and change?"

Gray hadn't left Cam's room since his first day in ICU.

"No. There's a shower in the bathroom." Gray stared off into space. She had to figure out who'd dropped a dime on her husband or else she'd be buried six-feet deep.

"I figured you'd say that." Mo pulled out a bag of clothes, underwear, and toiletries she'd put together for her. She felt terrible for her sister-in-law but Gray's dedication to her brother only reconfirmed that she was the right woman for him.

"Thanks Mo." Gray retrieved the bag.

Silence filled the room as they all looked at Cam, wondering when he would pull through. Mentally they offered up a prayer to God asking him to grant Cam a miracle. For they all were struggling to make it without him.

"Gray, let me holla at him for a second." Quan stuffed his hands inside his pocket.

"Sure." She slid off the bed and followed Mo outside.

When the door closed behind them, Quan inhaled and exhaled slowly. It was the first time he'd been alone with Cam. Seeing him look like a vegetable was gut wrenching. He and Cam were as thick as thieves. They'd been best friends since they were kids. He didn't know how to live without him. They'd been through everything imaginable with one another. Without him, he was lost. Cam was a big part of his world. He'd never suffered from grief this bad before. It all started when he learned Pastor Edris was Cam's attacker. Guilt swarmed him. It sneaked up on him quietly and took over his being. Every memory from his wedding week replayed like a song on repeat in his brain. He'd brought this madness into their lives. It was because of him his brother, his best friend, his boy was in this position.

"This all my fuckin' fault." Quan dropped his head. His eyes glimmered with watery tears. "I brought that nigga around you. I know the code. No new niggas. I thought cause the nigga was reformed and a preacher that he was good. I should've known shit wasn't right when his father dropped out of officiating our wedding last minute. Damn." He hung his head back and stared at the ceiling.

"The whole thing was a set up. Gunz got one up on us again but this time I was the one that walked us into the lion's den. How did I not see that shit? I'm supposed to be your blind spot. I fucked up, man. I fucked up." His deep voice croaked. Tears slid out the corners of his eyes and ran down the side of his grief-stricken face.

"I fucked up."

CHAPTER 5

"Cupid hit a bull's eye."- Syleena Johnson feat Common "Bull's-Eye (Suddenly)"

$\mathcal{T}$he sky blazed a vibrant shade of light blue and the sun was a festival of yellow as Aoki and her girls strolled leisurely down 22nd street. Like always it was poppin' on the block. The elders sat on the porch fanning themselves and drinking sweet tea while all the kids ran up and down the street chasing each other with water guns. Aoki's own brother and sisters played in front of Aunt Vickie's house as she sold plates to the neighborhood killers, scammers, and thieves. For the past week, the entire Parthens' clan had been coming over while Kema went to work from 3-11pm. Quan hustled all times of the day and night so it was a must they be somewhere there was adult supervision. Aoki thought she was old enough to watch the little kids but Kema and Quan thought different. If they would've known Aoki and crew would still be there after the wedding, they would've went to summer camp along with Li'l Quan, Makiah, Ryan and King. No one could've foreseen the unfortunate events that occurred at the wedding happening. It was a blessing in disguise that Kema and Quan had planned their honeymoon for the fall.

No, it wasn't home, but Aoki liked being at Aunt Vickie's house. She didn't mind being there at all. There was always good food, somebody getting their hair braided, bomb-ass music and fine niggas coming on and off the block. Even with all that going on, she would much rather be at the hospital with her mom and Cam. Aoki was worried sick about him. Cam was no longer the annoying man who'd married her mom on a whim. He'd become her friend and most importantly her dad.

She'd given him the blues when he first came into her life. Aoki was determined to push him away. At the time, she wanted nothing more than for her mom and Gunz to get back together. They were a family unit that, in her mind, Gray had broken. It wasn't till Gunz swore to be there for her no matter what, and went back on his word, that she finally saw him for the inconsiderate man he was. He didn't give a fuck about her. Gunz didn't even try to have a relationship with her little sister Press who was his biological daughter. Once he had his son, his namesake with the whore he'd cheated on her mother with, they quickly became a distant memory.

Despite being in jail Cam made it his business to be present in their life. There wasn't a birthday or holiday that went by where he didn't make sure he had a personalized gift from him sent. When he got out of jail, he invested all of his energy into making up for lost time. Cam was the perfect dad. He was extremely hood but sweet. He didn't take shit from anyone but was always there showing love in his own special way. He allowed Aoki to be who she was without trying to change her. He taught her right from wrong and encouraged all her hopes and dreams. He was funny as shit and would beat a nigga's ass in a minute. Yes, he was a menace to society. There were more people that feared him than loved him but to his family he was a hero. Aoki didn't know what she would do without him. If he didn't pull through she'd surely lose her shit. She'd never had her biological father and she'd already lost the only father she'd known the first ten years of her life. She couldn't lose another. Cam was all she had left. It had been hard enough knowing he was stuck in a coma and wouldn't wake up. Aoki was dealing with the news the best she could but Press and the triplets were a completely different story. Press wouldn't stop crying and the triplets asked for him nonstop. It was truly heartbreaking. They missed their daddy and Aoki couldn't blame them. She missed him terribly too. Usually, when she felt low she'd have her mother to lean on, but Gray might as well have been in a coma herself. She was good to no one. The last time she'd seen her mother, she looked as sickly as Cam. The sparkle that used to glimmer in her crystal blue eyes had dimmed.

In the movie *The Notebook* Noah and Allie died just minutes apart because they couldn't survive without the other. Aoki had always thought that to be some kind of made up fiction, until she saw the deep-rooted love between her parents. Love like that didn't come often. It was a once in a lifetime, fairytale, otherworldly type love. Aoki prayed to Beyoncé and Blue Ivy she'd never experience something so intense. She never wanted to love a nigga so much she'd die if she lost him. After her unrequited crush on Priest, she'd learned her lesson. Yeah, she still wanted to gag on his dick, but it was apparent he wasn't checking for her. She was thirteen and he was twenty-three. She never had a chance in hell of bagging him but as soon as she was legal, she was coming at him pussy first. Besides, he was too busy running in behind Britten's bobble-head ass to notice her.

With both of her parents out of commission, Aoki felt empty and lost. For the sake of her younger siblings, she had to keep it together but being strong came at a price. She had no one she could turn to when she wanted to vent out her frustrations. When she needed to cry or express her worries, there was no one there. She had to bottle that shit up and deal with it herself. She couldn't let her mother, Press or the triplets see her upset. Aoki had to keep on a strong face for the sake of everyone else. Gratefully, she had Princess Gaga and her new friend, Kiara, to kick it with and take her mind off things. Aoki needed to be around girls her age. Kiara was sixteen but that was neither here nor there. Being around toddlers and a 4th grader was not that deal. That afternoon, they broke out and made their way to the Arab store for drinks and snacks. Kiara and Princess were trying to be seen by the local dope boys on the block. Well, Princess was checking for chicks and dicks but that was none of Aoki's business. Love was love in her eyes.

Normally, Aoki's hot ass would be right on board with her friends' shenanigans, but that day, the heat pushed in making her feel claustrophobic. Aoki hadn't even been outside five minutes and she already wished she would've changed. Living in Paris the last three and a half years, she'd forgot how boiling hot the summers in St. Louis could be. It was 98 degrees and she was foolishly dressed in a black cropped sweatshirt with the word kisses written on the chest, a plaid print skirt that was made to look like a button-up shirt wrapped around her waist and black pointed toe Alexander Wang booties. Thank God she wore her 30-inch sandy-brown hair in a French braid to the back. She would've surely burnt up if all her hair was down. It was far too muggy and hot for that shit. Aoki was in dire need for her new favorite drink called a Quarter Water. They were literally twenty-five cent flavored drinks. The concept blew her mind. With the amount of money Quan gave her each day, plus the emergency debit card her mom laced her with, she could buy as many Quarter Waters as her heart desired.

Going to the Arab store was like going on a wild adventure. You could get soda, chips, candy bars, alcohol, fruit, vegetables, meat orders, fried chicken, cheese fries, cigarettes, Backwoods, money orders, cash your check, play the lotto, buy lashes, and cop a fake Gucci t-shirt. It was one stop shopping at its finest. There were always crackheads and corner boys that worked for Cam standing around out front. A couple of prostitutes even worked the area. To make matters worse somebody had gotten stabbed on the lot the day before. Considering she was raised in the lap of luxury, Aoki fit right into the rough environment. Nobody ever tried her. Not even Damya. They'd crossed paths a few times, but since the ass whooping Aoki laid on her, Damya had morphed into Ray Charles. She acted like Aoki didn't even exist which was fine by her. She had bigger things to worry about than Damya's trout mouth ass. She'd gotten a few side eyes from a few chicks, but bitches knew not to come outside their face, niggas too. Hell, Aoki could barely get a nigga to glance twice at her. Everyone was too afraid of Cam and Quan's wrath to step to her. That didn't stop the neighborhood dope boys from getting on Princess and Kiara. Princess, who was 5'4, Chinese with brunette hair, slanted eyes and full lips was down for the attention, but Kiara the Yung Miami look-a-like was already taken. She and her boo-thang, Meechi, had been together a year and homegirl was dangerously in-love. Since they'd left the house, she'd gone on and on about him. Aoki had tuned out most of her gushing until she started talking about the last time they'd smashed.

"Girl, I had that nigga toes curling. He was moaning like a li'l bitch." Kiara bragged, sticking out her tongue. "Niggas be acting so hard but turn into straight beauticians when you sucking they dick. They be putting your hair up in ponytails and shit. I was like nigga when you learn how to do a ninja bun?"

"So how long do you stay down there when you do it?" Princess whispered as if someone might overhear.

"Mmm . . . it depends. If I'm really into it, thirty to forty minutes."

"See I'm too lazy for all that. When I do start giving head, I'ma Black Chyna the dick and just lay there." Princess flicked her wrist.

"Umm this conversation is too NC-17 for my virginal ears." Aoki screwed up her face.

"You just mad that Priest won't knock the cobwebs off that pussy." Kiara teased.

"Eww he bet not." Princess curled her upper lip. "Have you not seen Surviving R. Kelly? My girl will not be the next Azriel Clary."

Aoki couldn't help but hold her stomach and laugh. Even if Priest wanted to be on some creep shit, he'd never get the opportunity to. Cam would shoot him between the eyes if he ever crossed the line with her.

"I just wanna know what y'all waiting on. When you gon' let a nigga hit? Well, Princess in your case, a nigga hit or a female lick?"

"My daddies raised me right." Princess put her hand on her hip and rolled her neck. "This pussy don't come for free. Ain't no boy or girl my age can afford a Birkin bag, so until then, this cootie cat is off limits." She patted her puss.

"Period." Aoki swiped her hand under her neck.

"How long you been fuckin' anyway?"

"Since I was 12." Kiara answered proudly.

"Damn, your vagina done been through some shit." Princess tuned up her face.

"Fuck you." Kiara playfully hit her arm. "What about you, Aoki? When you gon' bust it wide open?"

"Girl, sex is not on my radar. All I care about is my Pops getting better."

"Any update?" Princess asked.

"I talked to my mom this morning and nothing has changed." Aoki's eyes misted with tears.

She hated being all weak and shit, but it was Cam she was in her feelings over. He was the dad she'd always wanted. God had to work his magic and bring the big homey back to her, her sisters and brother.

"I'm sorry friend." Kiara wrapped her arm around her shoulder.

Aoki leaned into her one armed hug. She and Kiara hadn't known each other that long but as soon as they met they clicked. Kiara lived only two blocks over from Aunt Vickie and was always down with the shits. The day Aoki fought Damya, Kiara was right there ready to knock a bitch out if anybody jumped in. Although they were three years apart in age no one could tell. Because of her 5'7 height, Aoki easily passed for being seventeen.

"I know we just met but I hate seeing you so fucked up behind your old dude being sick. That shit be tearing me up for real."

"Thanks Ki." Aoki returned the embrace.

"Me too friend." Princess rubbed her back.

"Plus, yo' daddy gotta make it. He on my bucket list of niggas I gotta fuck before I die." Kiara boasted, scrolling through Instagram.

"Kiara, don't make me punch you in yo' throat." Aoki warned.

"What? You know yo' daddy fine."

"Cam can get it." Princess agreed.

"I'ma fuck both of y'all up." Aoki pushed them both away.

"I ain't Damya. I will Kung Fu Panda yo' ass."

"Oh, hell naw!" Kiara paused dead in her tracks.

"What?" Aoki looked over her shoulder.

"Look."

Aoki gazed down at her phone. Apparently, Meechi was up to no good again. He'd liked a girl Kiara had accused him of cheating on her with pic.

"I'ma beat his ass." She quickly dialed his number. By the third ring he answered the Facetime looking high as a kite.

High and all Meechi was fine as hell. Mad girls stayed on his dick. He was a young get money nigga with platinum blonde locs, round brown eyes, a slim build, and tattoos. He stayed dripped in blue and the latest hottest sneakers. He and Kiara made a cute couple, but because of his street status, he wouldn't stop putting his dick in other females.

"This what we doing today?" She arched her brow, tapping her foot.

"Hi Meechi. How you doing? Oh, I'm good." He mocked.

"You done?"

"Are you?"

"I haven't even gotten started." She shot back.

"That's the problem. You always on that bullshit."

"And you always on that bitch page!"

"What bitch?"

"Yara! That bitch!"

"Man, ain't nobody thinking bout that girl." He took a pull from the blunt hanging out the side of his mouth.

"LIES! Every day I catch you on her page liking shit."

"And? It's just a pic. You act like you pay my bill or something."

"I don't give a fuck if the Pope paid your bill. I'm your girl and what you're doing is hella disrespectful. What if I liked another nigga's pic?"

"Lose all yo' fingers if you want to."

"See. You full of shit."

"If you would stop barkin' at a nigga that monkey could be full of this dick."

"I wish I would fuck you."

"Quit frontin'. You love this dick. Put yo' pussy on the phone. I miss it." He smirked, licking his bottom lip.

"Ooh I hate you." Kiara narrowed her eyes.

"That's cool. I still love you."

"You don't love me if you looking at another girl's page. You got all of this." Kiara ran her hand down her shapely body. "You don't need to look at another bitch."

"You're right. All I need is you ma."

"Then why you lookin' at another bitch page?"

"Cause these hoes be thick." Meechi blew out a cloud of weed smoke.

Appalled by his response, Kiara gasped for air then ended the call. Meechi had her all the way fucked up. It pissed her off even more to see Aoki and Princess bugging up.

"That shit ain't funny." She pouted.

"Yes, it is." Aoki cried laughing.

"I put that on my mama next time I see him, I'm fuckin' him up." Kiara sent his incoming call to voicemail.

"Girl bye. You ain't gon' do shit but grin all up in his ugly ass face." Princess twisted her lips to the side.

"Y'all are crazy." Aoki wiped the tears from her eyes. She needed that laugh more than she knew.

"That's his ass. He get—"

"Aoki, watch out!" Princess yelled.

By the time she looked up it was too late. A tall, skinny figure came barreling around the corner, charging towards her at full speed.

Kiara and Princess had enough time to move out of the way, but she didn't. The boy slammed into her. Everything after that happened in slow motion. Aoki flew backwards and landed on her back. The impact of the fall was like being hit by a linebacker. All the wind was knocked out of her lungs. The back of her head bumped against the pavement, causing her to see stars. When her sight came into focus, the boy was on top of her gazing into her eyes. The lyrics to Iyla's hit song *Juice* came to mind as she gazed back at him.

I wasn't looking for you when you came along
When you came in
Where did you come from like
Out the sky into my life now
You just dropped out the sky
You just fell in my lap
You just crashed in my life
Run that shit, run it back

Outside of Priest, he was the handsomest nigga she'd ever been blessed to see. He had the kind of face that made your pussy cream on sight. Aoki's little panties were filled with juices she didn't even know she could produce. Her skin tingled from his firm chest being on top of hers. She'd never been this close to a boy before, but this was no boy. He was older than her. How much older she didn't know but he was out of her league. A blue Dodgers hat rested on his head cocked to the back. A tattoo of a gun was inked in the corner of his forehead. A set of silky brows framed his diamond-shaped, coffee colored eyes. Although his skin was the shade of butter, his broad nose let her know his ancestors were straight from Africa. His full pink lips were outlined by a mustache and beard that Aoki wanted to run her fingers through. A collage of tattoos decorated his neck along with a trio of chains and a blue rag. This nigga was hazardous to her health, but Aoki had always been drawn to trouble. She was so caught up in her attraction to him that she couldn't find her voice. When his weight became too much for her to bear she snapped, "Get yo' big ass off of me! Dickhead!"

Aoki tried to push him off, but he was too heavy to move.

"Watch were the fuck you going, Paris!" Kiara yelled from behind.

Paris ignored Kiara's loud-mouth ass and shot the Blasian lookin' bitch a menacing glare. Instantly, her slick talking ceased, and she sealed her plump lips together. The look he gave her told her she needed to shut the fuck up. Paris wasn't like most dudes his age. He didn't tolerate disrespect on any kind of level. Whether it be male or female, he had no problem getting your ass together. Now that he had her in check, he focused all of his attention on her features. Paris thought he knew every li'l bitch that ran around the neighborhood, but he'd never seen this beauty before. Even though she had a face of an angel and a mouth equivalent to an AR-15, she didn't look like she belonged. This girl looked like she should be walking the runway during New York Fashion Week. Her tall frame and slender body rivaled the highest paid supermodel. Her statuesque frame wasn't what tugged at his heart strings tho. It was her eyes. They were fucking mesmerizing. Her eyes were a rapturous shade of cerulean blue. They were emotionless and calm. Paris stomach became heavy with need. Gorgeous wasn't even the word to describe her. She was outright stunning. She was a masterpiece. From her butterscotch complexion to her perfectly shaped nose, Cynthia Bailey cheekbones and beauty mark above her heart-shaped lips, baby girl was the shit. She made feelings and other parts of him rise that he hadn't expected. At the same time, he and she looked down between them.

Aoki's cheeks flushed hot when she realized his strong man was stabbing her in the thigh. Shooting her a cocky grin, Paris winked his eye and took off running when the sound of the police officers who'd been chasing him footsteps neared. Dizzy with lust, Aoki's heart beat so erratically she thought it was going to fly out of her chest. The smirk Paris gave her was only a small smile, but it was enough to make her go back on her word. She didn't know who this nigga was, but she wanted to don his last name, birth his babies, cook him meals and fall madly, deeply in love. It was crazy but that quickly, she wanted everything her mom and Cam had with him. She felt like a sucka for lusting after a nigga who'd almost knocked her soul out her torso but that quickly he'd cast a spell on her. Taking her by the hand, Princess helped her off the ground as two out of shape cops chased behind the boy who'd unknowingly stolen her heart.

"MOVE! MOVE!" They yelled, wheezing past them.

"You alright?" Princess examined her for cuts and bruises.

"Yeah, I'm okay." Aoki dusted off her butt and legs. "Who the hell was that?"

"Paris bad ass." Kiara rolled her eyes. "He get on my damn nerves."

"How you know him?"

"He's Meechi's friend from New York. He moved down here this summer."

"Is that right?" Aoki said intrigued.

"Uh ah, bitch." Kiara shook her head while wagging her finger. "Don't even think about it. Stay away from that one. That nigga right there will ruin your life and I don't want yo' young ass crying to me when he do it."

"I'm young but I'm wise enough to know, that you don't fall in love overnight." Aoki sang lyrics from the old school Brandy song *Broken Hearted*. "Trust me, my mama didn't raise no fool. I know how to handle myself when it comes to the opposite sex. He's fine and all but I ain't checkin' for no nigga on the run from the police. My standards are way higher than that." She professed with confidence, but it was all a show. Aoki knew damn well if this Paris guy ever stepped to her he'd have her hook, line, and sinker.

CHAPTER 6

"I don't know what feels true, but this feels right so stay a sec."- Billie Eilish "Hostage"

DAY 12:

"Daddy! Daddy!" Beaux and Sky stood on the side of Cam's hospital bed jumping up and down.

Their little heads could barely see over the railing, but they were determined to wake up their sleeping father. Unlike in the past, Cam wouldn't open his eyes and give them the attention they so desperately craved. He lay as still as a statue unresponsive to anything around him.

"Mommy, tell daddy to get up." Sky played with the hem of his hospital gown.

"Yeah mama. Kiss daddy. He'll wake up like Snow White." Reign looked up at his mother's face as he sat comfortably in her lap.

On the verge of breaking down, Gray prayed internally, *"The light of God surrounds me. The love of God enfolds me. The power of God protects me. The presence of God watches over me. Wherever I am*

God is." Back on point, she held onto her little man tight. Moments like these she loved that he was a mama's boy. His positive energy seeped into her pores giving her the strength she needed to go on. Gray buried her face in the silky curls on top of his head. The scent of calming lavender and sweet almond shampoo wafted up her nose as she placed a series of kisses to his scalp. Reign was an exact replica of his father. He was long and lean just like him. A galaxy of freckles adorned his button nose. The only feature of his that resembled Gray's was his slanted ocean blue eyes. Closing hers, she wrapped him up in her embrace and rocked him from side-to-side. Each day that passed, life for Gray got harder. She was mentally and physically drained. If she could, she would sleep for a week. That's how tired she was. On top of needing rest, she still was at square one when it came to figuring out who'd set Cam up. Victor was an impatient man. There was only but so much time he was gonna give her. Gray needed a miracle asap.

"Remember mommy said daddy was tired and taking a nap?"

"But I want daddy to play with me." Reign whined, poking out his bottom lip.

"He will baby. . . soon." Gray prayed she sounded as convincing as she intended.

"Mama, you sad?" He picked up on her somber mood.

"A whole lot."

"Mama, I do not like you being sad." He rubbed the side of her face.

"I know, Reigny. You're such a sweet boy."

"You ain't gotta be sad, mama. I got you. You believe me?" He cocked his head to the side and waited for her reply.

"Yes, I believe you when you say that, but you're not supposed to be worried about me. It's my job to worry about you. I'm your mama. I'm the adult."

"Mama." Reign shook his head. "I'm yo' son and daddy told me to-to-to take care of you. So, smile girl. I ain't tryin' to see you cry."

"I'm okay Reign. I swear." Gray lied to ease his fears.

"Nah, mama. I gotta protect you. I'm not trying to see you sad. On blood. We can't have that mama. I got yo' back. For real-for real." He pointed to her chest then his.

"Oh Reigny!" Gray squeezed him tight. "I love you so much."

"Y'all gon' make my big ass cry." Stacy dabbed the corner of his eyes, glued to the wall.

He was almost sure he'd become physically ill if he stepped any closer to Cam's bed. His heart bled to see his bother from another mother laid up with tubes and shit all down his throat and on his chest. Being in a coma had started to wear on his best friend. Cam's hair had grown out of the short sponge twist box he wore for the wedding. His once neatly trimmed and lined beard was long and scruffy now. *I gotta get Trouble in here to get my man right,* he reminded himself. Before the day was over Cam would have a fresh cut and a shave. He couldn't have his man looking crazy. It wasn't like he could do anything else for him besides be there and pray. The least he could do is get him a shape-up. Emotionally exhausted, Stacy ran his large, calloused hand down his face. He hadn't been this drained since he'd been shot. The crew couldn't take another death. They all were still mentally reeling from the way Diggy was brutally shot in the head by Gunz. If Cam didn't come out of this shit, the loss of him would leave a gaping hole that no one would be able to fill. The crack was already starting to deepen amongst the guys. Quan had only been to the hospital to see Cam once. He couldn't stomach seeing his best friend in such a fragile predicament. Stacy had tried to talk him into putting his fears of Cam dying aside, but Quan couldn't do it. It was too much for him to bear. Stacy tried not to feel some type of way but he was lowkey disappointed in his homey. He was carrying the weight of their brotherhood alone. People often thought because he was 6'9, 400 pounds and covered in tattoos that he could tough his way through anything. But like everyone else, Stacy needed comfort too. He needed someone to pat him on the back and assure that everything would be okay. At night he went home alone. He didn't have a wife or a girlfriend to ease his worries. Yeah, Selicia had called a couple of times to check on him but nothing was like the comfort of lying next to a woman at night. Stacy was his own savior. He needed Quan and Cam more than they knew but his pride wouldn't allow him to cry out for help.

Next to him, Priest stood oblivious to his internal agony. From the outside looking in, the big guy seemed fine. Since what had been dubbed the bloody wedding, Priest had been doing fine. He wasn't that emotional of a person. Tragedies didn't affect him like everyone else. He might've been younger than his cousin and his pot'nahs but mentally and emotionally he was hard as steel. While everyone around him unraveled, Priest rose to the occasion and became the backbone of the crew. This was the perfect opportunity for him to prove that he could be trusted as more than an enforcer and guard dog to Gray and the kids. With Cam down and Stacy out of the game, he'd become Quan's right hand man. It was his responsibility to keep an eye on all the corner boys, trap houses, and keep count of all the product going out and money coming in. If somebody came up short or there was a potential beef, it was his job to handle it. Quan had enough shit to deal with. He didn't have time to police a bunch of low level knuckleheads. Priest, however, was happy to do it. The new title meant he couldn't spend as much time with his girl, Britten, but he didn't mind. Priest ate, shit and breathed this street shit. The goal was to one day replace Cam and become Victor's lieutenant. He would never be on some snake shit and ex his cousin out. He would earn the title and get Cam's blessing of course. In the meantime, he'd work his way up the food chain and guard his cousin and family with his life.

Across the room on the opposite of the bed, Aoki caressed Cam's cold hand. It was a hard pill to swallow but Iron Man had fallen and like Spiderman she wasn't ready to accept that Thanos had succeeded in taking her hero down. No man was greater, bigger or badder than Cam but the man that lay before her wasn't the Herculean figure that protected their family at all cost. This version of Cam was skinner and weaker. His heart still beat stubbornly inside his ink covered chest, but his skin was starting to turn a ghostly shade of grey. Cam was on his last leg. Aoki's eyes traced over his protruding collarbone and the veiny arm covered in tubes that once rocked her siblings to sleep. Even though he wouldn't wake, she knew her hero, her Iron Man was still in there, locked inside a body that wouldn't give up and chained to a heart that insisted on thumping despite the likelihood of him surviving.

Aoki tried to have faith that he would pull through but at thirteen it was hard to see the light at the end of the tunnel. It wasn't helping that the other man she adored was literally inches away, sucking the air out of her lungs. There wasn't a day that went by since the wedding that Priest hadn't come by to check on her and the little kids. When he did pull up on them, Aoki made it her business to avoid him. Ever since the pool fiasco, she'd been mortified to be in his presence. He didn't have to say it. The look in his eyes said everything. To him she was nothing but a pathetic little kid with a crush. Priest had it all wrong tho. She wasn't a little girl and her feelings for him went deeper than he would ever know. One day he would be hers. Aoki had never been surer of anything in her life. She and Priest were meant to be together. The only thing keeping them apart was their age difference. If she was older there was no doubt in her mind he'd be head over heels in love with her. Why did she have to be ten years younger than him? Why did God have to be so cruel? Didn't he know that seeing him made her heart twirl. Priest barely spoke a word but when he did the sound of his gravelly voice made her stomach drop. Aoki tried to get over her fascination with him but there was no helping the way she felt. Every time she was in his presence, she was reminded of just how fuckin' fine he was. Priest whiskey colored eyes told a story every time she looked at him. He was effortlessly handsome. Aoki glanced at him out of the corner of her eye. A white dad hat was cocked so low she could barely see his eyes. A gold diamond Cuban link chain, Off-White graphic tee, shorts, Nike socks and $450 Air Max 1 Parra sneakers made the buds of her nonexistent breasts sprout. He was perfection in human form. Aoki couldn't take how fine he was. *Jesus help me,* she silently prayed. Focusing back on Cam, she asked God to please wake up him.

"You have to come back to us." She whispered low so only he could hear.

"Daddy, look." Sky tried to push her new Emma Wiggles doll in his face. The triplets were obsessed with The Wiggles. They watched the show all day every day.

"She's the girl with the bow in her hair!" Beaux sang at the top of her lungs.

"Be quiet, Beaux. You're being too loud." Press shushed her.

"No! Daddy wanna hear me sing." She rolled her little neck.

"Mama, please get yo' child. She is working my nerves." Aoki glared at Beaux who was still singing.

"Everybody put your hands in the air!" Sky joined in and sang along with her. Twirling around in a circle, she shook her little tushy.

"If y'all gon' sing, rap some Meek Mill or something. Papa don't even like The Wiggles." Press popped her lips.

"Ah huh." Beaux balled up her face.

"Shut up li'l girl." Press argued. "Papa a hood nigga and hood niggas like hood music."

"Period." Aoki swiped her hand under her chin. *"I'm back in this bi — and I'm back on my shi—."* She bounced her shoulders. As if the holy ghost hit her, Aoki channeled Meek and rapped his hit song *Lord Knows* loud as hell. It was one of Cam's favorites.

"Man they tell me be humble, I'm cocky as hell
Shout-out my bitches that answered my calls
When I called 'em collect cause it got me through hell
Shout-out that judge that denied me my bail
It made me smarter and made me go harder
They locked me up and slowed my album up
But I did not give up cause I knew I would prevail!"

Totally engrossed in the lyrics Aoki and Press forgot they were in front of their mother. Cursing in front of her wasn't something they did but the spirit of Meek and Cam had taken over their bodies. There in the hospital room they put on their own private show for their Pop. Stacy and Priest stood back looking at them like they had lost their damn minds. Gray held Reign in her arms in a state of amusement and wanting to beat their asses at the same time. They knew damn well she didn't play that cursing shit. Cam thought it was funny, but she didn't.

Gray thought kids should stay in a child's place. The triplets seemed to love the show, however. Reign rocked back-and-forth as if he could hear the operatic beat while Sky and Beaux danced around in their Emma costumes like ballerinas. Gray might not have liked how they were behaving but apparently Cam did because out of nowhere his hand twitched.

"Oh my God! He moved!" She shrieked with excitement.

During the twelve days he'd been in a coma, Cam hadn't moved a limb. Stacy quickly pushed off the wall to get a better look. Sure enough, his best friend's hand was jerking. Everyone in the room was on pause. No one moved a muscle. They couldn't believe their eyes. It was finally happening. Cam was coming to.

"He likes the music." Stacy stated breathlessly.

"Aoki keep going." Gray urged.

Aoki didn't hesitate to resume rapping. If it was going to help Cam fight his way out of the coma, she'd sing every rap song known to man.

"All black Rottweiler, that Givenchy on
Drop-top Rolls Royce but the top is on
And the windows down like see y'all later
Mirror-tint on that bitch so you could see y'all hating
Champagne cork pop like we all made it
Y'all looking from the sideline we all hate it
Money don't make it real
Don't give a fuck if its eighty mil. . . pussy." She flowed like she was at Summer Jam.

"And just 'cause you got a Bentley
That Bentley won't make you thorough. . . pussy
Still hating me from my city
I'm thinking is they for real. . . pussies
'Cause all I got to say is kill
They'll come in like Navy Seals
That's word to my momma, I promise I ain't doing no block—"
Abruptly Aoki stopped.

Cam's legs had started to shake.

"Oh my God. He's waking up." Press rose to her feet with tears in her eyes.

Cam's left leg glided across the mattress then moved back into place. Shaking uncontrollably his big toe flexed. Then his right hand fell limp to his side. No one knew what was happening. He hadn't opened either of his eyes, but it seemed like a bolt of electricity had shocked his body. Any hope they had of him waking was washed away. It was abundantly clear that Cam wasn't coming out of his coma. Something totally different was occurring. Cam's frail physique shivered and convulsed like he was having a seizure. Gray swiftly placed Reign down and sprinted out of the room. Adrenaline pumped through her system. She would be damned if Cam died on her watch.

"Something is wrong with my husband! We need a doctor!" She yelled.

Dr. Waters and a nurse from the nurses station rushed inside the room on high alert. It was a madhouse within the four walls. The triplets had begun to cry. Their wails were high pitch like nails on a chalkboard. Press tried to console them, but she too had started to cry. Cam's body wouldn't stop jerking. He moved around like someone was sticking his body with thousands of needles. Gray wanted desperately to help him. Cam hadn't even been this bad off when he initially got stabbed. Was he going into shock? Aoki eased back; grief stricken. This was all her fault. Cam was going to die because of her. All she was trying to do was help but she'd made things worse. Fear gripped her throat. Only enough air seeped in to allow her body to function. The lack of oxygen was still crippling nonetheless.

"What's wrong with him?" Gray panicked.

The doctor checked his vitals before answering.

"Your husband is experiencing shivering in a coma."

"Is that bad?" Priest asked.

"Yes. Mr. Parthens has developed hypothermia because of a low ambient temperature. We need to get him warmed up and his temperature stabilized. Nurse Cindy, please get the patient some blankets and several dry compresses asap."

"Yes doc." The nurse speed walked out of the room.

"Will he be alright?" Gray questioned dizzy with worry. She'd never experienced anything like this before.

"We're going to monitor your husband's vitals closely over the next few hours. We'll have more information for you then." Dr. Waters assured.

Gray plopped down in her seat, breathing heavily. The palms of her hand were so clammy, she could barely grip the arm of the chair. Hypothermia was the last thing Cam needed. His poor body couldn't go through another ailment.

"I can't take this shit." Stacy tugged on his beard, stressed the fuck out.

"Mrs. Parthens, I hate to say this." Dr. Waters hesitated.

"Say it muthafucka!" Stacy barked, causing the poor doctor to flinch.

"It's my duty to inform you that you have to consider taking your husband off life support. It's been twelve days and we don't want him to suffer."

"Why would you even suggest that?" Gray balled up her face. "I'm not doing that." The mere thought of ending Cam's life almost caused her to pass out. She hadn't even considered taking him off the machines.

"It's something you're gonna have to consider at some point."

"Yo get the fuck out." Stacy damn near pushed the doctor out.

"He can't leave. He has to help him." Gray stressed, feeling numb.

Snot raced down Reign's nose as he raised his arms for his mother to pick him up. Gray roughly placing him down on the floor and running out of the room had scared him senseless. Beaux and Sky followed suit. Using the last of the strength she had for the day, Gray picked each of her kids up one-by-one. Their cries were ferocious. Each sob weighed heavily on Gray's wounded spirit. Lord knows she wanted to give up but having her babies close brought upon a peace that calmed the storm inside her heart. While she gained solace from her children, Aoki wasn't so lucky. She in fact was dizzy. What had occurred and hearing the doctors suggestion might've scarred her for life. The walls had started to close in. She had to go. She needed some air. Without a word, she raced out before anyone could stop her. Walking as fast as she could, she made her way down the long hall until there was nowhere else for her to go. Facing the wall, she sank down to her knees. The pain that flowed from her lungs was palpable. When would their family get a break? It had been nothing but one horrific incident after another. Crying wasn't enough. Aoki wanted to scream but the lion inside of her wouldn't allow her to break. She was stronger than this. She was tougher than her circumstances. Cam hadn't raised her to be a punk. She was a soldier in the making.

Gathering her emotions, she wiped her face when a set of muscular, tattooed arms wrapped around her feeble body and lifted her up. Notes of peach, may rose and jasmine engulfed her as she was spun around, and her face was pressed into a hard chest. Priest had come for her. Aoki would've betted money that he didn't care about her pain, but his actions proved he did. He might not have liked her the same way she liked him, but he cared and that was all that mattered. Countless nights she'd prayed for a moment like this. Sealing her misty eyes shut, Aoki held onto him for dear life. She prayed to Jehovah he never let her go. Priest's hug was life changing. His arms around her waist was heaven sent. She'd never been more content in her life. If Aoki could, she'd crawl inside his veins and take up space. As if holding him wasn't quite enough, she squeezed him a fraction tighter. Her heart thumped so hard that she swore it was audible. She prayed he didn't feel it, but he did. Priest needed to let her go but his arms stayed planted in place. Aoki was a little girl in duress. Most niggas he knew would've folded under the pressure she'd been through. He didn't want to encourage the inappropriate crush she had on him, but underneath all the murk, Priest had a heart. He couldn't see her in pain and not do something to help. One *innocent* hug wouldn't hurt.

"You straight Blue Eyes?" He held her at arm's length.

Aoki gazed up at his gorgeous face and lost her voice. You couldn't tell her Priest wasn't an African God.

"Yeah." She fanned her hair anxiously. Aoki hated how being around him always made her feel unsure of herself. Her hair was never shiny enough. She couldn't stop blinking. Her lips always seemed too dry. Her hands wouldn't stop shaking and her knees were always seconds away from giving out. Man did she want to kiss him. His lips weren't that far from hers. All she had to do was lift up on her toes and plant her mouth on his. Aoki's heart pounded in her throat as she licked her bottom lip. She was going to do it. If Cam being in a coma didn't do anything else, it showed her tomorrow wasn't promised. You had to live for the day. Fear and common sense be damned. Aoki wanted Priest in the worst way. Inching closer, she took in a gulp of air. Just as she was about to pucker her lips and close her eyes a female's voice interrupted her flow.

"Baby, is that you?" Britten called out.

Priest spun around and focused all of his attention on his girlfriend. Aoki's nostrils flared with fury. She was so tired of this beautiful ho. Everything on her was perfect, from her stupid hair, to her symmetrical face, big tits, round hips, and fat ass. Aoki hated her fucking guts. Whenever Britten was around she became an afterthought. It wasn't fair.

"What you doing all the way down here? Ain't Cam room back there?" She pointed.

"Yeah, I had to check on the li'l homey." He patted Aoki's shoulder like he was a coach and she was on his little league team.

Aoki was so mad she could spit. Taking her eyes off her man, Britten looked over at the curly haired teenage girl who'd obviously been in tears.

"Awwww! Aloha, are you okay?" She asked empathetically.

"My name ain't no damn Aloha. It's Aoki. Say it with me dummy. . . A-O-Ki." She enunciated each syllable.

Britten furrowed her brows and looked Aoki up and down. This child had her all the way fucked up. For some reason, her young ass scratched at her insecurities. She knew there was no way in hell Priest would ever cross the line with her but down the line Aoki would become a problem. It was best she get her in check now so she wouldn't have to do it later.

"Oh, wow. Now I remember you. You the li'l girl that jumped in the deep end of the pool and tried to kill herself. Baby, didn't you say she did it cause she had a crush on you?" Britten circled her arm around Priest's waist.

As if she'd been punched in the face, Aoki shook her head to shake off the sting of Priest's betrayal. She'd never be able to live down the embarrassment of that horrible day. Why did he have to go and make things worse by telling his bitch she liked him? They already took her as a joke. Priest spotted the look of hurt in Aoki's sapphire colored eyes. He didn't know why but a small part of him wanted her to know he hadn't told Britten about her crush to clown her. It was something that came up in conversation, but then he remembered that despite her looks, Aoki was a child. He didn't have to explain anything to her young ass. Lowkey, Aoki was glad this had happened. This was what she needed to come back down to earth. It was time to get over her silly obsession with Priest and let him go. It wasn't like she had him in the first place. As far as she was concerned, Priest and Britten's flat screen sized forehead could kiss her ass. Pushing them out of the way, Aoki made her way back to her dad's room. It didn't matter how fine he was. From that day moving forward it was fuck Priest for life.

CHAPTER 7

"Boy you'll be the death of me. Your my James Dean. You make me feel like I'm seventeen. You drive too fast. You smoke too much but that don't mean a thing. 'Cause I'm addicted to the rush."-Beyoncé "Rather Die Young"

ith her Apple EarPods in her ear, Aoki nodded her head to the rhythmic sound of Slum Village *Fall in Love*. Music was Aoki's lifeline. She loved all genres and was always on the hunt for the latest bop. *Fall in Love* was a hip hop classic and one of her favorites. The track had a cool, mellow vibe that matched her somber mood perfectly. Since the age of ten, Aoki felt alone. Once she'd learned the true identity of her father the feeling of isolation really set in. Being the product of rape made her feel dirty, like she was a mistake. It seemed like everyone had a place in this world but her. When Gunz abandoned her the pain she harbored multiplied. Anger festered in her soul. Through therapy, she was able to deal with the agony of feeling displaced. Aoki quickly realized that she wasn't alone. She was surrounded by love. Her biological father might've been a monster and the man who'd raised her might've replaced her with the son he'd always wanted, but through it all, her mother was there. Gray was always a consistent figure in her life. She'd jump through fire to protect her daughter. Aoki didn't always believe that. Hours of therapy finally convinced her of Gray's love and devotion. Now they were closer than ever. Their bond could never be broken, but with her mother on Cam duty, old feelings of being alone crept back in. Loneliness became a vice on her heart, squeezing with just enough pressure to be a constant pain. It killed her every day just a little bit more. Loneliness took what was once her inner light and replaced it with a darkness that overshadowed any good moment. That hot July night it was more of the same. Aoki sat on the front steps of Aunt Vickie's house. Crickets and cicadas made noises around her. The sun was still up but in another two hours the moon would light up the night sky. Oh, how she wished Makiah and Ryan were around. She missed her cousins like she missed 106 & Park. She needed them to get back from summer camp asap. She was bored out of her damn mind. Aoki couldn't be around her brother and sisters another second. Hearing them run around singing the Wiggles and playing with L.O.L. Surprise toys was driving her fucking insane. Every five seconds they were in her face begging her to play hide and go seek or to fix them something to eat.

Aoki was far too fly to be wasting her time and beauty on a bunch of kids. No one had even seen her cute outfit except Aunt Vickie's next door neighbor Miss Mary and the baseheads trying to barter for a free plate. The black leather beret, Dolce & Gabbana cross necklace, Gucci logo tee, black lace trimmed, mustard colored satin slip dress with a split, Doc Martins and Moschino fanny pack she rocked was a complete waste of an ensemble. She'd spent hours putting together the perfect look and for what, so crackhead Tony could ask her for $2. When she spotted Kiara walk up the driveway, Aoki practically pussy popped on a handstand. Thank God she'd have someone her age to talk to. She'd text her a few hours before to see what she was on but had gotten no answer.

"Why you sitting here looking like somebody stole yo' bike?" Kiara teased.

"Cause I'm bored bitch. Where the hell you been?"

"Girl." Kiara placed her Adidas by Stella McCartney sneaker on the bottom step. "My mama had me ripping and running to the store with her all day. We just now getting home. But she about to go to work. You wanna come over to my house for a while?"

"Hell yeah. I was hoping you'd ask." Aoki sighed with relief.

"Bet. Let me get a plate before we break out. What Aunt Vickie cook today?"

"Macaroni and cheese, curry chicken, sweet potatoes and hot water cornbread." Aoki rattled off the list as her stomach began to growl. She'd eaten twice in the few hours she'd been there, but Aunt Vickie's food was so good she could make room for more.

"Oh, I'm about to fuck this food up." Kiara rubbed her hands together like Birdman.

Minutes later, the two girls made their way down the street and around the corner to Kiara's crib. Aoki had only been over there twice. Kiara and her mom lived in a modest two bedroom, one bathroom ranch style home. There were two floors, the main level and the basement. They even had carpet and air conditioners that sat inside the window, which Aoki had never seen before. She thought all homes had marble floors and cool air that came out of vents. She soon learned that all people didn't live the same. Even though Kiara's home was low income it was clean and filled with love, which was all that mattered in the bigger scheme of things.

"Ma, I'm back!" Kiara yelled as soon as they walked inside.

"Good 'cause I'm about to go." Her mom placed her things inside her purse.

"Hi, Miss Andrea." Aoki waved taking a seat on the couch.

"Hey pretty girl." Andrea smiled, dressed in her hotel uniform.

She worked the night shift as the front desk manager at the Marriot

Hotel. Andrea was drop dead gorgeous and young. She'd had Kiara at the tender age of twelve. She was twenty-eight now. Aoki couldn't imagine having a baby at twelve. She still liked watching the Disney channel after school.

"How yo' fine ass daddy doing? He wake up yet?" Andrea quizzed, checking her makeup in the mirror.

It took everything in Aoki not to check the shit out of Andrea. Andrea's ratchet ass knew Cam was married to her mom. Twisting her neck from side-to-side, Aoki reminded herself that neither Kiara nor her mama knew any better.

"No. He hasn't."

"Ooh I hope he do. I been trying to sit on that dick since I was in the eighth grade." Andrea fanned herself with her hand.

"Mama!" Kiara shrilled, turning beet red.

"Oh, girl hush." Andrea waved her off.

"No. We discussed this. I got first dibs on that."

Aoki furrowed her brows and looked at the mother-daughter duo like they were fucking nuts. If they kept on talking reckless, she was gonna go heads up with both of them.

"Chile please. Yo' young ass don't know what to do wit' no grown man dick. Keep on fuckin' wit' these li'l niggas like Meechi and leave the big boys to me." Andrea gave Kiara a quick kiss on the cheek. "If y'all leave, make sure you lock up. Bye pretty girl." She waved over her shoulder and sashayed out the door.

"Y'all crazy." Aoki shook her head.

"That's her but c'mon." Kiara threw her plate in the microwave for later.

"Where we going?"

"To pull up on Meechi."

"Where he live at?"

"Not that far. C'mon." Kiara tried to lift her up.

"You still ain't gave up no location."

"Yo' Parisian ass wouldn't know the area no way."

"I ain't going nowhere until I get that address bruh." Aoki stood her ground.

"He live in Tower Village Apartments. You happy now?"

"Don't be on that bullshit, Ki. Aunt Vickie said I gotta be back by nine."

"I keep on forgetting yo' young ass is a tween." Kiara rolled her eyes to the sky. "Now let's go. You wasting time."

Groaning, Aoki eased off the velvet couch and strapped her Moschino fanny pack sideways across her chest. Having a friend that was older than her came with its ups and downs. One of the plus's was that Kiara had her own car. Yeah, it was a 2003 Chevy Malibu with chipped paint and a shotty motor, but they were able to get around. The downside was that Kiara always wanted to be around her boyfriend. It was bad enough they talked to each other morning, noon, and night. She had to be around him just as much. The shit was sickening. Aoki knew she was being a hater, but it was only because she didn't have a boo thang of her own. When they got to Meechi's apartment, Aoki quickly realized she'd made the wrong decision by coming over. She wasn't expecting it to be a kickback going on. The sound of music, loud voices and the overwhelming smell of weed hit her before she even got to the door.

"How I look?" Kiara posed.

Aoki eyed her friend. Like herself, Kiara always stayed on some fly shit. Andrea would be damned if her daughter didn't have the latest drip.

"Yo' ugly ass cute."

Flipping her long weave over her shoulder, Kiara threw up the middle finger then turned and knocked on the door. Giddily, she waited for Meechi to answer. It didn't take long before he swung open the door. A cloud of weed smoke smacked them in the face. Aoki clutched her chest and coughed profusely. Aunt Vickie was gonna kill her if she came home smelling like Kush, especially if she didn't bring her any. While she stood there hacking, Kiara and Meechi were oblivious to her distress. They were too busy sticking their tongues down each other's throats. Aoki wanted to gag on a fucking spoon. These horny niggas were practically clothes burning in her face. Meechi was groping her ass and Aoki swore she heard Kiara slip out a moan.

"Mmm hmm." She cleared her throat.

Finally, the two horndogs came up for air and remembered she was there.

"Oh, my bad. What's up, Aoki?" Meechi spoke as Kiara wiped her gloss off his lips.

"I can't call it." She replied, sounding like an eighty-five year old man.

"Y'all come in." He stepped to the side so they could get by.

Aoki followed closely behind her friend. It was so foggy she could barely see. The blue colored lights around the apartment weren't bright enough to light up the space. Shots from a semi-automatic rang from the 82-inch 4k tv mounted on the wall. A group of guys sat around the living room talking shit as they played Call of Duty. Aoki didn't know who they were but judging by the color blue they donned, she could surmise they were Crips. A blunt was being passed between the three of them. A bottle of Hennessy and Don Julio was devoured without any cups. Aoki almost gagged. She didn't understand how niggas could drink in behind each other. Niggas barely brushed their teeth and never flossed. On top of that they put their mouth on any bitch with a fat ass. She'd be damned if she got the coronavirus and died behind one of these niggas. Aoki hadn't been there five minutes and she was ready to dip. Meechi lived by his self so the place was barely clean. The trash needed taking out and the sink overflowed with dishes. She was surprised his ass didn't have roaches. According to Kiara, he grew up not having a stable living environment, so Aoki gave him a pass. Besides Meechi was eighteen and getting money hand over fist. He was barely home enough to clean anything.

"Friend." Kiara caught her attention. "Stay out here with them. I'ma holla at Meechi real quick."

"Holla as in a conversation or as in your legs about to be spread in the air." Aoki folded her arms across her chest.

"You already know that pussy about to talk to me real nice." Meechi pulled Kiara close.

Aoki swore she was about to throw up. Not only was she sick to her stomach at the thought of Kiara and Meechi boning, she was pissed the fuck off. Kiara was always on that bullshit when it came to him. Aoki's plan was to kick it with her girl, not sit around while she gagged on her boyfriend's dick. *I should've stayed my ass at Aunt Vickie house,* she mentally scolded herself.

"Girl, I ain't come over here for that. And what happened to you going upside his head the next time you saw him? I knew yo' ass was lying. Princess was right. Yo' scary ass wasn't gon' do shit." She quipped.

"Whatever bitch. Don't hate. Instead of worrying about what I'm doing with my nigga, you need to be seeing what's up wit' one of them." Kiara pointed to the three dudes in the living room.

"The fuck I look like?" Aoki curled her upper lip. "I don't want none of them dirt dobbers."

"Dirt dobber?" One of the guys named Rob tuned up his face. "Yo who you talkin' to?"

Aoki looked at the DC Young Fly look-a-like sideways.

"Well, first of all." She rolled her neck. "I wasn't talking to you. You all over here in our conversation."

"Facts 'cause yo' Big Bird lookin' ass called us dirty."

"If the shoe fits." She shot back on ten. Aoki didn't give a fuck if this dude was older than her and gang affiliated. She wasn't afraid of anybody with two legs and walking.

"I don't even know what the fuck that mean but you got me fucked up." Ole boy stood up.

"Nah nigga, you got life fucked up. Instead of worrying about me, you need to be concerned wit' yourself and that each-one-teach-one education you have. Wit yo' bum ass. You can't even afford no haircut."

"Haircut or not, I'll still smack the shit outta yo' dumb light skin ass." He pulled out his strap ready to backhand her with it.

"Chill. That's the OG Cam right there." Meechi tried to stop his homeboy.

"And? I don't give a fuck about that old ass nigga. Didn't that nigga Gunz just lay that nigga out?"

Rage rose in Aoki like an ocean wave. Within a blink of an eye, she became blind with fury. No one would ever disrespect her family, specifically not Cam. See niggas had the game fucked up. They thought her Pop was down for the count so muthafuckas thought they could talk slick at the mouth. But what they failed to realize is that Cam would be back, and when he was 100 percent, these same lame ass niggas talking shit would be buried six-feet deep.

"Nigga, I'll kill you." Aoki pulled a freshly sharpened switchblade from her fanny pack. She was always taught never to pull a weapon unless she was willing to use it. Aoki might've been only thirteen, but she wouldn't hesitate to slice a nigga's throat.

"Bet. Let's see who get to who first." Rob cocked the hammer back on his gun.

"Nigga, didn't you hear what the fuck I said?" Meechi barked, ready to fuck his mans up. "Gunz her Pops, nigga. You don't want that type of smoke."

Flaring his nostrils, Rob let Meechi's words sink in. Gunz was the big homey to most of the cats in the neighborhood. It was well known how Gunz got down. The wars he'd waged in the street were legendary. Rob respected his gangsta immensely.

"A'ight, you got it." He put his gun back on safety. "I'ma chill but let's be clear, she ain't gon' be in here disrespecting me just because of who her father is. I'll fuck her bulimic ass up."

"Nigga, try me and yo' mama will be identifying your body at the morgue." Aoki spat still on go.

"Ooh y'all got my blood pressure up." Kiara wiped sweat from her brow. "C'mon baby." She pulled Meechi by his arm.

"Uh ah. You ain't about to leave me in here with these niggas. I'm ready to go." Aoki blocked her path.

"Girl, chill. I ain't gon' be that long. I swear." Kiara rubbed Aoki's arm. "Besides," she whispered. "Meechi don't even last that long."

"I heard that shit. Now I'm really about to dig up in them guts." He dragged her up the steps.

Fuming, Aoki leaned up against the wall with her arms akimbo. Kiara leaving her with a group of niggas she didn't know and one who'd just threatened to shoot her was strike #1. Ryan and Makiah would've never played her like that. They rode for each other hard. It was obvious Kiara valued dick over friendship. All Aoki knew was that she had ten minutes to bring her ass on or she was leaving without her.

"Yo. You want something to drink?" A dude that reminded her of the rapper Li'l Baby held up a bottle of Hennessy.

"No. Fuck, I look like? I don't drink after niggas. There is a such thing called backwash. And them niggas in there look like they don't even know what Fluoride is."

"Damn cutie. You going hard on my mans." Dude grinned. "Since it's a no on the Henny, you want me to get you a bottle of water out the fridge?"

Realizing she was being a bitch for no reason, Aoki took a good look at the dude in her face. Unlike his dusty friends, this guy looked like he was well acquainted with a washcloth. The locs on the top of his head were neat and his outfit was up to her standards. He rocked a white fitted tee, Gucci belt, slim-fit Balmain jeans and blue and yellow Balenciaga track sneakers. The generic version of Li'l Baby wasn't her type physically, but his swag had Aoki intrigued.

"Nah, I'm good. I'm just ready to go." She pouted still in a foul mood.

"Why? You just got here."

"Cause I don't know y'all niggas and she upstairs being a ho." Aoki grimaced, ready to punch a hole in the wall.

"You gotta chill wit' using the N-word. We don't even know if you black or not." Rob jumped in her conversation again.

"*Nan dangsin-I ttong-eul ttaelilmankeum chungbunhi geom-eun-*

ibnida. (I'm black enough to smack the shit out of you.)" She shot in Korean.

"I knew she wasn't black yo! I knew it!" Rob gloated as his boy Chris slapped a $20 bill in his hand. "Up here cultural instigating."

"Appropriating dick head." Aoki corrected him. "And I am black if you must know."

"Fuck outta here." Rob waved her off. "I need to see your 23andMe."

"See this." Aoki mimicked jerking off a dick and coming on his face.

"I like her li'l sexy ass. She feisty as shit." Chris flirted.

"Will y'all niggas mind y'all business and play the game?" Blizz shot irritated. Rob and Chris were fucking up his flow.

"I see you over there tryin' to get your mack on. Ole lame ass nigga!" Rob pestered him.

"Anyway. Fuck them niggas. What's up wit' you?" Blizz focused back on Aoki. She was the prettiest girl Kiara had ever brought around. She was way out of his league, but he'd be remiss if he didn't shoot his shot.

"Who are you?" Aoki continued to give him attitude.

"I'm Blizz. You?" He stuck out his hand.

"Not interested." She glared back at him.

"That mouth shawty." Blizz grinned, entertained by her zero fucks attitude.

Liking his persistence, Aoki caved in and shook his hand.

"Aoki."

"I ain't never heard of no name like that. What you got Indian in yo' family or something?"

"No." She groaned, completely turned off.

"So, Miss Aoki. You gon' give me your number so I can call you sometime?"

"Mmm. . . let me think about it." She placed her index finger on her chin. "No."

"Damn, it's like that?"

"Like I said, I don't know you niggas."

"I'm tryin' to get to know you tho. You ain't got shit to worry about. I'm harmless." He pinched her chin and flashed a charming grin.

Aoki inhaled deep and rolled her eyes.

"A'ight, I guess but don't be blowing me up." She placed her number in his phone.

"I got you." He saved her contact info.

BOOM, BOOM, BOOM, BOOM, BOOM! A loud knock came from the door.

"Aye yo Blizz. See who that is." Rob kept his focus on the game.

"Nigga, I ain't Fonzworth Bentley."

"Just see who it is."

"I'll be back." Blizz walked to the door. Whoever was on the other side, was knocking like they were twelve. Hand on his pistol, he looked out the peephole.

"It's P." He unlocked the door. "What up?" He extended his hand.

A deathly scowl was plastered on Paris' face as he eyed Blizz open palm. He knew damn well he didn't fuck with him like that. Blizz was Meechi's friend not his. Paris didn't call anyone his boy except Meechi. He'd proven he was down ten toes. These other niggas would fold at a drop of a dime. They weren't about that life. They weren't no killers. He could tell by the glimmer of fear in their eyes they weren't real. Not in the mood for pleasantries, he bumped past Blizz like he wasn't shit. In Paris' mind he wasn't. He was there for one thing and one thing only: his bread. He had tunnel vision when it came to getting money. Deep pockets was the only thing that would better his situation. It wasn't like he had many people in his corner backing him. At a young age, Paris realized he was the only person he could depend on. Humans were fickle. That's why he didn't invest too much energy into them.

Blizz's face turned an embarrassing shade of scarlet red. He was hot that P had fronted on him in front of Aoki. He'd just softened her up to the point she felt comfortable to give him her number. He didn't want her to change her mind about him within a matter of seconds. If he had balls, he would've checked Paris, but his gut reminded him that he wasn't about that action for real. Paris was known for going ape shit. The nigga was a certified gorilla. Blizz would just have to eat him not speaking. It was humiliating but getting his ass kicked in front of a girl he liked would be something he'd never be able to live down.

Up against the wall, Aoki checked the time on her Apple watch. Kiara's ten minutes were up. Fed up with waiting on her, she pushed her body off the wall and linked eyes with a tall, lanky figure coming down the partially lit hallway. At first she didn't recognize the guy, but as he drew closer memories of the cutie with sad eyes who'd tackled her to the ground flashed in her mind. It was him. It was Paris in all his fine ass glory. Aoki wanted to sink her teeth into the skin of his tattooed neck. He was deliciously handsome. A strange jolt of electricity raced in-between her thighs as he neared. *Damn,* Aoki mumbled as her heartbeat erratically. This nigga had her straight tweakin'. His menacing eyes were a blazing red. The green dad hat hovering low made the rest of his features indistinguishable. The Cuban link chain, retro Shawn Kemp Sonics jersey, black ripped jeans, Air Jordan 10 "City Pack" sneakers and Louis Vuitton bookbag almost made her hyperventilate. It should've been against the law for a nigga to look so good. Ink covered every inch of his neck, chest, and arms. Physically, he possessed everything she liked in a boy. As he sauntered past, Paris' glare damn near sucked the life out of her. Aoki didn't cower to no nigga but when he cut his eyes at her she visibly wilted. There wasn't an ounce of softness to his gaze. It was a look that conveyed a bubbling hatred. Disgust perhaps. Whatever it was, it had Aoki questioning her sanity. This boy was the worst kind of nigga. He was a hoodlum, a killer in the making. She shouldn't want any parts of him but stupidly she did.

Paris scowled at the curly haired girl posted up on the wall eye fuckin' him hard. He knew who she was the second he walked in. He couldn't forget such a pretty face if he tried. She'd crossed his mind several times since he'd first laid eyes on her. He'd thought about finding out her name and how old she was, but Paris wasn't like most guys. He was a hot nigga. He didn't thirst after or trick on no bitch, no matter how beautiful she was, and this girl was fucking mesmerizing. Growing up in the hood you didn't see girls that looked like her roaming around. From her outrageously full curly hair, chinky azure eyes, Marilyn Monroe mole and mile long legs, she had him feeling some type of way. It was a good thing Paris was good at hiding his emotions. On the outside, he looked as frightening as a monster. He liked it that way. People responded to fear more than they did kindness. Plus, he didn't know why she was there. For all he knew, she could be a slut getting passed around by the homies.

"My nigga P?" Rob and Chris gave him dap.

"Sup." He dodged their hand. Paris was there for business. His mission was to get in and out. He placed his Louis V bookbag on the coffee table. From the outside, it looked like he was on some high fashion shit but inside the Louis bag were copious amounts of gas. Don't get it twisted, his favorite Glock rested comfortably on his hip ready to spit. Coolly, he unzipped the bag, pulled out six ounces of grade A Kush and tossed it onto Rob's lap.

"Good lookin' out fam." He happily placed a wad of money in Paris' awaiting hand. Holding the weed like it was precious glass, Rob placed one of the bags up to his nose and inhaled the strong aroma. "Yo this some fire."

"Oooooooooh wee!" Chris cheered, ready to roll up.

After counting the payment twice, Paris glanced over to Rob and said, "You short."

"I am? I thought you was running a special." Rob replied like he had no clue.

"What?" Paris growled.

Aoki and Blizz watched on from the hallway, knowing some shit was about to go down. She could hear the intensity in his tone. Paris stance said it all. Somebody was about to get their shit rocked.

"I heard you was selling an ounce for $85 a whop." Rob explained as his life flashed before his eyes.

"You ain't heard no shit like that."

"On God." He placed his hands in the surrender position. "Damya and them told me that. But you know what? My fault. I shouldn't have been listening to he say, she say. Since I'm short, how bout we do an I.O.U?" He reasoned.

"I got one better for you homey." Paris flicked his nose. "Let's just do an I."

"What's that? Some New York shit?" Rob asked genuinely confused.

Without warning, a sudden gush of pain jolted throughout his body. Paris had right hooked the shit out of him. The hard punch had landed directly on his eye. He couldn't even defend himself before another thunderous blow connected with the side of his face. Aoki could hear the sound of Rob's jaw cracking from where she was standing. It was the most grotesque, stomach churning sound she'd ever heard. The dizzying punch caused Rob to see stars. His tongue was soaked in the taste of blood. A searing pain soared through every crevice of his face. Nowhere near done with him, Paris grabbed him by the collar of his shirt and body slammed him onto the glass coffee table, shattering it into pieces. Shards of sharp glass landed in his back and scattered across the floor. Drawing his tatted fist back, Paris hit Rob with a Haymaker that shattered what was left of his already broken jaw. Niggas knew he didn't play about his money. Rob should've known he was gonna get his shit rocked. If he wasn't in such a good mood, Paris would've ended his life.

"Aye yo!" Meechi raced down the steps with just a sheet wrapped around his waist. "P, what you doing man? You broke my mafuckin' table? I just bought that shit!"

"Blame this goofy-ass nigga." He kicked Rob's leg viciously.

"Did you kill 'em?" Meechi peeked over the couch so he wouldn't get glass in his bare feet.

"That muthafucka still alive." Paris examined the damage he'd done to Rob's face. There was so much blood in his mouth that he'd started to gag on his own plasma.

"Oh, he crazy, crazy. Fuck Kiara. I'm out." Aoki threw two fingers in the air and left.

Blizz tried to stop her but she'd made up her mind. She wasn't supposed to be there anyway. It was funny how karma had come and bit Rob in the ass. She was high key happy that he'd gotten beat the fuck up and would've loved to stick around to see the aftermath, but Aoki didn't need further confirmation that it was time for her to bounce. Outside, the heat from the day smacked her dead in the face. Nightfall was in full effect. An eerie darkness stretched across the night sky. Milky speckles danced along the heavens in various patterns. Not one bird chirped. They all were silenced and not one soul walked the streets. For a second, it felt like Aoki was in the world alone. The alarming sound of gunshots ringing in the air quickly dispelled that notion. In her haste to leave, Aoki had completely forgotten that she'd be unaided in a neighborhood she was foreign to. Anybody could run up and try to rob, kidnap or rape her. Gray was gonna kill her if she wound up dead. Aoki couldn't put that kind of added stress on her mother. Come hell or high water she was getting back to Aunt Vickie's house in one piece and without anyone knowing the danger she'd placed herself in. Shook, she snatched her phone out her fanny pack to order an Uber. Once again, her mom had come through for her. The emergency debit card Gray had given her was about to save her life. As she logged into her account, the sound of the door slamming shut behind her caused her to jump. Ready to run, Aoki looked over her shoulder to see if a masked killer was about to chop her in half. It wasn't a masked killer, but it was a killer indeed.

Paris stormed out of the building with his Louis Vuitton backpack in hand. He looked even angrier than before as he huffed past. Yeah, he'd taken back the weed he'd sold Rob and kept the money after fucking him up but the fact that he'd even tried him got underneath his skin. *His fine ass need a hug,* Aoki thought as she watched him hop inside his 1960 blue Mustang. Aoki loved two things in life and that was music and vintage cars. When she grew up the plan was for her to become a world famous DJ. Paris' Mustang was gorgeous. Tommy from Power drove the same one. It had roughly 350-400 horses going to the rear wheels. This car dutifully represented the pinnacle of American muscle: raw, unadulterated power, in a fun but hard-to-contain body. Aoki wished she could get behind the wheel and take it for a spin. As much as she wanted to stand around and lust after Paris' flawless ride, she had to focus on not getting shot. Another round of gunshots echoed close, too close. Aoki ducked for cover. She thought about going back in and waiting on Kiara but her fake ass hadn't even come out to check on her. She could be dead for all she knew. If life couldn't get any worse, Paris abruptly pulled up to the curb with the window down. The loud engine of the Mustang roared. *Young Nigga* by the late great Nipsey Hussle bumped in the background as he glared at her with venom in his eyes. Aoki's heart thumped like a bass drum as she matched his gaze. He'd already proven he had a few screws missing. There was no telling what his next move would be.

"You fuckin' them niggas?" He barked.

"What?" Aoki responded, caught off guard.

"You heard me?"

"I did. I just wanted to make sure I heard you correct." Aoki replied aghast.

"If you heard me, answer the fuckin' question."

"Fuck nah. I don't know them. I don't even know you. Do I look like a ho or something?" She glanced down at her outfit. The split was a bit much, but she was tall, so it didn't come across slutty.

"Times done changed. Hoes ain't got no look no more. Shit my mama a ho."

"Well, I ain't yo' damn mama. And your rude ass need to learn how to talk to people." She spat heated.

"Yeah whatever. What you standing out here for? Prostitutes get ready for their shift around this time."

"I ain't Rob or none of them other niggas in there. I will fuck your big ass up. Keep playin' wit' me." Aoki warned on ten.

"Get out your feelings. Get in." He unlocked the door.

Speechless, Aoki eyed him perplexed. This dude was beyond

strange. How could he go from calling her a ho to offering her a ride? As much as Aoki wanted to throw caution to wind and hop in, the slogan *stranger danger* came to mind. She wasn't about to voluntarily put herself in harm's way. This panty-dropping psychopath had just crushed a man's face. If she made him mad what would he do to her? Aoki had no plans on finding out. She didn't want to fuck his beautiful ass up.

"What is up wit' you niggas? I don't know you." She tuned up her face.

"It ain't safe out here. I know yo' prissy ass ain't tryin' to get shot." His deep gritty voice boomed.

"I'm not prissy!" Aoki placed her hand on her hip.

"Using correct English, you are."

"Ain't you the same nigga that was running from twelve the other day? Hell nah, I ain't getting in the car wit' you."

"I'm tryin' to be nice to yo' waterhead ass. Come the fuck on. I ain't got all day." Paris raised the passenger side window up.

He didn't do a bunch of back-and-forth. The conversation was over. Unsure of what she should do, Aoki looked between the Uber app and Paris' car. There really wasn't anything to contemplate. Her Uber was nowhere near, and if she called Quan or Stacy to come get her, she'd be on punishment till she was sixty-five. Suddenly, another crack of gunfire sounded in the air. Paris had been in the hood long enough to know the shooting was less than fifty feet away. He wasn't concerned with anything happening to him. He never left home without his burner. A nigga would have to be deaf, dumb or crazy to try and take his life. They'd be dead before they could pull the trigger. Li'l mama with stilts for legs wouldn't be so lucky. She stuck out like a sore thumb. She looked like easy prey.

"Oh shit!" Aoki ran to the car, only to find the door was locked. "What is you doing? Open the fuckin' door!" She panicked, pulling the handle repeatedly.

"What's the magic word?" Paris fired up a blunt unfazed by her shrills.

"Now!"

"Wrong." He skirted off, leaving her standing there with her mouth wide open.

"Wait!" Aoki chased after his car.

Paris didn't stop until he reached the stop sign at the end of the street. By the time Aoki reached him, she was out of breath. Letting down the window he leaned back in his custom leather seat and said, "We gon' try this again."

Aoki glared at him. The stony expression on his face enraged her and turned her on all at the same time. She'd never encountered someone so cocky and confusing. If she didn't need his help, she would've given him her whole ass to kiss. Swallowing her pride, she caught her breath and replied, "Can you open the door. . . please?"

"Much better." Paris hit the unlock button.

Aoki promptly jumped in before he could change his mind. Safely inside, she placed on her seatbelt and canceled the Uber ride.

"Where to?" Paris took off doing 60mph down a residential street.

Aoki held onto the console for dear life. She quickly started to wonder was she safer back out on the street. Paris was whipping the Mustang like he was a race car driver. To make matters worse, the smell of the smoke coming out of the cigar was so bad, it was as if someone had put a piece of coal into her lungs.

"Twenty-second street and can you slow down?" She fanned the smoke from her face.

"Who you know over there?" He ignored her request.

"Damn, you nosey. Mind your business."

"You got a smart ass mouth for a bitch shaped like an Italian soccer player."

"First of all, I ain't no bitch." Aoki shot him a death glare. "Second of all, am I shaped like David Beckham? Yes, but that's neither here nor there."

A slight chuckled escaped Paris' pink lips. *I made him laugh,* Aoki smirked pleased with herself. The smile was genuinely sweet. An unexpected warmth rushed through her body. She didn't know why but seeing this side of him made her want to prove that she could make him laugh all the time.

"Why you pop off on ole boy like that?" She quizzed, intrigued by his hot and cold demeanor.

"That lame ass nigga was playing wit' my money." Paris got mad all over again.

"So, you just go around beating up everybody that make you mad?"

"Basically."

"I feel that vibe." Aoki nodded her head.

"Who you know at Meechi's house?" Paris felt like a sucka for asking but he had to know.

"He mess wit' my girl Kiara. Speak of the devil." She looked down at her phone. Kiara was finally calling her. Instead of answering, she forwarded her call to voicemail. Kiara was on her shit list. She'd deal with her when she didn't see herself wanting to snatch her by her 32-inch weave.

"Why?"

"No reason. I just thought you was there wit' that soft ass nigga Blizz."

Aoki's lips formed into a shit-eating grin. Paris could try to act unbothered, but it was apparent he was asking about Blizz 'cause he himself was checking for her.

"Nah, I just met him." She turned her body to face him.

The way he gripped the wood grain steering wheel while dipped low in his seat was sexy as hell. Aoki wished he'd place his hand on her inner thigh as he navigated his way through the city streets, but he didn't. Paris stayed focused on the road. It was like he had a million things on his mind. If Aoki could, she'd implant herself in his brain just to know what he was thinking.

"Why? That's your man or something."

"Them niggas are associates. I don't fuck wit' nobody except for Meech."

"That's good to know. Pull over right here." She pointed as they neared Aunt Vickie's street. There was no way on God's green earth she'd let him drop her off in front of the crib. On the corner was fine enough.

"Thanks for the ride." She reached for the door handle hoping he'd ask for her number.

"Yep." Paris gave her a quick head nod. He didn't even bother giving her any eye contact as she got out.

Unsure of what her next move should be, Aoki held the door. She wanted to extend their time together but couldn't find anything else to say.

"What you waiting on? Close the door." Paris scowled. She was letting all his damn air out.

Mortified, Aoki closed the door. It wasn't even all the way shut before he pulled off. Thoroughly confused, she began her trek up the street. If someone asked her to explain what had just happened, she wouldn't know what to say. Paris was an enigma wrapped up in tattoos and rage. Everything about him said proceed with caution, but like young Simba, she always laughed in the face of danger.

CHAPTER 8

"Baby I'm gang bout you. Ain't playing no games bout you. I'll go to hell and jail about you boy."-Summer Walker feat Jhene Aiko "I'll Kill You"

DAY 19:

*G*ray tried to keep her eyes open. She really tried her hardest but the warm blanket covering her body made her feel deliciously comfortable. Soon, sleep would be all she was aware of. Since she refused to leave Cam's side the hospital brought in a bed for her to sleep. She'd literally made his room her new home. She had a bag of clothes, toiletries, several pairs of shoes and food items organized in a corner. His court files, books and magazines were stacked on the nightstand by his bed. Flowers and balloons filled every available inch of the space. As sterile and cramped as the room was, Gray put aside her discomfort. She had to make the best out of the situation. Laying on her side, she relished the feel of the cushy mattress. The twin-sized bed was truly heaven sent. Yawning uncontrollably for the tenth time, her eyes began to drift close. Gray struggled to keep her eyes focused on the Ellen DeGeneres show, but the rhythmic sound of Cam's heart monitor was like a lullaby to her ears. He lay blissfully unaware of what was going on around him. Nothing had changed with his condition. Gray was disappointed of course 'cause she wanted him to wake. She kept telling herself that as long as he was still holding on that was all that mattered. At this point, she was just happy the doctors were able to get his temperature back to a normal degree. It took a few days for the shivering spells to cease. Now it was just a waiting game. A waiting game that was draining the life out of her. She missed waking up to her kids each day. She longed to see their smiles, hear them laugh and sit and listen to their day. Facetiming them every few hours was the only thing keeping her sane. It was tortuous being pulled in so many different directions. Gray was only one person. She wasn't a robot. Trying to accommodate her kids and her man was stretching her thin. Because of everything that was going on, she had to cancel several major fashion campaigns and missed out on a huge endorsement deal. Gray hated that she'd missed out on all the amazing opportunities but leaving Cam's side wasn't something she could fathom. All she could do was pray she was doing a good enough job of keeping everyone happy, even if it came at her own expense. Her own well-being and health was put on the back burner.

Gray was in a constant state of fear and fatigue. The level of tiredness she felt could only be equated to insanity. Most of days, she wished she could ask God to take her temporarily just so she could rest. There wasn't a moment she wasn't on high alert, which in turn, placed her brain at five percent. You couldn't tell Gray that all of her energy wasn't being drained as though she was leaking electricity. Exhaustion made her body hang limp like wet laundry.

Gray propped her head up on the palm of her hand and tried once more to focus on the television. Zendaya was a guest on the show. She didn't want to miss the interview. Euphoria had become her favorite new drama, but like the countless times before, she unknowingly drifted off to sleep. Tranquility was plastered across her face as she slept. Her chest rose and fell as gentle snuffles escaped her nose. The feel of her phone buzzing against her chest was what jolted her awake. Alarmed, she looked down at the screen. For a second, she thought about not answering the call. Noon was on the other end. Since their breakup, he'd reached out a few times to see how she was, which made Gray feel like shit. Even though she'd broken his heart, he still looked out for her wellbeing. Noon was a really good man. He treated her like a queen. It was the only reason why she decided to answer his call.

"Hello." She whispered just in case Cam could hear her conversation. If he could, he'd wake up and strangle her.

"Hey." Noon held the phone close to his ear to feel closer to her.

"Hi." Gray laid on her back and looked at the ceiling.

In New York, Noon swiveled in his chair from side-to-side, unsure of what to say. He'd told himself to fall back and let her be, but he missed Gray with a pain that multiplied every day she was out of his reach. No other woman could replace her, and if he had it his way, no other woman ever would.

"You good?" He finally asked.

"No." She answered truthfully.

Noon knew it was a silly question. He could hear in her voice that she was deeply troubled. He wished there was something he could do to make her feel better, but Gray had made it abundantly clear that she didn't want him or his help. Day in and day out he tried thinking of ways to get her to change her mind about him, about their relationship. They were good together. She was happy with him. Life was stress free before she came back to the states. They were building a solid future together. He loved her and you couldn't tell him that she didn't still love him too. Love just didn't disappear that quickly.

"Has there been any change?" He pretended to care about Cam's condition.

"Things are still the same." Gray closed her eyes. She felt a headache coming on.

"You need anything. I can have whatever you need sent to you."

"Thanks, but that's not necessary. Everyone here has made sure that I'm straight."

Noon massaged his forehead. There were so many emotions weighing on his chest. How could he support her taking care of her sick husband and convince her that with him was where she needed to be.

"I know I shouldn't be saying this—"

"Then don't." Gray cut him off. She knew he was about to say he missed her which was the last thing she wanted to hear. It wasn't because she didn't miss him too. She would be lying if she said a small part of her didn't. The residual feelings she had for him, however, just didn't compare to the undying love she harbored for Cam.

"Gray, I love you. Please, consider giving us another chance. I can make you happy. Let me show you what life can be like without all the drama."

Knock, Knock

Gray's baby blues popped open. By the door she found Kema, Tee-Tee, Heidi and Dylan standing.

"You got company?" Noon asked.

"Yeah, I gotta go." She sat up.

"Alright." Noon responded sadly. He didn't want their call to end but Gray's focus wasn't on him. It sucked to know another man occupied all of her time. Damn what he wouldn't give to hold her again. Noon tried convincing his self that this should be his last time reaching out. It was best he let her go and move on with his life, but Noon wasn't used to losing. He'd be damned if he let Gray go without a fight.

"Get you some rest. You sound like you haven't slept in weeks."

Gray let out a small chuckle.

"I haven't."

"Talk to you soon ladybug and please consider what I said."

"Bye." She exhaled breathlessly and ended the call. Every time she spoke to Noon it made her feel ten times worse. Snatching the cover off her body, she rose to her feet to greet her friends.

"Thank God she got on some decent clothes today." Tee-Tee said as soon as he walked in the room.

Usually, when they came to visit her and Cam, Gray was on her bummy shit. Looking cute was the least of her worries. A t-shirt, leggings or jogging pants had become an everyday look for her. It just so happened that day she decided to spruce up her attire. She wore a crème knit cardigan, crème cashmere tank top and fitted joggers. Black curls framed her makeup free face. The only jewelry she rocked was her wedding set. Three and a half years had passed since she last wore the gold Cartier Love ring, Maillon Panthere paved row ring and an 8 carat, round-cut diamond. Cam had outdone his self when he copped her the new set as a Valentine's Day gift years before. Gray nearly had to box the triplets to get the rings back. She wouldn't have taken them if she didn't have an overwhelming need to feel close to her husband.

"Forget him. Hey suga lump." Kema greeted her bestie with a hug.

"What? She look like death. She's giving me death becomes her tease." Tee-Tee mugged her with disdain.

Gray's eyes were red, they had bags underneath them and all of the color had left her face. She also looked like she'd lost weight.

"Well, that's an appropriate thing to say." Heidi rolled her eyes.

"Girl, fuck him. It's good to see you too loose booty." Gray playfully swatted Tee-Tee's arm.

"Ooh, you can tell?" He looked over his shoulder at his butt. "Me and Bernard just got a quickie in and I was on bottom."

"I did not need to know that bit of information."

"You just mad you ain't being stuffed like an Oreo."

"Don't remind me." Gray glanced over at Cam. The memory of the last time they made love flooded her mind. She and Cam might've had a tumultuous marriage, but sex was the least of their worries. Every time their bodies became one it was a movie. Cam did things to her body that left her sore and satisfied for days.

"How you doing boo?" Dylan gave her a loving embrace.

"I'm hanging in there."

"Slip on your shoes Chica. We're breaking you outta here." Heidi picked up her low-top Air Force 1's.

"I'm not going nowhere."

"Gray, you can't stay cooped up in this room forever. You haven't left in weeks." Kema argued.

"I know I haven't and I'm fine with that. As long as I'm next to him, I'm alright." She ran her hand across the top of Cam's head.

The mere thought of leaving him for a second was like her skin being sliced off with a knife. They'd spent enough time a part over the last three and a half years. She needed to make up for all the time they'd lost together.

"You might think that but boo you're gonna drive yourself crazy. You're not in jail love. You need some fresh air, get something to eat, see the sun."

"I'm not leaving." She clung to Cam's bedrail for dear life.

Knock, Knock

"Excuse me ladies." Nurse Jenni poked her head inside. She was a kind middle-aged woman that often was assigned to Cam's room. "Sorry to interrupt but it's time for me to change and bath Mr. Parthens."

Gray swallowed the lump in her throat. It still bothered her that Cam had a catheter and had to wear a diaper. He was too strong of a man to be placed in such a weak predicament. Cam was beyond prideful. Knowing someone had to physically wipe his ass every day would destroy him.

"See I can't leave. I normally help when he's being bathed."

"Nope. We're not letting you do this." Heidi shook her head.

"Listen." Dylan walked up and caressed her arm. "I've been the one in the hospital bed. I needed my husband to do everything for me, but Angel wouldn't have been any good for me if he didn't take care of himself first. Do you think Cam would want to see you like this?"

"Chile, he can barely stand to see you cry." Kema chimed in.

"Right. He ain't gon' kick our ass if he wake up and you in here lookin' like Alfre Woodard in Holiday Heart." Tee-Tee joned.

"I got the bike Holiday." Heidi imitated the character Wanda.

"Y'all ignorant as hell." Dylan grimaced in dismay.

"That's him. He started it." Heidi pointed at Tee-Tee.

"I understand what you guys are saying. I really do but I can't stomach being away from him. If something happens and I'm not here, I will never be able to forgive myself."

"So, instead of leaving the hospital, why don't we just stay here? Let's go grab something to eat in the cafeteria. That way you'll be close by if they need you." Kema tried to coax her into seeing things her way.

Gray let out a long sigh. She did need to eat and catching up with her friends would be a nice respite. *Lord, please don't let anything happen while I'm gone.*

"Just give us thirty minutes." Heidi begged.

"And that's all you're gonna get."

"Look at God. Won't he do it." Tee-Tee clapped his hands.

Once her shoes were on, Gray hesitantly grabbed her phone. She hadn't even left yet and was already having second thoughts. Kema could see her about to change her mind.

"C'mon Bernie." She referenced the movie *What's Love Got to Do with It.* "Let's go see what they have in this cafeteria. I'm dying for a burger." She took a hold of Gray's hand and led her towards the door.

"You guys have my number, right?" Gray asked Nurse Jenni.

"Yes ma'am. We do. Go have fun with your friends, Mrs. Gray. Everything will be fine."

"Okay." She reluctantly left.

Stepping out of Cam's room was like entering a whole new world. Gray literally hadn't left his side since he was admitted. Leaving Cam's floor was a death sentence within itself. She knew in her gut that something would go wrong as soon as she left. She tried to remain optimistic, but it was hard. Gray prayed to God her friends hadn't talked her into something she would soon regret.

"What you in the mood to eat?" Heidi questioned once they reached the floor the cafeteria was on.

"Nothing too heavy. Maybe a salad and some soup." Gray surveyed the space.

The cafeteria inside of DePaul was as spacious as a gymnasium. Several 'no smokin' signs decorated the walls. About twenty-five tables, a coffee bar, vending machines, and an array of kosher meals were available. The incoherent chatter of the masses overwhelmed Gray as well as the mixture of sweet and spicy aromas pouring from the kitchen. A glimpse of a small child heaping food into her mouth made her think of her own babies. As soon as she made it back to the room she was going to give them a call.

"Lunch is on me." Dylan massaged Gray's shoulder as they stood in line.

"Thanks boo." Gray smiled warmly. "I'm so sorry. I haven't asked how you've been. Are you okay? How is Angel and Mason?"

"My boys are well. Angel is the best husband in the world. He's still holding onto his heavyweight title and thinking about joining KFC."

"You mean UFC." Gray giggled as she picked up her tray.

"Oh yeah. That's it." Dylan snapped her fingers. "I don't really know how I feel about it. Boxing is already dangerous. UFC is even worse."

"Yeah, it is."

"He even got my baby boxing. Chile, I can't wait to have me a li'l girl so I can have somebody to do girly stuff with."

"Have you guys found a surrogate yet?"

"We did." Dylan beamed with pride. "In a few weeks we're going to do an embryo implantation."

"That's wonderful, Dylan. I'm so happy for you. I needed to hear that good news." Gray gave her a tender hug.

"Girl, I'm so excited. You know I thought after I had the hysterectomy it was over for me."

"God's plan for us is always bigger than our own."

"Amen." Dylan caught the holy ghost and waved her hand in the air.

For thirty minutes and not a minute less, Gray chatted with her friends, ate a little and even laughed a bit. For thirty minutes, she was able to take her mind off of all her troubles. Gray didn't know how much she needed her besties until they came to her rescue. There was no article of Chanel or luxury vacation that could match the smallest speck of joy her friends brought into her life. For no matter the weather or place, she found herself in they were always there. When lunch was finally over, Gray felt like a fool for thinking something bad would happen. Cam had been perfectly fine in her absence. Upon inspection, not one hair on his head was out of place. Gray let out a sigh of relief. She was worried for nothing or so she thought. It took her a minute to notice but Cam's court file and books were completely soaked with water.

"No! No! No! No! No!" She raced over and picked up the wet stack of papers. Majority of the ink had started to smear. Gray's entire life flashed before her eyes.

"Noooooooo!" She let out a loud cry.

"What's wrong?" Kema asked concerned.

Gray didn't even bother to answer. She allowed the darkness inside of her to swallow her whole. All of the emotions she'd kept bottled inside came bubbling to the surface at once. Gray couldn't help herself. All she saw was red as she stomped over to the nurses station. Several of them sat around laughing and talking like they didn't have a care in the world, which infuriated her even more.

"Where the fuck is Nurse Jenni?" She slammed the papers down onto the counter.

"She's with a patient." One of the nurses responded. "Is there anything I can help you with?"

"Bring her to me now!"

"Ma'am, we can't do that. What's the problem?" The nurse spoke kindly.

"Don't worry about what the problem is! Just do what the fuck I said!" Gray snapped. She was so angry, she was shaking.

"Ma'am, we're gonna need you to calm down and tell us what the problem is."

"Bitch, are you hard of hearing?" She gripped the nurse by the collar of her uniform.

"Gray, relax. What's wrong wit' you?" Kema pulled her off of the innocent nurse.

"These dumb bitches don't know how to do their jobs! I knew I shouldn't have left!"

"Mrs. Parthens, is everything okay?" Nurse Jenni asked coming out of a nearby room.

"No, bitch it's not! Do you see what you did?" She held the wet papers up to her face.

Shocked at her wrath, Nurse Jenni jumped back. She didn't even realize that she'd gotten them wet when she was giving Cam a bath.

"Oh my God. I'm so sorry. I had no idea." She replied sincerely.

"You had no idea? Nobody has any idea what the fuck I'm going through right now! Instead of y'all being helpful in this bitch, you might've just put me in the same position as my fuckin' husband!" Gray's hands clenched at her sides. She was two seconds away from dragging Nurse Jenni by her hair.

"What papers are those?" Heidi tried to take a look.

"You know what? It don't even fuckin' matter!" Gray held them close to her chest. "Going forward." She eyed Nurse Jenni with contempt. "Stay yo' stupid incompetent ass out my husband's room! And starting now I want a new nurse! Have I made myself clear?"

"Girl, bring yo' ass on." Kema grabbed her arm and pulled her inside Cam's room. She had seen enough. Gray was acting like a complete ass.

"What the hell is wrong with you? That lady has been bending over backwards for you. She didn't deserve that." Kema practically flung her across the room.

Gray caught her balance and shouted, "I don't deserve this! I don't deserve to have my husband in a coma! I don't deserve to have my life on the goddamn line! I shouldn't have to be worried about making my own funeral arrangements or thinking about my kids being motherless! Have you muthafuckas forgot that this nigga wanna kill me!" She shrieked at the top of her lungs.

"We get it friend." Dylan assured.

"No, you don't! Nobody does! Y'all rest easy at night! I don't! I gotta worry about him and me! I'm trying to keep both of us alive!" She heaved up and down.

Gray tried to reel in her anger, but she was experiencing system overload. Over the past nineteen days she'd kept it together the best she could, but stress and exhaustion had crept in and taken over. She no longer gave a damn about being polite or politically correct. She needed to scream and shout out her frustrations. She longed to be heard. It seemed like no one understood the agony she was in. Gray felt like she was in a bubble alone, fighting the good fight by herself. And yes, cussing out the nursing staff was wrong. She'd regret her actions later, but at that moment, she needed to release her inner demons.

"Everybody just calm down." Tee-Tee placed his hands in the air. "We can fix this. It was only water. The papers will dry, and everything will be fine."

"That's not the point. They're already ruined." Gray willed herself not to cry. "I needed these papers. They were the only connection I had to who the snitch is."

"We're here to help friend. We're gonna figure this out together." Kema swore.

"You promise?" Gray buried her face in Kema's bosom.

"I promise." She rubbed her back. "I love you friend. I'm not gon' let nothing happen to you."

"Right, if Victor kill you, he gotta kill all of us." Heidi assured, hugging her tight.

"Speak for yourself. I still got a lot of life to live." Tee-Tee folded his arms across his chest.

"And you wonder why can't nobody stand you." Dylan hit him with the middle finger.

Gray inhaled deep and placed a few of the papers that weren't ruined under the vent so they could dry. The cool air felt great against her skin as she held the papers over her head. Looking up to see if the documents were drying, she noticed how the light from the ceiling revealed the informants name under the blacked out area. Instantly, her face turned as white as snow. Gray couldn't believe her eyes. She was so stunned that her mouth was frozen wide open in an expression of stunned surprise. Swiftly, she pulled out her phone and called Quan. Nurse Jenni getting Cam's papers wet had been a blessing in disguise.

"Everything a'ight?" He asked instead of saying hello. Quan was fearful that he'd get a call saying Cam had passed on.

"Yeah, everything's fine. I got a question tho. I think I already know the answer but who is LaPorsha Angelique Wright?" Gray waited with bated breath.

"That's LaLa's name. Why?"

Gray bit her bottom lip, infuriated. She couldn't believe her ears.

"You ain't gon' believe this shit."

"What?"

"She's the fuckin' snitch."

CHAPTER 9

"You be chillin'. Laid all the way back. So causal, no. Unintentional, no. Way past mellow. Super relaxed. Not emotional, no. One dimensional, no. Make it make sense. Carefree is cool but not at my expense."-Alex Isley & Jack Dine "Gone"

"What yo' fake ass want?" Aoki held Aunt Vickie's screen door open and shot Kiara an evil glare.

Kiara stood on the opposite side with a guilty and sad expression on her face. Aoki couldn't care less. She'd iced her out and hadn't spoken to her in a week. One thing Gunz had taught her was that respect was something earned and not given. Kiara might've thought cause she was older than Aoki that she could get over on her, but she had another thing coming. Aoki might've been young, but she didn't tolerate disrespect. Kiara was gonna learn a lesson about friendship and that Aoki wasn't the one to fuck with.

"You gon' let me in?" She tried to pull open the screen door.

"No." Aoki snatched it close.

"I said I was sorry. Damn." Kiara whined, stomping her foot.

"I don't care. That shit wasn't cool. Them niggas could've did anything to me, and you obviously didn't care because you were too busy being a slore." Aoki called her a slut and a whore.

"You really think I would've left you alone if I thought they were gonna do something to hurt you?" Kiara cocked her head to the side.

"I don't know what you would've did. I know what you did do."

"Well, I'm sorry. You my girl. You know I got yo' back."

"Yeah way back." Aoki eyed her with disdain.

"Girl, whatever. Don't be like that."

"No, you don't be like that. I don't know what you're used to but you ain't got too many chances wit' me. I don't play that fake shit." Aoki warned.

"Let me make it up to you then. Let's get something eat. My treat." Kiara beamed brightly.

"Yo' greedy ass always wanna eat but that's gon' have to wait. I'm finna go." Aoki pushed open the screen door and stepped out with Kilo and Gram. They were a duo of Rottweilers with smooth black hair who were trained to attack on command. Melody had brought them as well as the rest of their belongings back from Paris a week before. Aoki was so happy to have her dogs back. Kilo and Gram were more than pets. They were a part of her family. Over the last three and a half years, they'd become her companions in quiet moments. On cold winter nights they were her heater and welcome wagon when she came home from school. In other words, they were her best friends.

"You cute." Kiara admired Aoki's outfit.

"I know." She smirked, feeling her cunt. One of Aunt Vickie's braiders had given her two feed-in braids that reached down to her butt. Silver chain link earrings dangled from her ears. A light blue denim dress with one black strap and a black color blocked hem was molded to her slim physique. The dress reached the center of her thigh and even had a split. Aoki's chest, arms and legs were on full display. Black, three-inch Phillip Lim booties completed her weather appropriate look.

"Ughn. Where were you going?"

"To meet up wit' Blizz. We can get something to eat afterwards." Aoki made her way down the steps with Kilo and Gram in tow. She figured she'd kill two birds with one stone and take them for their daily walk.

"See, being over there wasn't so bad after all. You done met you a li'l boo thang and er' thang." Kiara bobbed her head like a true ghetto girl.

"Calm down, Cookie." Aoki referenced the character from Empire. "I wouldn't say all that."

She didn't exactly know what she was doing with Blizz. He was cool for the most part, but she wasn't head over heels in like with him. When she was bored and wanted someone to talk to she called him. He was nice and tolerable. There wasn't a day that went by where he didn't check up on her. So far, he was doing everything right but the flame in the pit of her belly didn't burn for him. That blazing inferno belonged to Paris who was the total opposite of Blizz. He wasn't particularly nice and didn't seem to give a damn about her. Yet and still, he occupied every space in her mind and heart. She couldn't stop thinking about him, which gnawed at her ego. She hated herself for fawning over a guy that acted like she was gum stuck to the bottom of his shoe. It was the age old tale of having a good dude on your team but wanting the bad boy that didn't mean you any good.

"I mean, don't get me wrong. He seems like the kind of guy that has met his father more than four times in his life but I ain't that invested in him."

"I don't know friend. I think I see a love connection." Kiara nudged her with her shoulder.

"Ain't you damn near blind in one eye?"

"Girl, fuck you." Kiara laughed.

"Aoki, can I go?" Press yelled out the door.

Aoki thought about saying yes but she needed a minute away from her siblings.

"Not this time Pretty Girl. When I get back I promise I'll do whatever you want."

"Okay." Press poked out her bottom lip. What no one realized was that she too was having a hard time. With King gone she had no one to play with. The other kids in the neighborhood didn't like her. They made fun of her and called her four eyes cause she wore glasses and liked to read books about animals. Playing with the triplets usually got her through the day but there was only so much of The Wiggles she could take. Press wanted to roam free and have fun like her big sis.

"You get on my nerves. Bring yo' spoiled ass on." Aoki hid her grin.

"Yes!" Press pumped her fist in the air. "Aunt Vickie! I'm going with Aoki!"

"Bye and close my goddamn screen door! You letting out all the air!"

Press did as she was told, raced outside and caught up with her sister.

"Here." Aoki handed her Kilo's leash. "You walk him, and I'll walk Gram. Remember whatever you see or hear while you're with us stays between me and you."

"I ain't no snitch." Press sized her up.

"You bet not be."

"Where you wanna go eat?" Kiara interrupted their banter.

"Shell City Crab."

"Damn, bitch. That shit is expensive."

"I know." Aoki arched her brow. She wasn't letting Kiara off the hook that easily. A $30 crab broil meal would suffice for her pain and suffering. Soaking in the afternoon sun, she took in the tranquil summer vibe. The day was picture perfect, even the buses were running on time. The sky looked like it had been air brushed. The clouds were puffs of luminous joy. There was no wind, but it wasn't that humid, which was perfect for their walk. It took them almost fifteen minutes to make it to the strip mall where the barber shop Blizz got his haircut was located. That Saturday afternoon the parking lot was popping like it was an outdoors club. There were people standing around shooting the shit, eating, and bumping music from their cars. A small crowd was huddled in a circle while a few guys spit rhymes. Aoki had never seen anything like it except in the movies. If she would've known it was this live at the strip mall, she would've come a long time ago. Pulling her iPhone out of her pocket, she shot Blizz a text.

BLIZZ: I'm here

The message hadn't even delivered, and he was already walking out the door. It was like he was standing around waiting on her arrival, which Aoki liked. It showed he didn't take her time for granted.

"Yo." He extended his arms for a hug, which set off Kilo and Gram. A heart stopping, guttural growl roared from their chest. Canine teeth exposed they snarled ready to attack. All Aoki had to do was give them the word and Blizz would be lunchmeat.

"*Anjda* (Sit)." She spoke sternly in Korean. On command both dogs obeyed and sat back on their hind legs. Although they couldn't bite off a chunk of Blizz skin, neither dog took their eyes off of him.

"Damn they trained to go." He wiped sweat from his brow.

"Yep so don't try nothing slick." Aoki advised.

"Who is this li'l cutie you got wit' you?" He looked at Press.

"My li'l sister. Say hi Press."

"Sup?" She tipped her chin like Cam had taught her.

"Damn, y'all look just alike despite the eye color difference."

"Yeah, this my mini me." Aoki wrapped her arm around Press.

"You look cute. Let me find out you wore this for me." He tried to reach for her dress but was stopped by the sound of Gram's threatening bark.

"Don't get it twisted boo-boo. I don't dress for boys. I dress for myself 'cause I like to stay fly."

"Whoever you wore it for you look damn good." Blizz licked his lips.

"It's just a li'l light work." Aoki popped her invisible collar.

"What y'all finna get into? I'm tryin' to kick it."

"After we leave here we're going to Shell City Crab to get something to eat. You wanna roll?" Kiara invited him without asking Aoki.

Super annoyed, she glared at Kiara out of the corner of her eye. How did she know she felt like being bothered with Blizz? She didn't which was the problem.

"Hell yeah. I'm hungry than a muthafucka." He rubbed his flat stomach.

"You going, you paying." Kiara made it known.

"Don't even do me like that. You know I ain't no slouch." Blizz pulled out a wad of money.

"As long as you know and you putting some gas in my car."

No, this bitch didn't, Aoki eyed her in his disbelief. Kiara was supposed to be making it up to her by treating her to lunch but instead had finagled her way out of paying for their food and talked her way into getting a tank full of gas. This girl was truly a trip. Aoki was two seconds off her ass when the boisterous roar of several motorcycles nearing caught her attention. Everyone on the lot turned to see a crew of guys riding up the block on blue motorbikes and 4 wheelers. There was about twenty of them popping wheelies and doing tricks. Some were shirtless, others wore wifebeaters or white tee's. One guy in particular stood out amongst the rest. Despite the black ski mask covering his face she could spot Paris a mile away. His tall stature stood out like a sore thumb. Plus, he was the most daring out of the bunch. He was leaned all the way back while gunning the 4 wheeler he was on. Paris was so low to the ground the back of his Concord 11's touched the pavement. His black t-shirt flapped in the wind. Revving the engine, he placed his right foot on the ground and skated while flexing his muscles in the air. It was the sexiest shit Aoki had ever seen. She wished she were riding with him. Focused, he hopped down and sat on the seat of the 4 wheeler while in the wheelie position. Stretching his tattooed arms wide, he rode hands free. The boy was fearless. Aoki stared at him in awe. Her chin was literally touching her chest she was so shocked. Amazed didn't quite cover how she felt. It feel like someone took a spark of wonder and poured on kerosene. She and Kiara were damn near drooling as Paris, Meechi and the rest of the guys pulled up on the lot. Mad people walked over and showed them love. Paris didn't seem gassed by the praise. With his ski mask off, he shook very few hands and didn't crack not one smile. Aoki was truly stunned when he walked over to the cypher and started bobbing his head. The next thing she knew he was in the center of the circle spitting a rhyme.

Once again, Aoki was stunned by his abilities. Paris rhyme style was on par with Nas and Kendrick Lamar. The sixteen he spit had everyone in the cypher going nuts. Aoki didn't want to take her eyes off of him. She was in complete awe of his talent. Bars flowed from his pink lips like water ran from a faucet. It was effortless. Paris was in complete control. Confidence exuded from his pores. If Meechi wouldn't have come over barking at Kiara, Aoki would've stared at him forever.

"Yo what the fuck is wrong wit' you?"

"*Grrrrrrrrr.*" Kilo and Gram growled in the attack position.

"Aoki get yo' fuckin' dogs man." He pulled out his gun ready to shoot.

"Boy put that gun up!" Kiara looked at him like he was crazy.

"*Anjda.*" Aoki rubbed both dogs head to get them to settle down.

"Shut up. I should shoot yo' THOT ass." Meechi tucked his gun in the back of his pants. "Why the fuck you out here around all these niggas wit' this li'l bitty ass shit on?"

Kiara wore nothing but a neon green, deep V bra top and tie dye booty shorts that were so tight you could see her pussy print from a mile away. Aoki would've never left out the house in something so skimpy. She loved fashion and liked to dress for style and not sex appeal. Besides that, she was only thirteen. Gray would kick her ass if she even attempted to walk out the house in something that could be found in a Hustler magazine. Meechi absolutely detested that Kiara liked to rock ho shit all the time. Yeah, she had a dope body but that didn't mean she needed to show it off to every hood bugger with two eyes. If he didn't love her so much, he would've went upside her head. He had to remind himself that despite her thottish attire, underneath it all Kiara was a good girl. She and her mom had gone the extra mile for him. Meechi wouldn't have his apartment if it weren't for Andrea being his co-signer. Meechi couldn't depend on his family for shit. His mother was a dope fiend and his father was absentee.

"You look crazy." He shot.

"What?" Kiara looked down at her barely there clothing. "It's cute. I already got a thousand likes on Instagram." She posed, placing her hand on her curvaceous hip.

"Yo you hear yourself? You got all these nigga out here lookin' at you and shit. You act like I won't air this whole muthafucka out. A nigga already got two strikes as it is." Meechi barked enraged.

"Huuuuuuuh." Kiara groaned, rolling her eyes. "Can you please not start today? You blowing my high. You hungry? We about to go to Shell City Crab. You wanna go? Lunch is on me."

"Ain't this about a bitch." Aoki quipped. Kiara could pay for Meechi's food, but she couldn't pay for hers? This chick was truly a con artist. Aoki respected her gangsta but started to realize she couldn't rely on her for shit.

"I'm always hungry but that ain't got shit to do with what the fuck I said. You out here wildin' like you ain't gotta nigga. Like I won't bust yo' ass."

"You so violent. I love that shit daddy." Kiara grinned, rubbing his muscular chest.

"Y'all always arguing." Paris interrupted their conversation.

He was bold like that which Aoki loved. Everything about Paris was cocky and commanding. None of the other guys on the lot could fuck with him. From the Paper Plane snapback on his head to his gold chains he was the shit. All the air in Aoki's lungs caught in her throat as she watched him bend down and run his longs fingers through the hair on Gram's head. Flabbergasted that neither dog tore his head off Aoki looked on as Gram closed his eyes and whimpered. *What in the fuck,* she thought. Kilo and Gram didn't like anyone. What was so different about Paris? Aoki had no other choice but to feel this was a sign they were meant to be.

"Yo I'm about to get up wit' her real quick." Meechi told him.

"Nah, nigga we gotta go pick up that work." Paris rose to his feet.

"Aww shit. I forgot. My bad. I ain't gon' be able to go." Meechi rubbed Kiara's butt. "I'ma pull up on you later tho. In the meantime, change yo' fuckin' clothes." He ice grilled her.

"Damn, are you fuckin' Paris or are you fuckin' me? You always choosing him." She spat with an attitude.

"Yo on some real shit." Meechi pointed his finger in her face like a gun. "Keep showing out in front of your fuckin' friend and this shit gon' be a wrap."

"I'm just sayin'." She pouted like a child.

"You ain't sayin' shit. Now go home and do what the fuck I said." He stormed off before he snapped her neck.

"Yo stupid ass always doing too much." Paris used his index finger and mushed her in the forehead.

"Ain't nobody ask you to comment." She slapped his hand away.

"But I did and ain't nobody gon' stop me." Paris dared her to do something. When she didn't he smirked then stepped into Blizz face. "And yo' pussy ass gon' stand here like you don't see me?"

Paris towered over him by several inches. Caught off guard, Blizz eyes darted from left to right.

"I mean . . . last time I tried to speak you kept walking. Fuck you want me to do?" He shrugged his shoulders nervously.

Seeing that he had him shook, Paris chuckled.

"Just fuckin' wit' you chump. Take the wedgie out ya' ass li'l nigga." He lightly slapped the side of his face then turned to walk away.

Aoki couldn't believe that Blizz had let Paris punk him like that. He was a complete pushover which was a big turn off for her. She could never see herself liking a dude that didn't know how to stick up for his self. If Paris could run all over him she knew damn well she could. Blizz knew he'd fucked up the minute Aoki stepped to the side to distance herself from him. It was bad enough she'd been lusting after Paris ever since he'd walked up. He could see it in her eyes. She wanted him bad which meant he didn't stand a chance.

"You can't speak?" She called out. Aoki tried biting her tongue but there was no way Paris was gonna act like he didn't see her standing there. He made it his business to speak to everyone but her. *What kind of game is this nigga playing,* she wondered. He'd literally just given her a ride home the other day. She knew he saw how cute she looked. Halting his stride, Paris paused and said yep then continued walking. He knew it would get under Aoki's skin if he ignored her. Girls like her were used to niggas being all on their dick. He wasn't the one. He enjoyed keeping chicks on their toes. Aoki was mad cute, but her ego was out of control. He could tell by the way she carried herself that she knew she was the shit. It was a must she be brought down a peg or two. Over at their rides Meechi eyed Paris quizzically.

"What nigga?" He placed on his gloves.

"I see what type of time you on. Fall back nigga. This ain't that. Leave that girl alone."

Paris cocked his head back and laughed.

"Nigga ain't shit funny. Dead ass. That's Blizz girl."

"So. When has that ever stop me?" Paris frowned.

"Let that li'l nigga have that. You ain't even on her for real."

"Says who? You? You don't know what the fuck I'm on." Paris countered offended.

Meechi looked at him liked he was dumb.

"I'm yo' best friend nigga. I always know what the fuck you on and it ain't never good."

"Nigga, you don't know my life. It's something with shorty. I think she's cute." Paris replied honestly.

"C'mon man. You can't be going after that man girl."

"I ain't trying to be a home wrecker but I like her, and the dog was nice." He smiled wickedly.

"P man. You gotta chill out." Meechi shook his head. "Blizz act like he really feeling shorty."

"Fuck that lame ass nigga. She look better wit' me."

"You wild." Meechi hopped on his bike done with the conversation.

"Just wait. You ain't seen nothing yet." Paris gave Aoki one last look before riding out.

CHAPTER 10

Karma has no deadline.

*G*ray imagined she was stepping out of a SUV and heading into a five-star resort. That's where she would've rather been, somewhere on an island, sipping an ice cold alcoholic beverage and soaking in the sun. She envisioned her, Cam and their children frolicking along the beach, building sandcastles, and creating memories that would last a lifetime. Instead, she and Quan were being escorted inside Victor's estate by two armed guards. She would've much rather been on an island or back at the hospital. This would be the first and only time she left Cam's side. She didn't trust anyone to watch over him but Mo, who was there with him while she handled business. Gray felt nauseous as she rounded the steps and entered through the massive front doors. Armed guards were strategically placed all around the $165,000,000 estate that sat on seven acres of land. The mansion was approximately 20,000 square feet and afforded every possible amenity from high ceilings to large and formal gathering areas to small and intimate spaces. A four-plus acre backyard offered views to a pool, pool house, two-story guesthouse, tennis court and a walking/jogging trail that surrounded the estate. Everything at Victor's mega-mansion was grand. Not one detail was left untouched. He and Mina did a phenomenal job with the décor. Gray could give him that. It was the only compliment she'd dish out. She couldn't stand Victor Gonzalez. She didn't want to be anywhere near the man. He was a living, breathing, monster. He made her skin crawl. She wanted to claw his eyes out. But those things had to be set aside. She had to vindicate herself as being the snitch first.

After being patted down in-between her breasts, under her arms and in-between her legs, she and Quan were led into what she assumed was Victor's office. The man of the hour sat behind his desk like he was the president of the United States. Gray rolled her eyes. His smug ass didn't even acknowledge their presence as they sat down. For five whole minutes he continued to type on his computer like they weren't even there. Gray, Quan and the two armed guards sat shrouded in silence until Don Victor acknowledged their presence. Sitting back in his $3,000 chair he eyed his guests with contempt. His schedule had been thrown completely off because of this impromptu meeting.

"I hope you're interrupting my busy day because you have the information that I've been waiting for. Otherwise, I'm not gonna be happy about this." He addressed Gray.

Aggravated with his holier than thou attitude, she took the file and tossed it onto the desk. The file and its contents landed on the table with a thud. Victor clenched his jaw and inhaled deep. Gray was trying his patience. She knew he didn't tolerate disrespect. Victor would have a bullet lodged in her head if she kept it up. Satisfied that she'd gotten under his skin, Gray eased back in her seat and crossed her legs.

"I would tread carefully if I was you." Victor warned. Once it was clear he meant business he continued speaking. "What is this?" He pointed at the file like it was tainted.

"Proof that it wasn't me who snitched."

"Hold the papers up to the light, Jefe, and you'll see." Quan added.

Victor looked over the paperwork and got the answer he was searching for.

"LaPorsha Angelique Wright." He said slowly. "So, it was LaLa? Interesting." He placed the folder down. She was the last person he'd suspected. When Cam was with her, she'd been the epitome of a down-ass chick. They never even had an issue with her when they broke up. The fact that she'd switched up now was shocking. Regardless, she had to pay for her misdeeds. No one would get away with dropping a dime on the Gonzalez Cartel.

"Okay well, I guess our business is done. You can see your way out. I'll take care of this." He dismissed Gray and Quan casually.

Oh, hell nah, she thought. After weeks of being stressed out behind his threats this was how he responded? Gray was infuriated. She'd drove herself crazy thinking at any minute he'd have one of his hittas kill her. Gray had actually wrote goodbye letters to everyone close to her. That's how afraid she was. Now that she'd proven her innocence, Victor had the gall to act like the news she'd gave him was nothing. He had Gray Rose Parthens all the way fucked up.

"That's it?" She drew her head back. "You're not gonna apologize for trying to kill me in front of my kids at my best friend's wedding?" She snapped.

Victor rested his right ankle on his left thigh.

"Like I told you . . . it's just business and I'm not in the business of apologizing. Be thankful you're still breathing."

"Muthafucka!" Gray leaped out of her seat to attack him. She didn't get far. Quan immediately grabbed her by the shoulders and pulled her back. At the same time the guards cocked their guns ready to blow her fucking brains out.

"This ain't that. Chill." He coaxed Gray. If she kept on acting crazy she would never see Cam or her kids again.

Gray shook with anger. She'd been taking L after L. Somebody had to feel her wrath. She was tired of muthafuckas disrespecting her and getting away with it. Chest heaving up and down, she retook her seat and noticed one of the guards standing over her.

"What the fuck you think you about to do? Ain't nobody scared of yo' swole ass!" She spat with fury.

"Gray, I'ma tell you one more time." Victor tried to keep his composure. "Don't disrespect my home. Say one more thing and you won't leave here breathing."

"Jefe, if I may speak on Cam's behalf." Quan spoke calmly. Things were getting out of hand. He had to get the conversation back on track.

"You may."

"I think he would prefer to be the one to resolve this issue with LaLa."

Victor contemplated his request. LaLa had done the absolute most. She'd disrespected Cam in the worst way. He should be the one to exact revenge.

"If he survives." Victor arched his brow.

"Ain't no if. He's going to survive." Gray checked him.

Tired of Gray's mouth and the entire conversation Victor said, "I'll give him that. In the meantime, get your Chinese Pitbull and get the fuck out my house."

He didn't have to tell Gray twice. She didn't wanna be there anyway. The sooner she was away from Victor Gonzalez the better her life would be. If she never saw his face again she'd be alright. With the entire snitch situation behind her, she could focus solely on nursing her husband back to health.

CHAPTER 11

"I don't know what feels true, but this feels right so stay a sec. Yeah, you feel right so stay a sec."-Billie Eilish "Hostage"

*A*oki lay across Aunt Vickie's leather couch fanning her face with a paper plate. The back of her thighs and legs stuck to the leather, making her skin feel like hot glue. A heatwave advisory was in full effect. It was a 106 degrees outside. Aoki would give a million dollars if someone would turn the heat index down. It was like a dreadful ever present heat that lasted day in and day out. Even with the air conditioner on, sweat dripped from every pore on her body. It had been that way since the night before. She went to sleep sweaty, woke up sweaty and got out of the shower sweaty. She was uncomfortably hot. A singular drop of sweat made its way down her spine, leaving a path of momentary coolness in its wake. Since she'd arrived at Aunt Vickie's house, she'd been inside. There would be no going outdoors. Stepping outside for even a second was suffocating. Not one bird chirped, undoubtably too afraid to open their beak. Even the trees were defeated. Leaves that should be firm drooped like wet soggy lettuce. It was so hot that the grass started to look like hay. The air was equally dry. It had been weeks since rain fell, and when it did, the raindrops vanished as soon as they struck the scorching asphalt. Drinking copious amounts of water didn't even cool her off. This was one part of being back in St. louis she didn't miss. It was never this hot in Paris. The weather there was perfect. All she could do was lay in one spot and try not to move. Aunt Vickie's house was the quietest it had ever been. All business was shut down until the temperature dropped. The little kids lay on a palette, sleeping peacefully with a fan blowing directly in their faces. Press was up watching Mixed-ish and eating snacks. Aoki wanted to tell her to lay off the snacks since she'd gained a few pounds over the summer but didn't want to hurt her feelings. The stress of Cam being in a coma and their mother being away had really affected her. Instead, she focused on Tink's song *Treat Me Like Somebody*. The record put her in a romantic mood. It was the perfect slow groove.

'Cause I've been on the search and I'm losing my hope
Is that too much? Is that too much?
Trying to find love in a world so cold
Is that too much?
I just want an answer, I can't be the only one
Is that too much?
You ain't got to be perfect
Just give me a purpose to love

She was truly annoyed when a text message from an unknown person interrupted her flow.

314 555-5555: Come take a ride wit' me

Aoki looked at the phone puzzled. She didn't recognize the number, so she had no idea if the person reaching out had the wrong number or not.

AOKI: Who is this

314 555-5555: U got that many niggas hittin' u up

AOKI: I'm about to block u. Who is this

314 555-5555: P

Not believing her eyes, Aoki shot up in the upright position. This had to be a joke. Somebody was surely playing on her phone. She'd never given Paris her number so how was he calling her and what was he calling her for?

AOKI: How u get my #

314 555-5555: Kiara

Aoki rolled her eyes hard. She should've known.

AOKI: So now u know who I am

Paris ignored her quip.

314 555-5555: I'm up the street. Come fuck wit' me

Aoki's heart beat a mile a minute. Should she go or no? Her ego was telling her to leave him hanging. He'd dissed her the last time they ran into each other. She didn't want to look thirsty by jumping cause he called. Plus, it was going on 8:30 p.m. and already dark out. Her curfew was 9:00 p.m. If she was gonna go she'd have to go now. Aoki wanted to play hard to get but also didn't wanna miss the opportunity to see Paris again. She was dying to know what he wanted with her. Grabbing her Burberry mini bag, she stuffed her phone inside and got off the couch. As soon as she stood, a rush of heat swarmed her body. Quickly, she ran to the bathroom and freshened up as best she could. Satisfied with her appearance, she made the short trek to the sitting room and found Aunt Vickie asleep in her Lazy Boy chair. Her mouth hung wide open, and she was snoring. Briefly, Aoki thought about leaving without telling her but thought against it.

"Aunt Vickie." She shook her arm.

"Hmm?" She snorted half asleep.

"Can I go outside?"

"Mmm hmm." She turned to her side and fell right back into a deep slumber.

Now that she'd conned her way into leaving the crib with permission, Aoki tip-toed out of the room and out of the house. Gently, she closed the door behind her and locked it with the key she'd been given. She hadn't even been outside a full minute and she was burning up.

Aoki prayed she wasn't a sopping mess by the time she made it up the block. Applying a coat of lip-gloss, she walked swiftly down the street. A few people were out hanging around. She didn't understand how the stragglers could stand the heat. She hadn't even been out that long and was ready to go back inside. All of that changed as she neared the end of the block. Nervous energy took up space in her chest. There under the light of the moon, sitting sideways on his Kawasaki Ninja motorcycle was Paris. Aoki's mouth went dry as she took him in. He was dressed in a Mitchell and Ness White Sox jersey, wifebeater, black shorts and retro Jordan 10's. A black baseball cap with throwback written across it hovered low over his dreamy eyes. Aoki hoped he liked the gold accessories, Fendi t-shirt, black belt, tan high-waisted skirt and platform Doc Martins she wore. Being around Paris always made her feel unsure of herself. Maybe it was because she never knew what he was thinking or feelings. Even as she stood before him, she had no idea what was going through his brain.

Paris sat with a stone cold expression on his face. *What the hell am I doing here,* he wondered. Meechi had warned him to stay away. He should've adhered his advice, but he had to pinpoint what it was about this tall chinky-eyed girl that drove him insane. There had never been a girl who'd had a bigger impact on him than Aoki. She was strong-willed, sassy, unapologetic and tough. She was the female version of him, which was a recipe for disaster. There was no way either of them was getting out of whatever they were building unscathed. She'd be the death of him, if his feelings for her went beyond skin deep. So here he was trying to gauge if he was just infatuated with her looks or if there was something more to the blue eyed beauty. Was she just a pretty face or was there substance behind her sapphire orbs.

"How big is your head?" He asked out of nowhere.

"Excuse me?" She asked caught off guard by his question.

Paris grabbed the helmet off the back of his bike.

"I'm not getting on that death trap. More importantly, I'm not going anywhere with you." Aoki responded appalled by his gall.

Totally unfazed by her attitude, Paris took her purse from her hand

and placed it in the side compartment on his bike. Without saying a word, he pulled her hair up and placed the helmet over her head. Turning his back to her, he swung his long leg over the bike and revved up the engine.

"Get on."

Who does this nigga think he is, she thought eying him. Paris was rude, vague and didn't know how to talk to people. She wanted to pop him in the mouth. Riding on the back of his motorcycle while holding him tight shouldn't even be an option but Aoki would be lying if she said it wasn't something she'd been fantasizing about since she saw him do stunts. She'd never had skin-to-skin contact with a boy before. She'd be a damn fool if she didn't make Paris her first. Besides, this was a once in a lifetime opportunity. Throwing caution to the wind, she ignored the fact that she needed to be back at Aunt Vickie's house in fifteen minutes and hopped on. Her skirt rode up her thighs but there was nothing she could do about it. Anxiously, she wrapped her arms around Paris' waist and said a silent prayer to God she didn't fall off and die.

"You ready?" He gripped the throttle.

"Yea—"Aoki tried to speak but she couldn't even finish her response before he took off.

Holding on for dear life, she planted her chin on his shoulder and relished being near. Paris lowkey enjoyed having her chest pressed against his well-developed back. Pleased that she'd let him take the lead, he disregarded speed limits, opening the throttle wide. The full moon above lit the night sky bringing forth silver-sequin stars. Paris and Aoki's muscles worked overtime against the wind. Houses, trees and streetlights became a blur as they whizzed by. Aoki didn't know where they were headed—just that it felt good to be in his orbit. She didn't know it then, but from that moment on, her heart would follow him whenever and wherever.

An eternity went by before they pulled up to their destination. Paris parked his bike. Aoki pulled the helmet off and looked around. She had no idea where they were, except they were in a leafy suburb and a huge Olympic-sized pool was nearby.

"C'mon." He held out his tattooed hand.

Placing her palm against his, she jumped off and nearly collapsed. Aoki's legs had lost all the feeling in them. They were like Jell-O. She looked like a newborn deer trying to take its first steps as her knees buckled with each step she took.

"You a'ight?" Paris grinned.

"Yeah, I'm fine." She lied, straightening up. "Where we going?" She continued to examine the area. It was pitch black outside and the pool was closed. That didn't stop Paris from letting go of her hand and hopping the fence.

"What the hell are you doing?"

"Going swimming. You coming or what?"

If Aoki would've known they'd be breaking and entering on their excursion, she would've stayed her black ass at Aunt Vickie's house. Once again, she'd put herself in a position to be somewhere she had absolutely no place being.

"Don't think about it. Just c'mon." He coaxed.

Beyoncé please don't let me go to jail, she prayed. Throwing caution to the wind, she placed the toe of her boot in one of the holes in the fence.

"Don't look up my skirt." She demanded.

"You ain't got shit I ain't already seen before." Paris had smashed more bitches than he could count.

"Nigga please. This cootie cat is golden. You ain't never seen a kitty cat like this." She speedily climbed up.

Paris held out his arms to catch her as she jumped over. Chest to chest they gazed into each other's eyes until her feet hit the ground.

"This is crazy." She replied anxiously.

"Tell me about it." He reluctantly let her go.

"What made you bring me here?"

"It's hot as fuck. You know a better way to cool off?" He let his jersey slide down his muscular arms. With his wifebeater off, he revealed a chest full of vivid tattoos and a slab of concrete abs. Paris' shorts hung low off his waist, exposing a pair of Ethika boxer/briefs. Aoki could see a happy trail of smooth hair extend from his navel down to his crotch. Overridden with desire, her gaze slid to the side. This was too much for her young soul to handle. But like a moth to a flame, she was drawn to him. Sucked into a heady trance, she exhaled her fears. Aoki was determined not to let Paris get the best of her.

"What if somebody catches us?"

"We straight. I do this all the time." He stepped into her personal space. "Turn around."

Thousands of butterflies filled Aoki's belly as she gave him her back. Gently, Paris pulled her against his chest. His nose tickled her ear. Aoki let out a tiny gasp and fidgeted timidly. She didn't like being so intimately handled, for it was a foreign feeling to her. Paris' velvet lips brushed against the skin of her slender neck as his hands ran across her stomach. Aoki held her breath as he unbuckled her belt and slid it through the loopholes. Tossing it to the ground, he unzipped the back of her skirt. Aoki's face heated. Things were moving so fast, but she didn't wanna stop the pace. Summoning the courage to meet his gaze, she held her skirt in place and faced him.

"I'm not getting in naked."

"Put my tank top on." He dropped his shorts and dived into the deep end headfirst.

Aoki looked back at the shirt unsure. She'd have a lot of explaining to do if she returned to Aunt Vickie's house wet, but she was already out past her curfew and sure to be in a ton of trouble. If Cam's condition hadn't proved anything, it was that tomorrow wasn't promised for anybody. She might as well live it up while she could. Bending over, she picked up the wifebeater which smelled like Clive Christian cologne. If Paris wasn't looking at her, she would've buried her nose in the cotton and saved the hypnotic smell to memory.

"Some privacy please." She arched her brow.

Wading in the water, he smirked and faced the other way. Now that he wasn't looking, Aoki felt comfortable enough to let her skirt fall around her ankles. She then untied her boots and took off her shirt. In her bra and panties, she slipped on the tank top and pulled it down as far as she could. The shirt barely covered her butt, but it was the best she could do.

"You can turn around now." She clasped her hands in front of her private part.

Never before had she felt so exposed. This wasn't like wearing a bikini to the beach. This was far more intimate. Kicking his legs, Paris faced her. He didn't think he could be more enamored with her, but he was. She reminded him of a Frank Ocean song. Aoki's crystal blue eyes held such a tranquility that it was impossible for him not to be held prisoner by them. Her cheekbones were exceptionally high, and her nose was small like a bunny. Her long spirally hair fell down around her shoulders. Paris had seen ton of girls naked, but Aoki's legs alone had every chick before her beat. She was effortlessly stunning. It was all he could do not to stutter and blush when she addressed him.

"I can't swim in the deep end." She admitted. There would not be a repeat of the day she'd almost drowned.

"No worries. I got you." He swam to the edge of the pool.

He could see she was nervous. Aoki had that shy look girls often wore. Behind her slightly pursed lips was a smile just waiting to be tempted out. It was then that Paris knew he wasn't just physically attracted to her. He liked her. Underneath all of Aoki's bravado was a sweet innocence that he wasn't used to. She wasn't like all the hardened chicks he'd come across. The pitfalls of life hadn't jaded her. There was still a sparkle of wonder in her eyes that he hoped would never die. On her bottom, Aoki dipped her painted toes into the lukewarm water. Mesmerized by her supermodel legs, Paris tucked his hands under her armpits and helped her in. Despite the heaviness in her stomach, Aoki circled her arms and legs around him. She and Paris were completely submerged. Nine feet of water stopped at both of their chins.

"How you learn how to swim so good?" She asked.

"My brother taught me." He held her close as they waded in the water. "He used to take me to this YMCA in Harlem when I was little."

"What was it like growing up in New York?"

"It was the shit. Ain't nothin' like New York. Especially in the summertime."

"That's how I feel about Paris. Paris in the summer is fuckin' magical. We'd have picnics by the Eiffel tower, go to the Louvre—"

"I should've known yo' bougie ass wasn't from here." He cut her off.

"Actually, I am. For your information I grew up in St. Louis." She stuck out her tongue.

"Put yo' tongue back in your mouth unless you want mine on it." He warned.

"Whatever." She waved him off knowing damn well she wanted his tongue in her mouth.

"Yeah, a'ight. Think it's a game, but anyway, how you end up in Paris?"

"My family moved there a few years ago."

"I've always wanted to go there but I ain't never been nowhere but the five boroughs and the Lou." Paris said regrettably.

"If you're good to me, maybe one day I'll take you there."

"Is that right?" He chuckled.

"That's only if you're nice. Most times you act like you hate me."

"There's only two people I hate and you ain't one of 'em."

"What made you come get me then?"

"I wanted to see what was up wit' you." He studied the plains of her face. There wasn't a blemish in sight.

"And what's your assessment?" She tried to keep her nerves at bay.

"So far you're cool. You ain't as stuck up as I thought."

"You ever heard the saying don't judge a book by its cover?"

"Yeah, I've heard that a few times before." He smirked as they glided through chlorinated water. He'd somehow became Aoki's human floating device.

"How long you been rapping?"

"I ain't no rapper. I'ma street nigga, sweetheart. I just know how to put words together and make the shit sound nice."

"Well, you should consider taking it serious. You're good at it."

Paris took her words to heart. He'd heard that he was nice with his rhymes but coming from Aoki it meant more. Maybe because he viewed her differently. Unknowingly, he'd put her on a pedestal.

"You think so?"

"Real talk. I can see you blowing the fuck up. Me myself, I'm gonna be a world famous DJ when I graduate. I wanna prove that girls can rock the crowd as well as the guys. The DJ industry is so male dominated but I'm gonna be as big as Calvin Harris, DJ Khaled, David Guetta and my idol Steve Aoki."

By the optimistic look on her face, Paris knew she meant every word.

"What you listening to right now?"

"I was listening to Tink when you hit me up."

"I heard of her, but I don't listen to a lot of R&B."

"You should. I think you would like her. It's sad 'cause she still hasn't had the success she deserves."

"Who else you listening to?"

"Billie Eilish. She's a whole vibe. My mom also recently hipped me to Ann Peebles."

"Who is that?"

"She's the lady Missy got *I Can't Stand the Rain* from."

"Oh word?"

"Yeah, the original is a bop." Aoki gushed. "Pop Smoke song *Invincible* is my shit too."

"The whole *Meet The Woo* album go hard." Paris agreed.

"His voice is crazy. You know what else is a bop?" She quizzed.

"What?"

"Paul McCartney's *Arrow Through Me*."

"Ain't that the old nigga from Guns N' Roses?"

"No." She laughed heartily. "He's from the Beatles. You gotta listen to it. The bass intro is bananas and Paul got so much soul on the track."

"How you learn so much about music?" Paris asked captivated by her wealth of knowledge.

"My mom. She loves music too. She listens to everything and hipped me to a lot of artists. My love for music then grew from there. I love all genres. If you ever do take rapping serious, I know of some samples that will slap."

"I'll keep that in mind."

"So, what you gon' do, sell weed the rest of your life?" She challenged.

"I hope not."

"If rapping ain't what you're on then what you wanna be?"

"Alive." He answered truthfully. "Not in jail."

It saddened Aoki to know the future for him seemed so bleak. She wished he saw himself the way she did. Paris was so talented. In her mind there wasn't anything he couldn't do.

"You stay near 22nd street?" She died to know.

"Nah, I live downtown."

"By yourself like Meechi or with your mom?"

"I stay wit' my peoples. The bitch who birthed me back in New York with her weak ass boyfriend." His mouth formed into a deep scowl. The mere mention of his mother made Paris whole mood change. It was obvious there was a major rift there.

"You can't tell me a chick like you live in the hood." He changed the subject.

Aoki cracked a grin.

"I don't. My auntie live over there."

"Where yo' folks at?"

"My mom is taking care of my pops. He's not doing too well right now." She instantly became sad.

"Sorry to hear that." He pulled her closer.

"It's okay." She tried to make light of the situation.

"Stop frontin'. I can tell it's fuckin' wit' you."

"It is but I gotta remain strong for my family. They need me right now."

"While you're taking care of your family, who's taking care of you? Blizz?" He asked with a mean scowl on his face.

"No." She burst out laughing.

"What's up wit' you and li'l man?"

"He cool." Aoki shrugged.

Paris shook his head and chuckled again.

"What's so funny?"

"You don't like that nigga." He slowly whirled her around in a circle.

"You don't know what I like." She held onto his neck.

"I know you don't like him."

"How you figure that?"

"Cause if you did you wouldn't be here with me."

"Whatever. You don't know what I like."

"I know you better dead that shit." He clenched his jaw and gave her a look that was filled with desire.

Paris was bold with the shit. He focused on her plump lips then zeroed in on her mesmerizing eyes. There was no denying he wanted to kiss her. Aoki tried to seem unbothered. It wouldn't do her any good to let a nigga with an ego as big as his know how much power he had over her. Paris made her a nervous wreck. He was light years ahead of her when it came to intimacy. She could barely keep up.

"Can I be honest, and you not look at me different?"

"I don't expect nothing but the truth. Me and liars don't mix."

Aoki swallowed hard.

"I've never been kissed before." She admitted.

Paris drew his head back. It shocked him that someone as pretty as her who was around sixteen or seventeen hadn't been kissed. He would've bet money that niggas were beating down her door to get next to her. Quickly, he assessed that if she hadn't been kissed, she was also a virgin. Paris feelings for her grew even more. Aoki was further separating herself from the loose pussy hoes that usually crossed his path.

"You ain't gotta lie to kick it." He countered.

"It's true."

Now that the truth was out, the ball was in his court. No way was she gonna make it easy for him by making the first move. Paris didn't want easy anyway. He liked that she posed a challenge. It was one of the things that drew him to her. While other girls threw themselves at him, she gave him something to work for. Time stood still as he brushed her hair over her shoulder and moved in close. Aoki unknowingly held her breath. Swathed in his warmth, she swore his lips were already on hers, but they weren't. Instead of kissing her, Paris took his hand and caressed her cheek. Aoki's head started to spin. He was biding his time and making her wait. She didn't know how much longer she could hold on. Eagerness consumed her. She'd waited thirteen long years for this moment. Other girls her age had already kissed numerous guys, but she hadn't. Aoki didn't want to kiss just any ole boy. She wanted it to be special, something she remembered forever. Her crush on Priest led her to believe he'd be her first kiss, but now that she was with Paris, she realized that was a farfetched fantasy. Being with Paris felt right. It was everything she'd ever dreamt of.

Tenderly, he cupped the side of her face. Never before in his sixteen years on earth had he been hesitant to make a move, but with Aoki, things were different. She wasn't just some run of the mill girl. Nothing about her screamed jump-off. She was the kind of girl that was hard to get out of your system. Once he took it there with her, there would be no turning back. The nature of their relationship would change drastically. Fuck it. He'd suffer the consequences later. Unable to contain himself, Paris held Aoki's face in his hands and pulled her into a sizzling passionate kiss. Aoki's shaky hands worked their way around his back. If she didn't anchor herself she'd drown. Never in a million years did she think her first kiss would be like this. Her heart felt like it was gonna combust. She hoped she was doing it right. Paris seemed to be enjoying the way her lips moved against his. They were in complete sync. Each peck of his lips was fiery and demanding. Aoki thought about pulling away before she lost what sense of decorum her mama had instilled in her but letting go seemed like more of a punishment than a wise choice. She needed him as much as he needed her. Paris' minty tongue invaded her mouth and she could no longer think straight. After a few delicate strokes of his tongue, her hands started to roam his back. They couldn't get enough of each other. Aoki did something to him weed or alcohol couldn't do. She made him feel invincible. Her kisses were that addictive. Now that he'd had a taste of her, Paris was gonna make it his business to keep her in his web. Minutes later they pulled apart and took shaky, shallow breaths.

"Is it always like that?" Her lips quivered.

"It's never like that." Paris smoothed back her hair, astonished. Damn was he in trouble.

The next thing he knew, a blaring light was aimed at their faces. A security guard entered the gate holding a flashlight.

"IF YOU DON'T GET OUTTA THERE I'M CALLING THE POLICE!" He yelled.

"Oh shit!" Paris' eyes grew wide.

"I knew I shouldn't have listened to yo' ass!" Aoki hit him repeatedly in the chest as he swam to the edge. "I'm too skinny to go to jail! Them big bitches gon' eat me alive!"

"FREEZE!" The out of shape guard ran towards them.

Paris pushed Aoki out of the water. She almost scraped her knee but quickly landed on her feet and grabbed her clothes and shoes. Paris followed behind her. Beads of water dripped from their bodies as they ran across the grass and threw their clothes over the fence. Using his hands, he gave Aoki a boost so she could jump over first. Thankfully, she had long legs, so she was able to climb up rapidly. On the other side, she picked up her things and threw them on haphazardly.

"GET BACK HERE!" The guard tried to grab Paris' ankle, but he'd been running from the cops all his life. There was no way he was getting caught. Grinning from ear-to-ear, he hit the guard with the middle finger. Soaking wet, Paris slipped on his clothes and shoes then hopped on his bike. Aoki sat behind him with her helmet on.

"Go! Go! Go!" She nudged him urgently.

The flashlight cop was making his way out the gate with his hand on his taser. Paris took his bike off the kickstand and gunned the pedal. The wind whipped through them, causing Aoki to shiver. He could feel her clutching him with all her might. When they reached a red light, Paris looked over his shoulder.

"You a'ight?"

"Yeah." She smiled.

"That fat muthafucka was huffing and puffing wasn't he?"

"I swear he had an asthma attack." Aoki bugged up laughing.

"I told yo' scary ass, everything was cool. Was it worth almost going to jail?"

She sat and thought for a second.

"I wouldn't change a thing." She scooted closer.

The ride back to the neighborhood went by faster than Aoki would've liked. When they got back, she tapped him to stop at the corner. Paris parked his bike and let her off. Aoki handed him the helmet and tried to think of a reason to prolong her stay, but it was beyond late. She had to go. Unbeknownst to her, he didn't want her to leave either. The night had turned out better than he ever expected. Her damp hair clung to the back of her neck. Aoki prayed she didn't look like a wet dog. She had nothing to worry about. To Paris she was still beautiful.

"Here." He gave her, her purse.

Aoki took it and pulled out her phone. It was after eleven. She had several missed calls from Aunt Vickie and Kema.

"I gotta go." She sighed.

"Text me when you get in the house."

"I will." She turned to walk away on cloud 9. Even though she was in a world of trouble, it had been the best night of her life.

"Aoki." Paris called out her name.

"Yeah." She swiftly spun around.

"You seeing anybody?"

"No." She responded faster than she should've.

"Cool." He accelerated the engine and waited till she got halfway up the street before speeding off.

Oh, what a feeling to be in like with someone. Aoki felt like she was drifting on clouds made of pink cotton candy. If this was what the beginning of love felt like, she wanted more. Standing on Aunt Vickie's porch, she went to place the key in the lock, but the door was flung open.

"Where the hell have you been?" Kema barked with her hand on her hip. She'd been worried sick since she arrived. The last thing she expected when she got off work early and came to pick the kids up was for Aoki to be missing.

"I was at Kiara's." She told the first lie that came to her mind.

"At Kiara's huh?" Kema eyed her skeptically.

"I asked Aunt Vickie could I go."

"Yeah, while I was sleep." Aunt Vickie flared her nostrils. "You know damn well I say yes to anything while I'm sleep."

"I'm sorry. I didn't mean to stay out late." Aoki gave them her best puppy dog face.

"Save the sad look heffa." Kema grimaced. "And why the hell is your hair wet?"

"I let Kiara do my hair and it ended up looking wack, so I told her to wash it out." Aoki lied effortlessly.

"Mmm hmm. Help me with your brother and sisters so we can go." Kema shot her a death glare.

Once everyone was safely inside the car, Aoki placed on her seatbelt and let out a sigh of relief that she'd gotten away with murder. Kema placed on her seatbelt as well. She'd practice being a mama with Li'l Quan but policing a teenage girl like Aoki was a whole different playing field of parenting.

"Listen." She turned in her seat and faced her. "I promised your mama that I was gonna keep you guys safe while she takes care of Cam. I don't make promises I can't keep so whatever bullshit yo' ass is up to it needs to stop now. We got too much shit going on for you to be going M.I.A. I was ten seconds away from calling your mother. Do you know how upset she would've been?"

Aoki could only imagine the freak out her mama would've had if she'd received that call. She didn't want to stress Gray out. Her plan was to be a helping hand not a hinderance.

"I'm sorry for scaring you. It won't happen again." She swore, feeling bad.

"Good, cause Auntie Kema loves you." She pinched her cheek. "I don't wanna have to fuck you up, but if you lie to me again, on my unborn kids I will."

CHAPTER 12

"I had a dream. I got everything I wanted."-Billie Eilish "Everything I Wanted"

DAY 28:

"*H appy birthday to ya! Happy birthday to ya!*"
Cam's family and friends sang the Stevie Wonder version of *Happy Birthday* as he lay oblivious to the happenings around him. If he was awake, he would've been overjoyed and bashful by all the love in the room. Gray, the kids, Mo, Boss, their kids, Curtis, his wife, Cal, Cam Sr., Kema, Li'l Quan, Stacy, his daughter, Priest and Selicia were all there showing love. Selicia decided to come for moral support after talking to Gray. With it being Cam's birthday, she knew she'd need a few extra hugs. Quan said he'd be there but at the last minute changed his mind. Gray was disappointed that he hadn't shown his face since day three of Cam being in a coma but understood his grief. She knew despite his absence that he loved Cam as much as she did. Kerry was a whole different story. Once again, he was nowhere to

be found. He hadn't called or came to see his brother the entire time he'd been in ICU. As far as Gray was concerned, Kerry could be on fire and she wouldn't spit on him to save his life. He was dead to her. His absence, however, wouldn't take away from the happiness she felt. Nothing or no one would steal her joy. Cam was alive to live another day.

Everyone clapped their hands and rocked from side-to-side as she held the three layer, dark magenta, drip cake with blackberries and roses over his lap. Dylan had outdone herself with the design. Gray was sure it would taste as good as it looked. A number 4 and number 2 candle was lit to celebrate his 42nd birthday. It still amazed Gray that Cam was in his forties. He didn't look a day older than thirty. He had a boyishly handsome face and not a lick of grey hair. His face, neck, chest, back and tattooed arms only added to his youthfulness. But being in a coma for nearly a month was starting to wear on him. He lay in the bleached, aroma-filled ward on crisp but thinning sheets, immobile. The youthful glow that once radiated from his skin was no longer there. Cam looked as though he had too much skin to cover his wilting frame. His face had lost it's warm honey complexion. Over the past few weeks, his color had turned to an ashy grey. Gray's chest tightened into a knot. She hated seeing him this way. This was all Gunz's fault. Cam should've been awake so he could partake in the festivities. It had been years since they celebrated a birthday together. She swore that she wouldn't miss another. From that day moving forward they would spend every waking moment as one. Now more than ever, Gray was determined to get everything she'd always wanted and that was a loving husband and family. Nothing else mattered to her. Family was what she lived for. Hers might've been dysfunctional but it was hers nonetheless.

"Blow out the candles for daddy." She smiled lovingly at the triplets.

They sat on either side of Cam's legs. Leaning forward, they blew as hard as their little lungs could blow. When the flame was out, the rest of the family cheered. Mo helped pass out paper plates and plastic forks for everyone who wanted a piece of cake. By the time it was over there was only one slice left. Gray planned on saving it for herself for later. Together she and the kids opened the gifts everyone had brought for Cam. It was mainly cards filled with money. Stacy crazy ass had gotten him a brand new AR-15 rifle. Gray almost pissed on herself when she opened the huge box. She couldn't believe he'd gotten it past security. All the kids ooh'd and ahh'd over it.

"That's fucking ghetto yo." Selicia curled her upper lip.

"You know you love when I do ghetto shit." Stacy gave her his sexy face.

"Sure, I do. That's why I'm not wit' yo' ass."

"You ain't wit' me 'cause you scared of this DICK!" He grabbed his penis hard, causing Aoki to bug up laughing. "Fuck you laughing at?" He got in her personal space. "What you know about dick?"

"Nothing." She stepped back.

"That's what the fuck I thought."

"DICK! DICK! DICK!" Beaux bounced up and down on the bed.

"Look what the fuck you did." Selicia slapped his arm.

"My bad, Gray. Stop saying that shit, Beaux. It's penis. Say penis. Say it wit' Uncle Stacy. Pe-nis." He enunciated the word like it made it any better.

"DICK!" She giggled. "I. . . WANT. . . DICK! I. . . WANT. . . DICK!" She clapped her hands gleefully.

"No, the fuck you don't." Gray stopped her chant.

"Mama, I want dick too." Reign poked out his bottom lip.

"Ah nah." Stacy scratched his head. "Cam wake the fuck up dog. Ya' son in here saying he want dick. If don't nothing else wake yo' ass up that should."

"This all your damn fault. Get out!" Gray pointed to the door.

"I ain't even finish eating my cake yet."

"Yo fat ass don't need no goddamn cake." Selicia snatched it from his hand. "We on a diet, remember?"

"You on a fuckin' diet. I ain't on shit." Stacy took it back and ate a huge chunk. "This muthafucka good as hell. Dylan put her whole foot in this."

"That's why yo' ass gon' have diabetes. I ain't dating no nigga wit' high suga."

"It's been three and a half years. You got life fucked up. Bitch, we together."

"Call me another bitch." She balled up her fist.

While they argued, Aoki tried to pick up the rifle and shoot it but Kema smacked her hand away. After that, Gray insisted that Stacy take it back with him when he left. She didn't want to be accused of being a terrorist. Light banter and conversation filled the room until visiting hours were over and everyone packed up to leave. Gray hated to see everyone go. When the family came to visit, she didn't feel as sad. It almost took the jaws of life to pry her away from the kids. She could tell they longed for her as much as she longed for them. Gray hugged and kissed each child for what seemed like an eternity. When everybody was gone, she stacked all the gifts and stored her piece of cake. Silence caressed her skin, taking away her jagged edges. It had been one hell of a day. She didn't think she would've been able to get through it if it wasn't for her loved ones. Gray was overwrought with emotion. God kept throwing curve balls her way. Just when she thought she knew the direction in where her life was going, she was thrown off track.

Dressed in a long sleeve Beverly Hills shirt, grey jogging pants and high-top Nikes, she climbed into bed and curled up next to Cam. She was very careful not to lay on any of the tubes or wires attached to him. There under a soft shine from the moon she draped her arm around his waist. All day long she'd dreamed of the moment where it was just the two of them. Cuddling with Cam was how she got her release. Being next to him felt like a touch of heaven. Gray wished she could extend the night just so she could stay wrapped in his safe embrace. When they were like this, she had nothing to fear. Her head rested comfortably on his pillow as she lovingly examined his features. The lines on his face etched the story of a pleasant life. His crow's feet spoke of laughter and the smile lines around his mouth told of a man who gave away smiles like they were wishes. There wasn't a thing about this man Gray didn't love. The tattoo of her name on his temple made her heart swell with pride. They were so happy when he'd got it. If she could rewind time, she'd travel back to that day and start anew. She and Cam had made so many mistakes along their journey, but underneath all the murk, was an earth shattering love.

The safest place in the whole wide world
Is in the will of God;
Though trials be great, and the way seems hard,
It's in the will of God...

She sang while inhaling his natural scent. Gray could bask in the wonder of Cam for the rest of her days.

"I hope you enjoyed your birthday." She spoke softly. "Everyone was so happy to see you. The kids miss you so much babe. I miss you too, but you know that already. I tell you that every day." She ran her index across the backside of his hand.

"You got a ton of money. When you wake up, you're taking me shopping buddy. There's this Louis Vuitton bag I'm gonna need." She paused and gathered her emotions.

"I know you're wondering where my gift is. Don't worry. I didn't forget about you. I just wanted to give you my present alone. I hope you like it." She slowly pushed her hand inside her pocket and pulled out the small gift. Taking his hand, she wrapped his long fingers around a slender device.

"That Louis Vuitton bag I need is a diaper bag." Her voice cracked as several tears slipped from eyes. "I'm pregnant baby."

At first Gray thought her extreme exhaustion and headaches were because of all the stress she was under, but after weeks of feeling like a log, she knew something was wrong. For the life of her, she couldn't get her energy up. When the smell of the hospital disinfectant started to make her nauseas, it was apparent she was either ill or pregnant. Being at the hospital made it easy for her to learn her diagnosis. Her hormones were so high it didn't take long for the results to come back positive. There was no doubt the baby was Cam's because she and Noon hadn't had sex at all before she'd come back to St. Louis. Based on her due date, she'd gotten pregnant the night before the wedding. Being pregnant was the last thing she needed with everything going on, but Gray took the unexpected news as a good sign from God. There was no way that He would bless her with another baby, only for Cam to die. God would never be that cruel. At least that's what she tried to tell herself. Gray had to hold onto hope that Cam would come to and they would go through this pregnancy together. God knew she wouldn't be able to survive another pregnancy alone. Because of all the complications she had with the quads, she was considered high risk. Gray needed Cam now more than ever.

"I know this wasn't something we planned but Cam I want this baby. I need it. It gives me something else to fight for. Now you have something else to fight for too. We need you, baby. It's time for you to come back to us. It's time for you to wake up."

CHAPTER 13

"Nobody said it would be easy. It's such a shame for us to part.
Nobody said it would be easy. No one ever said it would be so hard.
Oh, take me back to the start."-Coldplay "The Scientist"

DAY 42:

"*S*ometimes mothers put their sons outdoors, and when that happened, regardless of what the son had done all sympathy was with him. He was outdoors, and his own flesh had done it. To be put outdoors by a landlord was one thing—unfortunate, but an aspect of life which you had no control, since you could not control your income. But to be slack enough to put oneself outdoors, or heartless enough to put one's kin outdoors—that was criminal. There is a difference between being put out and being put outdoors. If you are put out, you go somewhere else; if you are outdoors, there is no place to go. The distinction was subtle but final. Outdoors was the end of something, an irrevocable, physical fact, defining and complementing our metaphysical condition.*" Gray read a passage from Toni Morrison's *The Bluest Eye*. Toni was Cam's favorite author. She'd learned that right before the wedding but made sure to put the info to good use. In the time Cam had been in a coma, she'd already read Beloved, Sula, and Jazz to him. Normally, they were alone when she read to him, but that day Cam Sr. was there visiting. He hadn't said much since he'd been there. It was apparent that he didn't want to get to know his daughter-in-law. He didn't even talk much to Cam. He just sat there watching TV or reading the newspaper. Gray didn't mind his silence. She didn't have much to say to him anyway. To her, he and Kerry were in the same boat.

Yawning profusely, she rubbed her tired eyes and closed the book. The baby or babies she was carrying was wearing her out. She was only a month and one week along in her pregnancy, but it felt like she was further in the process. She could already tell the next eight months would be stressful as fuck. Gray was not prepared to be sick, constantly tired, out of breath, out of shape and on bed rest again. But for her unborn child, she was willing to take the sacrifice. As long as she had Cam by her side, things would be alright. She couldn't wait to get past the first trimester so she could tell the kids and her friends. Keeping the pregnancy a secret was killing her softly, but she didn't want to get everyone's hopes up if something went wrong and she lost the baby or babies. Just the thought of having multiplies again almost caused her to have a panic attack. How would she be able to handle one baby, let alone two or more? She'd most certainly need a nanny. Gray couldn't wait to see the look on Cam's face when she shared the news of their upcoming baby. It would be the best gift she could give him when he awaked.

Knock. Knock.

Dr. Waters peeked his head inside the room then entered.

"How is everybody doing?" He asked cheerfully.

"Oh, I'm making it." Cam Sr. stretched his legs.

"And you, Mrs. Parthens?" Dr. Waters clasped his hands in front of him.

"I'm here." She answered honestly. Gray wouldn't be 100% until Cam came back to her. "Do you need to check Cam?" She scooted her chair back so he could get by.

"No, I checked his vitals earlier, but I did want to speak to you regarding your husband's condition."

"What is it? Is something wrong?" Gray placed the book down. Sitting up straight she gave the doctor her undivided attention.

"Do you mind if I speak in front of your father-in-law?" He asked politely.

"If it's regarding my son, I have the right to know." Cam Sr. made clear.

Gray rolled her eyes and tried to keep her cool.

"Yes, sir. It's fine." She relented.

Dr. Waters took a deep breath and chose his words wisely before speaking.

"I know we spoke about this a few weeks ago and I in no way want to upset you, Mrs. Parthens, but it's time for you to revisit taking your husband off life support."

"I already told you no." Gray spat angrily. "Why are you bringing this up again?"

"Your husband has been in ICU for over a month now. To be frank ma'am, Mr. Parthens' condition hasn't progressed, and we need the space. So, we suggest either taking him off life support, seeing if he can survive on his own or moving him to another facility. You can also consider in home health care as an option."

"I'll do that before I even consider taking him off life support." She answered quickly. There was no other decision for her to make. The fear of taking Cam off life support and him not surviving was beyond terrifying. Gray thought her heart would explode from the notion alone.

"I have something to say about this." Cam Sr. sat up. "I know you're my son's wife." He made air quotes.

Gray jerked her head back from the insult.

"But I have some say so in this too. The decision isn't yours alone. He's my son—"

"Don't remind me." Gray interrupted with a snarl on her face.

"Listen here, li'l girl." Cam Sr. pointed his finger at her. "I know my son. He wouldn't want to continue suffering like this. I would rather he go on to heaven and be with his dear mother than be like this." He waved his hand over Cam's motionless body.

"That's easy for you to say. The only time you talk to or see your son is on holidays. You didn't even reach out to him when he was in jail."

During one of their long talks, Mo told Gray just how strained Cam and Cam Senior's relationship was now. Cam refused to talk to him, so it amazed her that his father thought he had so much say so over his life.

"What kind of father goes three and a half years without communicating with their son? When he needed you, you were nowhere to be found."

"Well, ain't that the pot calling the kettle black! You didn't talk to him for three and a half years either 'wife'!"

Hit with the reality of her own mistakes, Gray's mouth dropped open. She was speechless.

"You don't know what I've been through with that boy." Cam Sr. roared, causing the wrinkles in his face to deepen. "I stood by for years watching him go in and out of the system. I paid for lawyers, accepted long distance calls and all of that. I refused to stand by this time and watch him ruin his life. So yeah, I stayed away but don't ever think that I don't care about or love my son."

"You sure have a shitty way of showing it." Gray matched his energy.

"Okay listen." Dr. Waters interjected. "This conversation is getting out of hand. You two obviously have a lot to discuss. So, I'll leave you to do that. A decision needs to be made, however, in the next 48 hours." He exited the room.

Cam Sr. waited till the door was closed before starting up again.

"We're all suffering. Not just you." He shot up from his seat.

"I get that but taking him off life support isn't the answer." Gray argued. She'd tried her best not to disrespect Cam's father, but she'd had enough of him and his smart mouth.

"How long do you want him to lay here and rot? 'Cause that's what's happening. Cam is wasting away. Keeping him on a respirator is just prolonging the inevitable."

"See." Gray stood on her feet, infuriated. "That's your problem. You don't have any faith in him. You never have but guess what? I have faith the size of a mustard seed that he will pull through. Cam's gonna come back to us, and when he does, you're gonna regret ever saying we should end his life."

"Excuse me." Cam Sr. narrowed his eyes. "Don't judge me. Until you have a kid that you give everything to, but instead chooses to take on the persona of thug, you'll never know the depth of my pain."

"You're right but I've lost a child so what I do know is a parent's love should be unconditional."

"Taking him off the machines doesn't mean he will die!" Cam Sr. threw his fist in the air.

"But he might and I'm not willing to take that risk! If you can't back up my decision then I think it's best you go. Cam doesn't need your negative energy around him." Gray put her foot down.

"You're being selfish." Cam Sr. made his way to the door.

"I don't wanna play God!"

"And that's your problem. You're making this about you and what you want. You're not thinking about what's best for my son. I'm telling you now. You're making a big mistake." He stormed out in a huff.

"I'll take that chance!" Gray yelled behind him.

Alone, she wrapped her arms around her torso and tried to regain her composure. A million what if's flooded her mind. Was she wrong? The hooded vale of death had been hanging over the hospital room for quite a while. The grim reaper hadn't been this close since the passing of her mother. Death had ripped away a part of her that was most loved. Now here it was, again, trying to destroy her existence. Was Cam's father right? Was she making the wrong decision by keeping Cam on life support? Was she being selfish for loving her husband so much she wanted him to live? All Gray could do was think back to the moment she and Cam met. If Aoki wouldn't have smacked Makiah for jumping in front of her on the slide, she wouldn't even be there ruminating over whether to pull the plug or not. It was all because of Aoki that they'd met and fell in love. It was crazy because when she introduced herself to Cam, he was so rude she started to hate his guts.

"Miss Rose, we called Ryan and Makiah's parents but weren't able to reach them, so the next person on their call list was their uncle, Mr. Parthens." Principal Glanville pointed.

Gray placed her red, leather-trimmed, suede Gucci bag down and extended her hand to him.

"Hi, I'm Gray. Aoki's mother."

"Yep." Mr. Parthens nodded his head and kept his eyes focused ahead of him.

Gray screwed up her face to match his.

"Rude . . . but okay." She caught herself looking at his crotch.

She wondered if his dick matched the size of his cocky attitude.

Gray had never met a man so arrogant and mean in her life. Yeah, he was spine tingling fine, but Cam possessed all the qualities in a man that she detested. In the beginning, Cam didn't make it easy for her. The second time they ran into each other at his birthday party she wanted nothing to do with him. Because of his smart mouth, they went at each other all night. It wasn't till the Pussycat Dolls song *Buttons* came on that things changed. The undeniable chemistry they shared was no longer concealed. Cam made it known he wanted her. . . bad.

"Yo, don't play with me." He spun her around to face him.

"What?" Gray asked, caught off guard by his anger.

"You walked away like that shit was optional. Give me your fuckin' number." He ice-grilled her.

"I don't even know you, and most importantly, I don't even like you!" She lied.

"That's the third time you've lied tonight. I ain't gon' keep going back and forth with you about this. You either gon' give me your number or I'ma take it."

Gray paced the room with a smile on her face. Once Cam laid claim to her she knew then she was in trouble. Her feelings for him grew expeditiously. No matter how hard she tried to contain them they couldn't be held back. Cam was just too charming and commanding. Gray never stood a chance against him. He swept her off her feet, literally.

"I am not gettin' my big ass on yo' back."

"If you don't get yo' husky ass up here."

"BITCH, I AIN'T HUSKY!" Gray rolled her neck.

"Man, you know I'm playin'. You ain't husky. You fine as fuck and you know it. Now, c'mon. Get on my back, for real."

"You bet not drop me." She wrapped her arms around his neck and hopped up on his back.

Surprisingly, Cam was a lot stronger than Gray thought he was. He carried her down the street like she was as light as a feather. A smile a mile wide was etched onto her face. Gray felt like a little girl. An explosion of happiness exploded in her chest, as she held on tight.

Turning to face him, Gray gazed at Cam somberly. Since she'd meet him he'd done nothing but lift her up. Even when she thought she didn't need him or when she tried to back away, he came looking for her. When Gunz's Uncle Clyde died, he'd done just that.

"You really gon' make me fuck you up."

"What are you doing here? You can't just be poppin' up at my house." Gray stomped down the steps.

"Last I checked, I could always check up on what's mine."

"Cam, we together but—"

"But nothin'. I told you, you was mine, right?"

"Yeah."

Gray could never outrun or hide from him. From the beginning, Cam showed that leaving him wasn't an option so how could she possibly take the chance of letting him go? She couldn't. They were a team. That was clear the night they got into it and she chucked his phone out the car and then called herself trying to walk home. Cam wasn't having it. Without hesitation he parked his LaFerrari, threw on his hazard lights, chased her down, threw her ass over his shoulder and carried her back to his car.

Gently, he traced her lips with the tip of his finger. The urge to bite them, kiss them and suck them overwhelmed his senses. Cam gazed thoughtfully at each indentation of her lips, as if he could map out prehistoric seas and future plans. He was so wrapped up in her touch that he didn't wanna look up. If he did, he might find himself at the mercy of interrogative eyes, wondering what he was doing. Cam wished he was at liberty to say, but the truth was he honestly didn't know. His feelings for Gray were an enigma wrapped in fear but there would be no letting her go.

"You're mine. You hear me?" He said more as a command than a request.

Gray's lips stretched wide into a smile that reached her eyes. This was how Cam liked to see her. She had the kind of smile that made a man feel happy to be alive. Cam was going to do everything in his power to keep that same smile on her face every day.

"I've been yours."

She was a goner then, just as she was now but falling in love with Cam was always the easy part. She never doubted her feelings for him for one second. If you let Gray tell it her feelings for him were too deep. After only two months of knowing each other Cam was able to talk her into anything. Drunk in love, she'd follow him into the depths of hell if need be. That's how much she loved him. Gray looked down at her wedding set. The day Cam proposed to her was one of the most soul gratifying and scary days of her life. She'd always wanted to be someone's wife. For so long, she thought she'd carry Gunz last name then Cam came along and showed her what real love looked like. Yes, Cam had his flaws. So, did she but when he asked for her hand in marriage she knew that a life with him would be nothing short of entertaining. There was never a dull moment with him. He kept her on her toes.

"Tomor ain't promised, sweetheart. Let's just say fuck it and live in the moment. I love you. You love me. We ain't got shit to lose."

"But marriage? We just started going together."

"Look...I always said the next person I get wit' ain't gon' be just my girlfriend. She was gon' be my wife. I'm too old to be bullshittin' around. A nigga like me like to go all in or nothin'."

"But why you wanna marry me—"

"'Cause I want something from you that nigga ain't never had." He referred to Gunz.

"And what is that?" She asked, shocked by his response.

"The honor of callin' you my wife."

Retaking her seat by his bedside, Gray took his hand in hers. She could feel his blood pumping through his veins. Going down memory lane wasn't making it any easier on her. She and Cam shared so many memories; bad and good. Mist clouded Gray's eyes. Through the misty veil she could barely make out Cam's sleeping face. Death was so final. She didn't want to part from him in the physical world, but she also didn't want him to suffer. The problem was how could she possibly make the decision if the love of her life lived or died? Cam would never give up on her. He'd fight for her till the day he took his own last breath. She would bet her life on it. She'd tried several times to walk away from him and failed every time.

With nowhere to go, Gray's back was pressed into his chest as he hooked his arm around her waist.

"Let me go!" She tried to fight him off to no avail.

His physical and mental hold was too strong.

"Shut the fuck up. You ain't going nowhere." Cam's hand was still wrapped around her ponytail as he yanked her head to the side. *"You wanna a divorce, Gray?"* He passionately kissed the exposed skin of her neck.

Silently, she cursed herself for relishing the feel of his lips. She needed to continue to put up a fight, but her body was betraying her. Cam's masculine scent instantly had her feeling primal and feminine. Naturally, she wanted to submit to him. He was her man. He always knew how to take control of her body. Knowing he had her right where he wanted, he quickly spun her around to face him. Looking down into her lust-filled eyes, he pulled her in for a heated kiss. Gray's breath hitched. Cam was her drug. One touch from him and she was intoxicated. There was no stopping him when he wanted to have his way—not that she'd want to stop him. His scent alone sent her into a heady trance.

Conflicted by her emotions, Gray buried her face in the mattress on the bed. This was the biggest decision she'd ever have to make. She couldn't fuck this up. Her heart felt like it was ripping in half. Cam was as big a piece of her as the kids. She couldn't fathom life without either of them. Since day one of him being in a coma, she'd made it her business not to cry. Crying wasn't going to make him come to, but with the weight of the world on her shoulders and a new baby in her belly, the world became a blur. So did all the sounds, her taste and smell. It all vanished. Out of utter silence a gut-wrenching cry arose. Like a planted seed it began to grow. Leisurely, it rose to a moan and ripped from her heart. To the ends of the world the cry soared over lands, oceans, through woodlands and plains. Gray felt the heaviness of sorrow press into her chest as she sobbed. Her mind clouded with grief, her heart grew cold and numb with pent up emotion. Clogged with pain and anger all she could do was wail. So, she let it out in one long sorrowful bellow to the heavens.

Scorching hot tears slid down her cheeks. So many tears burst forth, she swore she was drowning. Gray's bottom lip quivered as her breathing became labored. Up and down her chest heaved as she gasped for air that simply wasn't there. The walls had started to close in on her. Bile filled her throat. For as long as she could remember, she'd been afraid of death. The more children she had the bigger the fear became. Sometimes, it kept her up at night. Gray tried to suppress the notion that one day she'd pass on 'cause she knew no matter how old she was she'd never be ready to depart the physical world. The sentiment went to her loved ones as well. She couldn't bear to see them die, especially not Cam. They'd just gotten started. They hadn't even made it a year together as a married couple. The time they had spent together was filled with so many ups and downs but damn did the ups make her feel high. Like the Mila J song if she and Cam weren't smoking, drinking or fighting they were making love or breaking up.

Cam was fucking her so good; she couldn't articulate a response. Harder and faster he pumped, intoxicating her mind. If a response was what he wanted, he was going to have to stop stroking her ass long enough for her brain to start working again.

"Talk that shit now, Gray." He gripped the back of her neck and went deeper.

Unable to speak, Gray blinked her eyes. Cam had hit an erogenous zone that caused her to temporarily go blind.

"You was gon' change the locks?"

"No." Her sweaty palms gripped the sheets.

Her vision had literally gone black. Cam pushed her face into the mattress and pumped in and out viciously.

"You ain't never gettin' rid of me. You're mine, you hear me?"

"Yes, baby. I'm yours. You got me forever."

"Fuck yeah, you mine. This ass is really mine." He bent down and licked her left ass cheek then bit it.

The longer she cried the more Gray could feel herself unraveling. The threads of every happy moment she and Cam shared weaved together in her mind. It was as if their entire love story was on play. She missed everything about Cam. His tongue kisses were the sweetest taboo. They left her in a tailspin of desire. Each word he uttered left her weak in the knees. She couldn't get enough of him. He was not only her husband , but the father of her children, her lover, her best friend, her shoulder to lean on, her man. Would she be able to go on if he weren't there to grow old with her?

The saying goes if a person lives fully they're not afraid of death. Cam had lived a life that most people could only dream of. He'd traveled the world, fell in love, bore children, and basked in his riches.

He'd also committed multiple sins. The biggest being murder. Would God condemn him to hell? Would he go to heaven, become a ghost or sleep on forever? Death was a painful truth that Gray didn't want to face. She couldn't be the one to send him to an afterlife of hell.

"What do you want me to do God? Whatever you want me to do, I'll do it." She lifted her head and glanced out the window. Sunlight seeped into the room like woven strands, free and united.

"I'll feed the homeless, I'll give blood, hell I'll give a kidney if you want me to. Just show me how to fix this. Don't take the only man who's ever loved me away. I can't lose him. I can't." She held Cam's hand in silence as salty tears soaked her chest. The pain that flowed from her lungs came in waves; minutes of sobbing broken apart by short pauses for recovering breaths. She couldn't imagine never seeing Cam's whiskey brown eyes again. She'd just gotten him back. After years of blaming each other for the downfall of their marriage, they'd finally reunited.

Gray closed her eyes. In Cam's hold she was cushioned better than any butterfly-to-be. He bathed her in his warmth and enthralling cologne. When the song ended it would be too soon. She'd want more but this was it for them. They'd hit the end of the road. There was so much that needed to be said and so little time. Apprehensively, Gray looked up into his whiskey brown eyes and cried.

"Why do you love me?" She died to know.

Cam was shocked by her question. He thought she knew.

"Cause I see you." He answered truthfully.

Now was not the time for a bunch of faking and fronting. He had to clear up anything that might've been misconstrued.

"Well, if you see me then why won't you leave me?"

"Cause I see you." He made it clear.

She was a mirror image of him. Even with all of her flaws his love would never waiver.

"You're an organ in my body, Gray. If you fail, I fail."

Gray dropped her head and let her tears fall where they may. Cam wasn't playing fair. He had no right to say these things to her now.

"Look at me." He demanded.

Doing as she was told; Gray gave him eye contact.

"I've been operating from a place of fear and not love. Fear of losing you. Losing the kids. Fear of the ramifications that come along with all that shit, but I refuse to let it happen. I need you to understand that you, me, and the kids are gonna always be alright. I got you, just have me."

Recalling their last moments together at the wedding only made her distraught with grief. Her heart felt as if the blood inside of it had become tar as it struggled to keep a steady beat. The rug was literally being pulled from her under her feet. It wasn't fair the predicament she'd been placed in.

"God, I'm so mad I don't know what to do!" Tears poured from her eyes at lightning speed. "Lord, I wish I could understand! How did we get here? I wanna know why! Why are you doing this to us? Whyyyyyyyyyyyyyyy?" Snot bubbled from her swollen red nose.

"It was supposed to be me laying here. Not him. I was supposed to go first! I was ready!" She wailed. "Lord don't make me do this. I'm not strong enough. I thought I was but I'm not. I won't make it God! I won't! It's not his time! We still have so much life to live together! My babies need him!"

When her life was on the line, Cam was right there by her side every step of the way. He wasn't fearful at all. He'd made it up in his mind. If she died, he was dying. Cam had her back all the way till the end.

Gray, go clean yourself up and meet me back here."

"Baby, it doesn't even matter." She sighed, not even realizing she'd called him baby.

"Yes, it does. We still have time."

Gray checked her watch.

"Not much."

It was 11:23. Cam took her hand in his.

"Have I ever let you down?"

"Is that a trick question?" Gray smirked, arching her brow.

"I got you." Cam said seriously.

Gray swallowed her anxiety. If she had any chance at survival, she had to open her heart and allow herself to trust him again.

"You believe me?" Cam's earnest eyes prayed she said yes.

Her answer would define their future.

Gray breathlessly said, "Yes."

Their last words were all the confirmation that Gray needed. She couldn't pull the plug.

"Wake up, baby." She lifted up on her feet and gazed down at his handsome face. He looked so calm, which made the crack in her heart widen. Even though she was hopeful of their future anxiety flowed through her veins.

I never dreamed you'd leave in summer
I thought you would go then come back home
I thought the cold would leave by summer
But my quiet nights will be spent alone

"Open your eyes, Cam. Look at me. I believe in you. I can't put you outdoors. I can't do it. I won't survive it. Don't make me choose. Please baby. Let me see those beautiful eyes." She caressed his cheek gently. Gray's eyes glimmered with watery tears. Cam lay unresponsive. No part of him moved. Gray's whole world started to crumble.

"Squeeze my hand. Move your leg . . . anything." She pleaded.

"Let me know you're in there. Please. You can't leave me hanging now. You never have before." She examined his body for any movement. There was none. Gray's breathing hitched as her knees grew weak.

"I lost you once, Cam. I'm not losing you again. Remember, I'm yours. Which means you're mine. There's no you without me. If you go, I go so who's gonna raise our babies?" She pulled on his nightgown frantically.

You said there would be warm love in springtime

'Cause that was when you started to be cold
I never dreamed you'd leave in summer
Oh but now I find myself all alone

"All we had was one good day. Twenty-four hours. That's not enough. I need more. So, you wake up goddamit!" She shook him profusely.

"It's not your time! Come back to me. Baby, please. Open your eyes, Cam. It's your turn to count my freckles. We have to come up with baby names. You have to be there to walk our girls down the aisle when they get married. I can't teach Reign how to be a man, only you can." She held the sides of his face and kissed his dry lips repeatedly. "A star can't shine without the moon. You're my moon. Without you there's no me. You light up our universe."

You said then you'd be the life in autumn
Said you'd be the one to see the way
No, I would never dream you'd leave in summer

And as if Cam couldn't take anymore of her heartbreak, he decided to put her out of her misery. Gray wouldn't have to play God. The choice was made for her as the heart monitor went from steady beats to one long blaring sound indicting his heart had stopped. Gray looked around confused. Her worst nightmare was coming true. Cam was leaving her for good.

"No. No. No." She panicked as Dr. Waters and several nurses rushed in.

But now I find my love has gone away
Why didn't you
staaaaaaaaaaaaaaaaaaaaaaaaaaaaaaaaaaaaaaaaaaaaaaaaaaaaaaaaay?

Pandemonium filled the room. Gray was swiftly pushed to the side as they tried to revive him with chest compressions. Push after push, breath after breath, Dr. Waters and the nurses took turns trying to resuscitate Cam. Gray stood by the door anticipating hearing the sound of his heartbeat again, but it was of no use. After twenty agonizing minutes he lay lifeless. It was over. A bone chilling silence filled the room. No one said a word. Gray's body shook violently.

To see him dead was to die herself. There was no her without him, no life after his love. He had been her all, her purpose. Tears rolled unchecked down her cheeks and dripped from her quivering chin. She was too blue to sob or wail. She just stood there like a mannequin while the magnitude of her loss seeped in. Her husband was gone. Decades later when asked to define her sorrow in the tragic moment she realized he was dead; her eyes would fill with tears once more. Losing Cam would never be something she'd get over. Heartbreak would forever come in harrowing waves, snatching her appetite and slumber. It would become a thorn stuck in her side that would never dull. A heart that was once whole was now nothing more than an echo of a love she once put her all into.

Then, suddenly, Cam's eyes opened like two flashlight beams and he shot up in the air, scaring the living daylight out of everyone. His heart pounded erratically as if a needle of adrenaline had been pushed into his veins. Gasping for air, he took in all the tubes and wires attached to his body, the hospital staff and then the blue-eyed beauty standing across the room. He'd asked God to return his soul to his body so he could have more time with her, and he'd answered his prayer. Together, they were both a beautiful dream and a catastrophic nightmare, but Cam wouldn't have it any other way. They'd always find their way back to each other. Not even death could keep them apart.

CHAPTER 14

"It's like all of a sudden your life is so cool. 'Cause everything in it is working for you. Your friends and your family are getting along. It feels like when you hear your favorite song."-Musiq Soulchild feat Kindred the Family Soul & Cee Lo Green "Momentinlife"

celebration of life commenced as all of Cam's immediate family and friends surrounded his bedside overjoyed that he was finally awake. When they received the call that he'd come out of his coma no one could believe their ears. It was nothing short of a miracle. Mo couldn't even get through the door good before she burst into tears. Holding her big brother tight, she sobbed for what seemed like hours into his chest. Cam's arms weren't mobile enough for him to hug her back. He was still very weak and being monitored closely. After performing a series of tests, it was concluded that he hadn't suffered from any memory loss. His vision, speech and hearing were intact. Cam had lost a ton of weight tho. When he'd come into the hospital he was 220 pounds. Now he weighed 182. For a man that was

6'4 in height with an athletic frame, that was frail. Cam looked like he was made of skin and bones. There was hardly any fat on his body. His speech was slow and measured. Dr. Waters made it clear he'd need speech therapy and that his body must be completely reconditioned, all while ensuring that his vitals stay in a healthy range, and that no part of his body reacted in a way it shouldn't. This included his vascular systems, skin integrity, cognitive function, as well as many other important signs that must be monitored to ensure a safe recovery. Because he was in such good physical shape before the coma, Dr. Waters was 100% sure that with extensive rehab Cam would be back to normal in no time.

Boss practically had to pry Mo off of her brother so the kids could get to him. Reign, Beaux and Sky were just happy Cam was awake to play with them. They were too little to understand the magnitude of the situation, but Aoki and Press did. When they walked into the room and saw their Pop awake, or as Press liked to call him, Papa, tears of joy flooded their eyes. Like Mo, Press held onto him for dear life. The girls no longer had to worry about losing another dad. Cam had kept his promise to be there for them always. Without him, their family wasn't complete. Now for the first time since he had come into their lives, they could be one big happy family. There would be no more worrying or sleepless nights without their mother and father. Finally, the drama was over.

Cam's eyes lit up as soon as he saw all five of his children. In his dreams, he heard the pitter patter of his kids' feet and their laughter. He would be so asleep and so awake in his soul, reliving those brief wonderful moments of fatherhood. His children were his world. He'd only had a week with them, which wasn't nearly enough time after being separated for three long years. On the outside it might not have seemed like it, but internally, he was fighting tooth and nail to get back to them. He wished he was strong enough to kiss them and hold them but now he had all the time in the world to do so. Cam closed his eyes for a second and thanked God.

"We missed you daddy." Beaux kissed her father on the lips. Sky and Reign followed suit. Cam instantly became overwhelmed with feelings. He could feel the tears rise from his stomach. This was the greatest moment of his life.

"Yeah, it's good to have you back." Stacy gripped his shoulder.

Cam mustered up the strength to give him a small smile. He couldn't have been more grateful to have such good friends by his side. No matter the circumstance, they were always there for each other. Stacy was his man fifty grand.

"I love you, son. I'm happy you're awake. I was worried sick about you." Cam Sr. ran his fingers through Cam's curly mane.

Surprised by the kind gesture, Cam looked at his father apprehensively. He couldn't remember the last time his dad had been so affectionate. Despite being slightly uncomfortable, he relished the moment anyway. Maybe this could be the start of them forming a new father/son relationship.

"You've always been a fighter. Even if your target was me." Cam Sr. chuckled. "But I knew you were gonna come through. You're not a quitter."

Gray's eyes bucked as soon as the words left his lips. *No, this old nigga didn't,* her mouth dropped wide open. If it were up to him, they all would've been crowded around Cam's bed saying their last goodbyes. It took everything in her not to blast his geriatric ass in front of everyone. Instead, she glared at him and rolled her eyes so hard she thought they'd fall out.

"Papa, what was it like being in a coma?" Press inquired, while fiddling with his cover. "Could you hear us? Did you know we were here?"

Cam swallowed hard and took a deep breath. It took a lot of his energy to complete one sentence. Everyone waited with bated breath for his answer. It was something they all wanted to know. Gray thought about asking him but didn't want to put too much pressure on him.

"I. . . could feel. . . when my hair. . . was. . . being washed. I. . . could." He paused to breathe. "Hear. . . your mama. . . singing. . . and. .

. counting . . . my freckles." Cam lovingly looked at Gray causing all the girls in the room to swoon.

Her unwavering love was what brought him through. Gray was his lover, his soulmate, his angel on earth. He'd never loved a woman as much as he did her and never would again. She was the one that made it safe for his soul to breathe anew. Gray possessed a strength and courage he thought had long extinguished from this world. Everything about her felt like home. She was his and he was hers: mind, body and soul. Making her his wife had been the best decision of his life.

"Everybody from the neighborhood and the church has been praying for you." Mo relayed the news.

"Abigail told me to tell you she was happy you're awake." Cam Sr. said. "She wanted to come visit you, but I told her that wasn't a good idea."

And just like that, Cam and his father were back at square one. All notion of a reconciliation went right out the window. He knew damn well that Cam didn't want anything to do with Abigail or her punk ass son, Kingston. This was why he and his father couldn't get along. Cam Sr. had no loyalty to him or their family. Gray noticed the expression of anger and aggravation on his face. Cam was pissed.

Quan picked up on the tension but chose to focus on the fact that his best friend was alive. He loved Cam like a brother. Let Mo tell it they were kindred spirits. Quan could no more abandon him than he could his own child. That's how close the two men were. It had been incredibly hard knowing Cam was laid up in the hospital and there was no drug or surgery that could help him. He'd never felt more help- less in his life. That's why he'd been unable to visit. He couldn't mentally or physically handle seeing Cam in such a vegetative state. Now that he was back, Quan's soul was at rest. That didn't stop the guilt that swarmed his chest. He thought his homey was done. He thought he was done for and that was all his fault. Making his way over to Cam's bed, he rested his forehead on Cam's thigh. Fuck his macho persona. He didn't care who saw. Quan broke down and let the cry he'd been holding in pour out. The sobs pierced through the years of being unaffected that he'd perfected. Men, specifically black men, were taught that crying was weak. Since as far back as he could remember, he'd watched most of the men around him hide their emotions and refrain from expressing them even when they'd been hurt. It was mechanism he'd adapted as a shorty. Quan quickly realized if he wanted to continue to keep up this tough guy image, he'd have to perfect the part of being a hard, non-emotional black man. If he did show emotion, he was called a pussy, a punk, a fag, or a lame. It was normal for black boys and men to embrace and conform to the traditional gender norms of manhood such as being stoic, strong, dominant, and not displaying traditionally feminine characteristics. But Quan was a grown, forty-plus-year-old man. He now knew that showing emotion wasn't a sign of weakness or being gay. Life was too precious not to show his loved ones that he cared. So, he pressed his forehead into Cam's skin and began to let his heart yank in and out of his chest. Kema watched on as her husband cried. For weeks, she'd observed him walk around numb. He needed this release like he needed air to breathe.

Cam could barely lift his arm, but he had to put his friend out of his misery. Seeing Quan in a heap of tears was worse than seeing Gray cry. It took what felt like hours to place his hand on his back, but the palm of his hand finally landed. Feeling Cam's hand on his person, only made Quan cry harder.

"Real shit dog." He lifted his head and looked at his boy. "You cause too much trouble. You been taking me through since we was kids. How you gon' try to die at my wedding? You always trying to take the spotlight from me." He joked.

"Word." Stacy agreed. "I ain't never seen nobody try to die at somebody wedding. That shit outta pocket, dog."

Cam glanced over at him and said slowly, "Shut . . . yo . . .fat ass . . . up."

A roar of laughter filled the room.

"Keep talking shit." Stacy licked his lips. "I'ma unplug all this shit. This nigga a'ight."

"Nah, for real. This on me. I—" Quan began before Cam cut him off.

Sluggishly, he shook his head no. Pastor Edris stabbing him was in no way his fault.

"It is." Quan disagreed, wiping his face and nose. "I should've been paying attention. I should've never let that flaw ass nigga get that close to us. You know that shit hit home when Diggy was murked, but you don't understand the turmoil I been through the last 42 days, counting every minute thinking I'm gon get the phone call that you ain't here no more."

"But. . . I. . . am. . ." Cam muttered as a single tear fell from his glossy eye.

He and Quan were brothers, for better or worse. The kind of bond they had was a union of souls, a feeling that to lose the other would be worse than death. Whatever life threw their way, he knew they'd be there for one another. He only relayed that kind of trust to Gray, Mo, Stacy and Priest.

"Yo, I'm tired of you niggas crying." Stacy said fed up with all the dramatics. "It's enough of that shit. It's a celebration bitches. Where the bottles at? We need to make a toast." Stacy looked around the crowded space. There weren't any bottles of champagne, but Sky offered up her sippy cup by placing it in the air.

"Yep, you know the vibe ma-ma." Stacy kissed her chubby cheek.

For as long as the hospital would allow it, the family loved on Cam. The kids didn't want to leave but after a while he grew tired and was ready for bed. It was hard saying goodbye to everyone. Even though he wasn't 100% conscious during his time in the coma, when he was aware of his surroundings he yearned to see his loved ones faces. Family was everything to Cam, especially the one he had with Gray. They'd gone through hell and back to get this marriage of theirs on track. Now that he was alive and well, the two of them together would be unstoppable. Nothing or no one would ever tear them apart again.

Once they were finally alone, Gray kicked off her shoes and

climbed into bed with him like she did every night. Snuggled close, she tried to fall asleep but couldn't wipe the smile off her face. God had answered her prayers and she couldn't have been more elated.

"Go. . . to sleep." Cam said with his eyes closed. He could feel her grinning from ear-to- ear.

"Okay-okay." She wrapped her arm around him and settled herself. "I'm just so happy. I got my moon back. My world is complete again."

Cam couldn't agree anymore. God had given him a second chance at life, and he swore this time not to take it for granted or fuck it up.

"I . . . love you . . . Star."

"I love you too."

CHAPTER 15

"Many men, wish death upon me."-50 Cent "Many Men"

The heavy slumber Gray was in was the best sleep of her life. She hadn't slept that soundly since Cam was assaulted. Having him back gave her the peace she needed to rest at night. Five hours had passed since their family and friends had left. She would've slept through the night if her bladder hadn't filled with pee. It was so full it hurt to stand. Slowly, she eased her way to the bathroom. As soon as she stood, she realized she had to do more than pee. Her belly started to ache. It was apparent she'd be in the bathroom a while so she took her phone and EarPods with her so she could listen to music and scroll through Instagram while relieving herself. Gray tried not to make too much noise. The last thing she wanted to do was wake Cam. He needed all the rest he could get. Once the door was closed, she pulled her underwear and jogging pants down. The cold toilet seat sent a chill throughout her bottom. Clicking on her Tidal app she played Donny Hathaway's *Jealous Guy*, the live version. Tapping her foot to the beat, she brought up her Instagram page and handled her business.

While Gray used the restroom, the door to Cam's room creaked open. The room was pitch black as an unknown woman dressed in a nurse's uniform tip-toed in. For hours, she'd waited for Cam to be alone. Now was the perfect time to strike. Taking hold of the pillow on Gray's cot, she lifted it up and smashed it down onto Cam's face. His eyes immediately popped open. Cam struggled to fight back but could barely move his limbs. All he could do was scream but his shrills came out as muffled mumbles. Cam couldn't believe this was happening. He'd survived 42 days in a coma just to die twenty-four hours later from suffocation. Frantically, he tried reaching for the nurse's button, but without his vision, he couldn't find it.

"Gray!" He called out her name. Where was she? Cam didn't know how much longer he could hold on. The person trying to kill him wasn't letting up. The attacker pushed the pillow down with force. No air was getting in. She had a job to do and she was going to accomplish it.

Gray pulled up her pants, sat her phone down and washed her hands. She couldn't wait to get back in bed with Cam and rest. Once things settled down some, she'd tell him they were expecting another child. Gray knew beyond a shadow of doubt he'd be elated to hear the news.

Pulling back the door, she stepped back into the dark room only to find some woman smothering her husband with a pillow. For a second, Gray was so taken aback she froze. She didn't know if she was hallucinating or dreaming. When she heard Cam's cries for help, she knew what was happening was real. Moving swiftly, she grabbed one of the glass flower vases and cracked it across the back of the woman's head. Knocked unconscious, the hitta sent to kill Cam knees buckled and she tumbled to the floor. Breathing heavily, Gray rushed over to Cam to make sure he was okay. After clicking on the light, she examined him. The color had drained from his face but he was alive and that's all she could pray for. Looking down at the woman, she wondered who could she be. Cam's entire hospital stay had been peaceful. Now when he was awake, all of a sudden, someone wanted to kill him? None of it made sense. Bending over, Gray took a good look at the woman and that's when she saw it. Right there on the side of her neck was an MCM tattoo.

~

Ring. Ring.

GUNZ COULDN'T ANSWER THE PHONE FAST ENOUGH. THIS WAS THE call he'd been waiting for all night. After learning Cam had awakened from the coma, he didn't hesitate to make his move. Gunz wanted Cam gone. He refused to let him live another day.

"Hello?"

"Hello. This is a free call from—"

"Veeta." The girl that he'd chosen to kill Cam used her alias instead of her real name.

"An inmate at St. Louis City Justice Center. This call is subject to recording and monitoring. To accept this free call press 1. To refuse this free call press 2."

Gunz quickly pressed the number one. Veeta calling from jail meant one of two things. Either she'd succeeded in killing Cam and gotten caught or she'd failed and caught. For her sake, it better had been the first option.

"What the fuck happened?" He growled into the phone.

"I failed." She sighed.

"Fuck you mean you failed? Failure was not an option! I fuckin' told you that!"

"His bitch came in the room while I was in the middle of handling it and hit me with a vase. When I came to I was handcuffed and being placed in the back of a squad car. But look, you gon' come bail me out."

Gunz didn't even bother answering her dumb ass question. Veeta could rot in hell for all he cared. His main concern was Cam. The nigga must've had a horseshoe up his ass. The muthafucka wouldn't die for shit. Defeated, once again, Gunz decided to go back to the drawing board. The next time he made a move against Cam he wouldn't miss.

CHAPTER 16

"I hate when niggas be lying, especially when shit be so small. If you ain't gon' ride then don't waste my time. I told you I'm not to be fucked with."-Tink "I Ain't Got Time Today"

There was no more disarray. Everything in Aoki's young life had fallen back into place. Her pop was in the hospital on his way to a full recovery, soon he and her mom would be returning home. Gray and Cam made the conscious decision to keep the attempt on his life a secret. The kids had been through enough. They didn't want to scare them. With Cam out of the coma, Aoki was living her life like it was golden. The twins were back from summer camp and they all were attending their first kickback a.k.a. house party at Kiara's crib. Everyone from the neighborhood would be there but of course Aoki was most excited to see Paris. He'd text her several times since their night at the pool. He didn't even know how much their conversations helped her through the last days of Cam being in a coma. She anticipated his calls and relished every second of communicating with him. Her feelings for him grew enormously. She was deep in like and lust for him. The conversations she had with Blizz just didn't compare. She wanted to give him a fighting chance at gaining her affection, but Paris had already taken up space in her heart.

Boss parked the car in front of Kiara's house. The party was already in full effect. A crowd of kids were out front laughing and talking. Boss turned around in his seat and looked back at the girls. Makiah, Ryan, Aoki and Princess sat side-by-side dressed to the nine with hoop earrings and heels on. It fucked his head up to see his daughters, niece and Princess, who was practically his niece too, look so mature. They were no longer little girls running around with barrettes in their hair. They were young ladies now and for Boss that was a hard pill to swallow.

"Y'all be good, a'ight."

"Yes, daddy." Ryan groaned, rolling her eyes to the sky.

"You can roll 'em but you sholl can't control 'em." He snapped. "And don't yes daddy me. I don't even want y'all going to this bullshit. Ya' dumb ass mom talkin' about y'all *mature enough*." He mocked Mo.

"My mama ain't dumb." Ryan rocked her neck from side-to-side.

"Yes, the fuck she is! Letting her thirteen year old daughters go to a fuckin' house party on the northside unsupervised at that. Matter fact, fuck that. I'm coming in there wit' y'all." He opened the driver side door.

"NO!" Ryan, Aoki, and Princess shouted at the same time.

"Why the fuck not?" He slammed the door shut. "Fuck y'all tryin' to hide in there?"

"We ain't hiding nothing but that's embarrassing going in there wit' our dad." Ryan whined on the verge of tears.

"No, it'll be embarrassing if I shoot that shit up."

"Uncle Boss, you ain't even no thug, for real." Aoki waved him off. "Don't you own a gas station?"

"That's besides the fuckin' point! You know what? Mind your fuckin' business!" He pointed his finger in her face. "Wit' yo' grown ass." He looked her up and down. "Now I want y'all to go in here and act y'all age and not your shoe size—"

"Seven?" Ryan looked at him liked he was dumb.

"It's not too late for me to turn this car around. Keep fuckin' playin' wit' me. Looking like yo' damn mama. Nah, fuck that. Y'all ain't going." Boss started up the engine.

"Daddy, no!" She grabbed his arm. "I promise we gon' be good. We ain't gon' even be in there long. You're coming back to get us at nine o'clock. You bout to have us lookin' like we in middle school anyway."

"News flash! Y'all are in fuckin' middle school!"

"They don't need to know our business." Princess smacked her lips.

"Keep that shit up and I'ma call Bernard and tell him that I socked you in the mouth. They already gave me permission to beat yo' ass."

"Calm down, Uncle Boss. You gon' raise your blood pressure. Mess around and be in the hospital wit' my Pop." Aoki cautioned.

"You got one more time." He warned on the verge of smacking her.

"Daddy, chill. By the time you come get us the party will just have started poppin' off." Ryan reasoned.

"You damn right. Y'all hot asses gon' be at home watching Life After Lock Up wit' me."

"Trust me, I would much rather do that." Makiah pouted, looking out the window. She didn't even wanna go to the stupid ratchet party. Being around a bunch of wannabe, damn near illiterate thugs and over-sexual hood bitches wasn't her thing. Makiah was much different from her twin and cousin. Sure, she liked boys, but they didn't rule her world. She was more into drawing in her sketchbook and studying up on different painters like Kehinde Wiley, Jacob Lawrence, Basquiat, and the famous sculpture Augusta Savage. She prayed one day her name would be just as big as theirs. Art was a way of living for Makiah. There was nothing else she wanted to do with her life than draw, paint, and sculpt. Shaking her ass to trap beats wasn't her idea of fun. On top of that, she and Kiara didn't really get along. They simply tolerated each other for the sake of Aoki. Kiara wasn't Makiah's cup of tea. She was loud, ghetto, loose with her puss, fake and always had some slick shit to say. It was only a matter of time before she had to pop her in the mouth.

"You wanna go back home with me baby girl?" Boss eyed his daughter quizzically.

"Yes." She answered eagerly.

"No twin. You gotta come. It ain't gon' be the same without you." Ryan poked out her bottom lip. She hated being separated from her sister but Makiah was far more independent. She liked her alone time. She savored the moments where she stood on her own merit and wasn't lumped in to being a twin. Ryan, on the other hand, loved for them to be attached at the hip.

"*Pleaaaaaase.* Come for me." She begged, tugging on her arm.

"Okay." Makiah sighed, pulling away. She had a hard time telling her sister no. Ryan could practically talk her into anything.

"If anybody offers you drugs or alcohol what you gon' do?" Boss quizzed all the girls.

"Daddy, Kiara's mom is gonna be there—"

"What the fuck that's supposed to mean? That bitch been a ho."

"You think everybody a ho." Ryan mumbled under her breath.

"Watch your fuckin' mouth." He popped her in the lips.

"Dang, daddy. You messed up my lip-gloss." She pulled out her Dior compact mirror.

"Up here dressed like Dainty Kane. Now what you gon' do if somebody offers you drugs?"

"Ain't nobody gon' be drinking, smoking, or drugging." Ryan lied. Andrea was going to be supervising the party, but she knew damn well Andrea didn't give a damn what Kiara and her friends did, as long as she was aware of it.

"Unc." Aoki chimed in. "You have nothing to worry about. None of us even want to do drugs. We gotta preserve our pretty." She flipped her long braid over her shoulder.

"Yeah a'ight. Just know when I pick you up I'm administrating these." He pulled out the at home drug test called Prime Screen.

"Really, daddy?" Ryan cocked her head to the side. "It ain't even that deep."

"Yes, the fuck it is. My daughters ain't gon' be no dope fiends."

"Can we go now?" Makiah huffed. The quicker they got inside the party, the faster they'd be able to go home.

"I guess." Boss reluctantly let them leave.

"Bye daddy!" The twins gave him a kiss on the cheek goodbye.

"Bye Unc." Aoki climbed out the truck.

"Bye Boss." Princess waved.

"Make sure you keep your phones on and you bet not pop no pills, or no pussy or I'm poppin' you!" Boss shouted out the window 'causing the other kids to laugh.

Totally embarrassed, the girls avoided eye contact with the older teens and ran inside the house. Kiara was upstairs playing Beer Pong with a few of her friends. If Boss would've known this was the kind of shenanigans going on, he would've shut the whole party down and it wasn't even his house. Aoki looked around for Paris. She'd been waiting all week to see his face. Outside of the phone conversations they'd had, she hadn't seen him in person since they're late night rendezvous. Since this would be their second time kicking it, Aoki had to come with that sauce. Her fashion game had to be on point. It took her days to curate the perfect look. After heavy contemplation, she finally decided on wearing her hair in two French braids to the back, Dolce & Gabbana vintage bronze earrings with red jewels, a black choker, fitted white baby tee, black fishnet stockings, two-tone skintight jeans, Dolce & Gabbana t-strap bejeweled heels and a velvet cobalt blue Elie Saab purse. You couldn't tell her she wasn't the shit. She and her girls were dressed to kill.

"Bout time y'all got here. For a second, I thought y'all wasn't coming." Kiara rushed over and gave all the girls a hug, except Makiah. From the moment they'd met, the vibe between them had been off. Kiara and Makiah were total opposites. They had absolutely nothing in common from the company they kept, to the things they liked to do and the way they dressed. Case in point. Kiara wore a platinum blonde 40-inch, lace-front wig, mink lashes, a Fendi logo dress that zipped up the front and boots. Embracing her natural hair, Makiah rocked her hair in two afro puffs. Her ensemble had a 70's vibe to it. She wore gold hoop earrings, gold coin necklaces, a blue off-the-shoulder, long sleeve top that tied in the front, flowy shorts and gold thong sandals. To Kiara, she looked like an extra from that 70's Show. She wished her, her weird outfit and her stuck-up attitude would've stayed at home.

"So, you don't see my sister standing here?" Ryan caught her shade.

"Oh no. Hey." Kiara replied dryly.

Makiah didn't even bother responding. She didn't care if Kiara spoke or not. She had no intentions on speaking to her anyway.

"Is that my boo?" Andrea sauntered out the kitchen tipsy drinking a vodka cranberry.

"Hey Miss Andrea." Aoki gave her a quick hug hello.

"*Heeeey* Pretty Girl." She slurred her words. "These Boss girls ain't it?" She stared at the twins.

"Yes ma'am."

"Girl, I'm too young to be anybody's ma'am. Hey twins. Y'all fine ass daddy drop y'all off?"

"Yes." They answered in sync.

"Ooh." Andrea fanned her face. "Just thinking about yo' daddy got my coochie beat boxing. That damn Zaire baby. . . is fine as shit. He and yo' mama still together?"

"Yes." Makiah screwed up her face.

"Mmm." Andrea pursed her lips. "They been together forever. You can't tell me he don't be cheating."

"I will punch the shit outta this old bitch." Makiah's nostrils flared.

"C'mon y'all. Let's go downstairs. Everybody's down there." Kiara led them to the basement.

On the way there Aoki noticed a full table filled with desserts, chips, a crockpot of Rotel, fried chicken, pizza and more. People were straggled around everywhere drinking and hooking up. When they made it downstairs she took in the décor. Christmas lights, an old couch, folding chairs, a dart board, washer and dryer was all there was. It was so packed that nothing else could fit. Everyone was dancing and throwing their red Solo cups in the air. A cloud of weed smoke hovered over everyone's head. The music was so loud it made Aoki's skin tingle. She'd been waiting her whole life to experience a high school party. Ever since she'd saw Bow Wow and Omarion's video for *Let Me Hold You Down* she'd wanted to attend one. The energy in the room made her feel like she was high. Yo Gotti's *H.O.E.* was bumping, hyping everyone up. Aoki couldn't stop her shoulders from bouncing. The song had pulled her in and wouldn't let go. She had no choice but to join the crowd and dance.

"I'ma ho, you know I'ma ho (I am)
But don't call me that li'l nigga, that shit come with the smoke
I'ma ho, got bitches galore"

Princess, Ryan, and Kiara joined her. Forming a semi-circle, they all got their life on the makeshift dancefloor. Makiah refused to dance to a song that objectified women, even though she liked the beat and Yo Gotti's flow. Leaning against the wall, she pulled out her phone and scrolled through Instagram. Kiara glared at her and shook her head. This was why she couldn't fuck wit' Makiah. She was a fucking wet blanket. The girl wouldn't know how to have fun if it bit her in the ass. Song after song, the DJ had them hittin' the Woah and twerkin'. The only thing that stopped them from dancing was the sight of Meechi, Blizz, Chris, Rob and ten other niggas mobbin' through the crowd like Nas and DMX in Belly. A throng of people parted like the red sea so they could get through. The entire vibe of the party went up a notch when they arrived. A bright smile spread across Kiara's face as Meechi came near. Aoki wasn't happy at all. Her mouth had formed into a deep frown. Paris wasn't with them. She wondered where he was. He didn't go anywhere without Meechi. They were joined at the hip more than Ryan and Makiah. Kiara wrapped her arms around her boo's neck and kissed him passionately on the lips. Meechi placed his hands under her skirt and gripped each of her ass cheeks like they were basketballs. Kiara didn't even care. She loved the attention and didn't mind him groping her like she was a piece of meat. Makiah couldn't believe her eyes. This was the ho shit she couldn't get with. She wished she would let a nigga disrespect her like that. Her father had taught her to have self-respect. Meechi's ass wouldn't live to see another day if he tried some shit like that with her.

"What's good, Miss Lady?" Blizz spread his arms wide for Aoki to give him a hug.

"Hey." She begrudgingly obliged his request. She would've much rather been hugging Paris. She thought about asking where he was but didn't want to come across thirsty.

"Baby, let me introduce you to Aoki's people." Kiara kept her arm around Meechi. "You've met Princess before but this Aoki cousin Ryan."

"What up?" He gave them a head nod.

"Again." Ryan placed her hand on her hip. "You don't see my sister standing here?"

"Oh nah, I forgot she was there. Bae, that's Ryan's 'woke' sister." She threw a whole shade tree.

Meechi looked over at Makiah. He'd heard of the infamous Carter twins but had never met them face-to-face. They looked like two chocolate Barbies. They were as bad as he'd heard.

"Asalamalakim." He spoke.

Makiah looked at him like he was dumb.

"Nigga, I'm intelligent not Muslim, but you wouldn't know nothing about that, fake ass Li'l Wayne." She curled her upper lip.

"Actually, I'm taking all AP classes this year, Shirley Chisholm."

"That's so fuckin' disrespectful." Chris bugged up laughing.

"I'm not finna go back and forth with this hoodrat." Makiah walked away beyond ready to go.

"I'll be back." Aoki followed her. "Kiah, wait up!"

Makiah stopped and waited for her to catch up.

"Don't mind Kiara. That's just how she is." Aoki tried to ease the tension.

"You mean a bitch? 'Cause that's exactly what she is. I don't even see why you like her. That bitch is flaw as fuck."

Not in the mood for a bunch of I told you so's, Aoki decided to keep it to herself that Kiara had violated girl code two times before. She had one more time to be on some shady shit before she cut her off for good. Together both girls went upstairs to grab something to drink. It had started to get hot in the basement. A cooler filled with soda, water and juices sat by the back door. Aoki twisted open a bottled water and chugged half of it down before coming up for air. As soon as she swallowed the cold water, her crystal blue irises noticed the bathroom door open and Damya walk out pulling down her skirt. *What a whore,* she thought. Aoki hadn't seen her since after the fight. One day she saw her coming out of Mama Lucy's house. Damya avoided eye contact at all cost. Aoki found the shit funny. She must've had some liquid courage that night cause she gave her the dirtiest look she could muster. Never the one to back down, Aoki drew her neck back and side eyed her until she disappeared down the steps. She didn't even understand why she was there. Kiara knew they didn't get along. Kiara claimed not to like her too. Unexpectedly, a sharp pain spread through her stomach. Aoki felt the sting of betrayal before she saw it. The pain was so intense she wanted to double over in agony. She couldn't even return to the party and inquire about Kiara's third and final betrayal, before she got the shock of her life. Paris exited the bathroom with a satisfied grin on his face, wearing a Pittsburg Pirates cap, a Chinatown Market tee-shirt, Balenciaga khaki shorts, socks, and low-top Puma sneakers, buckling his Off-White belt. Never did he expect to see Aoki standing there. Inches away from each other they connected eyes.

Paris felt like a piece of shit. He knew that Aoki was gonna be there but let his alcohol infused brain and hard dick cloud his judgement. He knew she'd eventually find out about Damya, but he didn't want her to find out the way she had. With other bitches he didn't care but with Aoki things were different. He found himself actually caring about her feelings. The night at the pool had changed everything for them.

For Aoki, things had changed for the worse. That quickly, any anticipation of seeing him vanished. Aoki allowed the negative emotions he'd placed in her heart to swallow her whole. Seeing him with her nemesis was like acid being poured into her soul. She tried to remember the good memories they'd created in the short amount of time they'd known each other but all Aoki could envision was her ripping his esophagus out of his tattooed throat. Damn, she felt stupid. He'd completely pulled the wool over her eyes. He made it seem like he liked her, and she'd actually believed him. Here she was thinking they were working towards something and the whole time he was fuckin' the op. Now Aoki knew the true meaning of the term niggas ain't shit. What was the point of the night at the pool or the phone calls before he turned in for bed? All she could do was glare lifelessly into Paris' chocolate eyes as he strolled past her. Aoki saw no trace of the boy that night who'd held her under the stars. Her heart cracked at the sight of his unforgiving gaze. Her legs tried to give out on her, but she summoned the strength her mother had instilled in her and tipped her chin up. She'd be damned if she let him see her crumble.

"Yo daddy know you here?" Paris stopped in front of Makiah.

"Yo' brother know you here?" She hit him with a question of her own. After a brief stare down, she and Paris cracked a smile and threw their arms around one another. Confused as to how he they knew each other, Aoki eyed them both with a confused expression on her face.

"That nigga don't give a fuck what I do. Who you here wit'?" Paris glanced over at Aoki.

"Ryan's downstairs but this our cousin Aoki. She's Cam daughter."

"Cousin?" They said in unison.

"Who he related to?" Aoki questioned, shook.

"This Priest li'l brother P." Makiah looked from her to him.

"You have got to be fuckin' kidding me." Aoki doubled over and held onto the edge of the table. Her life couldn't get any worse. How had she possibly fell for two brothers?

"Am I missing something?"

"I thought Cam ain't have no kids." Paris furrowed his brows. He was just as stunned by the news as Aoki.

"Aoki is his wife Gray's daughter, but he and Gray have triplets together that we just found out about before Quan's wedding."

"So, we're not blood related?" He wanted to make sure.

"No. Please tell me y'all ain't talkin'." Makiah eyes damn near popped out of their sockets. "What the hell is wrong wit' you, Aoki? You got some kind of sick fetish for niggas you're related to and older than you? You need to have a sit down with Iyanla or something."

"How old are you?" Paris died to know.

"None of your damn business." Aoki stomped down the steps. She wasn't about to make a bigger fool out of herself by revealing her age. Catching Paris fucking Damya in the bathroom and learning they were family through marriage had to be some kind of sign. With each step she took, her heart broke a little bit more. She was head over heels in like with him. Those feelings wouldn't just go away. She was going to have to do something about them tho. Paris hadn't lied to her, but he'd omitted the fact that he was seeing and sleeping with other girls. If she would've known the truth, she would've moved differently. She wouldn't have allowed herself to get so invested. Learning he was Priest li'l brother didn't help either. They hadn't even gotten started and the odds were already stacked against them.

"Yo, how old is she?" Paris asked Makiah. He hoped she didn't say eleven or some shit like that.

"Thirteen but she'll be fourteen in two months."

Paris let out a sigh of relief. An almost three year age difference wasn't that bad, but no matter how much he was feeling Aoki, he still couldn't fuck with her. They were family through marriage, and she was younger than he assumed. Everything made sense now. The aunt's house she was staying at was Aunt Vickie's. That's why she was always in the hood.

"Real talk cuzzo." Makiah began. "I don't know how deep things are between y'all but if you ain't serious just fall back. She's going through enough."

Paris ran his fingers through his chin hair. Maybe Aoki catching him with Damya was a blessing in disguise. Maybe it was best he leave her alone now while he still had the chance. Knowing his self, he knew things between them would only end bad. She didn't deserve to have a nigga like him come and turn her world upside down. Maybe it was best they both move on.

"I hear what you saying. Even though I'm feeling the shit outta shorty, I'ma fallback."

Kiara's parties were always a movie but that night it was lit. It took Paris forever to get through the crowd and over to his mans who were posted up in the corner blowing trees. Damya and her girls were right by them, turning up. Paris kinda wished she would go do her own thing. Whenever they were out, she was always up in his face. Sometimes it was cool but most times he found the shit annoying as fuck. Damya was always doing the most, trying to be seen. Paris liked to lay back in the cut. He didn't have to draw attention to his self, it naturally came his way. Plus, he didn't want to hurt Aoki's feelings more than he already had but he had to remind his self that they're li'l friendship was over. Things had gone from 0 to a 100 real quick. He needed something to numb the anxiety he felt. Digging into his pocket, he pulled out an Oxy. Popping it into his mouth he chased it down with a cup of Lean. As if that wasn't enough, Paris eyed the blunt in the Meechi's mouth. He needed to smoke.

"Let me see that." Meechi passed him the blunt. Taking several long drags, Paris let his mind settle as Damya stood in front of him and rubbed her ass on his dick in a circle. Her hot ass hadn't gotten enough. If he let her, she'd get on her knees and gag on his dick in front of everyone.

A few feet away, Aoki tried not to seem pressed, but she was dying on the inside. After doing some digging, she learned that Paris and Damya had been on and off for years. The fact made her sick to her stomach. Why was it that every guy she liked was already taken and lowkey related to her? She should've known Paris wishy-washy ass was Priest's brother. They were exactly alike. She should've put two-and-two together when he said his brother taught him how to swim. Priest was a freaking lifeguard for God's sake. Determined to get out of her feelings, she went over to the DJ booth and asked could she play a couple of tracks. Music was the only thing that would help her out of this funk. Needing a break, the older guy stepped to the side and let the young girl do her thing. He didn't think she would know how to rock the crowed. Because of her age, he took Aoki as a joke. He thought she'd get up there and play Ariana Grande, Lizzo or The Jonas Brothers. The DJ was fully prepared to watch her make a fool out of herself while he rested for a few minutes.

Ready to take things up a notch, Aoki kicked things off by playing Pop Smoke's hit record *Dior*. Everybody lost their mind and started grabbing their waistband and swaying from side-to- side. Music was a drug that brought Aoki higher. Getting her entire life, she played the big homey Jay-Z's *Allure*. All the young dope boys bobbed their heads and rapped along. From where she stood she could see Paris and his boys rapping the song word for word. Like the stunned DJ, he too was shocked at Aoki's musical choices. Aoki really knew her shit. Even Damya was grooving.

Now that she'd showed loved to the fellas, Aoki focused on the girls and bumped 2 Live Crew's *Hoochie Mama*. It was a throwback classic that was sure to get any party rockin'. All Aoki saw was booties tooted in the air shaking. It was an all-out twerk fest. She even spotted Makiah bent over popping her pussy. Aoki was totally in her element. She had complete control of the crowd. The party was electric. Showing love to her cousin, she played some shit no one was expecting. Taking the party from Miami to Africa, Jidenna's *Sufi Woman* blasted from the speakers. It wasn't your typical party song but it's Afro beat took you right back to the motherland. You had no choice but to bob your head or move your hips. Surprisingly, everyone knew the words to the song.

"Sufi woman
Read me Rumi 'til I fall asleep upon your bosom (yeah, yeah, yeah)
Sufi woman
You're a lion, but you walk around so unassuming
You go shine your eyes; you go put it on me
Put a little spell on me
Wetin you do to me?"

Now that she had something she could vibe to, Makiah broke out of her shell. During summer camp she'd taken up dance. Hours of training paid off when she took center stage and started rolling her torso and hips like a snake. High as a kite, Meechi licked his bottom lip and focused on her every move. Makiah was a certified bitch, but he had never seen a girl move her body so fluidly. She unknowingly had his full attention. Meechi couldn't take his eyes off of her. Kiara tried to gain attention by shaking her ass, but booty shaking wasn't the kind of dance you did to a song like *Sufi Woman*. Showing her how it was done, Makiah busted out a sickening 8 count, spread her legs, rolled her hips to the right, lifted the opposite leg then repeated the move as Jidenna sang:

"You go, you go see
You go, you go ni, ni, ni
You go, you go shekere
You gon' see that God is in la bruja, la bruja"

Everyone was amazed when she ticked and did some fancy foot-work. By the time she was done, Makiah had worked up a sweat. Fanning herself with her hand, she looked over at Aoki and smiled. She knew she'd played the song for her. It was the only bright spot of the entire night. To close things out, Aoki really went dumb and played Omeretta The Great *Pressure* freestyle. Makiah and Ryan went stupid and started rapping and dancing together. The song was their shit.

"I don't like niggas
I don't like bitches
Might slap the fuck outta ho with these millions
Might drop a bag on yo' head, if you dissing
Might put yo face on a plate but I'm picky
Ho if you ever stand in my face with that talkin'
I might pull my Glock out and wet ya
Get to the point
If you want me up in yo shit
Then I might need a 20 or better
I'm sick of tired of being humble
I kinda just wanna go rumble
Oh, that's a threat, you talkin' shooters
Mmm, let me go call up my uncle"

Both girls hit the Woah and bounced to the beat. Pointing their fingers like a gun they pretended to wet up the crowd.

"I know some killers and robbers
I will come make this shit awkward
I will treat you like my daughter
Ho go sit down before I give you a whooping
Bitch, I am yo' muthafuckin' father"

Over across the room, Paris was a ball of emotion. He was supposed to be putting Aoki in his rearview mirror, but by the time she was done taking over the song selection, she'd sucked him right back in. Once again, she'd proven she was a rare gem. Girls like her didn't come a dime a dozen. Not only had she taken the party to whole other level, she even had the nerve to flex and scratch a little bit. He'd be a fool to let her go. Everything Paris was feeling for Aoki, Blizz felt it too. She'd captured his undivided attention from the moment he laid eyes on her. Homeboy was on a mission to make her his girl. That night he planned on doing just that.

"You did your thing ma-ma." He applauded Aoki on her mini set.

"Thanks." She beamed happily, jumping up and down in his arms. She felt like she was floating on a cloud. For the rest of her life she wanted to feel that way.

Paris watched from afar with a furious scowl on his face. Even though he was supposed to be falling back, it pissed him off to see Aoki with another nigga. Specifically, a soft ass nigga like Blizz. He'd told her to cut that nigga off and here she was grinning all in his face like shit was sweet.

"Ooh Aoki! You did that." Her cousins raced over and wrapped her up in a congratulatory hug.

"Come dance wit' me." Blizz took her by the hand.

The DJ had started spinning Kanye West *White Dress* to slow down the mood. The music spun around them lifting away gravity. Aoki couldn't count how many times Blizz stepped on her feet. Despite the pain she endured, he smiled as they swayed to the beat. He was the man. Aoki was by far the prettiest girl in the room. He peeped how every nigga had been eye fuckin' her. Even Paris was in his feelings. Life couldn't get any better. This was perfect. Nothing else mattered except him, her, and the music. Trying to get under Paris' skin, Aoki spun around and faced him. Closing her eyes, she bent her back and wind her hips. Blizz held onto her tiny waist and watched her small ass grind on his dick. His cock instantly bricked up. Aoki didn't really like the feeling but kept on dancing. Blizz was in heaven. He never wanted the song to be over, but all good things must come to an end. When the song was done, he asked her if she wanted something to drink. Aoki was dying for another water. Wanting to make sure she was comfortable, Blizz told her he'd be right back. No longer able to hide his anger, Paris walked up on Aoki and got in her personal space.

"Didn't I tell you to dead that shit?" He clenched his jaw. Jealousy radiated from his pores.

"What?" She played dumb.

"You heard what the fuck I said."

"Nigga, if you don't get the fuck out my face. Your girlfriend is over there. You don't check me. You check her." She bypassed him and left him standing there.

"Aye yo' P. Come get in on this dice game." Meechi tried to take Paris mind off Aoki. He could see his violent temperature rising. Besides that, Damya was watching his every move. If he didn't distract his boy there was sure to be an altercation.

The dice game was in full swing by the time Blizz returned with Aoki's drink. Paris tried to focus on the game but just knowing that she was entertaining this nigga made his blood boil. On one knee, he rolled the dice and barked, "Walk away." Paris didn't even bother turning around to face Blizz. To him, he didn't deserve the respect. The nigga was weak. And yes, he knew he was being an asshole and a bully, but Paris simply didn't give a damn.

At first Blizz didn't know it was him Paris was talking to. Since he'd arrived, he hadn't said one word to him. It wasn't until the energy shifted around him that Blizz realized he was Paris' target.

"You talkin' to me?" He pointed to his chest as everyone focused on them.

"Yeah nigga. Who the fuck else would I be I talkin' to? Walk away." Paris threw the dice.

"Man, I ain't going nowhere." Blizz asserted himself. He was over Paris trying to punk him all the time.

Rising to his feet, Paris stormed over and got in his face. He towered over Blizz by several inches.

"What you say?"

"You heard me." Blizz voice squeaked. "I ain't going nowhere. I ain't even do nothing. What's yo' problem with me, my nigga? Have some respect."

"Respect who and respect what?" Paris crossed his hands in front of him. "What am I respecting?"

"Since day one you've had a problem with me, and I haven't said shit about you."

"Cause you can't." Paris stood firm, causing everyone to fear what may happen next.

"Well, I chose not to." Blizz nodded his head.

"You can't, nigga. Why would I respect you? I'm not yo' friend, nigga. I don't know you."

"You right. We're not friends. We'll see how this shit go after the party."

"Ay, yo homey." Paris put his hand in Blizz face like a gun. "Don't get fucked up trying to play tough in front of all these people. Because we both know you ain't that. So I'ma say this shit one more time. Walk. The. Fuck. Away."

Blizz could see the devil in his eyes. Not wanting to cause a scene or get swung on, he regrettably gave Aoki her bottled water and made his way back up the steps. He didn't want to stick around to see the look of disappointment on her face. Everybody was already laughing at him. Aoki glared at the back of Paris' head, seething with anger. Every time he opened his fucking mouth bullshit came out of it. He was such a fucking hypocrite. How dare he cock block her when his bitch was only a few feet away.

"Thought so. Stay in yo' muthafuckin' place." Paris turned his back.

"What the fuck is your problem?" She pulled him back by his shoulder.

"I'm good. You?" He looked up at her beautiful face with a smirk on his lips.

Aoki wanted to slap the shit out his tall sexy ass. Paris was a dickhead and he knew it.

"You got a girlfriend *and* you just fucked her nasty ass in the bathroom. You don't have the right to interrupt my conversation like me and you together."

"What she talkin' about? Is there something I need to know?" Damya interrupted their tête-à-tête.

"You on a need to know basis. Until then, get the fuck out my face." He checked her while never taking his eyes off Aoki.

Not expecting such a harsh response, Damya stood frozen with a dumb look on her face.

"That could never be me." Aoki shook her head in disbelief.

"Exactly. That's why I'm giving you my undivided attention, so what's up?"

"Oh, nigga you sick if you think I'ma be a seat filler for her or any other bitch. I'm number one or there's no need for this conversation." Aoki made clear. She might've been young, but she had all of the confidence of a woman twenty times her age.

"Why you think I'm standing here? You all on some rah-rah shit like I did something to you."

"You did!"

"What I do?" Paris folded his arms across his hard chest.

"You know what? Bye. I'm not playing this game with you. You know exactly what the fuck you did." Aoki tried to walk away but Paris pulled her back.

"Nah, come here. You wanted to talk. You wanted to come over here on your City Girl shit. Don't bitch up now."

"Bitch, I ain't bitching up." Aoki balled up her face, annoyed.

"A'ight say it wit' ya' chest then li'l nigga."

"Yo Paris, leave her alone." Meechi spoke up, feeling bad.

"Nah, her li'l ass think she tough and that shit is cap."

"I ain't cappin'. That's you nigga." Aoki shot back.

"Then say what it is and quit beating around the bush. Your feelings are hurt. Admit it."

At a loss for words, Aoki eyed him with contempt. Her heart shattered into a million pieces. Yes, her feelings were hurt but he didn't have to put her out on front street. Did he care about her at all? As her heart broke so did she. Paris was treating her like she was the enemy, but she wasn't. Like all of his other victims, she was just an easy target.

"Damn, you went too far." Meechi sighed, rubbing his forehead.

"As usual." Rob mumbled with wires all in his mouth from his broken jaw.

"Shut the fuck up before I crack your shit again." Paris cautioned with his fist balled.

"You one angry nigga." Meechi shook his head.

"Stay outta this Meech."

"Yeah, Meechi. I got this." Aoki stood back on one leg. "Let me tell you something." She pointed her finger in Paris' face. "You got me all the way fucked up. I will smack the shit outta you, your broke ass friends and your gonorrhea infected ass girlfriend."

"Bitch, I ain't got gonorrhea." Damya found her voice again.

"Yes, you do. Shut the fuck up."

Paris lowered his head and chuckled.

"Really nigga?" Damya rolled her neck.

"What? The shit was funny." He shrugged, really not giving a damn about her feelings.

"I don't know if you know who the fuck I am but I ain't none of these Northside hoes." Aoki's rant continued.

"What the fuck is that supposed to mean?" Damya's friend named Cliché jumped in.

"Exactly what the fuck I said."

"Well, you can take yo' wee-wee croissant eating ass back to London or wherever the fuck you from."

"Bitch, who the fuck you talking to? You ain't talkin' to my cousin like that." Princess stepped up.

"You got Chinese cousins all of a sudden? Everybody wanna be family." Damya groaned, twisting her lips to the side.

"Bitch, I'm Korean and black. Fuck outta here." Aoki snapped.

"I'm the Chinese one bitch." Princess said ready to fight. She'd been practicing Judo since she was three. Her black belt was well intact.

"Shrimp fried rice, shrimp Lo Mein, Egg Fu Young gravy, it's all the same thing." Damya flicked her wrist.

"Oh no bitch. Step into the street." Princess started taking off her earrings.

"Mya, go sit yo' ass the fuck down. You ain't fighting nobody." Paris tuned up his face.

"Yeah, ain't you got enough of her beating yo' ass?" Ryan interjected.

"Obviously not but I'ma beat her ass again she keep talking shit." Aoki charged at her, only for Paris to hold her back.

"You know what P, fuck you! I wish you would take your stupid ass back to New York." Damya stormed up the steps, pissed. Her friends followed suit.

"You done being mad now?" Paris held Aoki in his strong arms. He knew he needed to let her go but she felt right in his hold.

"Let me make something clear." She pushed him off of her. "I don't play number two and I'm not about to be chasing you or be all on your dick. If you want her be with her. Leave me the fuck alone."

"You done?"

"Are you?"

"Put your mouth to good use and blow on these." He revealed the set of dice in the palm of his hand.

"I wish the fuck I would." Aoki snatched them. Moving him out the way she bent down, shook the dice, and then rolled a four and the number three. All the guys roared, shocked that she'd rolled a seven on the first try. Little did they know but she'd been shooting dice since as far back as she could remember. Gunz had taught her and Press. Paris stood back and watched her win five times in a row.

"Y'all we gotta go. My daddy five minutes away." Makiah announced.

"Damn, we just got here." Princess stomped her foot like a child.

Aoki gathered up all the money she'd won, which added up to be $3,000.

"Gimme my money thief." Paris took the bands from her hand.

"I won that fair and square." She tried to take it back.

Taking in the somber look in her eyes, Paris clenched his jaw.

"You better be glad I fuck wit' you the long way." He gave her some of the money. Not wanting the conversation to end, he pushed aside his ego and revealed the side of him he'd kept hidden since the night at the pool.

"On some real shit, I ain't mean for you to see what you saw. I wouldn't do no corny shit like that in your face. It's just me and her been dealing wit' each other for the last couple of years."

Aoki took a deep breath and looked off to the side. She wanted to believe what he was saying but the wound was so fresh she couldn't get past her emotions.

"I'm just tryin' to keep it real wit' you and tell you what it is. I like you but I also like her."

"Like I said. I ain't number two." Aoki turned to leave.

"And that's on menstrual. . . pooh." Princess smacked her lips.

"I wasn't done." Paris grabbed Aoki by the wrist.

"I was." She broke free and followed her folks up the steps.

"Let me walk y'all out." Kiara led them out the door.

Damya, Cliché and their girl Hepiphany were huddled up talking on the walkway.

"What the fuck is Paris' problem?" Hepiphany died to know. "That shit he pulled was real corny."

"Girl, he got a thang for bitches that shop at Rainbow and wear DSW shoes." Damya played it off like it was nothing to save face.

"I know she ain't talkin' about you!" Kiara said loud enough for them to hear.

"Bitch, you still out here talking shit?" Makiah said ready to square up.

"I mean, I ain't say no names but if you know your friend shop at Rainbow and wear DSW shoes that's not my problem." Damya spoke nonchalantly.

Done talking, Aoki dropped her Elie Saab purse and punched her in the eye with all her might. Caught off guard by the blow, Damya started to see stars. Aoki couldn't even get another good lick in before chaos exploded. Cliché grabbed one of her braids and tried to yank her to the ground, but Ryan grabbed her from behind and threw her in the grass. Hepiphany then snuck behind Aoki and punched her in the back of her head. That's when Makiah lost her mind and right hooked the shit outta her. The punch landed directly on the side of her face, causing her to stumble to the side. Princess then followed up with a two-piece to the dome, dropping her instantly. Meanwhile, Kiara stood on the porch with her iPhone out filming the entire brawl.

"WORLDSTAR!" She shouted thoroughly amused.

Going heads up, Aoki and Damya scrapped but Damya was no match for Aoki's lightning speed and reach. Dazed by her brutal blows, she lost her footing and fell backwards. Aoki quickly got on top of her and kept tagging her face. Seeing that Aoki was getting the best of her friend, Cliché tried to jump in again and pull Aoki off her by her hair.

"Let her hair go!" Ryan yelled about to get her, but she was too slow.

Irate, Makiah slid out her sandals and swung on Cliché repeatedly. Toe-to-toe they started banging. Makiah was taught by her mother to never put her head down during a fight. Cliché obviously hadn't been taught that lesson. She was so afraid to get hit in the face that she kept ducking her punches.

"BITCH YOU GON' TAKE THESE LICKS!" Makiah whapped her in the temple. Cliché tried to block her blows by covering her face, but it was of no use. Makiah had completely blacked out. Viciously, she took a chunk of her hair and dragged her across the pavement. The sound of Cliché's skin peeling against the concrete could be heard from a mile away.

"What the fuck is going on?" Boss jumped out the car. "I knew I shouldn't have let y'all come to this ghetto shit!" He pulled the girls apart.

Out of breath, Aoki and Makiah fixed their clothes and gave each other a high five.

"Where the fuck yo' ho ass mama at?" Boss barked at Kiara.

"She somewhere in the house."

"And why the fuck you just standing there looking stupid letting them fight?"

"I was just trying to make sure they ain't get hurt." Kiara shrugged sheepishly.

WHAP!

Unable to control herself, Makiah hauled off and open-hand smacked her. A red welt from her ring was left behind right below Kiara's eye.

"Bitch, that don't even make sense!" She yelled incensed.

"Get yo' ratchet ass in the car!" Boss popped her in the back of her head.

"This ain't over!" Aoki pounded her fist in her hand while glaring at Kiara. Their friendship was done. Kiara's snake ass wasn't a friend to anyone. She was as fake as a Chanel bag on Canal Street.

"Get in the truck, Anna Mae!" Boss popped her in the back of her head too.

Not wanting to get hit, Ryan and Princess ran and hopped inside the truck before he could get his hands on them. The evening hadn't gone the way they'd planned but it had been one hell of a night. For years to come, the girls would recall the events and laugh.

CHAPTER 17

"Don't wanna see you no more. I'm ready to let this go but never will I ever not wish you well."-Jhene Aiko "Pray for You"

The road to recovery for Cam wouldn't be easy by any means necessary. Coming back to consciousness after a coma wouldn't be like in the movies or in most books he'd read. He wouldn't just miraculously be up walking and talking like nothing had happened. His speech was still sluggish at times. He could barely move his limbs because they'd been out of commission for 42 days. Because of his condition, he'd been transferred to the SSM Health Rehabilitation center. After the third attack on his life by Gunz, he had his room surrounded by security. No one including the staff was getting in without his permission. Cam didn't trust anyone except his immediate family and friends. Once he was 100% well, niggas was gon' feel his wrath for real. Until then, he'd go through the necessary steps to get his body back where it needed to be.

Inside his new hospital room, the lighting had to be kept low and the temperature cool. He learned the term for this was called "keeping the stimulation low" so that the brain can rest and recover. With the help of the staff, Cam was starting to establish a normal pattern of being up and out of bed with the help of a wheelchair. Every day Gray accompanied him and a nurse's aide as he was wheeled around the halls several times. Soon, the goal would be for him to sit on the edge of the bed and use a table to put weight on so he could stand. Cam couldn't wait to be moving about on his own. He missed being able to move around freely. Even eating for him was a task. He had to work on swallowing his food without choking. Everyday his arms and legs had to be stretched to combat abnormal muscle spasticity that occurred when the brain was injured, which could cause his joints to get tight. Despite all the obstacles ahead, Cam was determined to get better so he could get back to his life. He hated feeling like an invalid. He'd fought in the war. He'd witnessed his entire squad be gunned down. He'd went toe-to-toe with some of the hardest niggas in the streets. He'd survived jail. He'd conquered PTSD. There was no way he was gonna let this defeat him.

More than anything, he was thankful that his Star was by his side. She hadn't left him once. Her dedication to him and his well-being was unbelievable. It took Cam back to the reason why he proposed to her in the beginning. Her loving, nurturing spirit and unwavering devotion to the people she cared for was what pulled him to her. Gray was a replica of his mother. She was a gift from God. She was made to be his soulmate, his helpmate. She was his everything.

Laying on his back, Cam gazed up at her pretty face. Gray stood next to his bed, holding his hand as his left leg was stretched outward and then inward towards his chest by a Physical Medicine and Rehabilitation Physician. Age couldn't touch the kind of beauty Gray possessed. There was a glow about her that he hadn't seen before. Her caramel skin was completely flawless. It had a golden shine. Cam could only attest it to her being happy about their new start. Maybe that was why her skin shined so bright. Being happy lit her eyes and softened her features. When Gray smiled you couldn't help but smile along too, even if it was just on the inside.

Gray took her eyes off of the doctor and caught him staring at her. Tenderly, she leaned down and placed a loving kiss on his forehead. Cam had been awake for almost a week. She'd been bursting at the seams to tell him they were adding another addition to their family, but between his health and the attack on his life it hadn't been the right time. But then when would there ever be a good enough time. She had to tell him and let the chips fall where they may. It wasn't like she expected him to be upset about the pregnancy. Actually, it was the opposite. She knew he'd be ecstatic. Gray was apprehensive on telling him because she knew Cam. Once he learned she was pregnant, he would push himself to the limit to get back to his old self so he could be there for her. Gray didn't want him over-extending himself. They'd been through enough. She couldn't bear them suffering another setback. Things were peaceful and she wanted to keep it that way.

"You did wonderful today, Cam." Dr. Keaton smiled warmly. "I'm astounded by your progress."

"That's great." Gray beamed, overjoyed.

"If you keep this up you should make a full recovery within the next three months."

"How long will it be before he can go home? I don't think our children will be able to last much longer without us."

"I would love to give you a firm date Mrs. Parthens but I don't want to make you, or your husband upset if we don't reach the deadline so let's just play things by ear."

Gray's eyes shifted to the side. She wanted to hide her disappointment but couldn't muster the strength. She was dying to get back to their kids. Cam noticed her change in demeanor. His heart ached for his wife. He could only imagine the stress she'd been under the last month and a half. He didn't want her to suffer anymore. It was his turn to take care of her.

"For now, I want you to rest up. Later on today, your speech therapist will be by to work with you." Dr. Keaton announced before leaving the room.

"Lala better be lucky." Cam grimaced. He'd been made aware that Victor knew she was the snitch and was allowing him the pleasure of offing her himself.

"I don't condone Killa Cam resurfacing, but that dirty bitch deserves it." Gray shook her head. "And so does Gunz."

"Facts. You know if you want you can go be with the kids." Cam ran his thumb slowly across the back of her hand. The small gesture was the equivalent of running a mile for him.

"You're not getting rid of me that easily." Gray arched her brow and smiled. "I told you. I'm not leaving until you are."

"But—"

"No buts sir."

"They miss you."

"I know they do." Gray's face dropped into a frown. "I miss them too. I feel horrible we didn't do anything for the little kids' birthday."

The triplets had turned three four days before Cam's birthday. Gray promised once he returned home they'd throw them a lavish party. But after what the doctor said, there was no telling when that would be. Gray needed to be around her babies now. She needed their love and carefree energy to rejuvenate her.

"I still have to get the kids registered for school and move us back into the old house since we'll be staying here." Gray became over-whelmed with everything she had to do.

"You're not gonna move into the house I bought us?"

Gray hadn't thought about the mansion Cam purchased for her since the day she left. She'd literally pushed it out of her head, espe-cially since the house held so many bad memories.

"I was thinking it was best I go back to my old house. I could never sleep in a house you had that skank whore in."

"I get it." Cam agreed, disappointed. He wanted his family under one roof, but he understood the house held negative energy. He'd destroyed her on the steps of the home, he'd fucked Devin in the bed he bought for them and he'd been arrested in the wee hours of the morning there. It was best they start anew. He didn't want Gray to be uncomfortable.

"How about." She sat up. "I swing by Kema's and surprise them with a visit."

"They'll . . . love that."

"I'll stop by Popeye's and get their favorite meals." Gray quickly threw on her shoes and grabbed her purse. "You want me to bring you something back?"

"Mash potatoes."

"Ooh that do sound good." Her stomach began to growl. "I'ma get me some too and that new chicken sandwich everybody been raving about. You sure you'll be good while I'm gone?"

"Meagan Good." Cam smirked.

"You so silly?" Gray laughed, shaking her head. "I love you Cameron Parthens." She placed her face inches away from his. For a second, they gazed into each other's eyes silently. Cam's expression was stone. Even in a hospital gown and socks his aggressive nature still dominated her. There was nothing soft about her husband. Killa Cam was still there waiting patiently to get out. Turned on by just his handsome face alone, Gray pressed her lips against his. She wanted to feel every inch of his skin on hers. Together they shared a passionate sweet kiss. Fireworks erupted. A whimper of pleasure escaped Gray's lips as she became lost in each swipe of his minty tongue. Oh, how she'd missed this. Everything good in her life came from this man. It was time to lay all her cards out on the table. When she came back from seeing the kids, she'd bring him a gift announcing the birth of their 6th child.

"I love you." Cam croaked once their lips parted.

"I won't be gone long. I promise." Gray stood up straight. "If you need me don't hesitate to tell one of the nurses."

Cam nodded and watched as she drifted out the door like an angel. He never wanted to see her go but it was for the best. He had a lot on his mind anyway. He needed the time alone to think. Some big decisions had to be made. Decisions that would affect him and Gray for the rest of their lives. A few hours later, he'd come to the conclusion on what he wanted to do moving forward. He prayed Gray understood the choice he'd made. He hoped she understood that his decision would benefit them both in the end.

"Baby, guess what?" She entered the room holding a Popeye's to-go bag, drawings the kids made, a gift box and her purse. The entire time she was gone, Gray had been itching to get back and give him the onesie she'd picked up.

"That damn chicken sandwich been sold out for weeks. I ended up getting a three-piece wing meal and a biscuit. Don't be mad but I ate yo' mash potatoes. You can have mine tho."

"You always eating something. Don't you ever get full?" Devin grinned mischievously.

Gray was so caught up in her excitement that she didn't even see Devin sitting next to Cam's bed. Frozen by the sound of her irritating voice, she paused stunned. Devin was the last person she expected to find when she returned from seeing the kids. There she sat tho in all her stank ass glory. Thoroughly confused Gray asked, "What the fuck is she doing here?"

"I told you I was here to stay." Devin waved her fingers, wickedly. "Your time is up, sweetheart. Wifey's home and you can't get me kicked out this time." She crossed her legs, satisfied with herself.

"What the fuck is she talking about and why is she here? Did you call for her?" Gray placed down her things just in case she had to start throwing hands.

"Tell her baby." Devin took Cam's hand in hers.

"Give us a minute." Cam sluggishly pulled his hand away from hers.

"But I'ma be able to come back, right?" She asked eagerly. Devin would literally die if she got kicked out again.

"Yeah . . . man." Cam groaned.

Pleased with his answer, Devin happily got up, sashayed past Gray and walked out the door.

Once they were alone, Gray glared at Cam. A million and one thoughts ran through her mind. She was angry, hurt, perplexed, nervous and shocked all at once.

"Can you please tell me what the hell is going on?"

Cam took a long deep breath. He could barely look her in the eyes but what he was about to say needed to be said.

"I just been thinking. Ever . . . since I came to . . . things . . . just. . . been moving at lightning speed. I haven't had time to . . . really think."

"Think about what?"

"Everything . . . us. . . the kids—"

"What the fuck are you saying, Cam?" Gray yelped in a huff. Her heart was damn near beating out of her chest.

"I'm sayin' before all this shit happened . . . you . . . was. . . on your divorce shit. You ain't even . . . wanna be wit'. . . me."

"That was then. This is now. You said you loved me."

"I'ma always love you, Gray . . . but—" His chest heaved up and down like he'd ran a marathon.

"But what?" Gray threw her hands up in the air then slammed them down onto her thighs.

"I." Cam took a big gulp of air. "Just think we need to fall back for a minute."

Tears formed in the corners of Gray's eyes. Distraught, she placed her hand on her stomach. Suddenly, she'd started to feel weak. She couldn't believe her ears. This had to be some kind of cruel joke. They were fine before she left. What had happened to make him change his mind about them?

"Where is all this coming from?" Her voice cracked.

Cam squeezed his eyes shut. Seeing Gray cry was worse than almost dying. He never wanted to see her unhappy or in distress because of him. If only he could tell her the truth. He didn't really want to end things. Cam was being forced to.

"Mr. Parthens you have a visitor." One of the guards peeked his head inside the room.

"Who. . .is it?"

"A Mr. Aubrey Simmons."

Cam lay confused as to why Noon would be there to see him. Interested in what he had to say, he allowed him in.

"Well. . . well. . .well." Noon strolled into his hospital room with a huge smirk on his face. He looked like a million bucks in his three thousand dollar Brunello Cucinelli suit. A tan leather Maxwell Scott briefcase swung from his hand. His Bleu De Chanel cologne filled the room with the aroma of cedar and sandalwood. The scent instantly made Cam feel sick to his stomach.

"What the fuck . . . do you . . . want? Pussy ass nigga.".

"I . . . see . . . a near . . . death . . . experience . . . hasn't . . . changed you." Noon mocked his exacerbated speech. He really wanted to take one of the cords attached to Cam's body and choke him with it. The last time he reached out to Gray, he expected to hear about funeral arrangements not her rejoicing in him being awake. Noon knew with Cam being alive and well he had a slim chance in hell of getting Gray back. He couldn't take the chance of losing her for good. He had to pull out all the stops to get her away from Cam and back into his awaiting arms. And yes, he loved Gray. He cared for her immensely. But this wasn't just about his feelings for her. His obsession with her went deeper than that. This was about his ego. Noon wasn't used to the chase. Women flocked to him. They died to be on his arm, to attend gala affairs. They yearned to bear his last name. But Gray was different. She could take him or leave him. Noon had never been left before. He was the one who switched women out like dirty underwear. In his mind, Gray should've been grateful a man with his background and tax bracket even looked her way. She was a chubby, married woman with five children. Men like him weren't just knocking down her door. Then she had the gall to throw him to the curb for an ex-convict with an infinity for murder. The bruise to his ego was wider than the Pacific Ocean. Losing a woman to a common street thug was foreign to him. Didn't Gray know that men like him didn't lose? Noon always got what he wanted and right now he wanted Gray.

"Ain't nothing gon' change me. Now what the fuck do you want?"

"Me and you have some things to discuss."

"We ain't . . . got shit to discuss." Cam became more enraged by the second. He knew he shouldn't get worked up but couldn't help himself.

"Oh, on the contrary, we do." Noon placed his hand inside his pants pocket. "It's been brought to my attention that you are a member of the Gonzalez cartel. The lieutenant at that."

"Is that what you came here for? You better get the fuck out my face . . . wit' that bullshit. I don't know what the fuck you talkin' about." Cam played dumb.

"Oh, I think you do, Archibald."

"Who the fuck you callin' Archibald? Nigga I'll . . . kill you." Cam's nostrils flared angrily.

"From the looks of things, you won't be doing much of that for quite a while. But that's what brought us to this conversation." Noon paced the room deep in thought. "Seems like you have a pension for murder. A little birdie told me that you were the one behind the brutal, violent, gut wrenching murder of all those innocent people at Emilia Marciano's 80th birthday."

"Emilia Marciano's dead? Damn, I ain't know shit about that." Cam lied. "My . . . baby ain't said nothing. May her old ass rest in peace."

"I still can't believe she chose you." Noon sneered, disgusted by Cam's behavior.

"Believe it."

"Back to the matter at hand." Noon waved him off. He couldn't let Cam's nonchalance get him off track. He was there for a reason; to bring Cam to his knees.

"Not only did you commit a mass murder, but you also betrayed your Jefe." He glared at him with malice.

Cam's silence let him know that he had him by the balls. Cam swallowed hard. He needed to refute Noon's claim, but no words escaped him.

"Oh, cat got your tongue. None of that hood talk now." Noon chuckled.

"Like I said. I don't know what the fuck you talkin' about. Why . . . would I wanna kill that old ass lady? That bitch . . . ain't do nothing to me."

"Oh, she didn't?" Noon quizzed, calling his bluff. Placing his briefcase on the table near Cam's bed, he popped it open and retrieved the folder inside.

"Does this ring a bell?" He placed several photos on Cam's lap. The pictures showed him sitting on a park bench next to a well-dressed man. *"Are my eyes deceiving me or is that you meeting with Don Valentin Francois?"*

"Nigga, that ain't me. That's a clone." Cam came up with the first lie that came to mind.

"So, this isn't you?"

"Nah, that gotta be photoshopped or something."

"If that isn't you, is this you?" Noon held up a picture of Cam giving Asinine to the head chef at the Botanical Gardens.

All Cam could do was bite his bottom lip. If he could, he would've yelled, kicked and threw things.

"You're fucked. Not only did you kill all of those people, but you went behind your Jefe's back to do it. How do you think Victor will feel when he finds out that you went to Don Francois for a favor without his permission?"

Cam wished he could fall back into a coma. Noon literally had him by the balls and there was nothing he could do about it. The nigga had physical proof of his betrayal. The last thing he ever wanted to do was disrespect Victor, but at the time, he felt like he had no choice. Gunz had threatened the lives of his children. He couldn't let that slide. He needed to get rid of him at all cost, even if that meant making a deal with the devil. When he learned Mother Emilia's 80th birthday party would be held at the Botanical Gardens, Cam knew it was the perfect time to strike. The only problem was the Botanical Gardens was owned

by the Francois family. In order to commit a hit on Don Francois terri-
tory, Cam needed permission. He knew if he would've asked Victor to
grant him a meeting with Don Francois to take down Gunz, he
would've said no. Victor made it clear that he wanted no parts of the
war between him and Gunz. With his back against the wall, Cam had to
do what he had to do. So, he went to Don Francois on his own behalf,
which was punishable by death in their world. It was Cam's luck that
Don Francois was in town on business. The two men met at the park
during the middle of the day. Cam had no idea they were being
watched when he asked the infamous Don for a favor. His plan was to
take the meeting to his grave. After his request was granted, Cam was
informed that he would owe the Don a favor. A trained killer like Cam
would come in good use for a man of Valentin's stature. In order to
protect his family, Cam sealed the deal with a shake of the hand. The
saying goes what happens in the dark shall come to the light. That
analogy had never been truer. Secrets always had a way of being
exposed. Now that his biggest secret was being dangled in front of him
like a grenade, Cam only had one move and that was to concede.

"Who the fuck are you? How did you get these?"

"Wouldn't you like to know." Noon smirked, loving the fact he had
the upper hand.

"Okay, so what the fuck you want?" Cam clenched his jaw.

"It's simple." Noon came close to his bed. "I want what's rightfully
mine."

"Yours?" Cam drew his head back into his pillow.

"Mine." Noon made clear with a low growl.

"And what's that?"

"Gray."

"Nigga please. That's my fuckin' wife."

"Not for long." Noon patted his shoulder mockingly. "If you want
your freedom, if you want to live, I think it's best you let Gray go."

"I ain't just fight for my life . . . to wake up and let my wife go. You
might as well kill me."

"The thought crossed my mind, but I actually care about the well-

being of my future step kids. They've been through enough. Don't you think?" Noon sneered, rubbing his jaw.

"Pussy, do you know I will 6F you out this muthafucka?"

"The question is do you know what I will do to you?" Noon took his index finger and pushed it into Cam's incision.

Cam let out a strangled squeal as he bit his tongue in a vain attempt to remain quiet. The pain Noon was inflicting on his stab wound throbbed deep within his gut. The pressure felt like he had his hand inside Cam's stomach and was squeezing his intestines with all his might. Cam sucked in his abdomen and curled his fist into a tight ball. He wanted to fight back but he didn't have enough strength to lift his arms. Cam had never felt more helpless in all his days. If Noon pressed any harder his stiches would pop. It wasn't until sweat began to form on his forehead and his heart monitor started to increase that Noon finally let up. All Cam could do was inhale and exhale slowly, until the pain waned.

"So, what's it gonna be?" Noon clasped his hands in front of him. "I don't have all day, Archie."

"Fuck! Fuck-fuck-fuck-fuck! Fuck!" Cam roared, enraged.

Spit flew from his mouth, but he didn't care. There was no way out of this. Noon had established dominance. He'd threw down the gauntlet and Cam had taken the L. In that moment of loss his entire world collapsed. This was supposed to be the start of a new beginning for him and Gray. They'd finally found their way back to each other. How would he be able to endure losing her again? He wouldn't. This would be the thing that killed him. The only way he'd be able to make it through this was by reminding his self that it would be only for a while. He'd let Noon think he'd won, but once he was 100% healthy, Cam was gonna kill Noon and get back his girl.

"You got it."

"I'm happy we could come to an understanding." Noon packed up his belongings and left the room as quickly as he'd came.

So here Cam was doing the unthinkable to the person he loved the most. Breaking up with Gray was bad enough but adding Devin into the mix was icing on the cake. Cam knew he wouldn't have been able to push her away with his words alone. Gray would've fought him tooth and nail. He needed to make it seem like he'd rushed things with her and made a grave mistake. It was the only way to place distance between them, until he could reveal the truth.

"Why are you doing this?" Her eyes blurred with tears.

"I need a minute to get myself together. I just went through some near death shit."

"I know. I've been here with you every step of the way!" Gray stabbed her chest with her hand repeatedly.

"And I can't . . . say thank you enough for everything that you've done."

"You know how you can thank me?" She rushed to his bedside. "By getting rid of Devin and giving our marriage a second try like we said we would. Don't you get it? I love you! I wouldn't have been here day in and day out if I didn't."

"I know you love me." Cam looked away.

"Then act like it. Prove it. Love me back." She begged, gripping his jaw. She was determined to make him face her.

"I wish it was that easy." Cam swallowed the cry that filled his throat.

"It is!"

Cam's mind clouded with pain. His heart grew numb with pent up emotion. Out of complete silence a spine tingling cry arose. Out of complete reverence angels stilled to listen. From the pit of his belly to his throat it flowed. Slow and gentle his cry rose to a sob that reached far away countries and the seven seas. Gray would never understand that this hurt him more than it ever would her.

"I love you, Gray, I do, but I got love for her too." He lied. "She was there for me when I ain't have nobody. You left remember."

"Wow." She stumbled back horrified. His words were worse than any smack to the face. "We going there again? You know why I left."

"And when you did . . . everything changed. We can't . . . just act like the past three and a half didn't happen."

"Look, I'ma give you one last chance to fix this shit. Either we gon' be together or we're not. 'Cause I'm not going through this back and forth shit with you anymore." She asked once again. After this, there would be no turning back.

Cam hung his head. He didn't want to remember the look on her face when he answered her question.

"I ain't got a choice, Gray, and that's the honest to God's truth."

Gray's feet stayed rooted in the spot she stood. What is love? She thought she knew but now the concept seemed foreign to her. There was a time she would've gladly taken a bullet for this man. Yet he gave up on them within a blink of the eye. Had she tricked herself into believing they shared this great love? Maybe it had been one sided this whole time. It had to be. This wasn't love, or at least not a version Gray could respect. Through thick and thin she was always there for him, but as she stood there begging him to save her, he was nowhere to be found. Noon was right. As soon as she let her guard down, he broke her heart and let her down. Cam was never gonna be the man she wanted him to be. It seemed like he took pleasure in breaking her down bit by bit. There wasn't a woman on the planet with common sense and self-respect that would sit around and take this kind of abuse. Gathering her dignity, she held her head high. There would be no sulking after she spoke her peace.

"We all have a choice and you just made yours. What's funny is Noon said you would do this to me. But here I am stuck on stupid, thinking that you'd changed." She grabbed her things, including the gift with the onesie inside of it. "You don't know how to love a anybody but your damn self. You selfish muthafucka. You the worst type of nigga there is. I sat here 42 days straight, every hour on the hour by your side. I barely ate, I barely slept, I didn't even go outside. I barely had time to wash my ass. I took time away from our kids to be here for you. Do you know how hard that was for me? No better yet, do you know how difficult and excruciating it was to explain to our children that you might not ever wake up? My life was on the line because of you and your fuck shit. When your father wanted to pull the plug and give up on you, I was the one that said no. Nigga, if it wasn't for me you wouldn't even be breathing right now. And the sad part is even after all of that, I would do it all over again 'cause that's how much I love you. But you don't know shit about love. You only know how to play with people's hearts. You ain't shit and you ain't gon' never be shit. I wish I never—"

Cutting herself off, Gray stopped herself from saying something she would later regret. The old Gray spewed hate when hurt or rejected. The new God-fearing Gray knew better so she was going to do better. Turning the other cheek proved to be difficult but it was not a weakness as some perceived it to be. Turning the other cheek was a position of power. This time she would lead with compassion. There was no need to wish him ill will. If he didn't want her that was fine. She was willing to let him and their relationship go. She couldn't be in this marriage alone. And yes, she should tell him about the baby, but she'd be damned if she put herself through his denial of her pregnancy. This was déjà vu all over again. For all she knew, he'd accuse of her lying and saying she was pregnant to keep him.

"You promised me but it's okay. Lord knows I wanna hate you, but I can't. It is what it is at this point. I'll keep you in my prayers. Just know if it's not regarding the kids, I don't have anything else to say to you." She turned her back to him and left for what would be the last and final time.

Cam lay prisoner inside his bed wishing he could run after her. If only things were that simple. The pain in his wound from which Noon had pushed in paled in comparison to seeing the love of his life walk out the door. Not having Gray by his side during his road to recovery would make the journey ten times harder. Cam vowed to himself, when he returned to full capacity, he was gonna get his wife back and eliminate everyone that stood in opposition.

CHAPTER 18

"I know what it's like to lose. Do you? Have you ever loved someone,
then lost that one?"-Jhene Aiko feat Nas "10k Hours"

ace-to-face, Gray and Kema lay. Gray left the hospital and
went straight to her. She needed the one person besides
Cam that knew her best. When Gray was at her lowest the mere
thought of Kema lightened her mood. She felt content knowing she
would always be there to protect her and rescue her from any harm that
came her way. No matter the trial or tribulation Kema was there ready
to lift her after she'd fallen. Their friendship was everything to Gray.
Outside of her children it was the only stable force in her life. Men
came and went but Kema was steadfast. She was the person who
hugged her when she was dejected, the person who wiped the gloomy
tears from her swollen eyes. Gray would forever be grateful for her.
More than ever she needed someone to lean on and give her comfort,
so they lay. A dim light cascaded over the room as the afternoon sun
began to fall. A patchouli scented candle flickered from the credenza in

front of the bed. In the fetal position, Gray rested comfortably in her best friend's arms as she cried a million tears.

The sound of heart break was etched in each whimper that seeped from her throat. But hearts don't break like old candy or burst like an overfilled balloon. A heart breaks in the throbbing waves of a new frightening reality that has arrived uninvited. For Gray, things would never be the same again. A part of her had to die so the rest of her could carry on. It was terrifying to come to terms that she and Cam were over for good this time. He'd said he loved her, and like a dummy, she held him at his word. Gray really thought they were soulmates. Over the years, pieces of her personality had morphed into his that's how in sync they were. Then out of nowhere, he announces that he wants to be with Devin of all people. Gray wished he would've killed her instead. The deed would've been quicker and less painful.

For everything she knew to be true had blown up into a black cloud of smoke. There wouldn't be a third chance at making things right. Their future wouldn't be spent as a couple in love raising their family. He'd finessed her and made her look foolish for the last time. That didn't stop the tears from falling at lightning speed from her eyes. Breakups were painful, especially when there was still loved involved. Gray didn't know when she'd be fully whole again. How had she ended up in the same position from three and a half years before? Here she was pregnant, again, by a man that proved repeatedly he didn't want her. And here she was thinking Devin was stuck on stupid. No, she was the stupid one.

"He's an idiot, friend. Fuck him. You deserve better." Kema rocked Gray back-and-forth like she was a child she was trying to put to sleep.

"You know what's fucked up? I saw this shit coming a mile away. I knew I was in for pain, but I wanted the happy ending so bad that I ignored all the warning signs."

"Look at it this way. At least he was honest with you and didn't string you along like most of these niggas do."

"Yay me." Gray spat sarcastically. "I wasn't gone five minutes before he just threw us away. The first chance he got he went crawling back to that retail working whore. Can you believe that? And do you know when he said we needed to fall back I argued with him. I tried to talk him into loving me." Gray's voice quivered. "I tried to talk him into it. I tried to talk him into loving me like I love him." Salty tears rolled down her cheeks as she retold the story for the third time.

Kema didn't mind tho. Gray could tell it as many times as needed. That's what best friends were for. It wasn't always about giving advice or saying I told you so. Sometimes, a friend was needed to be a sounding board, a listening ear. So, as Kema watched Gray shake with grief, tears streaming unchecked, there was a part of her heart that broke too. If her girl was hurt so was she. That's what happens when you love someone, right? Their sadness or happiness becomes a part of your own. Just when she was about to give Gray a word of encouragement the door creaked open. In walked Press. Gray sat up and quickly wiped her tears away. She refused to let her kids see her cry. They'd seen enough of that to last a lifetime. With a worried expression on her face, Press eased over and crawled onto the foot of the bed. Gray took her in. Boy, was her precious girl getting big. Press wasn't her little nugget anymore. She was a li'l lady with curly brown hair that kissed her shoulders and slanted cinnamon colored eyes that hid behind glasses that were slightly too big for her slender face. Press was absolutely stunning, even though most times she begged to differ.

"Eomma, is appa okay?" Eomma meant mom and Appa meant dad in Korean. Press had decided recently to call Cam that instead of papa.

"He's fine." Gray held out her arms for a hug.

Press quickly crawled on her knees to oblige her request. Affectionately, she wrapped her small arms around her mother's shoulders and pulled her close. A sense of relief washed over Gray. This was what she needed. Press always gave the best hugs.

"Eomma?"

"Yes." Gray stifled her cry.

"I don't know what's wrong but you're gonna get through this. Time is your friend. It heals all wounds even the ones that seem like they'll never mend. There's a quote by Cayla Mills that says you never know how strong you are until being strong is the only choice you have. Eomma, you're the strongest person I know." Press eased back and looked at her.

"Whatever is troubling you, it's only temporary. Remember God will never take anything away from you without replacing it with something better." And with that being said, Press planted a tender kiss to her mother's forehead and caressed Kema's tear stained cheek. Her job was done.

"I love you, Pretty Girl."

"I love you too, eomma." Press smiled as she left.

"From the mouths of babes." Kema replied astonished by Press' profound wisdom. "I can't believe you gave birth to her."

"Same." Gray leaned back against the headboard.

"The world doesn't deserve her."

"I couldn't agree more."

"Gray." She twiddled her thumbs.

"Yes."

"I'm pregnant."

Gray's head spun in Kema's direction.

"Me too."

"Oh my God!" Kema clutched her chest.

"Congratulations." Gray gave her a closed mouth grin.

"Ditto." Kema reached for her hand. "We're pregnant together. Can you believe it?"

"No." Gray burst out into tears all over again.

"Did you tell Cam?"

"I was gonna tell him, but he broke up with me before I could." She wept, buckling over.

"Damn, friend, it's okay. When the time is right you'll tell him. Until then, I got you. I'll be the pappy." Kema pulled her back into her embrace and squeezed a fraction tighter.

Gray breathed slowly as her body melted into Kema's arms. In her mind, she kept telling herself that this too shall pass. It had to because she didn't have the strength to weather another storm.

CHAPTER 19

"It's not closure if it was never over."-Chari' Joy "Fed Up"

𝒶 month and a half had passed since Cam last seen or heard from Gray. She'd kept her word and completely disappeared from his life. During the rest of his hospital stay, Quan brought the kids to see him or either he contacted them via Facetime. When he was released Gray let him have the kids three days out of the week with the assistance of Melody. Cam had worked diligently to get back on his feet. The doctors had never seen anything like it. What was supposed to be a three month hospital stay was reduced to a month because of all Cam's hard work. His speech was back to normal and he was able to walk but with the help of a cane. His legs still gave him a bit of trouble when he tried to walk without it. Cam knew it wasn't healthy to push himself to get better but every day he spent without his entire family under one roof was complete and utter torture. After Gunz latest attempt at killing him, he needed to have his eyes on Gray and the kids.

Since she wouldn't fuck with him, he made sure her and the kids were heavily guarded.

He hated being away from Gray. The short amount of time they'd spent together when he woke from his coma wasn't long enough. He had to get his strength back and get rid of Noon once and for all. Being blackmailed by a cooperate snob was worse than walking with a cane. Gray not knowing the truth behind their breakup was equally unbearable. This nigga had to be 6F'd immediately. Cam had just got his life back. He'd be damned if it was taken again just because he was trying to protect his family. Victor wouldn't give a damn about his motives. He'd only focus on the betrayal. And yes, he could've had Quan or Priest take Noon out, but much like LaLa, his death would come from his hands only.

Dressed in an orange beanie, gold chain, a black Mets jersey, black joggers and retro Jordan 3's, Cam stepped out the back of his SUV as his driver held the door open for him. He didn't know how much longer he would be able to handle not being able to drive. Being chauffeured around wasn't his thing. Regardless, he'd made it to his kids' first day of school. The morning sun shined down on his freshly shaven skin. Cam's beard was lined so precisely it looked fake. Despite the limp in his stride, he looked like his old self. As he made his way around the vehicle married and single moms salivated over his panty dropping good looks. Cam was next level fine. Not only was he tall and tatted from his neck down to his waist but he had a GQ cover face and a big dick with a crook it. Men like him were unicorns. In the past he would've got off on all the attention, but Cam had grown past that place in his life. He only had eyes for one woman and that woman was Gray Rose Parthens.

Look at my baby, he admired her with wonder in his eyes. Cam's heart grinned gleefully as she stepped out of the passenger side of her car. Damn did she look good. Cam couldn't pinpoint it but something about her was different. Maybe it was the way she wore her hair. Gray rocked four cornrows to the back. A simple light beat of penciled in brows, lashes, foundation, a little blush, and gloss decorated her face.

Gold hoop earrings, a white Balmain t-shirt tied in a knot exposed a sliver of her stomach. Boyfriend ripped jeans, white Fenty strappy heels and the gold dog tag necklace he'd bought for her 36th birthday swung from her neck. On each dog tag was their mother's name, birthday, and death date. For someone that didn't want anything to do with him, Gray sure kept pieces of him close. She even still wore her wedding rings. Gray could act like she was done with him, but it was obvious she wasn't as over him as she claimed. She loved him just as much as he loved her.

Damn it sucked not to be able to talk to her, hold her hand or call her on the phone and see how her day had been. After nearly dying, Cam cherished the people in his life more than ever. Nothing in life was guaranteed. Time hadn't been on his side in the past and it wasn't right now either. There were so many obstacles ahead of him that needed to be cleared. Was it too much to have Gray by his side as he fought off his enemies?

"You need help with the kids babe?" Noon asked from the driver seat of the car.

Cam gripped his cane so tight his knuckles turned white. He'd heard through Quan that she'd gone back to him but to see it with his own two eyes was like a steak knife to his irises. This square ass nigga had really weaseled his way into his family's life. Cam had to remind his self that Gray had only gone back to him cause she thought he didn't want her anymore, which was the furthest thing from the truth. With each day that passed he longed for her. At night he dreamt of her. Noon couldn't have his love. Gray was merely settling. She didn't know her worth. She for damn sure wasn't in love with Noon. He was nothing but a replacement that was added to Cam's kill list, which was growing by the day. The only problem was the nigga was a literal walking ghost. No matter how much digging he did, Cam couldn't find any real information on the guy except that he was a portfolio manager that resided in New York. There was no info on his birth date, where he was born or who his family was. It was like the nigga popped up outta nowhere. This muthafucka was far more dangerous than Cam had expected. How was he supposed to go up against an opponent he knew nothing about? How was he supposed to plan his attack when he didn't know his opponents weak spot?

One by one the kids filed out the back of the truck. They all were attending Forsyth Academy, which was the most prominent predominantly black private school in St. Louis. It was the same school Cam met Gray at after Aoki had fought the twins on the playground. The school was located on one big campus that ranged from preschool to high school. The preschoolers and elementary kids were in one building. The middle school kids were in another and students that were in 9th through 12th had their own separate building. Cam looked on with pride as his girls got out and situated their uniforms. Each of them wore a white button up, navy, green and yellow plaid blazer, vest, and pleated skirt. Gold buttons and the school crest was embroidered onto the breast of the blazer. Aoki, of course, jazzed her ensemble up by rocking big gold earrings, a green Bottega Vanetta bag, grey socks and lace-up booties. Her long hair was pulled back to the nape of her neck in a sleek ponytail. Cam had to fight back his tears. She wasn't the little loud mouth ten-year-old girl he'd met nearly four years before. Aoki was a young lady now. If he didn't know any better, he would've sworn she was a high school senior and not the thirteen year old girl she was.

"Appa!" Press ran towards him at full speed.

The triplets ran as fast as they could to him too.

"Daddy!" They sang in harmony.

Gray watched on as her heart cried. Like a mirage Cam stood before her. It was hard to see him for the stranger he'd become. He was so beautiful yet unreachable. Life without him was so sad. She didn't wanna live this way, but her love wasn't enough, and neither was she. Gray had tried to prepare herself for this moment, but she still wasn't ready. The last time she'd laid eyes on Cam he was confined to a hospital bed. Now he was up on his feet looking like the man she'd fell in love with. The transition was alarming, but she was thankful that his health was improving. She just hated that their relationship was still at the place it had been when she returned for the wedding. Why after all this time did he not love her the way she loved him? It was truly heartbreaking to give your all to a man and the feeling not be reciprocated. Not even a near death experience could get them back on track. After he'd destroyed her for the umpteenth time, she'd thought about running again but this time she put the needs of her children before hers. The kids needed their father more than ever. So, going to back to Paris was no longer the answer to her problems. In St. Louis is where they would be.

"Be careful." She cautioned. Cam's balance wasn't steady. Even though she couldn't stand the sight of his face, she didn't want the kids to knock him over. She hated herself for even giving a fuck about his wellbeing. She had to remember that he was the enemy. Cam was nothing more than the father of her kids.

Cam held out his arms and scooped Press up in his embrace. His Pretty Girl was going to the fifth grade. Cam wished he could turn back the hands of time. He missed the little girl he used to read bedtime stories to.

"Aoki, you gon' leave me hanging?" He reached out his arm for her as well.

"Like you left us." She snarled with revulsion. When she'd learned he'd broken his promise on them being a family again, like her mother, Aoki was done with him. She was tired of the men in her life disappointing her. She needed consistency. She expected it to come from Cam but like Gunz he'd proven not to be trustworthy or dependable.

Cam's heart sank. This was supposed to be the happiest time of his life. Because of Noon everything in his world was falling apart. The last thing he wanted to do was disappoint his kids, especially Aoki. He'd finally won her trust. Knowing that he'd hurt her added another scar to his already bruised and battered heart. The smug look on Noon's face as he sat in the driver's seat of Gray's car made Cam want to slice the skin off his face with a butter knife. Cam almost had the mind to do it. Priest pulling up stopped him from acting too quickly. Loud music blasted from his Jaguar F-Type Coup as he turned off the engine. Paris begrudgingly got out. School was the last thing on his mind but the one rule his brother put in place was in order for him to live with him, he had to attend school. With nowhere else to go after getting kicked out of their mother's house, Paris had no choice but to comply. Until he could get his own place, he'd play by Priest's rules. He'd go to the bougie, over-priced private school but that didn't mean he'd actually pay attention or do any work. School was meant to prepare you for the real world and the work force. Paris was already making bank by selling weed. The fuck did he need school for? The only upside of attending Forsyth Academy was getting new customers. He knew for sure the white kids would cop weed from him by the pound.

"Bye ma." Aoki gave her mother a quick hug. She didn't want to be around Cam or Paris if she didn't have to be. Hell, Priest either.

"Bye baby. Have a great day." Gray waved goodbye as she walked quickly up the school steps.

"Be good Li'l Boosie Bad ass!" Cam called after her.

Aoki rolled her eyes and kept going.

"What's good, cuzzo?" Priest slapped his palm against his.

"Shit . . . maintaining." Cam said happy to see his family.

"P. Come speak."

Paris released a long sigh. He didn't feel like a bunch of pleasantries. Cam was his older cousin, but they barely spent any time with each other. Not only was he ten times older than him but Cam was a Blood and he was a Crip. Because of their affiliation they had to keep their distance. Cam eyed his little cousin. Paris li'l bad ass was sixteen and had just as many tattoos as him and Priest. As he approached them, Cam couldn't help but notice how uncomfortable he looked in his uniform. The fabric seemed to itch his skin. Paris was used to attending public school, where he got to wear what he want. Donning a white button up, tie, gray V-neck sweater, navy blue blazer and white khaki pants made him feel like a stuffy politician. The only thing cool about his uniform was that it was the color blue.

"Sup?" Paris barely gave him eye contact. He hadn't gone to see his big cousin the entire time he was in a coma. Going to hospitals wasn't his thing. Paris threw a prayer up to God on Cam's behalf and went on about his life. Life and death didn't mean that much to him, particularly since he didn't feel he had that much to live for.

Cam examined his little cousin closely. It was always awkward when he saw him. Because of their age difference, they weren't particularly close. Paris would never know how much he reminded Cam of his self. When he was his age, Cam walked around with a chip on his shoulder too. It was sad because it took him damn near forty years to brush it off. He didn't want that for Paris. He prayed he found happiness before it was too late.

"You good?" He quizzed.

"Yeah, just ready to get this shit over wit'." Paris grunted, wishing he was anywhere but where he was.

"Appa, c'mon. I'm gonna be late for class." Press tugged on Cam's shirt.

"Well, let me get these kids to class. It was good seeing you. Priest, I'ma get up wit' you later."

"Yep." Priest gave him dap. "And make sure you're standing out front at 2:30." He told his brother.

"I could've drove myself." Paris spat with an attitude.

"If I would've let you drive yourself, you would've never shown up. You gotta prove to me that I can trust you to handle your business before I let you do that."

"You the wrong muthafucka to talk about trust." Paris quipped, giving his brother his back.

With a solemn look on his face, Priest watched as Paris disappeared amongst the crowd of high school students. Paris had been with him since the middle of July and there had been no progress in their relationship. The once solid bond they shared was completely gone. Priest couldn't blame anyone but himself. He'd done this to them. He was the one who'd left his baby brother behind when he needed him most and for that he'd have to suffer the consequences.

Once Press was safe in her seat, Gray and Cam led the triplets to their preschool class. Inside there was an American flag, chalkboard, wooden tables, colorful chairs, cubbies for their things, books, games, computers and more. In the middle of the floor was a huge rug where the entire class would gather to listen to the teacher read. Cam thought the kids would be scared and start to cry, but unlike their classmates, the triplets were fine. It was Gray and Cam that was a nervous wreck. They both kept asking the kids were they okay and did they want them to stay. To make matters worse, Gray wouldn't stop crying. Her babies weren't little anymore. Soon, they'd be in kindergarten, middle school, then driving, going to college, and getting married. It was all too much for her to handle. Her pregnancy hormones weren't helping the situation either. She'd been throwing up all morning. It was a miracle she'd even been able to get dressed. The bell signaling the start of the school day rang and Cam and Gray were still glued in place, unable to leave the triplets behind.

"Mom and dad we're going to start class now." Miss Bianca smiled ready for them to leave.

"Oh." Gray sniffed back her tears. "Mommy's gonna go now, okay."

"Bye mommy." Sky and Beaux waved as they sat on their square.

Cam was so proud of his big girls. They were fearless just like him. It was his mini me, Reign, that started to have a hard time. As soon as they said they were about to leave, tears welled in his crystal blue eyes. Gray crouched down to his level.

"Mommy and daddy are gonna go so you can meet your new friends."

"I don't want you to go. I'm scared. But I'ma man, mama. I ain't supposed to be scared." He tucked his face into Gray's bosom and held onto her for dear life.

"Don't cry, Reigny." Gray's voice cracked.

"No, mama. A real man ain't no punk. Ain't that right daddy?"

"You damn right."

"Cam!" Gray stressed.

"What?" He shrugged.

"Listen, Reigny. Don't cry. I love you, okay." Gray said on the verge of tears herself.

"O-tay." He whimpered, poking out his bottom lip.

"Wipe your eyes buddy." Cam took his small hand in his. It was breaking his heart to see his son cry. Reign was way more sensitive than his sisters. He needed a lot more reassurance and attention. Most fathers would be irritated or embarrassed by this but not Cam. Reign had something he didn't have until recently. A heart.

"Everything's gonna be okay. If anybody fuck wit' you, you know daddy will shoot 'em."

"In they pinky toe?" Reign rubbed his eyes back-and-forth.

"And they big toe."

"Can I have a kiss?" Gray held Reign by the stomach. His little round belly poked out.

Reign wiped the rest of the wet tears from his sad face and pecked his mom on the lips. Gray's heart did several summersaults in a row. Oh, how she loved her son.

"Can daddy have one too?" Cam leaned down slowly. He wished he could bend down but his legs weren't strong enough to support his weight. Reign gave his father a tender kiss.

"Daddy loves you buddy. You know you're my best friend, right?"

"I thought Uncle Quan and Uncle Stacy was?"

"Uncle Quan is but Stacy just a fat ass nigga that I tell to shut up all the time. You're my best-best friend."

"What about mommy?"

"She's my star and I'm her moon. One can't exist without the other."

Were the two most important men in her life trying to kill her? That's what it felt like. Reign and Cam were tugging on Gray's heart strings like they were playing a game of Tug-of-War.

"You ready to meet your new friends now?" Gray tried to keep her composure so Cam wouldn't see she was affected by his sweet sentiment.

"Yes." Reign answered with his head down.

"You're gonna love it buddy, I swear. Have I ever lied to you?"

Reign's head shot up.

"That one time you . . . you said the tooth fairy wasn't real. But he is mommy. The Rock is the tooth fairy. I saw it on da movie."

"Let me tell you something I had to learn the hard way." Cam interjected. "Your mama is a fuckin' liar. She wouldn't know the truth if it smacked her in her pretty ass face."

"*Oooooooh* he said a bad word." Some little girl pointed her tiny index finger.

"Stay away from her li'l ass. She a fuckin' snitch." Cam snarled at the child. "What's our family motto?"

"Snitches end up in ditches." Reign grinned proud of himself.

"That's my boy. High five." Cam raised his hand.

Reign happily smacked his palm against his fathers. Not ready to go, Gray placed several more kisses on Reign's cheeks. She even thought about taking him home with her. Miss Bianca literally had to push them out to get them to say goodbye. Outside the door, Gray wiped her face and took a deep breath. Time was moving too fast, but she was thankful for her health and her children.

"Here." Cam held out a tissue he'd stolen from the Kleenex box.

"Thanks." She took it and blew her nose.

"You need me to come help you with they homework after school?" He asked. Cam knew it was a dumb question, but he couldn't think of anything else to say. Gray hadn't said a word to him the entire time they'd been together.

"Nigga, they're three." She slammed the snotty tissue in his hand.

"Gray, I swear to God. If you give me the Rona I'ma bust yo' ass." He threw the nasty tissue in the trash.

"I'm pretty sure I can handle coloring and tracing letters by myself." She quipped, still irritated.

"I'm just saying that shit can be hard."

"Have a nice day, Archibald." Gray tried to bypass him.

"Hold up. Hold up." Cam swiftly took ahold of her arm. "I ain't done talking to you."

"Well, I'm done talking to you." She pulled away.

"When you gon' give me another baby?"

"What?" Her eyes damn near bulged out their sockets.

"We got some pretty ass kids, Gray. We should have like ten more of 'em."

"You better go have a baby with Quack-Quack. I'm sure she'll give you a whole tribe of birds."

Gray knew the truth would have to be revealed sooner rather than later but wrapping her mind around the fact that Cam was alive and still not hers was something she still hadn't mastered. Nothing in her life was as she'd hoped it would be. Never did she want to be pregnant again and not with her child's father. Being back with Noon wasn't something she truly wanted either. That's why she'd made it known that she didn't want to be anything more than friends right now. Noon respected her wishes but still made it known that he wanted to be with her.

"Why you gotta be so mean? You too pretty to be so angry? You hungry? You know you get angry when you're hungry."

"No, I get angry when I get played by fuck boys who waste my time."

"Why you bringing up old shit?"

"Mutha—" She stopped herself before she cursed. "Bye Cam." She marched down the hallway.

"Wait-wait-wait!" Cam limped behind her with his cane. This was the first time they'd had some alone time together since she left the hospital. He couldn't let it end that quickly. "On some real shit. What we gon' do about the triplets' birthday party?"

Gray spun around and faced him. Cam halted in his tracks.

"I already got it handled. Anything else?"

"Yeah, I wanna be involved. They my kids too."

"Okay perfect. You can be involved by cutting the check and I'll send you an invitation."

"Say no more. No expense needs to be spared for my babies. I can write you a check right now. How much you need? Fifty stacks . . . a hunnid."

"Matter fact. Just give me your Amex and I'll take care of it." Gray arched her brow and held out her hand.

"Anything else?" He handed it over.

"Nope. This will do." She turned to leave. She was so sick and tired of walking away from him. If given the chance, she'd run to him and lay down all her burdens. All she really wanted to do was leap in his arms and place sweet kisses all over his gorgeous face. Gray missed everything about him. She no longer wanted to pretend like she was okay without him. That game was tired and boring. Yet, here she was putting up a front like she was fine with moving on. Yes, it was pathetic but what was she supposed to do? He'd made it abundantly clear that they were through. Even though Gray would give up her left lung to be his girl, she couldn't continue to play herself. Desperation looked good on no one.

"So, this how it's gon' be moving forward?"

"You made it this away." She power walked so he couldn't keep up.

"I'm just saying. I know you miss the kid 'cause I damn sure miss you."

"Fuck outta here." She caught him off guard and pointed her finger in his face. "Play with my pussy but don't play with my emotions. You said it was over so keep that same energy playboy."

"On everything. I miss the fuck outta you." He used his free hand to pull her into his personal space.

"Let me go!" Gray pounded her fist into his steel chest.

"Will you stop all that fuckin' yelling. You loud as hell in these people hallway."

"Like I give a damn about these people. What do you want, Cam?" She tried to ignore the scent of his cologne, but the heady aroma had already made her nipples hard. Why was she so stuck on stupid when it came to this nigga?

"I get you mad but it's a lot you don't understand right now."

"I understand perfectly. You're the perfect father but that's all you'll ever be. You'll never be the perfect man for me."

"And that bitch ass nigga is?" Cam pushed her out of his hold.

"Least he ain't never lied to me or played with my heart."

"You don't even know that nigga for real. Look, I know shit is fucked up between us but it ain't what you think. I wanna explain what's going on—"

"Is there a problem here?" Noon interrupted their conversation.

Cam stopped speaking and scowled. This muthafucka had to go.

"Nah, we good. Ain't that right Cam?" Gray wrapped her arm around Noon's waist. She knew the gesture would piss him off. It did.

Cam chalked this up to being nothing but the devil. Only He would try him this way. With nothing to say, he simply curled his upper lip and shot Noon an evil glare. Playing along, Noon took advantage of the situation and tilted Gray's head back. Looking Cam square in the eye, he planted a soft kiss to her sumptuous lips. Cam's stomach started to churn. The sight of another man kissing his wife not only made him want to vomit but commit murder in the 1st degree.

"You be good, Cam. It's a lot of *poison* out here. You don't wanna get caught up." Noon patted Gray on the butt and winked his eye. Once they were out of ear shot of Cam, Noon started going in. "I thought you were done with him."

"I am." Gray groaned.

"It doesn't look like it."

"I ain't got nothing to do with that. I told you it's over between me and him. We're strictly co-parenting."

"If that's the case, why won't you give me another chance?" He pushed open the door for her.

"I don't want to be with anyone but my kids right now. They're my main focus."

"I get that but if we're together, I could help you with the kids."

"I don't need your help. They have a father to be there for them."

"Damn, Gray. Give me something here. I love you."

Halting her steps, she stopped before him.

"And I told you that I care about you but we can only be friends. I can't handle anything else right now. You're either gonna respect that or stop being my friend."

"You know I can't let you go." He caressed her arm. "I'm committed to making you mine again. We will get back to where we were. I'm sure of it."

AOKI'S FIRST DAY BACK AT FORSYTH HAD GONE NOTHING LIKE SHE'D expected. The hallways seemed more chaotic, the students weren't particularly kind and the teachers didn't care that she didn't remember her way around at all. Walking the halls plastered with people she didn't know, while trying to make it to each period on time was a daunting task. She didn't have any classes with the twins, Princess or Li'l Quan. All the kids she used to be friends with were now all cliqued up. In Algebra class when she'd turned to speak, they acted like they barely remembered her. At first Aoki was offended but then she remembered that she'd up and left them behind without any warning. Life had gone on and she'd become a distant memory. As she sat at her desk, all she could think was she should be back in Paris with her friends where she belonged. In Paris she was the 'It Girl' the most popular girl in school. Here, she was nothing. She was just another girl in the crowd. Being the new girl with a weird first name made her stick out like a sore thumb. When she was a kid it didn't matter that people made fun of her name. Now that she was older, she instantly felt like an outcast. It didn't matter that she was half black, had a great sense of humor and loved music more than life. All the other students saw was a chinky, blue-eyed girl with a head full of frizzy hair and mile long legs. Without getting to know her, she was instantly labeled stuck up just based off her looks. Aoki realized it was going to take a lot more than a wave and smile for her to fit in.

Relief came when the lunch bell finally rang, and she was freed from the Spanish class she was unable to understand. Aoki slung her

Goyard backpack over her shoulder and headed to the cafeteria. It took what felt like forever, but she finally made it. Students raced past her in an effort to get in line first. As Aoki walked into the lunchroom alone, she prayed to God that her family would be on the same lunch schedule as her. As she searched the busy room desperately for the twins, Aoki took in the atmosphere. The cafeteria reeked of bleach. Even the aroma of the mediocre food was overpowered by the scent. The students didn't seem to mind tho. The food was always piping hot and arrived on time. Amongst the processed food, the cafeteria was a disharmony of loud banter. Each table consisted of kids talking loudly so they could be heard over the racket. The food came second to the information that was exchanged. Over cheese fries and nachos cliques were formed and gossip was traded like cigarettes in jail. High school was a dog-eat-dog world. Much like jail you were either the hunter or the prey. Aoki would be damned if she was a target. She had to solidify herself as the big dog on campus. Somebody you didn't want to fuck with. As she tried to come up with a game plan someone tapped her shoulder. Aoki turned to find a familiar face.

"You looking like somebody stole your bike." Blizz joked, happy to see her.

"Please tell me you have lunch during this period."

"I do. Come sit wit' me." He laced his fingers with hers.

Aoki didn't even mind that he was basically marking them as a couple by holding her hand. Having someone she knew by her side made her feel secure. She'd take that any day over being alone. When they neared the table, they'd be sitting at Aoki's heart dropped. Everyone she had beef with was there. Paris and Damya sat side-by-side. They were so close; she was practically sitting in his lap. Seeing them together further made Aoki wonder was anything they shared real. It didn't help that Paris looked incredibly handsome in his uniform. Somehow he'd given his outfit a thugged out appeal. He made the preppy ensemble look cool. Damn, did she miss him. Aoki felt stupid for feeling such a way, but she couldn't help herself. Next to Damya was her ugly ass friend Cliché. Meechi and Kiara sat across from them too. Aoki would rather gag on a spoon than sit with their fake asses. She didn't even expect to see any of them there but remembered that even though Forsyth was a $17,000 a year academy, they provided funding for low income families. That was how kids from the neighborhood was able to attend.

"What's up, Aoki?" Meechi spoke, scooping the last of his fruit cocktail into his mouth. This was his last year at Forsyth.

"Hey." She reluctantly sat next to Kiara.

Blizz sat on the bench right beside her. On the outside, Paris made it seem like he wasn't fazed, but in reality, he was boiling on the inside. The last thing he wanted to see was Aoki all boo'd up with Blizz's corny ass. She was too good for him. Hell, she was too good for Paris as well. Neither of them deserved her. He'd thought about speaking to her that morning when they were dropped off, but she'd ran into the building so fast he didn't have a chance to get to her. Aoki acted like he had the plague or something. It really fucked with his mental that they were in such a fucked-up space. There was no one else to blame but himself. He'd done this to them. He should've kept it a hunnid. But like most guys his age, he decided to have his cake and eat it too. For weeks he'd come up with ways to get her back in his life. Nothing seemed good enough. Aoki wasn't some regular ole girl from around the way. She had standards. He had to come correct or not at all. With her it was all or nothing, which was the problem. Damya didn't demand anything of him. Things with her were easy. He could fuck around with other girls, she'd pop her shit, he'd dick her down and they were good. He could never try Aoki like that. She wouldn't take any of his shit. So, the question remained. Was he ready to give his heart to a chick and risk getting it broken?

"Bae, look at this." Kiara showed Meechi a meme on her phone so he would stop talking to Aoki. After her Kunta Kinte looking ass cousin snuffed her, Kiara wanted nothing to do with Aoki. If she didn't fuck with her, Meechi couldn't fuck with her either.

"Oh, I don't just be sitting with anybody." Damya crossed her legs and screwed up her face. "Especially not no eighth grader."

"Exactly. Ain't the middle schoolers supposed to be over there?" Cliché pointed across the room.

"Why they even in here? Fuck is the world coming to." Damya sneered, causing Kiara to laugh.

"I'll smack the shit out of all y'all." Aoki made clear.

"Who?" Damya and Cliché said at the same time.

"You. You and you." She pointed at Damya, Cliché and Kiara.

"Chill y'all. Chill." Meechi groaned. He was not in the mood to hear a bunch of bitches arguing.

"That's her." Cliché snapped.

"Yeah Kiara, get yo' friend." Damya mean-mugged Aoki. It had been a month and a half since their last fight, but she was still salty. She couldn't stand the fact that she'd gotten beaten up twice by a spoiled, high yellow, rich girl.

"She ain't my friend and ain't nobody gon' get me." Aoki rolled her neck.

Out of nowhere, Paris started rapping to an imaginary beat. She knew he'd done it to stop them from arguing and it worked. The rhyme he spit immediately took everyone's mind off of fighting. Meechi joined in and flowed bar-for-bar. Back-and-forth they went. Everyone was amazed at their lyricism and rhyme pattern. Aoki was really awestruck. She loved to hear Paris rap. If he perfected his craft, he could be as big as Drake and Kendrick Lamar. By the time they were done, a round of applause erupted.

"Baby, that was so good." Damya wrapped her arms around his neck.

"A'ight chill. You doing too much." Paris scooted away from her. He hated when she was all over him.

"You always acting funny when Coronavirus come around."

"Who the fuck you calling the Coronavirus?" Aoki leaned forward, ready to swing.

"You. Trump said it was a Chinese disease so y'all need to get the fuck up outta here."

"Yo, don't even argue wit' her. She ignorant as fuck." Blizz stopped Aoki from reacting violently.

"Damn Blizz, so this your best friend now?" Damya questioned.

"Mind your fuckin' business." Aoki answered for him. "And for the last time, I'm Korean *and* black. Not Chinese. Wit' yo' dumb ass. You got your nerves. You the last person to say somebody got something. Your whole fuckin' family is one big walking venereal disease. Didn't I see your mother standing outside the corner store trying to sell her pussy for crack rock? Your own mother doesn't even want you."

"Hold up." Paris interjected. "Now you doing too much. You on some li'l kid shit." He eyed Aoki with disdain. Yeah, she had the right to clap back 'cause Damya was being petty but bringing her mother into it was taking shit too far. Everybody wasn't lucky enough to have a mother that was loving and responsible. Some people like him and Damya had to deal with the cards they were dealt with. Their mothers chose the drug of their choice over their children. Dope ruled Damya's mother world and going from man to man was his mother's drug of choice.

"You think I'ma sit here and let her talk crazy to me?" Aoki eyed him, hurt. She couldn't believe he was taking Damya's side. She was obviously the one in the wrong.

"Why would you even come over here?" He barked. "You know she don't like you. You came over here looking for a fight? You don't fuck wit' nobody at this table except this clown ass nigga." He threw his chocolate milk at Blizz.

The open container smacked him in the forehead. Cold chocolate milk trickled down Blizz's entire face. He couldn't breathe without inhaling the liquid. Everyone in the cafeteria except, Meechi and Aoki laughed. Blizz pursed his lips together angrily. He was getting real sick and tired of Paris and his bully shit. There was only but so much more he could take before he exploded.

"You know what fuck you, her and everybody else at this damn table." Aoki threw the milk back at him as she got up to leave.

Blizz wiped his face with his hand and followed behind her.

"Bye Corona!" Damya and Cliché waved.

"Yo, shut the fuck up." Paris snapped, annoyed. "You the one acting like an eighth grader. How about you act your fucking age. You always on some immature shit. That's why I don't be fucking wit' you like that now."

"No, you don't be fucking with me because of her." Damya corrected him.

"You might be right. Keep it up and I won't be fucking with you at all because of her."

CHAPTER 20

"Life is but a dream that you manifested slowly. So, fuck a fantasy. This your muthafuckin' moment."-Victoria Monét "Moment"

"*W*here in the hell are y'all taking me?" Gray sat in the back of the limo along with Mo, Boss and Kema. They were all dressed to the nine in high-priced, after-five attire.

"You didn't tell her where we were going?" Boss chuckled, looking at Mo.

"No. I knew if I told her she wouldn't come."

"Y'all wild." Boss shook his head.

"Boss, what the hell are they up to?"

"Leave me outta this Jack."

"Listen." Kema turned to face her bestie. "Quan is throwing Cam a belated birthday party and its . . . tonight."

"Oh, hell naw. Pull this muthafucka over." Gray tugged on the door handle.

"If yo' crazy ass don't stop." Kema pulled her back before she unlocked the door and fell out.

"Y'all know damn well I don't wanna be at his party."

"Lowkey you do." Mo gave her a stern look of disbelief.

"That's neither here nor there." Gray waved her off.

"It's more here than there. I know the real. You still love my brother girl."

"I will always love him. He's the father of my kids—"

"And your husband." Kema added.

"Until we get a divorce."

"Is that really what you want?" Mo questioned, worried. The last thing she wanted was to see Cam and Gray legally part. Seeing the way she cared for him when he was at his worst let her know there wasn't another woman on the planet who'd love her brother like Gray. They were meant for each other. They balanced each other out. Cam needed a stable force like Gray in his life. Her love was unwavering and pure.

"No." She replied honestly.

In the past Gray would've lied and said yes for appearances sake. She hated to look or feel dumb. However, at this stage in her life she no longer cared about saving face. Her feelings were her feelings. She loved her husband. She wanted their marriage to work. She wanted to be with him forever. The only problem was the feeling wasn't mutual.

"But it's not about what I want. I can't be in a relationship by myself. Your brother made his choice. He chose . . . Devin." She damn near choked on her words.

"He don't want her funky ass." Mo scoffed. "That bitch on the unemployment line because of Rona."

"Yeah well, he chose that unemployed bitch." Gray sighed, somberly.

Softly splashing water droplets hit the car window as she looked out into the night sky. Steady rain fell from a sky made of black velvet. Car rides usually calmed Gray but that night things were different. Her stomach clenched as she watched rain race down the window. She was nervous and weary about seeing Cam with the whore he'd left her for. After all she'd done for him, after all the sleepless nights, heartfelt prayers and worry, he pushed her to the side as if it all meant nothing. The shit hurt. It cut her deep. This wound was one that would probably never heal. Now her best friend and sister-in-law wanted her to party the night away with him like none of it had happened. Were they completely oblivious to her pain? Kema couldn't have been. She knew firsthand what she was going through. Every day it was a struggle to get out of bed. Gray's life had been turned upside down. Nothing was as she'd hope it would be. Her modeling career was on hold until God knows when. She was back living in the home she'd left behind nearly four years before. Gray was used to her life being in order. Everything was chaotic and out of place. She needed balance. She needed peace but it seemed like relief was nowhere in sight.

"We're here." Mo rubbed her palms together, excited.

It had been ages since she hit the club. With six kids at home, going out was a rarity. Boss climbed out first and helped his wife, sister-in-law and then Kema out the car. The ground was slick with rain, so the ladies were cautious with their steps. None of them wanted to fall or break an ankle. Gray wondered where the party was being held. The limo driver had let them out in an alley with hanging lights. The shit looked sketchy as hell. Gray didn't feel safe at all. All was well when Boss led them to a door in back of a theatre. The sign above the door read Thaxton Speakeasy. After ringing the doorbell, they were greeted by a friendly staff person. The cute girl escorted them down a dimly lit flight of steps and into the venue where the décor and music was lively. Quan had rented out the entire space. Only close family, friends and the who's who of St. Louis were invited. The art deco venue was the perfect place to hold the black tie birthday bash. Thaxton Speakeasy was a ritzy cellar haunt located in a historic building with a Prohibi-tion-era theme. On regular nights, a password entry was required to take part in the live music and libation. Gray examined the room. The lighting, artwork, décor, and architectural details all came together, to create a truly unique vibe. No added décor was needed. The space was already stunning. To add to the ambiance, Chef Pierre executed the perfect menu of all Cam's favorite foods. Guest wet their palette with flavored moonshine served in mason jars.

Wall to wall there were people. Quan, Stacy, Priest, Britten, Heidi, Tee-Tee, Bernard, Curtis, Elizabeth, and Cal were there to show love. Cam had grown ten times closer to his two brothers since his coma. Kerry, however, was dead to him. *Vivrant Thing* by Q-Tip had the crowd going wild. DJ Nice was on the ones and twos. Feeling the energy from the music, all of the tension in Gray's body dissipated. The bass thumped in time with Gray's heart beat as though they were one. Instantly, she started feeling her cunt. Gray bobbed her head to the beat as she sashayed through the throngs of people on the dance floor. The music was as loud as thunder; it made the cutlery on the tabletops rattle. Neon lights flashed everywhere like police sirens, but much more colorful.

On the second level Cam stood with a Cuban cigar in hand amongst his mans. They all looked like kings in their tuxedos and suits. Because he was the man of the hour, Cam didn't don black like his boys. Red was his color of choice. In a blood red satin Dsquared blazer, black cashmere t-shirt, black dress pants and calf suede Christian Louboutin loafers with a tattoo patch detail he looked sexy and debonair. His edge up-high-low fade and beard had been cut and lined to perfection. Two iced-out Cuban link chains gleamed from his neck. On his left arm he accessorized with a gold bust-down Rollie, a $298,000 diamond Juste Un Clou Cartier bracelet and his blinged out wedding band. On his right wrist were two gold Cartier Love Bracelets dripped in diamonds.

He'd officially been out of the hospital two and a half months. October was in full affect. Time was flying by. The time was needed because Cam was only 80% back to full capacity. The good thing was he no longer needed to walk with a cane. His arms and legs still had spasms from time to time and every now and then he'd become winded. The stab wound in his stomach had fully healed. A scar was the only evidence left behind. Other than that, his progression had been great. Every one that had seen him during his hospital stint was amazed at how far he'd come. Dr. Keaton's prognosis was that in a few more weeks he'd be given a clean bill of health and cleared from attending rehab. Cam hadn't shared the good news with anyone yet. He wanted to save the moment for the woman who'd loved him back to health. Just as he thought of her she appeared.

Gray was the last person he expected to see that night. He thought she'd be home finalizing the plans for the triplets' birthday party which was that weekend but there she was stepping through the crowd like a goddess. She'd never looked more beautiful. He couldn't keep his eyes off of her. Neither could any of the other men in attendance. Her face was beat to the gods. Celebrity makeup artist Priscilla Ono had given her a smoky cut crease with pale pink shadow on the lids and mink lashes. Rosy pink blush enhanced her high cheekbones. Nude pink lipstick adorned her full lips. Extensions were added to her hair to give her a sleek pulled back fishtail braid. A silver metal chain was wrapped around it.

Cam was fine with all of that. It was the racy outfit she rocked that he had a problem with. Gray was practically naked. The top she wore was barely made of anything. One side was made of sheer chain metal that draped over her arm and across her bare breast. The other side of the top was made of black circle disc chained together. From where Cam stood it looked like her nipples were exposed but she wore nude nipple covers. A biased cut black leather mini skirt showed off her toned peanut butter colored legs. A Valentino Garavani clutch and black patent leather Marsell ankle boots pulled the rest of the risqué ensemble together. Cam wanted to run down and cover her with his jacket. Every inch of her curvy physique was out for the world to see. Was she trying to send him to an early grave? Was this payback for him leaving her? She would've never pulled this shit if they were together.

Gray's curvaceous hips seemed to sway in slow motion as she waved and smiled at the people who knew her. By the time she made her way up the steps to the private section he was in, Cam's anger had rose to an explosive level.

"Happy birthday boo!" Mo cheerily wrapped her arms around him.

"Thanks, li'l ugly ass girl." Cam hugged her back.

"You wish, nigga. I look good." Mo pushed him lightly.

"Happy birthday bro." Boss gave him a warm embrace. He was truly happy to see his brother-in-law doing well.

"Hey Cam." Kema kissed his cheek.

"What's up?" He rubbed her back while never taking his eyes off Gray.

"Where's my husband?"

"His ass over there." Cam pointed towards the back. "Congratulations on the baby. You know this is the happiest my boy has ever been."

"Thank you. We're both really excited." Kema rubbed her flat belly. She was only two months pregnant whereas Gray was three.

"I'm trying to have another one with your friend but she ain't fuckin' wit' me."

"Stop playing games and do right by her. You never know what could happen. Now if you'll excuse me. Let me go give my man some suga." Kema skipped off.

Cam clenched his jaw. Placing his hands in front of his crotch, he put one over the other. His legs were spread inches apart in a dominate stance. He was heated and he wanted Gray to know. Unfazed, she stepped into his personal space with the same confidence. Cam didn't pump any fear in her heart.

"Happy belated birthday."

"I know the fuck you ain't come in here dressed like a Soul Train dancer."

"ALL ABOARD! TOOT! TOOT!" Gray giggled, mimicking a train conductor.

"You real funny. Yo nigga let you out the house like that?"

"What he doesn't know won't hurt him. And plus, I'm a model. This is fashion, darling." Gray snapped her finger like a queen.

"Yo, you for real right now?" Cam stepped so close she could smell the hint of Hennessy and mint on his breath. "Yo' whole fuckin' titty out." He tapped it. "The same titties me and my kids suck on."

"They look good don't they?" Gray jiggled her breasts.

"Them muthafucka's sitting up too!" Heidi raised her glass of champagne in the air.

"Stop! You bet not shake a nan nother titty." Cam cupped Gray's breasts, so they'd stop wiggling.

"You betta move your hands before yo' li'l girlfriend get mad."

"What girlfriend?"

"*Devin.*" Gray nudged her head in her direction like he was dumb.

She and her girls were huddled in a circle giving her the evil eye.

"Go home." Cam growled, menacingly.

Gray covered her mouth and chuckled.

"Good one, nigga. I ain't going nowhere and give me this damn cigar." She tossed it to the ground and stepped on it. "You know damn well you ain't supposed to be smoking."

"You buying me another one."

"I ain't buying you shit."

"Whatever. You know how this shit gon' end. One of these bum ass niggas gon' disrespect you and I'ma end up back in jail. Is that what you want?"

"I want you to get out my face. Remember nigga, I'm grown."

"On my mama, Gray. Take yo' ass home."

"*On my mama. On my hood. I look fly. Nigga, I look good.*" She rocked from side-to-side and snapped her fingers. Mo and Kema started dancing with her.

"Y'all muthafucka's think this shit a game?" Cam barked, livid.

"Fuck it up, Gray! Fuck it up!" Stacy joined in.

"*Jenny Craig! Jenny Craig!*" Devin sang, bopping towards them.

"Watch yo' mouth, bitch. That's what got you fucked up at the barbeque." Kema squared up, forgetting she was pregnant.

"You gon' let them talk to me like that?" Devin snapped her neck towards Cam.

"Hell yeah. You doing too much. Go sit the fuck down!" He

snapped on ten. Cam didn't even know why she was there. Yeah, they were supposed to be "together" but he didn't even invite her to the party. She'd basically invited herself and showed up with her homegirls.

"*Ooooooooooh!*" Devin stomped her feet like a child. She was outraged. She thought since Cam had chosen her over Gray things between them would change. But everything was still the same.

Before Cam could say another word, Gray dipped past him and made her way to the bar. Discreetly, she asked for a mocktail. If she made it known she wasn't drinking, everyone would know she was pregnant. And yes, telling Cam would be an unforgettable birthday present but she still wasn't ready to reveal her secret. She really refused to tell him while Devin was around. She would beat her ass if she ruined such a precious moment.

Needing to smoke in peace, Cam made his way outside. Plain clothed security was right behind him. He couldn't risk Gray breaking another one of his cigars. If she did it again, he'd have to push her wig back and he didn't wanna do his baby like that. Plus, Devin was getting on his fucking nerves. He appreciated everything she'd done for him while he was locked down, but he couldn't stand the sight of her face. The bitch was fucking annoying. All her ass did was complain and start shit knowing damn well she couldn't fight.

The cool night air breezed against his face as he leaned against the building. Cars whizzed by as he lit a freshly rolled blunt. Inhaling the potent weed, Cam blew out a breath of smoke and watched until it evaporated into thin air. On his second pull, he ended up coughing so bad it felt like he'd hacked up a lung. Gray was right. He shouldn't be indulging but damn did getting high feel good. He needed something to calm his nerves. Not being able to figure Noon out was getting under his skin. His goofy ass was a complete enigma which posed a problem. Before he could set his sights on LaLa and Gunz, he had to eliminate Noon first. He was an immediate threat that needed to be deaded quick. It was a shame he wasn't well-enough to take him out. At night he fantasized about the many ways he could kill him. The disrespect he'd shown him while in the hospital couldn't go unpunished. He'd insulted his manhood and attacked him during his weakest state. Cam would never forget the feeling of his finger pressing into his wound. He thought about the shit every day. That's why he couldn't let someone else handle his dirty work. Noon was his for the taking and so was Gunz but Cam was going to mark him off last on his kill list. When he got his hands on Gunz, his death would be a slow and tortuous one. While he fantasized about the many ways he could kill Noon and Gunz, the sound of a woman yelling caught his attention. Cam looked to his right and spotted a man and a woman down the street having a lover's quarrel.

"Is that. . ." He spoke out loud while trying to make sure his eyes weren't deceiving him.

A chick that looked a lot like Tia was going off and waving her finger in a man that resembled Kingston's face. He hadn't seen either of them since that day at the community center, so he wasn't sure if his eyes were playing tricks on him. Any doubt he had was put to rest when he heard the girl say, "I'm tired of being a fuckin' secret Kingston! You told me years ago you was gon' tell my auntie about us! Nigga, I'm tired of waiting! Gavin Jr. needs to know who his real father is!"

"I told yo' stupid ass I was gon' tell her. I just need more time. Now stop actin' like a fuckin' brat and give me a kiss." He pulled her to him.

"Ooh you get on my nerves." She planted her lips on his. "But for real. I'm not playing. You need to tell LaLa so we can be a real family."

"I am." Kingston groaned, dragging her down the street to his car.

Little did either of them know but Cam had recorded the entire encounter. The video footage along with the photograph he had would come in handy later. Mind blown, he tucked his phone inside his jacket pocket and headed back inside. He didn't expect too much from Mama Lucy's offspring but Tia having a baby by her auntie's baby daddy was some low down dirty shit that even he didn't see coming.

An hour later the party had really started jumping. There wasn't an empty space on the dance floor. Gray was dying to go down and shake her ass. The distraction was necessary. The whole time she'd been in Cam's section, Devin and her silly ass friends kept giving her dirty looks. On top of that, the air was filled with weed and cigar smoke. She could hardly breathe, and the second-hand smoke wasn't good for her or the baby.

"Come dance wit' me." She took Tee-Tee and Heidi by the hand. Both of them gulped down their drinks and rose to their feet.

"Where the fuck you going?" Cam ice grilled her as she strutted by.

"Ughn you nosey." She balled up her face and kept going.

As soon as Gray stepped onto the dance floor, she was transported to another space and time. She and her friends fed off each other's smiles and dance moves. Teyana Taylor's song *How You Want It* had started to spin. Gray clapped her hands and two-stepped. The record was her shit. She wondered did the DJ know 'cause it seemed like he'd played it specifically for her. Moving her hips like she was in a 90's music video, she dirty wind to the mid-tempo beat. Gray loved to dance. She could go on like this for the rest of the night.

Cam gripped the steel rail and watched her do her thing. Seeing Gray groove was better than any strain of Kush. The chain metal and black shiny disc on her top shined under the sultry lights as she bent over and did a grown and sexy twerk. Grinding his teeth, Cam tried to keep his composure. The short skirt she wore barely covered her booty meat.

Feeling someone staring at her, Gray looked up and spotted Cam eye-fuckin' her. The moment reminded her of his birthday party four years prior. She couldn't stand him then and she couldn't stand him now. The only thing different was love was added to the equation. Since she had his attention, Gray decided to put on a show. In the squat position with her hands on her knees, she squeezed her thighs in and out, making her ass arch up and down. Visions of when he used to hit it from the back flashed in Cam's mind, making his dick hard. In the zone, Gray methodically rolled her torso to the beat while running her hand across the top of her head. Then on some nasty shit, she turned her back to him, leaned forward and slid her hands through the opening of her thighs. Speedily, she slid them back out on some peek-a-boo type shit. Rolling back up, she placed her index finger inside her mouth and sang the naughty lyrics.

Tell me what you want (how you want it?)
Ass up and face down (with the loving)
Baby let me know (when you need it)
Four-course meal, chopped down (when you eat it)
Make me curl my toes (toes)
What's the quickest way to turn you on?
Morning, middle of the night
Tell me what you want

Cam adored every second of his private dance until one of his drunk soldiers from the neighborhood creeped up behind Gray and started grinding on her. The young nigga must've not been aware of who she was. Gray immediately tensed up when she felt a random hard dick in-between her butt cheeks. Cam was about to step in until Gray looked over her shoulder and moved to the side.

"Back up." She ordered.

"Damn, it's like that?" The young bull uttered, surprised.

"Exactly like that. Now move ugly." She shooed him away.

"Yeah. A'ight. Remember that." He gripped his dick, backing away.

After the weird encounter, Gray was completely over being on the dance floor. Niggas didn't know how to respect a woman's space. Once she let Heidi and Tee-Tee know she was leaving, she walked back up the steps. The first thing she saw was Devin all in Cam's face. He seemed irritated but it didn't take away the sting. Gray wanted to throw up. Rolling her eyes, she sauntered past them only to be stopped by Kema.

"You good?"

"Mmm hmm," she lied.

In all actuality, she felt like a dumb, thirsty, third wheel. *Why am I here,* she wondered. The mixed signals she received from Cam wasn't worth the emotional turmoil he put her through.

"I know you lying but we'll talk about that later. Right now, the real party is about to begin. C'mon." Kema led her over to the rail.

Stacks of money were handed to the entire crew as they lined up front. Suddenly, the lights went black and the sound of a fire alarm went off. After the club massacre she'd been involved in years before, Gray didn't know whether to run or hide. She had nothing to worry about tho. A few minutes later, a spotlight shined down onto the infamous stripper Pole Assassin. She stood in the center of a custom circular stage holding onto a 20 foot pole. Blonde faux locs reached down to her waist. The amber light made the metallic pink bikini and 5-inch lucite stripper heels she wore glow. Gray's mouth dropped. Pole Assassin's body was crazy. Not one ounce of fat could be found anywhere. In top physical shape, she climbed the pole all the way to the top. Once she reached her destination, Cam's favorite song *Dreams and Nightmares* by Meek Mill started playing. Cam instantly started rapping like he was a Philly nigga himself.

> *I used to pray for times like this, to rhyme like this*
> *So I had to grind like that to shine like this*
> *In a matter of time I spent on some locked up shit*
> *In the back of the paddy wagon, cuffs locked on wrists*
> *See my dreams unfold, nightmares come true*
> *It was time to marry the game and I said, "Yeah, I do"*

Hanging upside down, Pole Assassin whipped her locs around in a circle better than Willow Smith. Gray watched on amazed at her athleticism. The girl was literally holding onto the pole by her thighs. Wanting to see Cam's reaction, she took her eyes off the entertainment and looked over at him. He was in absolute heaven. A grin a mile wide was etched onto his handsome face. Cam thought the beginning of the party was cool, but this was his kind of fun. Him and strippers were always a good time. As the song built to a crescendo, Pole Assassin began her routine. As soon as Meek rapped, *Hold up wait a minute, y'all thought I was finished,* she started flipping up and down the pole like a crazed monkey. The crowd went nuts. There wasn't a fireman in the world that could fuck with her as she slid down the pole and landed into a perfect split. Climbing the pole again, she held on by one leg and extended the other. Then she started alternating legs at lightning speed as she made her way back down head first. When she jumped up, held onto the pole by her hands, lifted her legs into the air and started smacking her stripper heels together like it was some kind of mating call, Gray threw what was left of her stack at her. Pole Assassin deserved that and more. The girl was everything.

The crowd really went dumb when ten of the industry's baddest big booty strippers dressed in red thong bikinis came out and started twerking to *I Wanna Rock (Doo Doo Brown)* by Luke featuring 2 Live Crew. An array of asses of all different colors and sizes bounced to the old school classic. Cam gleefully threw dollar bills in the air. Stacy stood next to his boy puffing on a cigar turning up big time. It felt good to be back in their element with his best friend. He thanked God he hadn't lost him. Stacy needed fifty more years of nights like this. Feeling sentimental too, Quan came over and gripped Cam's shoulder.

"This shit lit ain't it?"

"Yeeeeeeees sir!" Cam continued to rain down ones onto the dancers. Money was everywhere. The entire floor was covered. A hundred g's had been thrown without breaking a sweat.

"Y'all bitches better go in!" Kema shouted, having the time of her life.

"Let's go!" Stacy yelled.

"Here." Quan handed Cam his present.

A grey Patek Philippe box rested in the palm of his hand.

"Not the Patek." He pulled the top off and pulled out the shiny wooden box.

"It's the big Patek too. Not the li'l one."

"Aww man." Cam flipped open the case. Inside was a limited

edition 5303 Minute Repeater Tourbillion Patek Philippe timepiece. Only twelve of them had been made. Cam couldn't believe his eyes. The watch was a work of art. The skeletal structure of the dial exposed its hammers and gongs, as well as the tourbillon carriage. The red-lacquered, sapphire-crystal minute ring decorated with white stars was inspired by the Singaporean flag.

"This some grown man shit. Preciate that big bro." Cam thanked him with a big bear hug. "I love you, bruh."

"I love you too." Quan relished the celebratory moment.

On que, Cam's cake as well as fifty bottles of Ace of Spade were brought out by scantily clad waitresses. The bottles were given out to the guests. The intention was for them not to be opened until after Happy Birthday was sang but the dude Gray dissed took the moment to shake one of the bottles, pop the cork and splash the entire bottle of champagne on her. The liquid landed all over her legs and shoes. Cam saw the whole thing go down. Before Gray could react, he leaped over the rail and Superman punched the li'l dude. The blow knocked him out instantly. That didn't stop Quan, Stacy, and Priest from jumping down too and stomping his young ass out. Security ran out but even they couldn't get them to stop. Disrespect towards the women in their lives wasn't tolerated on any level. Blood covered each of their designer shoes but none of the men cared. They ate, shit and breathed violence. All the women raced down the steps to get their men, including Gray. She couldn't risk Cam hurting his self or going to jail. She'd never forgive herself. He'd warned her something like this would happen. She should've listened.

"Cam stop! Stop!" Devin tugged on his arm.

It was of no use. Cam had blacked out. He'd gone to that dark place hidden deep inside. His long legs rammed into the young boys rib cage with brute force. He savored letting out all his aggression. He needed this release after everything he'd been through. Niggas kept testing him like he wasn't a trained merciless killer. Niggas were gon' learn why his name rang bells in the streets. Niggas were gonna feel why he'd gotten the name Killa Cam.

"Baby stop!" Gray pulled him back. She didn't care that she'd called him an endearing pet name. It came natural and it got him to snap back to reality. Huffing and puffing, Cam gazed down at her face, but he wasn't all there. He still had a vacant look in his eyes. He was still in kill mode.

"Just breathe." She caressed the side of his face gently. "It's okay. I'm alright. It's just alcohol." She spoke in a soothing tone.

Slowly, Cam's breathing evened, and he calmed.

"Much better." Gray smiled with her eyes. "You're just determined to send me to an early grave."

"Not if you don't send me there first."

"Move!" Devin bumped Gray out the way. "Are my eyes playing tricks on me? Why the fuck you keep fighting her battles? She shaped like a whole Sumo wrestler. She big enough to fight for herself."

"And I'm big enough to beat yo' ass too. Play wit' me." Gray lunged in her direction, but Cam held her back.

"Move Cam! I should'a been fucked her up."

"Whew . . . the ghetto." Tee-Tee fanned his face.

"I don't understand why you always making it your business to save her!" Devin's anger rose.

"That's my fuckin' wife!" Cam roared in her face. "Fuck you mean."

"If she's your wife then why the fuck are you with me?"

"Good point." He took Gray by the hand and power walked towards the exist. The party was over.

"Cam wait! Where you going?" She went to race after him but was stopped by her friends.

"I know you ain't gon' chase after that nigga." Her girl Angie spat.

"Every chance he get, he play you to the left. Let that man be with that Beluga whale if he want to." Her other friend Naomi added.

"Y'all don't understand. *I love him.*" Devin whined, on the verge of a nervous breakdown.

"You better learn how to love yourself."

"Or Jesus 'cause this is sad." Angie shook her head as Devin cried into her arms.

Gray's heels clicked against the roadway as she tried her best to keep up with Cam. His long legs were able to stride much faster and wider than hers. Stars shined like sugar over black marble as he unlocked the passenger side door to his maroon colored Mercedes Benz G-Wagon.

"Get yo' hot ass in the car." He slung her forward.

"I ain't one of your kids. Don't tell me what to do."

Cam clenched his jaw and exhaled an irritated breath.

"Gray. . . I'm not in the mood for your shit. You heard what the fuck I said."

"Yeah-yeah-yeah." She flicked her wrist dismissively and climbed in.

Cam slammed the door and rounded the car, incensed. He was starting to think life was much easier when he was stuck in a coma. Life back in the real world was full of drama and unwanted chaos. Hopping into the driver seat, he sat back and took another much needed breath. He was still riled up from the fight. All of it was in vain. Before he could do his breathing exercises, Devin started blowing up his phone. Cam didn't hesitate to block her calls and throw his phone in the cup holder. Having to deal with Gray and her bullshit was bad enough. He didn't have the strength to put up with Devin's shit too. The charade of pretending they were in a relationship was draining him.

"Just like old times, right?" Gray smirked, placing her phone and purse on her lap.

"Don't start your shit. I'm not about to let you raise my blood pressure."

"You always threatening somebody. When are you gonna learn?" Gray placed her face next to his. "Unlike these niggas, I'm not scared of you."

"You scared of this dick tho." Cam grabbed a handful.

"LIES! I ain't never been scared. I rode that dick like a champ." Gray grinded her ass in her seat.

"Do it now then." Cam challenged, leaning back. "I'm wit' whatever. What you wanna do? I'ma slut. What's up? Get me lit. I dare you."

"Cam, you don't want this smoke."

"Yeah a'ight." He pushed the ignition and sped off into the night. "It's a whole different story when I got these 11-inches in you."

"Nigga, please. I could barely feel it."

"Bitch, you tried it."

"Call me another bitch!" She punched him in the arm with all her might.

"Instead of hitting me, I should be knocking yo' ass out." He thumped her in the head. "Why the fuck you come to my party with this bullshit on?"

"Don't flatter yourself. I didn't even know I was coming to your li'l funky ass party. And last I checked, whatever I wear is none of your concern. You don't wanna be with me, remember?"

"As long as you're my wife that shit gon' always concern me. Every time you come out the house wit' ya' ho shit on, I gotta knock a nigga the fuck out 'cause you wanna walk around like you Kash Doll or some shit. You a mother of five, Gray. Don't nobody need to be seeing your ass and titties but me."

"I wouldn't give a fuck if I were a mother of fifty-five. What I wear is none of your business. Worry about what Devin be wearing. That is who you want to be wit', right?"

"I don't give a fuck what she wear." Cam gripped the leather steering wheel.

"Yeah, okay." Gray scoffed. The fact that he kept avoiding her question was annoying the hell outta her.

"I don't care. Who the fuck I leave with? You."

"Didn't nobody ask you to take me home!" She turned around in her seat and glared at him. "You made me leave with you."

"Like somebody can make you do something you don't wanna do.

You the most hard headed muthafucka I know." Cam focused on the road.

The night rolled over bringing a threat of a storm. Gleaming stars lit up the moonless, onyx sky, as if to remind the world that even in darkness there was still light. The air was heavy with dry warm air. Fluffy white clouds covered majority of the sky. Even shadows were swallowed by the never-ending darkness. Gray sat gazing aimlessly out the front view of the truck. For once she didn't have a snappy comeback. Cam got on her nerves. It drove her crazy when he was right.

"Exactly. That's what I thought. You wanted to get in this car wit' me." He placed his hand on her inner thigh.

"If that's what you need to sleep at night." She smacked his hand away. "Just hurry up and get me home so I can go to sleep and get up for the kids' soccer game in the morning."

"While you call yourself having an attitude, I should be the one mad. Where the fuck my gift at?"

"I already gave you your gift." Gray avoided eye contact. Memories of her placing the pregnancy test in his comatose hand filled her mind. It was the saddest and happiest day of her life.

"There you go lying again. You ain't gave me shit." He stopped at a red light.

"How you gon' tell me what I did? You was in a coma, nigga."

"Cause you're a fuckin' liar, Gray." Cam drove up the ramp and hopped onto the highway.

The tires on the G-wagon made a monotonous hiss over the rain-washed pavement as he accelerated the engine. Neither him nor Gray made a sound. The only thing that could be heard was the radio. Each of them were deep in thought. The unexpected sound of her phone ringing disrupted their rumination. At the same time both of them looked down at her phone. Cam's face contorted into a deep scowl. It was Noon on the other end of the line.

"You better not." He warned on the verge of losing his shit.

Always the one to test the limits, Gray answered the phone call anyway. Why should she protect his feelings when he wasn't protecting hers?

"Hey babe." She turned down the volume and held the phone close to her ear. She didn't want Cam to hear Noon's end of the conversation.

"Huh?" Noon said caught off guard by the way she answered. "You alright?"

"I'm fine. What you doing? Why you up so late? Let me guess. You miss me?" She crossed one leg over the other and leaned towards the door. Cam glanced over and saw her exposed thigh. Just the thought of Noon's bitch ass touching it made him want to crash the truck into the median.

"Yo, what's good wit' you? You been drinking?" Noon questioned, caught off guard by her flirtatious nature.

"A little," she lied.

"I mean don't get me wrong. I like this sudden change but you're throwing me off."

"Hang up the fuckin' phone." Cam demanded. Any second he was gonna lose it.

"Who is that?" Noon sat up in bed. If it was who he thought it was, the gloves were coming off and he was going to destroy Cam.

"Nobody. Just some weird ass nigga trying to get my attention. I can't wait to see you Sunday. You gon' stay at my place when you get in town?" Gray continued to be extra.

"What's going on, Ladybug? You never let me stay at your crib."

"Miss Kitty miss you." She purred.

That was it. Gray had gone too far. Letting down the driver side window, Cam snatched the phone from her ear and threw it out into the darkness.

"You and Miss Kitty gon' die fuckin' around wit' me."

"Have you lost your fuckin' mind? I just got that phone!"

"So."

"So? Nigga, this ain't 2016!"

"But you still got me fucked up like it's 2016."

"Oh yeah?" Gray challenged, ready for war.

"Yeah nigga." Cam shrugged his shoulder before he caught onto what she was about to do. Before he could stop her, Gray grabbed his phone and tossed it out the passenger side window. Pulling the car over onto the shoulder, Cam deaded the engine and eyed her dumbfounded. Minutes passed while they just stared at each other. Finally, Cam broke the intense silence.

"So, we just gon' be two phoneless muthafuckas?"

Gray erupted into a fit of laughter. Cam followed right behind her. They needed this. Holding his stomach, he admired her gorgeous face and smiled. Gray's laughter was like summer rain, soft and tranquil. Every time he heard it, no matter the weather, his world brightened. Gray always said she hated her laugh, but every time Cam heard her sniggering through her nose, snorting adorably, he fell a little more in love with her.

"I guess so." Gray's laughter trailed off.

"I can't stand yo' water head ass."

"Feelings fuckin' mutual." She teased, enjoying their banter. Years had passed since they last had a moment like this. Cam didn't want to fuck up the mood, but he was dying to know one thing.

"On some real shit. Why you wit' that nigga?"

Instantaneously, Gray's entire vibe changed. She was so over him playing with her heart.

"Now you about to piss me off for real. Don't ask me no stupid shit like that. You know damn well why."

"I'm just sayin'." He massaged his jaw. "Even though me and you ain't together right now, don't mean you gotta be with him."

"So, I'm just supposed to be alone while you're with somebody else? You have rejected me twice. At some point I have to move on."

"No, you don't."

"What?" She jerked furious.

"You don't need to do shit but be patient wit' a nigga. Like I said before, it's a lot of shit you don't understand."

"No, I understand just fine. You wanna string me along when it's convenient for you. You wanna fuck me whenever you want and do you on the side and I'm not going for it. I'm Gray Rose, nigga." She pointed her hand like a gun. "I'm a fuckin' prize and should be treated as such." She mushed him in the forehead again.

"Parthens, my nigga. Gray Rose . . . Parthens." He stressed. "And I agree you are a fuckin' prize."

"I know am. You ain't telling me nothing I don't already know."

"It's a lot of shit you don't know. You have a right to be upset but it's just a lot you don't understand right now."

"Make me understand then!" She yelled as *Moment* by Victoria Monét came on.

I got a feeling that yoooooooou
Brought me to you

Unable to keep his feelings at bay, Cam gripped the back of her neck and pulled her close. Without permission his lips crashed into hers. He was supposed to be keeping up the façade of him and Devin being together but the emotions he harbored for his wife couldn't be contained. Gray wanted to protest, but as soon as his mouth landed on her lips, the whole world fell away. The kiss was everything she craved and more. It was soft, slow and comforting in ways that words would never be. It was as if their celestial souls had been in captivity and were finally breaking free. Falling stars gathered at their feet as their tongues beautifully danced. In the depth of euphoria moans dripped from their lips like confessions at a Catholic church. Cam and Gray wore the fragrance of long lost lovers as he pulled her body onto his. Gray straddled his waist as the driver seat was pushed back. Greedily their hands roamed each other's bodies. They were starving for one another's flesh. Erratic heartbeats pounded like bass drums. Cam bathed himself in the fervent swipes of her tongue.

Look what your mind's imagination can dooooooooooooooo
Making shit true

Yeah, you do, babe

Gray couldn't believe she was allowing this to happen. Having sex with Cam was the last thing she needed but it had been months and her body needed to be replenished. Hastily, he undid the piece of cloth she called a top. In the semi-darkness, Cam's eyes journeyed from her face to her neck, then to her breasts. The nipple covers she wore were swiftly removed. Without support, her bountiful breasts sat lower and further apart, but each were perfectly sculpted to her physique. Cam didn't let his eyes linger there too long, just enough for her to see how magnificent she was to him. It was her indigo eyes that he wanted to focus on. Her eyes were like candles in that night, their light a spark of desire. Palming her full breasts, he sandwiched them together. There was nothing more bewitching than Gray in naked form. Her nipples were like mountain peaks. He couldn't wait to devour them. Mesmerized by her erect nipples, he ran his thumb across them then took each into his sweltering mouth.

The hairs on the back of Gray's arm rose as the sensation of his tongue flickering across her nipples caused her temperature to spike. Her head drifted backwards as Cam sucked his way from her breasts to her neck. Any hesitancy she had about taking it there with him vanished. In that moment she was alive in the present. All thoughts of past and future melted away. This was their moment. This was black love at its finest.

So, let me take away your pain
Give me all of your emotions

Caught up in the rapture of her love, Cam roughly palmed the crease of her hips. His face was tucked in the base of her neck as his dick grazed her slit. With each stroke, Gray's butter cream threatened to leak from her center. Cam slid his hand inside the front of her skirt. It didn't take long for his fingers to find her dampness. Parting her wet fold, he slowly eased two fingers into her warm cave. Gray inhaled a gulp of air. Her heart thudded inside her heaving chest. But don't be mistaken. The acceleration of her heartrate had nothing to do with fear and everything to do with what her body yearned for. It had been so long since she'd been touched. This was bliss. Heaven had to feel like this. Her entire body shuttered with delight as he thumbed her firm clit. Round and round he massaged her into a frenzy. Gray wind her hips and matched his rhythm. A kaleidoscope of colors developed behind her closed eyes. This was an addiction. It had to be. Only he could have her naked and exposed on the side of the highway. Anyone could see them, but she didn't care. Cam could have her anyway he wanted. Fuck, chivalry. The shit was dead. Gray was a lowkey freak and he knew that.

There wasn't a glimmer of a smile on Cam's face. The hot intensity of his gaze penetrated her soul as he pushed her skirt above her waist. Next her thong was ripped off and thrown out the window. The ripping of the fabric stung her hips, but she didn't mind. Everything Cam did to her turned her on. Gray's pussy lips were damp with dew as she placed her heels on the seat, pushed back, and rested her shoulder blades against the steering wheel. Her mound of Venus was smooth and bare. Naughtily, she spread her pussy lips apart with her fingers. She'd waited weeks for him to taste her. Cam ate pussy like it was his last supper.

The rest of the world became an irrelevant blur that was exiled into the far recesses of his brain. The scent of her muskiness overwhelmed his senses. The only thing that mattered more than touching her was making her climax. It was his mission to make her scream his name. Cam needed to hear it. Had to hear it. His dick bricked up on sight of seeing her pretty pink flesh.

"Look at this shit." Feverishly, he kissed her clit as her juices crossed his parted lips. "Look how pretty she is. Miss Kitty miss me?"

"God, yes." Gray's eyes rolled to the back of her head. "You miss her?"

"I miss the fuck out her pretty ass."

Still thirsty, Cam raised her ass in the air and took deeper sips.

Gray's hips bucked forward from the spine tingling sensation. Cam wasn't playing fair. Like the devil, he was there to kill and destroy.

"Ooh shit." She bit into her lower lip.

Cam was wreaking havoc on her pussy. He ate her out like he hated her. The erotic assault brought Gray to a writhing orgasm that rocked her to her core. Needing the D, she unzipped his pants and pulled them down to his knees. A river of wetness flooded her silky smooth thighs. Gray wanted Cam in the worst way. Sweat started to form all over her body. From there on in it was all passion and intense animalistic love-making. Cam's 11-inch dick stood at attention, tall and strong. He had the prettiest dick she'd ever seen. Not only was the length astonishing but the girth was equally astounding. The crock in it made it even more special. Her mouth watered from the sight of it. Cam's dick was deli-cious. Gray wanted to taste all 32 flavors of his cum. This dick was hers. It was made for her. It was art in human form. Gently, she wrapped her hand around the crown. After a few soft strokes, Cam lined his dick up with her center. Thrusting upwards, he pushed through her warm flesh and entered her completely, stretching her wide. He was only one stroke in and already wanted to bust. Gray's pussy was extra gushy. She'd never been this wet before. Cam didn't know if he was just super horny or if there was something truly different about the way she felt but damn did she have his head spin-ning. Sex between he and Gray had always been next level. Being with her was like having a glass of cold lemonade on a hot summer day; it always quenched his thirst, but this shit was other worldly. Gray held onto him tight and gasped for air. She was filled to the brim. His rock solid veiny cock felt like it was rising up her throat. The feel of him hurt so good. All those nights in the hospital she dreamed of a moment like this. Gray would've gave all her worldly possessions, hell her life, just to feel him inside of her again. When she was in Cam's arms she'd never felt more loved, more secure or beautiful. It was truly devas-tating that during sex was the only time they could emotionally connect.

Life is but a dream
Here we are inside of it
and you're inside of me
Until you actually fall asleep
Finally you can add this moment
to your memory

"Shit, I missed this." She moaned as tears welled in her eyes.

"Me too, baby. Me too." Cam pumped with reckless abandon.

The faster he stroked the louder Gray cried. To quiet her whimpers, he kissed her with such raw intensity that it took her breath away. Arms and legs entangled, Gray rode the wave of passion. Cam was fucking her brains out. She was sure she wouldn't be able to walk afterward. The tightness of her pink was of no consequence to him. He stroked his way through that shit.

"Oh my God. Please don't stop. I'm almost there." She held onto his neck.

Cam's eyes searched hers. Gray blushed and kissed him back as he knew she would. With his lips he could feel her mouth stretching wider than it should, fighting between a grin and a French kiss. She was enjoying this just as much as he was. It was inevitable. Their bond was eternal. A love like theirs couldn't be extinguished by the likes of Gunz, Lala, Noon or Devin. When he was in her arms he felt love, safety and passion too. It was what brought him back to life. Only his Star could revive what was lost and restore what was shattered. They were born to love each other unconditionally. In a whirlwind of pleasure and pain, Gray continued to ride him despite the fullness she felt. Cam's cock was at its deepest. She could feel him in the center of her lungs. All she could do was dig her nails into his skin. An unstoppable snowball began to form in the pit of her belly. Gray couldn't concentrate on anything else but it. Thrusting deeper, Cam bucked and humped his way to her sweet orgasmic center. The honey pot of nectar he discovered caused his body to quake. Gray squeezed her pussy tight as they both reached their orgasmic high. Like a volcano, Cam's dick erupted deep within her womb. He prayed one of his seeds connected to one of her eggs. Cam wanted another baby more than anything.

Gray felt every drop of cum splash against her walls. If she wasn't already pregnant she'd damn well be that night.

"Fuck." He held her tight as she convulsed.

Gray's stomach contracted violently as she experienced the best orgasm of her life. No matter how long they were married, they were always lovers first. Life brought so many changes, from babies to youthful teens to breakups to makeups. There were ups and downs and periods of closeness that linked them together forever. Despite the bickering and arguing, Cam and Gray always found a way back to being lovers, to passion's first true kiss, to that moment of union that made their love everlasting. Couples like them were meant to be. Things that were meant to tear them apart only made them stronger.

CHAPTER 21

"You say I'm selfish, get it all off your chest. If we're being honest, without you I'ma mess."-Pink Sweat$ "No Replacing You"

*B*right eyed and bushy tailed, Cam chirped the alarm on his candy apple red Porsche 911. He hadn't felt this good in years. For the first time in forever his mind and body were relaxed. Happiness tingled from his fingers to his toes. He felt it rush through him like an ocean wave. He'd had the best sleep of his life. By sunrise he was up and at 'em. He couldn't wait to see Gray, so he got dressed in an army fatigue baseball cap, a long sleeve white shirt with a short sleeve khaki button up over it, fitted khaki pants and custom made brown leather Louis Vuitton Jordan mid retro 1's. Gold frame Cartier shades, a gold chain with a picture of his mother and his wedding ring was the only jewelry he wore. Not only did he look good enough to eat but he smelled even better. Notes of gardenia, rosewood, honey accord and plum from his Byredo Casablanca Lily cologne permeated from his pores. With a dip in his stride, he made his way up the walk way to Gray's house. The last time he'd been there was the night before the wedding when they'd made passionate love. He'd also signed off on the divorce that night, which made him wonder what Gray had done with the paperwork. Did she file them in court? He prayed to God she hadn't. But there was no telling with her. She was a live wire. She acted off emotion. He couldn't risk her taking legal action. That would be yet another problem he'd have to deal with. He had to get the ball rolling. His enemies were piling up and his marriage was holding on by a thread. Niggas had to meet their maker and quick. Taking out his key, he placed it in the lock and opened the door. Cam wasn't even two steps in when a 12 gauge shotgun was aimed at his head.

"Freeze muthafucka!" Mrs. Mariam cocked the hammer. Her bifocal glasses sat on the tip of her nose by a silver chain. The yellow floral duster she wore ballooned over her small frame. Mrs. Mariam was 110 pounds soaking wet. The wrinkles and folds of her skin were now so noticeable it was hard to tell what she might've looked like as a young woman. Apparently she was once admired, courted and coiffed. Now she looked like a saggy and deflated balloon. Cam furrowed his brows, shocked to see the racist old lady. The shotgun was bigger than her. She could barely keep it up, her arms were so frail. She would probably end up shooting herself before she shot him.

Never the one to let a person pull a gun on him, Cam quickly pulled out his and aimed it back at her. He didn't give a fuck that she was his elder. He'd shoot her ass dead and not think shit about it.

"What the fuck yo' old ass doing here?" He curled his finger around the trigger.

"Keeping your kind outta my neighborhood. And what the hell are you doing here DJ Jazzy Jeff? I thought we got rid of you!"

"And I thought you was dead."

"You got five seconds to hightail yo' high yellow ass outta here or I'm pulling the trigger." She tried to keep the gun up right even though the weight was wearing on her arms.

"Yo' decrepit ass can barely see let alone shoot. Gray come get this old bitch before I pump two in her chest!" Cam yelled ready to fuck Mrs. Mariam's old ass up.

Surprised to hear his voice in her home, Gray rushed from the back. He hadn't told her he was coming by. The plan was for him to meet them at the soccer game. She wasn't at all prepared for what she was about to see. There her elderly neighbor and husband were holding each other at gunpoint.

"What the hell are y'all doing? Mrs. Mariam, put that damn gun down!" She ordered.

"Why you got this racist bitch around my kids anyway?" Cam barked.

"Bitch? Well, I never." Mrs. Mariam faced the gun towards the floor.

"Melody had a family emergency and had to return to Paris. I needed help with the kids and Mrs. Mariam offered to help." Gray explained.

"You know she don't like black people." Cam argued.

"Well, they're only half black so I like the other half of them." Mrs. Mariam corrected him.

"Mrs. Mariam, I have told you about your mouth." Gray shot her a look. "And how did you get in here?" She focused on Cam. "Did you use your key?"

"I sure did." Cam tucked his gun back inside the waistband of his pants.

"You can't just be walking up in my house." Gray sprinted over and snatched the keys from his hand. Just because they'd slept together didn't mean that he could go all alpha male on her and boguard his way back into her life. He'd made his choice. Now it was time for him to live with the outcome.

"Our house."

"My house." She took her house key off his key chain. "My name is on the deed. Not yours."

"Gray, you need to get a better handle on these coloreds. They have no respect." Mrs. Mariam shook her head.

"Who you calling colored?" Cam charged towards her.

"You're the only one standing here."

"That's enough." Gray jumped in-between them. "Mrs. Mariam, what did I tell you. You can't call black people colored."

"Well, I can't say the other word. Everybody makes such a big deal about it nowadays." She huffed.

"Thanks for your help, Mrs. Mariam." Gray said ready for her to leave. "We're about to go. You wanna take a plate of food home with you?" She'd made a big breakfast for her and the kids.

"Oh nooooooo. I like you, but I know about your kind." Mrs. Mariam pursed her lips together, disgusted.

"Mrs. Mariam, you tap dancing on my last nerve." Gray warned, ready to go off.

"I'm sorry, Gray. I'm trying to do better." The old woman apologized.

"Mmm hmm." She side-eyed her. Kids, come say bye to Mrs. Mariam!"

The pitter patter of tiny feet rang in the air as the kids ran from their rooms. The triplets were dressed in their red and white soccer uniforms and cleats. It was the cutest thing Cam had ever seen. Press walked into the living area with her face planted into a first edition copy of Moby Dick Cam had bought for her. Like Mrs. Mariam, her glasses swallowed her face. Press was enthralled by the story, but when she looked up and spotted her Appa standing there, a grin spread across her face. Just as quickly as her smile appeared it disappeared. Press was self-conscious about her new set of braces. Life was already hard for her because she was a mixed girl that wore glasses. Now things were ten times harder. The kids at school had dubbed her Brace Face. No matter how much Gray and Cam affirmed her beauty, Press hated the way she looked. When she looked into the mirror she hated the reflection staring back at her. All she saw was a dorky, four-eyed girl with a pudgy stomach. It wasn't surprising that King had chosen Sanya over her. At school Sanya made her life a living hell. She thought about telling Aoki but changed her mind. She didn't want to make things worse for herself. Press tried her best to keep a low profile. She mostly kept to herself. The only friend she had besides King was Stacy's daughter, Kyla. They had lunch during the same period and sat together every day. Kyla was the exact opposite of her. She was beyond confident. She was the Queen Bee of their 5th grade class. All the girls flocked to her. Press hoped one day she'd have as much self-confidence as her. Aoki was the only one that didn't bother to come out and speak. She refused to be fake. She didn't see it for Mrs. Mariam or Cam.

"Bye, Mrs. Mariam." The triplets hugged her.

"I swear Gray, you got some of the prettiest Oriental kids I've ever seen." She hugged them back.

"Oh, hell no! You gotta go! Get the hell out before I go to jail for fucking your old ass up!" Gray pushed her out the door. She'd had enough of her bigoted verbiage to last a lifetime.

"Crazy bitch!" Cam barked behind her. "Here." He handed Gray a brand new iPhone 11 Pro Max. He'd gotten them both new phones.

"Thank you. I thought I was gonna have to go to the Apple store today."

"Y'all ready for y'all birthday party tomorrow?" He asked.

"YES!"

"I'm wearing my princess dress, daddy." Sky beamed.

"You are? You gon' look so pretty baby girl. Daddy can't wait to see it."

"Daddy, you going to the game with us?" Beaux excitedly hopped up and down. Her energy was through the roof.

"No." Gray responded on his behalf.

"Yes. Y'all go get y'all stuff ready."

"Cam, you are not riding with us. You have your own car."

"Y'all want daddy to ride wit' y'all?"

"Yes!" The triplets jumped around.

"No." Aoki appeared out of nowhere.

"Shut up, Aoki." Press sneered, rolling her eyes. She didn't want her to push Cam away with her negativity. Her real father hadn't made an effort to be there for her. Press needed Cam in her life more than anyone would ever know. His unconditional love meant everything to her. Gray was her mother, she had to love her, but Cam wasn't obligated to. He was just her step-father. He didn't have to make her a priority, so the fact that he went above and beyond to be a stable force in her life gave Press the fatherly love and security she'd lost with Gunz.

"It's settled then. Let's go." Cam grabbed the kids' soccer bags and jackets.

"Cam, I'm not playing with you. You're not going with us." Gray picked up her black leather Hermès bag. The purse paired well with her black Celine shades, gold hoop Ippolita earrings, black Frame tee, vintage Gloria Vanderbilt jeans, Christian Dior belt and Isabel Marant black leather slouchy boots. Cam looked at his wife with admiration in his eyes. He loved her effortless beauty. Gray had the kind of looks that put supermodels to shame. After locking up the house, the entire family headed over to Gray's electric blue Mercedes G-Class. While she wasn't paying attention, Cam stole the key fob from her hand.

"Give 'em back!" She yelled not in the mood for his antics.

"Nope." He opened the back doors so the kids could get in.

"Why do you want my keys?"

"Cause I'm driving. Get in the passenger seat."

"This my car. You get in the passenger seat." She snapped.

"Like I give a fuck. You can get in the passenger seat or the pumpkin seat for all I care. Either way you ain't driving me."

"C'mon mom, we're gonna be late." Beaux whined as Cam strapped her into her car seat.

"Ooh, you better be lucky." Gray snarled at Cam.

"Lucky my ass. You ain't gon' do shit. Wit' yo' cute ass." He pinched her cheek.

"Get off me." Gray swatted his arm.

When the entire Parthens clan was strapped into their seats, Cam got in on the driver side and started the ignition. *Love on Top* by Beyoncé started playing. There was no way Cam was listening to that girly shit. Without asking, he connected his Bluetooth to her system and started to play some music of his own. King Von hood anthem *Crazy Story* bumped loudly. The little kids started going dumb when the track came on. Every time they were with Cam they asked him to play it. Gray looked over her shoulder and spotted Beaux bouncing her tiny shoulders to the beat. Sky was rocking her booty from side-to-side with her hands in the air. Somehow Reign had gotten ahold to a giant red Lego piece. Screwing up his face, he pointed the Lego like it was a gun while he rapped the lyrics to the song.

But this what happen, I got to the door, I thought I was capping
I was lacking, 'cause there go the opps, yelling out: what's cracking?
I'm like, "What?" I'm like, "Nigga who?" I was born to shoot
I got aim, I'm like Johnny Dang when it comes to chains
So I rise, hit one in his arm, hit one in his thigh, this no lie
Bitch it's do or die, you said you gon' slide
You got some nerve, your shit on the curb, boy we put in work
From 64th, and from 65th, we not from 63rd

Gray was dumbfounded. Her precious baby boy had morphed into a baby goon. This was all Cam's fault. To make matter worse, Cam looked through the rearview mirror with a shit eating grin on his face, encouraging the nonsense. And to think she was about to have another baby with him. All Gray could do was lean her head against the window. They couldn't get to the soccer game fast enough. She needed Cam to give her fifty feet.

In the backseat, Aoki gazed absently out the window. It was a sunny fall day. Besides summer, autumn was her favorite time of the year. Not only was her birthday that month but the weather was perfect. The sun rose and set as if on fast-forward, as if there was some divine rush to reach the winter. Sidewalks were awash with multi-colored offerings from the trees. Though the sunrays beamed from the sky, it was still cooler on the days that lacked clouds. Dazzling shafts of sunlight shined down on the streets filled with reds and gold leaves. Each breath of fresh air that drifted through the window filled her with a sense of life that made her want to shout. Adjusting to a new school and making new friends was tough at first but she'd found her way. She'd taken a squad of girls and deemed them worthy enough of being a part of her squad. They mobbed together like they ran the place. Blizz was still trying to shoot his shot but she'd seen him get bitched out by Paris too many times to call him her boo thang. And just like that the boy that tormented her dreams text her. Aoki swore the breath in her lungs evaporated. The palms of her hands began to sweat. Her mouth went dry. She could feel her heartbeat . . . every single pound in the center of her chest. Aoki didn't move a muscle. This was what he did to her. He made her a nervous wreck. She was frozen stiff. A militia of chills marched down her spine. The booming of her heart got louder with each pound. He hadn't hit her up since the day of the party. That had been two months before. What did he want now? She'd never know until she opened up the text. Queasily, she tapped the message.

PARIS: Yo

Aoki paused and stared at the screen. No, he didn't. This nigga was so rude. They hadn't spoken in weeks and this was what he decided to text her? Instead of responding right back, she waited a few minutes before replying. She refused to seem pressed. What she didn't know was that Paris didn't know what else to say. All he knew was that he missed her more than a nigga like him should. Distancing himself from her had been a harder task than he expected. There was an ongoing ache in his chest that came and went, but no matter what, it always returned. Paris would give anything to keep her close, to talk and laugh like they once did. And yes, her absence in his life was his fault. A decision had to be made that he wasn't ready to make. Aoki wouldn't settle for anything but the best of him. The problem was Paris didn't know how to be good to anyone, not even his self. He had some shit with him that a girl like Aoki wouldn't be able to understand. He didn't want to taint her with his bullshit. She didn't deserve that, but damn did he miss the sound of her voice.

AOKI: What

PARIS: WYD Thief

AOKI: With the fam

She responded dryly.

PARIS: What y'all doing

Aoki curled her nose. She didn't understand what his motive for texting her was. Placing her head down, she tried to figure out what her response would be. She had no idea that Cam was staring at her through the rearview mirror. His heart sank. The look on Aoki's face was the same one he'd placed on hundreds of girls. Some li'l knuckle head nigga had infiltrated his baby girl's heart. Cam wasn't ready for this shit. Aoki was only thirteen. He thought he had a few more years before he had to deal with some shit like this. He should've known better. Aoki was a gorgeous girl. She didn't even look thirteen. Niggas were most definitely checking for her. He made a mental note to have a talk with her as soon as possible. It was important that he see where her brain was at. Whoever this boy was, the li'l nigga had already dug his claws into her. It was one thing if she was just infatuated with the nigga, but if he had her mind, it was a wrap. There wouldn't be a thing Cam could say to get her to slow down. He prayed to God he wasn't too late.

AOKI: Why

She finally replied.

PARIS: Cause I wanna know . . . the fuck

AOKI: Who u cursing at

She typed back quickly.

PARIS: U . . . nigga

AOKI: Why don't u ask that bald-headed bitch where she at wit' her family.

PARIS: Stop discriminating against bitches wit' no edges. Everybody can't have pretty hair like u.

AOKI: Just cuz I have a silky grade of hair don't mean it's prettier or better than anyone else's. Stay woke li'l nigga.

PARIS: A'ight Angela Rye

A roar of laughter erupted from Aoki's belly. Paris got on her nerves. She hated the effect he had on her. Thank God he wasn't in her face to see her reaction. She couldn't let a cocky nigga like him know he'd gained an inch because he'd take a mile.

"What the fuck you laughing at?" Cam shouted, causing her to nearly jump out of her skin.

Aoki clutched her chest. Cam had scared the shit outta her.

"None of yo' business. Pay attention to the road. Traitor!" She remarked, placing her attention back on her phone.

"Call me another traitor. I'll kill everybody in here."

"Don't be saying no stupid shit like that!" Gray mushed him in the side of his head.

"You ain't gon' be Ike 'ing me li'l girl. This all yo' fault anyway. You be calling me a fuckin' traitor behind my back?"

"I'll call you one to your face."

"Yeah a'ight." Cam sucked his teeth.

"*Yeah a'ight.*" Aoki taunted him. "You've been threatening to kill me since I was ten and I'm still alive. When you gon' pull the trigger, bruh? I'm starting to question yo' gangsta."

"That's your word?" Cam stared at her through the rearview mirror.

"On blood gang, nigga." Aoki formed her fingers into the letter B.

"Sky . . . get the strap."

"No daddy. I don't wanna get the strap. You can't kill sissy." She began to cry uncontrollably.

"See what you did. Dumb ass." Gray turned around in her seat and faced her angel. "Sky stop crying. Daddy's not gonna kill Aoki."

"You promise?" She hiccupped.

"I promise."

"The fuck I ain't." Cam put his foot down.

"It's okay, Sky." Aoki wrapped her up in her embrace. "Yo daddy all talk and no action."

"Wait till we get out this car. I'm busting yo' ass." Cam pointed his finger over his shoulder.

"You can't even catch me wit' yo' wheezing ass. *Huuuuuuuuuuuuh ha-ha-ha huuuuuuuuuuuuuuuh.*" She started breathing heavily like Biz Markie.

Gray and Cam erupted into a fit of laughter. Even he couldn't pretend that the joke wasn't funny. Aoki and the rest of the kids giggled hysterically too. Their family was nothing short of dysfunctional, but she wouldn't have it any other way. Aoki was so caught up with going back-and-forth with Cam, she'd forgotten all about her conversation with Paris.

PARIS: HELLO!!!!! Fuck u doing

AOKI: My pop watching me like a hawk. I'ma hit u when I get to my destination

PARIS: U better

The rest of the car ride Gray zoned out and pretended like she was on an island in Tahiti. The noisy rap music, screaming kids and Cam starting fights with everyone was driving her nuts. All she wanted to do was go back home and lay down. The little munchkin in her tummy was making her super tired. When they got to the soccer field she leaped out of the car. Homegirl was in desperate need of some fresh air. Cam followed suit and exited the vehicle as well. They both helped get the triplets out of their seats. Cam held Beaux and Sky by their hands as they walked across the parking lot. Gray carried Reign.

"If you don't put his big ass down."

"Leave me alone, Cam. I'll carry my baby as much as I want." She nestled Reign's head against her chest. He would never understand their relationship. So far, Reign was her only son. Their mother/son bond was special. For Gray, it was the purest form of love. She vowed to protect her prince at all cost. It was impossible but Gray wished he could stay this small forever. In Reign's young world nothing was more important than his mommy. He held onto her every word. And much like his father, he thought she was the prettiest girl on earth. Once they reached the field, Gray placed him on the ground. His sisters raced over to their team, but Reign clung to her leg for dear life.

"Mommy, I don't wanna play." He whined.

"But you have to buddy. Your team needs you." She rubbed his back lovingly.

"That's his problem. You keep babying him." Aoki typed on her phone as she sashayed by.

"Facts." Cam agreed. His little man had to toughen up. He didn't mind him expressing his feelings and being vulnerable. He was a toddler. That's what they were supposed to do but Gray was gonna make him hella soft.

"We ain't on teams, bruh. I don't need you agreeing with me." Aoki hit him with the screw face.

"Aoki, don't make me wear yo' ass out in front of all these peoples." Cam pointed his finger at her. He was two seconds off her ass.

"Mmm hmm." She sat next to Press on the bleacher.

"Come on, Reigny! We need you on the field!" Coach Roberts clapped his hands.

"Go head, baby. Make mommy proud." Gray edged him onto the grass.

Reign walked with the speed of a turtle. That day their team the Tiny Tykes were up against the Bumblebees. Gray placed her purse down beside her and watched as the kids lined up on either side of the center circle. The Bumblebees player kicked the ball and the game began. All the kids ran after the ball as fast as they could. There was no coordination. Everyone was going in different directions. It was a mess. The kids were having a grand old time tho. Gray rested her chin on her hand and smiled. It was the cutest thing she'd ever been blessed to see. Sky and Beaux were all into it, but Reign didn't move an inch. He just stood there in the center of the field pouting while all the other kids ran by him.

Cam sat next to Gray. They were so close his arm brushed up against hers. The side of her that wanted to play tough died to tell him to move but the soft pink side of her liked having him so close. *You so damn stupid,* she mentally chastised herself. How had she gone from being his enemy, to his lover, to his wife, to his baby mama, to his soon-to-be ex-wife, to his side chick? Everything was so confusing. Cam claimed to want Devin but every chance he got he was up in her face. Was all of this game? Was he stringing her along and playing with her emotions to pay her back for everything she'd done? That had to be the reason because nothing else made sense. If it was the last thing she did, Gray was gonna figure out a way to get from under the spell he'd cast on her.

"Yo' big bobble head ass gon' sit there and ignore me?" He studied the plains of her face. *My god she is beautiful*, Cam lustfully licked his bottom lip. He could stare at Gray for the rest of his life and never get tired. He was truly a lucky man. The big homey upstairs was really looking out for the kid when he blessed him with her. He couldn't wait to freely love on her, kiss her and hold her hand. Too much time had been spent apart.

"Go Beaux!" Gray placed her fingers in her mouth and whistled.

"Star, I know you hear me." Cam tried to get her attention.

Hearing his nickname for her almost made her blush but Gray held her composure and kept a straight face. As an alternative, she treated him like a ghost and raised to her feet. Beaux had gotten possession of the ball.

"Way to go Beaux! Get it girl!"

"You really gon' act like last night didn't happen?"

"It didn't. *It was all a dream. I used to read Word Up magazine. Salt-n-Pepa and Heavy D up in the limousine.*" She sang lyrics from a Biggie Smalls' song.

"When did everything become a joke with you?" He mean-mugged her.

"Well, ain't that the pot calling the kettle black." She retook her seat.

"You play too much, Gray. Then you wanna get mad when I cuss you the fuck out."

"Cause you go too far."

"You wasn't saying that last night."

"I don't know what you talking about." She played dumb.

"There you go lying again. At this point I think you gotta problem.

You just like to lie." He scoffed, annoyed by her passive aggressive behavior.

"Look at Reign." Gray pointed onto the field. He'd finally gotten into the game, but he and several other kids went for the ball at the same time and collided into each other. Like a set of a bowling pins they all fell down. The other children rebounded and resumed playing as if it was nothing. Reign, however, being the dramatic child he was lay sprawled out on the grass like a dead fish.

"C'mon buddy! Get up!" Cam encouraged him. "Dust that shit off li'l man!"

Reign didn't listen at all. He simply lay there with his arms and legs spread wide. The funny thing was he wasn't even hurt. He just didn't wanna play. To make matters worse, the soccer ball was kicked in his direction. Instead of going after it Reign just lay there and let it roll over his leg. Coach Roberts literally had to go onto the field and help him up.

"That's right! Get back in the game son!" Cam clapped his hands with exuberance.

Reign went after the ball again. This time he was doing good. He'd almost gotten to the ball, but another kid side swiped him and kicked it first. Once again, Reign went tumbling to the ground. The crowd let out a collective sigh. Cam threw his hands up in the air defeated. What happened next would be something they'd laugh about for years. As Reign fell, all Cam saw was his little legs fly in the air and him roll over onto his side. It was the saddest thing he'd ever seen. Cam couldn't do anything but massage his temples and laugh. Soccer was obviously not Reign's sport.

"Get up buddy!" Gray shouted from the sidelines.

All the kids ran around him as he lay on his side with one of his arms behind him. Gray didn't know what to make of it. She'd never witnessed anything like it.

"Reign, are you hurt?" She asked.

"No!" He answered rolling all the way over. Gray watched on

mortified. Instead of dusting himself off and trying again, he started rolling down the field like he was on fire.

"Oh God." She shielded her face from the other parents. Gray had never been more embarrassed in her life.

"That's yo' son." Cam bugged up laughing.

"No, he ain't. That's yo' son." Gray snickered too. "I love him, but he is terrible at soccer."

"I think that's the first time you've told the truth." Cam teased.

"Whatever."

Together they sat back down and continued to watch the game. The last thing Gray wanted to do was have a deep, heartfelt conversation but she and Cam needed to get real with one another. Boundaries had to be set in place. If they weren't, things between them would continue to spiral out of control.

"On some real shit, last night was a mistake."

"Don't piss me off, Gray." He clenched his jaw.

"You the one that brought the conversation up. I didn't even wanna talk about this shit. I was gonna go on with my life and pretend it never happened."

"You always on that bullshit. Well, guess what? You got your wish. I don't wanna talk about it either."

"Every time somebody say something you don't like they always on that bullshit. No, you were on some bullshit last night when you fucked me, knowing damn well you're with loose puss." Gray shot with venom.

"I haven't touched that girl." He told the God's honest truth. He would never violate or disrespect her like that. Not now. Not ever. "But don't act like you ain't wit that Poindexter looking muthafucka." Cam called her out.

"And whose fault is that?"

"Yours. Didn't nobody tell you to start back fuckin' wit him."

"Even if I wasn't fucking with him, I still shouldn't be fucking with you. Like I said last night, you only want me when it's convenient for you."

"Spell convenient, since you know everything." He challenged.

"I'm for real, Cam. I'm not gon' keep repeating this same fucked-up cycle. We've been on this merry-go-round for four years now. It's time for me to get off. Moving forward we just need to figure out a way to co-parent."

Tired of arguing and fighting, Cam decided it was time to tell her the truth. He would let the chips fall where they may with Victor. If he had to go head-to-head with him then so be it. Nine-times-out-of-ten, he would die in the process, but he couldn't let Noon continue to play puppet master with his life. It ate him up that Gray thought he didn't want her. In all actuality, he wanted her more than life itself. Before he could even reveal his secret, Sky landed her first goal. The crowd erupted in a wave of applause. Gray and Cam immediately shot up and cheered her on.

"That's my girl!" Cam yelled like the proud father he was.

"Yay Sky! Get it mama!" Gray jumped up and down.

Sky searched the crowd for her mother. It didn't take her long to find her. Gray was the only mom there dressed like she was about to rip the runway.

"I did it, mommy!" She waved her hand enthusiastically. Then things went left when a little boy from the opposite team picked up the ball and threw it directly at the side of her head.

"Oh shit." Aoki gasped. Sky had gotten her shit rocked. "He knocked the shit outta her."

"She gon' have a concussion." Press shook her head.

Immediately, Sky burst into a heap of tears. Cam couldn't get to his baby girl fast enough. Before he could reach her, Reign who'd been playing a game of stop, drop and roll for the last ten minutes stopped playing possum and raced over to his sister. Sky held the side of her head as she cried hysterically. Reign didn't hesitate to wrap his arms around her neck and kiss her cheek.

"It's okay, sissy. Don't cry. You're strong, remember?" He made a fist.

Sky nodded her head. Reign was right. She was strong. In no time she stopped sobbing. Reign used his thumb and wiped away her tears.

"All better." He kissed her cheek again. Reign hated to see his sisters cry. While he comforted Sky, Beaux balled up her tiny fist and socked the boy from the Bumblebees in the eye. The little boy released a loud wail which caught the referees attention. The whistle was blown, and Beaux was ejected from the game. Cam saw red.

"Yo, is you dumb? That li'l muthafucka was the one who hit my daughter on purpose. He should be the one getting kicked out the game." He stepped to the referee.

"I didn't see that, and we don't condone violence." The middle-aged white man replied.

"Honey, are you okay?" The little boy's mom caressed the side of his face.

"No." He sobbed.

"Don't worry about it son. She can't hurt you anymore. She was put out the game." The boy's father shot Cam an evil glare.

"All y'all got me fucked up today! You gon' put his Opie lookin' ass out the game! If my daughter can't play that muthafucka can't play neither!"

"Period!" Aoki yelled from the stands.

"Sir, your language is unacceptable. If you don't calm down and go back to your seat, I'm gonna have to ask you to leave." The ref said.

"What the fuck you mean we gotta leave?" Gray ran up. "You ain't gon' sit here and tell me you didn't see him hit my daughter with the ball!"

"Like I told your baby daddy, I didn't. Now please have a seat."

"No, he didn't." Gray looked at Cam.

"Oh, yes did." Cam responded back.

"Get 'em." Gray let him off his leash.

"I ain't her fuckin' baby daddy. That's my wife." He gripped the referee up by his collar. All the parents gasped.

"Somebody call the police?" The little boy's mom yelled.

"Bitch, shut the fuck up before I smack the shit outta you." Gray warned.

"I knew we shouldn't have let him play on a diverse team." The mom pursed her lips.

"You're right, honey. This was a bad idea." The father agreed.

"Mrs. Parthens, you guys gotta go. This kind of behavior is not tolerated. I'm sorry to say but this is your kids last day on the team." Coach Roberts announced.

Cam released the referee from his grip and kicked over the tub of Gatorade.

"Man, fuck this team! Y'all a bunch of racist muthafuckas anyway! Fuckin' Trump supporters! C'mon y'all. We out this bitch." He stormed off the field but not before jumping at the little boy's father. Scared for his life, the man flinched so hard he accidently wet himself.

"Fuckin' pussy."

CHAPTER 22

"Yeah, we knucking and bucking and ready to fight. I betcha I'ma throw dem thangs. So, haters best to think twice."-Crime Mob "Knuck If You Buck"

Bang! Bang!

Heated, that someone was infringing on his time with his kids, Cam stormed down the steps and swung open the door. He couldn't imagine who'd be crazy enough to bang on his door like they were the fucking police. Only close family and friends knew where the mansion he'd bought Gray was. To his utter dismay, Devin was on the other side. She stood with her arms folded across her chest, tapping her foot against the concrete. Even though she looked like a snack, Cam dropped his head back annoyed. The kids were whining cause they were hungry. He too was grouchy and starving. This was the last thing he wanted to deal with after the debacle at the soccer game. Gray was tired and wanted to go home and take a nap, so he dropped her off. After everything she'd done for him, the least he could do was let her rest for a few hours while he watched the kids. The plan was for him to drop them off later and give her back her car.

"What is it, Devin? Why are you at my house unannounced?"

"Maybe if you wouldn't have blocked my number I wouldn't have to pop up."

Cam had completely forgotten he'd done that. After Gray had chucked his phone out the window, all he cared about was digging in her ass.

"What's up?" He held the door.

"*What's up? What's up?* No, nigga what's down? You left me." She bent forward and pointed towards her chest. "For the Pillsbury Dough girl and in front of my friends at that. I was humiliated. Do you know how dumb I looked?"

"Yeah."

"What?" She shrieked.

"I'm just fuckin' wit' you." He chuckled. "What's up?"

"Cam, I'm dead serious. Why do you keep doing me like this? I was there when that bitch was nowhere to be found. Now you're just pushing me to the side like none of it even matters? I love you. Can't you see that?"

The sessions he'd had with Pastor Edris had really worked their magic because Cam genuinely started to feel bad. Despite her reckless mouth, Devin was a cool girl. She'd been loyal to him and held him down. His intentions was never to hurt her. Using her for his own personal gain wasn't cool. She didn't deserve that. He had to keep it a buck with her and let her know what was up. It was over between them and it was high time she knew.

"Look man, I hear what you saying. Let me go run an errand and grab these kids something to eat. You mind keeping an eye on them until I get back?"

"You couldn't answer my calls all night, you left me in the club for your *wife*." She made air quotes with her hands. "And now you want me to be Mrs. Fuckin' Doubtfire. You are a piece of work, Cameron."

"If you can't watch 'em I'll have to get up wit' you another time."

"Fine!" She stamped past him angrily.

"Bet. When I get back you'll have my undivided attention. I swear." Cam grabbed his keys and locked the door. Gray would kill him if she found out he'd left the kids with the one woman besides LaLa that she hated the most. He hoped she'd understand it was either gather up all the kids and their car seats, which would take forever, or let Devin watch them for an hour max.

Making herself comfortable on the leather couch, Devin crossed one leg over the other and took a look around. She hadn't been at this house since the night it got raided by the Feds. If Devin had it her way, she'd move out of the condo Cam had bought her and move into this place. She was the kinda girl that was born to live in a mansion. Devin was tired of struggling. Cam's financial help had been a godsend. Before she met him she'd been living paycheck to paycheck. And now that Forever 21 had filed for bankruptcy, she didn't know what she'd do with herself. She'd heard The Gap was hiring. Maybe she could apply for the management position there. It wasn't like she didn't have the experience. Until she could get Cam to fully commit and forget about Gray and her tribe of children, she'd have to do what she had to do.

Aoki sauntered down the staircase with her phone glued to her hand. She and Paris had been texting nonstop since that morning. The last thing she expected to see when she walked past the living area was her Pop's mistress. The heffa had made herself extra comfortable too. She'd taken off her shoes and everything.

"Where my Pop go?" She asked, confused.

"*Cam* is gone to get y'all hungry asses something to eat. Gunz . . . oops I forgot he ain't yo' daddy either." Devin snickered. "Your sperm donor was a nut ass rapist."

Aoki was about to pass out from rage. Inhaling deep within, she steadied her emotions. Through therapy she'd learn that people would try to trigger her by making nasty comments about her paternity. No matter what anybody said, Cam was her father. They didn't have to share the same blood. And even though she was mad at him right now, he was her dad in more ways than one. She refused to let a bitch like Devin who still made minimum wage get under her skin.

"Tread lightly, bitch. I'll dog walk you." Aoki made clear.

"Oki!" The triplets and Press came running down the steps.

"We hungry." Beaux rubbed her belly.

"Pop gone to get us something to eat now."

"In the meantime, y'all go sit y'all asses down somewhere and be quiet." Devin ordered.

"But I'm hungry now." Press poked out her bottom lip. It had been hours since she last ate.

"Girl, you don't need to be eating nothing. In a minute you gon' be just as big as yo' damn mama."

Press drew into herself. She would give anything to be invisible at that moment. Lately it seemed like no one looked at her twice unless it was to make fun of her or sneer. This was why she hated her reflection. Being chubby on her mother was cute but on her it was a burden she didn't know how to get rid of.

If there was one thing Aoki didn't play about it was her mama, her daddy, the triplets, and her sister. Hearing this grown ass woman talk bad about sweet innocent Press pushed buttons inside her she didn't even know existed.

"Fuck you." Press seethed before Aoki could react.

"What you say?" Devin spun around. All that could be heard was the sound of her butt squeaking against the leather.

"You heard me." Press stood up for herself. She was tired of letting people bully her. If she didn't start setting folks straight now they'd continue to harass her for the rest of her life. "Fuck you." She spat again.

"Oooooooooooh Press. You gon' get a whoopin'." Reign said scared for his sister's life. Unlike their father, Gray didn't play when it came to cussing. Kids were meant to stay in a child's place, even though all her kids acted like they were ten times older.

"She sure is." Devin shot up from the couch. "Ya mama might

tolerate disrespect but I don't." She grabbed Press by the arm and swung her around so that her butt faced her. Taking her hand, she swatted her behind several times. The sting was unbearable. The smacks to her bottom were as hard as punches. Tears spilled from Press' russet brown eyes. She'd never been spanked in her whole life. She'd never done anything to warrant one.

"Get the fuck off my sister!" Aoki dropped her phone and pushed Devin with all her might.

Devin stumbled back but recovered quickly. Lifting her hand in the air, she smacked Aoki in the face. Devin's palm cracked across her cheek, snapping it back with the force of its blow causing Aoki's head to slam into the wall behind her. Aoki cupped the side of her face. The slap made her feel dizzy. Unlike Damya, Devin was a lot taller than her and had more weight on her. Being hit by her was like being hit by a grown ass man. Thinking quick on her feet, Press grabbed her sister's phone off the floor and ran into the downstairs bathroom. After she'd locked herself inside, she called her mother. It took a few rings before Gray finally answered.

"Hello?" She answered groggily. She'd been knocked out asleep.

"Mama!" Press yelled frantically.

"What's wrong?" Gray shot up.

"Devin just whooped me and smacked Aoki."

"WHAT?!" Gray shouted so loud the sound hurt Press' ears. "Is she hurt?"

"No, I don't think so."

"Where's your daddy?"

"He went to get us something to eat."

"Go check on your sister. I'm on way." Gray hung up the phone without saying another word.

Press did as she was told. When she made it back to the living room, Aoki was still on the floor. The triplets surrounded her.

"Aoki, you okay?" Press got down on her knees.

"I'm fine. My head just hurt a li'l bit." She groaned, rubbing where her head had hit the wall. A huge lump had formed there.

"I called mama."

"You can call the police for all I care." Devin spat. "Yo' fat ass mama don't scare nothing over here. Y'all bad asses need to learn how to stay in a child's place. Play wit' ya' mammy. Don't play with me. Now, do like I said and go sit the fuck down."

Press helped Aoki off the floor. Her head was pounding. She swore Devin was gonna pay for putting her hands on her. Together they all went into the kitchen until their mom or Cam arrived. Twenty minutes hadn't even gone by before Gray pulled into the driveway and parked her car recklessly. She was so pissed she didn't even bother turning off the ignition. Devin had tried her entire life. For years, her ass had deserved an ass whooping but that day she was gonna die. Gray had only committed murder once and that was in self-defense. This was different. This was premeditated. Neither Cam nor the man up above would be able to stop her. Using her fist, she bammed on the door. Press ran out of the kitchen and unlocked the door before Devin could stop her.

"Where she at?" Gray seethed with venom.

Devin walked down the stairs with her phone pressed to her ear. Her homegirl Angie was on the other end.

"She gon' call her mama." She chuckled. "I'm like li'l girl, I will fuck you and yo' mama up. Ain't nobody scared of Gray ass. Just cause the bitch shaped like a deep freezer don't mean nothing." She spotted Gray standing at the door. "Oh, here her ass go now."

"You hit my daughter?" Gray barged inside.

"I sure did." Devin placed the phone down to her side. "What the fuck you gon' do? Her grown ass deserved—"

Before she could get the word out, Gray reared her fist back and punched her with so much force she summoned the spirit of Sharkeisha. The punch could be heard around the world. Devin and her phone went torpedoing to the ground. Pain erupted from the point of impact. The hit was so hard that Devin saw stars and other galaxies. On the ground in the fetal position, she covered her face. That didn't stop Gray from using her fists to punch her in the back of the head.

"I have waited fourteen long years to beat yo' ass!" Gray rained down blow after blow. She'd never envisioned fighting while pregnant but some ass whoopings couldn't be prevented. The insults Devin spewed were one thing but hitting her children was the last and final straw. Hearing her mother fighting, Aoki raced out the kitchen to help. The little kids tried to follow but she made them stay behind. Her mother needed her, but Gray was good on her own. She didn't need any help at all. She'd completely blacked out. Devin lay on the floor screaming for help.

"Ain't nobody gon' help you bitch!" Gray used her foot and kicked her in the face. The grotesque sound of Devin's nose breaking filled the room. Blood instantly began to pour from her nostrils.

"Okay mama. That's enough." Aoki pulled her back. She'd never seen her mother fight before. To her surprise Gray had hands.

"I'ma fuck you up!" Devin struggled to get off the floor. Crimson leaked from both her nostrils and her nose was twisted to the right. The triplets could be heard crying in the kitchen. Gray would tend to them in a second. At that moment, she was laser focused on bodying Devin.

"You gon' fuck who up!" Gray pushed Aoki to the side and charged her again. Speedily, she ran up on her and landed several more punches to her face. Devin tried to fight back but it was of no use. She was no match for Gray, especially when she was this angry. Drawing her fist back, she ploughed it into Devin's stomach. The punch was like being hit by a freight train. It felt like all the air had been sucked from her body. Her guts smashed together, and several blood vessels popped.

"Ahhhhhhhhhhhhhhh!" Devin screamed as Gray hit her with so much visceral force she lost her footing and slammed backwards into the wall. A huge dent was left behind. Aoki pulled her mom back again. But Devin wasn't done. She was determined to get a good lick in. Back on her feet, she ran towards Gray and started swinging wildly. Gray countered by grabbing a fistful of her hair and dragging her to the ground.

"Ahhhhhhhhhhhhhhh!" Devin screeched from the pain. Her

screams were as loud as Joycelyn Savage when Azriel Clary beat her ass.

"You gon' learn today." Blood hummed in Gray's veins as determination and anger took over. Still gripping her hair, she drug Devin across the marble floor, ripping several patches of her hair out along the way. All Devin could do was kick and scream.

"Get the fuck off of me you crazy bitch!"

"I ain't crazy. You just mad 'cause I know how to fight!" Gray unleashed a no holds barred attack on her. She wasn't going to stop until Devin could officially no longer breathe.

"The fuck is going on?" Cam dropped the bags of takeout, spilling the contents of it everywhere. Speedily, he pulled the two ladies apart.

"Let me go, Cam!" Gray tried to break loose. She was nowhere near done fucking his whore up.

"Devin hit me and smacked Aoki." Press told it all.

"What?" Cam's nostrils flared.

"Wait Cam. I can explain." Devin held her broken nose. Her face was a battered bloody mess. Blood left the artery it belonged to in surges. It came gushing out thick and strong through the seams of her fingers.

"And she called Press fat." Aoki added.

"They wasn't listening." Devin whimpered, barely able to stand.

"That don't mean you put your fuckin' hands on them. Bitch, have you lost your mind?" Cam growled.

"I didn't even hit them that hard." She lied.

"Yes, you did. Pop look." Aoki showed him the lump that had formed at her temple.

"Cam, please let me explain." Devin walked up on him. "They were being disrespectful."

"I don't give a fuck what they were doing. Bitch, are you dumb?" He yoked her up by the collar of her shirt.

"Yes." Gray replied.

"You always taking everybody else side but mine! These bitches ain't even your kids!" Devin spat heatedly.

Without warning, Press picked up the remote control and chucked it at Devin's face. The device hit her directly in the forehead. Gray and Aoki followed up by rushing her. Together they landed punch after punch to her face. Devin tried to protect herself by covering her head with her arms, but Gray wasn't having it. Since she wanted to cower, Gray took what was left of her hair and held her in place as she rammed her knee into her mouth. Outside of having the wind knocked out of her, the vicious blow caused Devin's front tooth to pop out. Aoki hit her with a body shot to her ribs that sent fresh ripples of pain through her torso. Now that they'd gotten their shit off, Cam stopped the fight and pulled them off of her.

"Get your shit and get the fuck out my house! This shit is a wrap!" He grabbed her phone, shoes and purse and threw them out the door.

"Cam, please don't do this. Just hear me out." Devin limped in his direction.

"Bitch!" He back handed her face, causing her to fall to the floor again. Gripping her hair, he yanked her head back. Devin winced from the pain. "I will fill your entire upper body with holes. And let me make this shit perfectly clear. Don't go back to my condo. You not getting shit out of there."

"What about all my stuff?" She held her face and cried.

"Bitch!" Gray snapped. "That shit cost $5.99 anyway. You better use your employee discount and get you some more shit. Oh, I forgot Forever 21 gon' bankrupt. Sucks for you, bitch."

"Cam, can I at least get my stuff?" Devin pleaded.

"FUCK NO! Bitch, you better be glad you even fuckin' breathing after putting your hands on my kids. Now get the fuck up and get the fuck out my house!"

Devin sluggishly rose to her feet and hobbled out the door. Cam slammed it behind her and checked on Gray.

"You alright?" He cupped each of her cheeks.

"Get the fuck off me! Why in the hell did you leave them here with her in the first place?" She yelled still on ten.

"I just went to run an errand and grab something to eat."

"And you thought it would be a good idea to leave her here with my kids and in this house. The same house you bought for me?"

"I was gon' tell her I was done fuckin' wit' her when I got back." Cam tried to explain. He was lowkey afraid. He'd never seen Gray this mad before.

"I don't give a fuck what your plan was. You would've had a fit if I left them with Noon."

Cam didn't have a rebuttal. She was right. He would've killed them both.

"I'm sorry." He apologized sincerely.

"Don't ever do no shit like that again. You hear me?" She pointed her blood-soaked finger at him. "Or the next time we'll be jumping you."

"Y'all ain't never gotta worry about that bitch again. On my mama, I'm done with that ho for good." He confessed sincerely.

"You better be." Gray warned. "Or I swear to God, I'm done with you."

"Daddy, I'm scared!" Sky trotted out of the kitchen with tears strolling down her cheeks. Reign and Beaux jogged behind her.

"It's okay. Daddy's sorry." Cam scooped her up in his arms and kissed her all over her face.

"That lady hit my sissies."

"I know. It's all daddy's fault."

"Sure is." Gray rolled her eyes. "C'mon. We're getting ready to go home."

"Daddy, come with us." Reign wrapped his arms around Cam's leg.

"Yeah, Appa spend the night at our house." Press pleaded.

"I don't know if that's good idea, Pretty Girl." Gray replied for him.

"I would love to spend the night with my babies." Cam spoke up.

"Yay!" The triplets cheered.

"Cam." Gray stared at him. After fighting, she was physically and emotionally exhausted. This was the last thing she needed.

"C'mon, Gray."

"No."

"I know it's a lot but I really wanna spend time with you and the kids."

"Noon will be here in the morning."

"So." Cam balled up his face.

"Mommy, please." Beaux batted her big brown eyes.

How could she say no to that? Gray rolled her neck in a circle and rolled her eyes. She couldn't get away from this nigga if she tried. They were supposed to be separated but here he was inserting himself into her personal space. The mixed signals he was sending her was killing her softly. Sooner rather than later, she'd have to put her foot down.

CHAPTER 23

"Everything I do you're still distant. I am asking for your attention."-
Chari' Joy "Porcelain Doll"

*a*fter spending all day with her family, Aoki relished her alone time inside of her room. The rest of the Parthens' clan were scattered about the house. She was beyond happy no one was bothering her. After the day she'd had, she needed the reprieve. Sitting Indian style in the center of her bed, she held her iPhone above her head. The flower wallpaper and white tufted headboard was the perfect backdrop for her Facetime call. Her right arm was hurting but she'd be damned if she let it drop. Nothing was worse than having a double chin on Facetime. There was no way she was gonna risk looking a mess while video chatting with Paris. It was bad enough that every time he called she started shaking. Thank God, she looked cute or she wouldn't have answered at all. Although she was dressed down, she still slayed the pink silk headscarf, gold hoop earrings, gold Aoki nameplate necklace, white tank and Nike fitted joggers. The scarf did a good job of hiding the knot that was at the front of her head. She prayed it would be gone by the next day. The last thing she wanted was everybody at the party gawking at her and asking a bunch of questions she didn't have the energy to answer.

Baby girl, the late great Aaliyah, old school hit *At Your Best* bumped softly in the background as she gazed into the screen. Paris puffed on a blunt and blew a cloud of weed smoke into the air. Aoki admired the way his pink lips puckered into the letter O. It was the sexiest shit she'd seen. Paris was fine beyond measure. He oozed sex appeal. He had the kind of face that should be immortalized on canvas. If Makiah wouldn't clown her, she'd have her draw a sketch of his handsome face so that she could look at him forever. There wasn't any trace of him on social media. So, Aoki spent all of her spare time sitting up in her room fantasizing about him and what they could be. Everything from his slim build, tattoos and symmetrical face had her in a tizzy. If he knew how deep her feelings for him went, it would probably push him away. Aoki was in deep. She found herself wanting him, feenin' for him and missing him more than she should. He was everything she wanted in a boy and more. As usual, he was surrounded by a bunch of niggas that used all their free time ass kissing. Paris wasn't fazed by the fanfare at all. He was used to niggas riding his dick. Aoki loved all the attention he got. She wouldn't have had it any other way. Aoki wasn't born to be with a dude that was second best. She came from hood royalty. She was destined to be with the nigga other niggas wished they could be. The problem was she wasn't his girl. She and Paris were nothing more than associates. She couldn't even label them as friends. They were in that weird grey area where there was an obvious attraction and feelings but no title. She and Paris had been cakin' all day and the topic of them being together had yet to come up. Aoki didn't know what was up with him. She'd made herself perfectly clear at Kiara's party. She hoped he didn't take her demands as a joke. She wasn't going to change her mind. It was either him and her and no Damya or no her at all.

"So, what's up?" She asked tired of beating around the bush. "You been talking to me all day. Does that mean you handled your situation? Cause if not we don't need to be talkin'."

Paris stopped bagging up and stared at her. Traces of the girl she was lingered in the innocent features of her face and in the thinness of her body, but Aoki had all the other trappings of a woman. She was strong and cunning. Most girls her age would be easy to finesse. But Aoki wasn't a rookie to the game. She possessed confidence that women ten times her age didn't have. Paris was in trouble. This thirteen-year-old girl literally crashed into his world and changed all the rules. Paris was used to having his cake and eating too. Girls didn't put demands on him. But Aoki stepped up to the plate and knocked his player ways out the park. She wasn't having it, and because of that, she'd gained his respect. Not only did he respect her, but he really liked her and didn't want to lose her. Being her friend wasn't good enough. He wanted more. Sooner or later, he'd have to stake his claim before another nigga came along and made her his.

"You know what your problem is, Thief?" He swiveled side-to-side in his chair.

"No, but I'm sure you're gonna tell me." She leaned back against her pillows.

"You need to stop being so concerned about other people and worry about what we doing?"

"And what exactly is that?" Her chest rose with anticipation. Outside of Priest, Paris was the only boy that made her nervous.

"We getting to know each other. We friends, right?"

Aoki rolled her eyes to the side. Nothing about their dynamic had changed. Paris was still playing the same old tired game he'd started months ago.

"I got enough friends." She made clear. If he thought she was going to participate in his nonsense he had another thing coming.

"Well, add another one to the mix, muthafucka." He put his face close to the phone. Aoki tried not to grin but was unsuccessful.

"I ain't going nowhere and neither are you?"

"You sure about that?" She contested.

"I ain't never been so sure about something in my muthafuckin' life." He challenged at her sexily. Aoki hid her smile behind her hand. There was something about Paris, a slight confidence and inflated ego, that had her muddling her words and blushing uncontrollably whenever he was around. She needed to learn how to control her emotions or he'd never take her seriously.

"What you got on? Pan the camera down. Let me see something."

"Nigga, please. I ain't Damya." She lay on her side.

"Here you go on that bullshit." He resumed smoking. "On some real shit, what you getting into tomor? I wanna see you. I ain't used to all this Facetime shit." Paris was used to pulling up, smashing hoes and jetting. Aoki had him acting all out of character. He hadn't talked to a girl on the phone this much since he was in the sixth grade.

"I don't know what you're doing. I'm going to my li'l brother and sisters birthday party. If you wanna see me you can see me Monday through Friday at school. But oh, I forgot you barely come. You need to get that shit together. Being a high school dropout ain't cute."

"Don't worry about me. I got my shit under control." He dug inside his pocket and pulled out a wad of money.

"You know I've always been confused by people who know their purpose but refuse to walk in it."

Aoki's words hit Paris like a ton of bricks. He knew he could be much more than a dealer but when you've been told your whole life that you're nothing you start to believe it.

"Not everyone is equipped to walk in their purpose." He responded back.

"But some of us can't afford not to." She dared.

"Let me get up wit' my folks." He dropped the subject. Aoki was conjuring up emotions in him that he didn't wanna deal with. "I'ma pull up on you tomor."

"No, you're not." She jumped up in a panic. Her mom and pop would string her up if they saw them together.

"Watch me." He hung up before she could respond.

~

IT HAD BEEN AGES SINCE CAM LAST COOKED A MEAL IN GRAY'S HOME. After that horrific night on his doorstep where he told her he never wanted to see her again, he thought they'd never have a moment like this. But there he was cleaning up the kitchen. Dinner had been served and eaten. The entire Parthens' clan bellies were full of home fries, corn on the cob and fried chicken. Cam didn't get in the kitchen often, but when it was time to burn, he knew how to throw down. The kids loved everything. There wasn't a piece of chicken left, only bones with the gristle left on them. As he cleaned up the mess, Gray gave the little kids their baths.

The rich airy voice of Chari' Joy flowed throughout the house sere-nading everyone's ears. Cam didn't fuck with many female artists, but he liked her music a lot, specifically her song *Yours Truly*. The slow groove put everyone in a chill mood. This felt good. This was what he wanted his everyday life to look like; him at home with his wife and children. Being out in the streets, hitting up the club and bagging bitches no longer enticed him. This was what he'd searched his whole life for.

While Cam cleaned up the kitchen and Sky and Beaux played with their dolls in the living room, Gray went to go check on her Pressy Pooh. She was in her room reading as usual. On the outside she seemed fine, but the day's events had to be jarring for her.

"Hey Pretty Girl." She eased inside the room.

"Hi mommy." Press placed the book down onto her lap.

Gray sat beside her on her vintage daybed.

"You feeling okay?"

"Yeah." Press fibbed. She was far from fine. Devin's mean words were still ringing in her head.

"It's okay if you're not. No one should have to go through what you went through today." She rubbed her knee.

Press placed her head down and exhaled. It was a struggle to get her words out.

"Mommy . . . do I need to lose weight?"

Gray felt the crack as it etched into her heart. Press was only ten. They shouldn't be having conversations like this. Her life was supposed to be joyful and carefree. She shouldn't be worried about what size she was.

"No." She responded quickly. "Why would you say something like that?"

"Cause . . . all the kids at school and Devin called me fat." Press' chin quivered.

Taking her by the hand, Gray pulled her into her arms and held her close. Press rested the side of her face against her mother's warm bosom. She didn't wanna cry, but her vision clouded with tears anyway. She used to think of Press as a wallflower waiting to bloom, but she was much more than that. She was a young lioness. Press had invisible wings that were dying to spread and fly. There was an inner strength hidden deep within that she'd yet to tap into. As her mother, Gray knew where all vulnerabilities lye. It was her job to shield her from the vultures that would try to pick at her weaknesses. At some point, she'd have to let go and let Press fight her own battles and find her own way. Until then, Gray would continue to be her protector.

"You are perfect just the way you are. You hear me? There is nothing wrong with you. You're beautiful. You're the prettiest girl in the whole wide world. Not only are you beautiful on the outside but the inside too." Gray squeezed her tight. It tore her up inside that her baby girl viewed herself so negatively. She wished Press saw herself the way she did. She was extraordinarily pretty. Press had nothing to worry about. The little belly fat she'd gained over the summer would melt away in no time. Until she gained the confidence to know that she was perfectly made in God's image, Gray would continue to affirm her worth and beauty.

"You're drop dead gorgeous. You're exceptionally smart, kind, caring and you have the biggest heart of anyone I know."

Press let her mother's words sink in. It felt good to hear so many positive words of affirmation about herself. But it would still take time to feel comfortable in her own skin.

"Fuck them kids and Devin too." Cam's bass-filled voice flooded the room.

Gray looked over her shoulder and found him standing in the doorway.

"Check this out, Pretty Girl. I want you to give me the name of everyone that said something slick about you. I'ma come up to that school and fuck 'em up."

"Cam, you can't fight a bunch of ten-year-olds." Gray shot him a deadpan expression.

"The fuck I can't. Age ain't nothin' but a number."

"And let me guess? Going to jail ain't nothing but a thang."

"You damn right." Cam stood next to Press' bed. "I already did one bid. I can do another. Listen, Pretty Girl. Papa about to drop some jewels. You gotta learn how to talk shit. When they fuck wit' you, fuck wit' they ass back. Don't let nobody talk to you crazy. Be aggressive. Start knockin' they fuckin' heads off. Put them li'l baby bitches in they place. Once you do, I swear they ain't gon' fuck wit' you again."

"But I don't like being mean, Appa. It's not in my nature."

"And that's what I love about you." Cam ran his long fingers through her hair. "Never lose that kind spirit you have but sometimes, Pretty Girl, you gotta put a bitch in their place. Sometimes, you gotta push a muthafucka wig back. Sometimes, you gotta put yo' foot so far up a ho ass they'll be shitting leather for weeks. Sometimes—"

"Okay!" Gray stopped him. "That's enough. I think she gets it."

"I was just making sure." Cam placed his hands inside his pocket.

"Basically, what Papa is trying to say is that you have to learn to be your own protector. Me and Papa won't always be around to defend you, so you have to learn to do it yourself. When you stick up for yourself it not only creates boundaries for others, but it'll make you feel better about yourself. It'll build your confidence."

"And if all else fails." Cam interjected. "Papa will make it, so they wind up six-feet deep."

"You can't kill a kid, Appa."

"Yes I—"

"No, he won't. Ain't that right, *Appa*?" Gray arched her brow.

"Yeah, I guess." Cam huffed.

"You get thirty more minutes to read. Then it's time for you to go to bed, okay?" Gray brushed Press' hair away from her face.

"Okay." She gave her mom and dad a hug goodnight.

"Love you, Pretty Girl."

"Love you too, Appa." Press got comfortable under the sheets.

Gray and Cam walked down the hall one after the other.

"Let's go get Beaux and Sky. It's past their bedtime. I don't want them to be tired tomorrow during their party."

"What kind of party are they having anyway? You ain't told me shit." Cam complained.

"You'll see when you get there. It's a surprise." Gray smirked. The slight grin didn't take away the fact that he was still on her shit list. Cam had violated her in the worst way possible. A simple I'm sorry dinner and help with the kids wouldn't fix her attitude. Cam knew that. Gray was a tough nut to crack when she wanted to be. The entire time he'd been there, she'd acted like he was a ghost. He hated when she gave him the silent treatment. It was almost as bad as when she cried. God must've been on his side tho, cause when they made it to the living room Ghostface Killah's soulful rap song *Done It Again* had started to play. The song was a romantic love letter to the woman he loved.

"Hey, excuse me." He tapped Gray on the shoulder while mimicking the words. Wondering what he wanted, she turned around and looked him up and down. To her surprise, Cam took her by the hand and led her to the center of the living room floor. Not in the mood for whatever he was up to, she tried to pull away, but he wouldn't let her. Cocking his head to the side, he licked his bottom lip and said, *"Excuse me, love, can I have a word wit'chu?"*

Now that he had her attention, Cam took ahold of her other hand and started to two-step from side-to-side. It took Gray a minute, but she reluctantly joined in and moved with him. Staying mad at him was pointless. She'd been trying for years and failed every time.

"Not to be rude though, you know, I mean I just seen't you." Hand-in-hand Cam started rapping the verse as Sky and Beaux danced around them.

"Sometimes you my psychiatrist, others my philosopher. Feelings in my heart as deep as Phantom of the Opera. Heal me wit'cho cookin', you can be my doctor, herbalist. But I'ma be the one to keep you calm when it's turbulence. We was buyin' hella houses, we was territorial. Give you a tutorial, teach you somethin' historical. Tourin' through the Matrix, we was Neo and the Oracle. Watchin' sunsets on the beach, that's adorable. But oral deep and she was wetter than the coral reef. Scuba dive up in her raw and then she'll snore asleep. You my wavy lady, but really, you make me crazy. If we stay another day, we gon' make another baby, yeah."

Cam was smooth, real smooth. Gray could feel the heat growing on her cheeks. Trying to be hard, she tried to suppress her smile, but the attempt was futile. Her usual even peanut butter skin had a rosiness to it that was cute as hell. Throwing caution to the wind, she allowed Cam to whisk her around the room. He spun her around in circles, causing her to grin and giggle. It had been ages since she'd done anything like this. The pressure of Cam's warm hand on her back and the feeling of her bare feet gliding across the floor made her feel like she was Ginger Rodgers and he was Fred Astaire. The words he rapped to her only made the moment better.

"Hey, miss lady, maybe you can have my baby. Nice long flight, first class, out to Haiti. Even bake you cookies, throwin' frosting on the cakie. Gucci bags, mad flavors, steppin' outta Macy's. Yeah, these fake niggas like to talk about it. Celebrate, we could pull a cork up out it. Beef? You know we gon' walk up out it. Swagger, don't let me bring New York up out it."

The piano keys and sounds from the horn twirled like thread around them. Caught up in the moment, in him, his woodsy scent, the feel of his brawny arms, Gray rested her head on his broad chest.

Together they swayed 'round and 'round. A million thoughts plagued her. It was time to tell him. This was the second time Cam had brought up having another child. She couldn't keep it a secret anymore. It wasn't fair to him that she'd kept quiet this long.

"Cam." She spoke just above a whisper. Her heart was pounding so fast she could barely speak. She knew he'd want the baby, but it was a good chance he'd rip her head off for keeping him in the dark. Gray just couldn't find the right time to tell him. Fighting was the last thing she wanted to do but an argument was sure to ensue. No matter the outcome, she deserved every bit of what he was gonna give her.

"Yeah." He soothingly rubbed her back.

"There's something I need to tell you."

"Shoot."

"I'm—"

Gray couldn't even get the word pregnant out. Somehow Beaux had gotten ahold of the remote and started blasting *Baby Shark*. She and Cam immediately stopped dancing and turned their attention to her. Sky and Beaux were having the time of their lives jumping around and clapping. Instead of being mad, Cam released Gray from his hold and turned up with his baby girls. They danced as if they were bursting with liquid sunshine. Gray joined into the fun. As a family they had the time of their lives. The only person that was missing was Reign, but he was in his room playing with Kilo and Gram. Everything was cool until Sky placed her hands on the wall, poked out her bottom and started bouncing her botty to the beat.

"Look at me daddy! Look at me!" She looked over her shoulder and twerked.

Not to be outdone, Beaux bent into the Downward Facing Dog position, and started shaking her butt like a King of Diamonds stripper. Cam halted dancing and clutched his chest. All the color left his face. It felt like someone had wrapped their hand around his heart and began to squeeze. Cam's worst nightmare was coming true. As a father, he only had one job and that was to keep his daughters off the pole. His baby girls were only three and he'd failed them already. Gray covered her mouth and giggled loudly. She was laughing so hard she almost pee'd on herself. The expression on Cam's face was priceless. She'd never seen him more afraid in his life.

"Aye! Aye!" He pointed. "Stop that shit! Ain't gon' be no ass shaking in here unless It's ya' mama. Get y'all asses up and get ready to go to bed!"

"Aww, daddy. You no fun." Beaux curled her upper lip.

"Keep it up. Daddy gon' beat yo' ass."

"You so funny, daddy. You ain't gon' do nothing." Sky snickered.

"Why these kids take me as a fuckin' joke?" He looked at Gray.

"I don't know." She continued to laugh.

"Yes, you do. It's all your fuckin' fault. You always think something funny."

"Sure, blame everything on me."

On their way to the girls' room, Cam stopped at Reign's bedroom door which was cracked wide open. He lay on his back with Gram right by his side howling at the moon. Every time he howled, Gram would raise his head in the air and follow up with a howl of his own. Reign would then chuckle like it was the funniest thing on earth. Cam watched them do this this several more times before walking into the room. At least one of his kids still acted like a toddler. In a fit of giggles, Reign continued howling like his father wasn't even there. Cam sat on the foot of the bed where Kilo lay on his side resting and scratched his belly. He missed his dogs as much as he missed Gray and the kids. Kilo and Gram were his first family. They were his savior. Whenever he was down and out or in a state of panic they were always there to give him a sweet cuddle. Their dark liquid eyes, black coat of hair and loyal spirit were the things he loved about them most. Cam couldn't have asked for anything more. In spite of the altercation, this had been the best day he'd had since waking up from the coma. There was nothing better than seeing the smiles on the people he loved the most faces.

"Get up." He patted Kilo's stomach, but he lay there playing dead.

"C'mon get up." Cam scratched and rubbed his belly to entice him. He still wouldn't budge.

"C'mon you gotta go to your house." He lifted his head and gave him a kiss on the cheek. Cam then lifted him all the way up and placed him on his legs. Kilo stood for a second and then plopped right back down onto the bed. At that point Cam gave up. Kilo had made it clear he wasn't going anywhere. Fed up with him he focused on Reign.

"It's time to go to bed buddy." He ruffled his curly hair.

"Do I have to, daddy? I'm having fun." Reign pouted.

"You gotta get a good night's sleep so you can be ready for your party tomorrow."

"Oh yeah." He looked off to the side. "I forgot about that. We gon' get poppin' daddy. We gon' fuck the club up." He pumped his fist in the air.

Cam hid his face and laughed. His kids were a trip. Once he'd regained his composure, he turned back to Reign.

"You can't say the F word buddy."

"Why not? You say it."

"I'm grown. I've earned the right to cuss."

"So, when I get big like you I can curse too?"

"You can curse all you want."

"Pinky swear." Reign held out his tiny finger.

"Pinky swear." Cam intertwined his pinky with his. "Now close your eyes li'l man. It's time to pray."

Reign closed his bright blue eyes and pressed his palms together. Cam got down on his knees and did the same.

"Heavenly father, please hold those I love as they sleep. Bless them with peace that surpasses understanding. Sow in them hope that can't be put out. Grow in them dreams and visions for their future and protect them with your unconditional love. Lord, help us to learn your ways, your ways that are only love. We are humbled by your gift of life. We will only move our lips to say good words. We understand that your creation is divine and to be cherished. We will only serve the power of love and work every day to bring your heaven on Earth, healing your children."

Mid-way through the prayer Cam found himself saying more than a nightly prayer. His soul was crying out to God. Overcome with emotion, tears trickled from the corner of his eyes. Being stabbed by a man of the cloth had tested his faith. Cam found himself wondering why God had preserved him and God answered, "All things are new. Your path is now behind you." God not only spared his life but added more years to his time on earth. God had greater things for him than he did his parents. It was Cam's duty to rewrite his family's history. Every curse, sickness, disease, weakness that was attributed to his family's name would be killed through him. Cam was a walking testament of what a miracle was supposed to look like. It was only right that he thank God and praise his name.

"Let your spirit speak to our mind and hearts while we sleep. So, that when we wake in the morning, we find that we have received in the night-time, light to lead us on our way, peace for our worries and forgiveness for our sins. Lord, grant us sleep tonight, and tomorrow power to live. In Jesus name I pray, Amen."

"Amen." Reign opened his eyes to find his father overwrought with tears.

"Daddy, it's okay. Don't cry. You're strong, remember?" He spoke the same words he'd said to Sky earlier that day.

"Daddy is strong but sometimes daddy feels weak." Cam confessed, wiping his face.

"When you're weak daddy, I'll catch you." Reign planted a loving kiss on his forehead.

Cam gazed upon his handsome son amazed. When he looked at Reign he saw an achievement that made all the years of pain he'd endured worthwhile. Reign was truly a blessing to everyone lucky enough to know him. For Cam, he was his biggest blessing. Through Reign he'd get to have the father/son relationship he'd never had with his.

"I wouldn't want anybody else to." Cam kissed him back. "Rest up. You gotta big day ahead of you."

"Can Kilo and Gram come to the party?"

"I don't know about that buddy."

"Aww man." He smacked his little hands against the sheets.

"We'll party with them when we get home."

"That'll work." Reign gave him a thumbs up.

After tucking Sky and Beaux snuggly inside their bed, Cam kissed them goodnight and headed to what used to be his and Gray's bedroom. Cam looked around. Everything was still the same. The king-sized bed they'd made love on numerous times sat in the middle of the room in front of the floral print wallpaper and alongside two night-stands. Gray was inside her huge walk-in closet pulling out pajamas to wear. Spent from crying, Cam threw his self into the comfy chair in the corner of the room. Difficult emotions rushed through his body. He breathed in slow and let out an exasperated sigh. Feelings he'd yet to deal with swarmed him. Cam took the time to soak in the calm and peace of silence. Gray came out of the closet with her things and found him sitting with his eyes closed and legs spread wide apart. Cam looked like he'd been through it. Exhaustion covered him from head to toe. She hoped he hadn't pushed himself too hard that day. He wasn't 100% well yet.

"I ain't been in this muthafucka in a minute." He announced, catching her off guard.

"Yeah, it was weird for me when we first moved back in too."

"You ever think about moving into the crib I bought you?"

"Absolutely not. I ain't laying my head nowhere that's been exposed to orgies, chlamydia and the Feds."

"The orgies was at the condo, not the crib. And I ain't never had no fuckin' chlamydia."

"That you know of." Gray joked.

"Aye, let me ask you something. What you do with the divorce papers?"

Gray stilled. She knew the conversation would come up eventually. She just wasn't expecting to talk about it then.

"I tore them up." She answered nonchalantly.

"Is that right?" Cam massaged his jaw. He wondered what that meant. Did she wanna stay married to him? Did she do it for medical reasons? Now that he was well would she bring the subject up again?

"I mean, I can get a new set drawn up if you like." She spun around on her heels and faced him.

"Did I say that?"

"Whatever. How are you feeling? You look really tired."

"I'm cool."

"Cam . . . stop. This is me. I was there with you the whole 42 days. What happened to you was traumatic. Let's not pretend that you aren't still dealing with the aftermath of everything. Hell, I'm still fucked up, so I know you gotta be. You ain't gotta put up a front for me. Remember, we said we were gonna keep it real with each other moving forward so tell me how you really feel." She placed her things on the bed and sat before him on the ottoman.

"To keep it a hunnid the shit still fuck wit' me. The whole time I'm thinking this nigga Edris gave a fuck about us and the whole time he was plotting and I ain't even see the shit. I let that nigga prey on my family. I let him get close to us." Cam screwed up his face, disgusted. "That nigga knew my deepest darkest secrets and shit. That nigga broke bread with my kids. I can't believe I let that shit go down like that. This whole thing is my fault. I was supposed to see that shit coming from a mile away. I put you and the kids at risk thinking his grimy ass had our best interest at heart. I ain't never fucked up and did no nut shit like that. I been on my P's and Q's my whole life. So, to answer your question no I'm not good. This shit sit wit' me every day."

"None of this is your fault." Gray ran her hand up and down his thigh. "How you gon' put all of that on your shoulders? We all were blinded by him."

"Yeah, but it's my job to protect my family, Gray. It's my responsibility to make sure snakes don't get through our grass. I'm always supposed to be ten steps ahead but the whole time this nigga was a hundred feet ahead of my dumb ass. I let my family down. I ruined what was supposed to be the best day in Quan's life." Cam continued to beat himself up.

Getting up from the ottoman, Gray sat sideways on his lap and wrapped her arm around his neck. Through couples therapy she learned that marriage was a deep and loving friendship, one in which the love is so strong that each partner would sacrifice for the other. The only way to a lasting and happy marriage is via friendship. It was one of the things that they lacked in the beginning. They didn't have a solid foundation. After his near-death experience, they both realized more than ever that all the arguing they'd done in the past came from the hurt they both harbored. Now that they'd gotten past that the friendship they were building could grow. Gray could honestly say that outside of Kema, Heidi and Tee-Tee, Cam was her best friend. As his friend she couldn't sit back and watch him fight his demons alone. She vowed to be there through thick and thin. Right now, they were in the thick of it. No matter the status of their relationship, she'd be there to be his shoulder to lean on.

"Everything we've gone through falls back on Gunz. We were just casualties of the sick game he started. You have done a great job protecting us." Cam pursed his lips and gazed off to the side. Seeing that she still wasn't getting through to him, Gray tried another tactic.

"Look at it this way. Even though what Pastor Edris did was terrible, the words that he gave us in counseling was true. Neither of us were much of a believer before our sessions. His guidance honestly gave me the strength I needed to stick in there with you those 42 days. After witnessing everything you went through, there ain't a person on earth that can tell me there isn't a God. Somebody up there is watching over us. Pastor Edris might've let the devil use him but God is most certainly real."

Cam nodded his head. Slowly, he drew circles on the sliver of skin from her stomach that was exposed. Gray tried her best to keep things PG, but Cam was making it extremely hard. Feeling his wood against her thigh and his hand on her stomach had her thinking nasty thoughts she shouldn't. Cam was the only man who made her dizzy with lust. When they were close she melted like ice cream in a warm porcelain bowl.

"At the end of the day, none of this is on you. What are the odds that a pastor would be working for MCM? None of us saw that coming. I don't even know how Gunz pulled that shit off. The nigga ain't that bright. So, please stop blaming yourself. You didn't let us down. You did the opposite. You protected us to the best of your ability and for that I can't say thank you enough." She gazed at him adoringly and caressed the side of his face. Cam took hold of her delicate hand and kissed her palm. Gray blinked her eyes and remembered to breathe.

"But I will anyway." She croaked, clearing her throat. "Thank you for being an extraordinary father. Thank you for being the father that my daughters needed. I honestly don't know what I would've done if you hadn't been here for us. From day one you've been the best provider and protector. I tried to raise five kids on my own and I did a good job, but I wouldn't have made it this far without you. Having you here by my side to lesson my burdens and lift me up has been a godsend. Even when I tried to push you away, you still were there for us. The only time you remotely came close to failing us is when you flatlined and I thought I'd lost you." A single tear slipped from her eye. Gray yearned to hold back her cry, but her tears and emotions were raw. Cam rocked her silently as her tears soaked his shirt.

"I wouldn't have been able to make it without you, but your stubborn ass found a way to come back to us. Knowing you, you probably got kicked out of heaven." Gray laughed, despite how melancholy she felt. "I can see you now telling Noah or whoever built that ark, you'll pump two in his chest."

"I ain't that crazy. I would never disrespect the big homey Noah like that." Cam chuckled.

"Seriously, I think now that you're back and we're establishing order things will be better. In the past, I struggled with allowing you to lead. But I trust you to lead our family now. So. . . as you follow God, we will follow you."

Cam's brain stuttered for half a second. Had he heard right? Did Gray really just bare her soul and say she would fall back and let him lead? Had he died and gone to heaven 'cause the Gray he knew and loved would never. Taking his index and thumb, he pinched her forearm. Gray squealed. He wasn't dead. She was right. God had to be real because only He could get her to open up to him like this.

"You a'ight?" He placed the back of his hand against her forehead. "You sick? You gotta fever?"

"Move fool." She swatted his hand away and got up.

Turning on her Beats Pill, she picked up her pajamas and headed into the master bath. To her detriment *Porcelain Doll* by Chari' *Joy* was the first song that played. The song was ungodly sexy. It instantly put you in the mood. Gray tried to put all thoughts of being intimate with Cam out of her mind and turned on the shower. Stripping bare, she stepped inside and let the water beat down onto her sore muscles. It wasn't until then that she realized the fight had done a number on her. Gray closed her eyes and asked God for forgiveness. She had no business fighting while pregnant. Thankfully, Devin hadn't hit her in the stomach. If she would've lost her baby behind defending her children, Devin would've wound up buried next to Truth. After a soothing twenty-minute shower, she exited relaxed and clean.

In front of the sink she wiped the steam from the mirror and turned on the faucet. Water streamed into the basin as she grabbed a face towel. Gray drenched it with hot water. Once it was fully soaked, she placed it over her face so that her pores could open. The feeling was sensational. It was exactly what she needed. Suddenly, she felt a presence behind her. She didn't have to see to know it was Cam. The scent of his cologne wafted up her nose alerting her that he was present. Shivering with excitement, she opened her eyes and dropped the towel in the sink. Gray didn't have to be a rocket scientist to know what was about to go down. Cam had that animalistic look in his eye. He wanted her and she didn't have the willpower to stop him. Looking into the mirror, she stared at their reflection. They made a stunning couple. Where his honey complexion ended hers began. They were perfect together. Cam towered over her making her feel small. His gaze was intense and demanding. He watched her as she watched him. Gray swallowed the lump in her throat. She was both terrified and turned on. This was the part of foreplay she loved the most. That split second before he touched her always electrified every nerve ending on her body. It was the anticipation of being together in a way that was completely tangible. Wet in more ways than one, she stood waiting for him to pounce.

Cam stood so close she could breathe in his scent. Without warning, he moved in so close she could feel his lean physique pressed up against her back. Gray felt his body heat and imagined his lips were on hers. But it was all a fantasy. Cam hadn't made his move yet. He knew she enjoyed the hunt. He couldn't give her all of him at once. So, without saying a word he watched her watch him. Cam and Gray were a wonderous sight to behold. Their bodies fit together as if they were made just for this. And they were. Falling into a natural rhythm of lovemaking was second nature to them.

In one gentle pull their skin finally became one. Cam wrapped his arm around her waist. His hand squeezed her waist then landed on her stomach. A slight bump was there that he hadn't noticed before, but he didn't think much of it.

Gray closed her eyes. This was insane. She'd swore not to go there with him again, but Cam was like the sun. She orbited around him. Affectionately, he placed his lips on her wet skin and brushed his lips from her shoulder to her neck. Cam tried to be gentle and take his time but the water droplets on her skin tasted like Nutella. Electricity jump started Gray's heart. Slowly, she raised her hand and rubbed the back of his head. Cam savored the feeling as his hands sliding over her water slick body. Bodies pressed together they both disregarded the fact that she was wet and naked, and he was fully clothed. All that mattered was the kisses he planted on her skin. Cam had to have her.

He'd do whatever even if it meant he'd have to get down on his knees and crawl. He was down for whatever.

A quiet moan escaped Gray's plump lips. It was so low he could barely hear it. Roughly, he took hold of her hair and yanked her head back. Her mouth was right there for the taking. Diving in headfirst, he devoured her rosy lips. Gray's mouth was like a taste of heaven. Cam's tongue slipped in and out of her mouth with ease. Drawn by her ripe fruit, he slipped his right hand down her stomach and ventured into her secret garden. It didn't take long for him to find her bulbous clit. Hanging heavy and swollen on swaying boughs, it rested between his fingertip throbbing wet from her juices. Cam rubbed it vigorously in a circular motion until she bloomed. He could feel her labia harden as he leisurely inserted his middle finger in and out of her velvety walls. Tempted by the sweet taste of her skin, his tongue danced across the vein of her neck. Gray's breathing came in long hard spurts as he worked her into a frenzy.

"You're mine." He growled into her ear.

"I'm yours." She moaned, coming undone.

Gray's cheeks flushed red from desperation. Each stroke of his hand felt like sand slipping through an hourglass. Soon she'd explode but Gray didn't want this to end. She wanted them to stay like this forever. Soft harmonic love notes floated from her throat. Gripping her shoulder, Cam bent her over the sink. Gray trembled from the inside out as she spread her legs apart. Cam needed better access to her carnal ambrosia. Thankful for the space, he played in her wetness until her legs almost gave out. This was love at its finest. For years, he'd longed for it and now he couldn't bear to lose it or her. The love he and Gray shared made him feel complete. He could take on the world with her by his side. Nothing was impossible. He prayed she never gave up on them.

Gray's breathing became slightly heavy as he unzipped his pants. When they hit the floor a shutter of ecstasy washed over her. She didn't want to admit it, but she needed his dick. She ached for it. Running his fingers through her slick folds, Cam coated his dick with her juices.

His hand glided up and down his shaft until he was lubricated from the tip of his dick to his balls. The musky scent of Gray's arousal filled the air. Cam couldn't hold out any longer, so he positioned his manhood at her womanly door. Inch by aching inch, he slid his 11-inch crooked dick into her hungry vagina. Gray's walls felt like a vice grip around his dick. Filled to the brim, she gasped for air. The thickness of his cock filled her up to the point her throat constricted. Holding onto the sink, she bit into her bottom lip as he dug his way in deeper. She prayed to God he never let her go. Delirious from pleasure she pushed back against him. Cam's deep strokes were almost too much for her to handle but she maintained a steady rhythm.

With each grind of his hips, Gray's brain turned to mush. Cam was fucking away all her strength. By the time they finished there would be none left. Desire burned all around them. Cam was killing her shit. Gray's moans became more ferocious and frequent with each stroke of his cock. Cam pounded into her center. With each thrust her body disenagrated into a million pieces. Roughly and dominantly they forced themselves back-and-forth. Gray could feel her soul levitate above her body. Cam was digging into the truth of her. He wasn't going to stop until she was completely cracked open. Squeezing her waist, he pumped feverishly. Gray screamed like he was out of line for fucking her with such intensity. From hilt to tip, he pulled out then sank back in until he hit bottom. Her silken walls rained down juices onto his cock. Orgasmic sounds were like melodies to his ears as she thrashed before him in distress.

"Ooooooh Cam. Wait-wait-wait." She begged as her body became weak. "Oh God, it feels so good. I can't take it."

"Be a big girl. Take it for daddy. You can do it. Take it. It's all yours."

"It's mine?" She whimpered, gripping the sink.

"I'm yours, this dick yours, my heart is yours. Everything I got is yours." He sucked her earlobe.

It was no secret she was his friend, his lover, his wife and his whore. She loved when Cam abused and used her pussy. She was his porcelain doll. He could pick her up whenever he wanted her and put her back down. His dick was that good. Melting with liquid desire, Gray's body began to tremble. Cam could feel her walls tighten around his shaft. She was about to come. A tidal wave of euphoria swept over her body as her pussy juices drifted free. A bomb denotated in her belly that erupted in her clit. Screams of ecstasy bellowed from her lips as she came. Creamy sap drenched his rigid shaft. Gripping her hips, Cam hit corners of her walls she didn't know existed.

"Fuck this pussy." She begged.

Cam did just that. Not one inch of her pussy went untouched. Shuddering, he worked her shit. A raging primal heat overtook him. Wrist stationed behind her, Gray arched her back as he plummeted deeper. Cam's muscles tensed. The nut he'd been trying to hold back had reached its peak.

"Say you love me." He drilled in and out of her at a feverish pace.

"Ooooooooooh I love you." Gray confessed wholeheartedly.

"Say it again."

"I love you."

"Again."

"I love you, Cam. Baby, I swear I do."

"Louder!" He fucked her relentlessly.

"I LOVE YOU!" She shrilled overcome with desire.

Dripping with fire, he released a volcano of milky white cum into her womb. Cam's body shook viciously as he stuffed her to the brim. The orgasm was so intense his soul visited the seven wonders of the world from the Hanging Gardens of Babylon to the Great Pyramids of Giza. Sweat covered their bodies. Neither he nor Gray knew where things would go from that moment on. The only thing they knew for sure was that their love was ever present and growing fast.

CHAPTER 24

"Even if it means that I'll never put myself back together. Gonna give you my heart to break. Even if I'll ends up in shatters, baby it doesn't matter. Gonna give you my heart to break. I try to fight, but I can't help it. Don't care if this is my worst mistake."-Kim Petras "Heart to Break"

*A*mazement didn't quite cover what Cam felt when he gazed upon the wonderland Gray had created for the triplets' birthday. It felt like someone had took a spark of wonder and doused it in gasoline. After an hour drive they pulled up to what was once a vacant piece of land. The area had been turned into every child's dream. Gray had gone all out. She'd created a day that no one would soon forget. She didn't have one party planned but three. There was a party venue set up for each of the triplets. Each one fit their personality to a T.

For his baby boy, Gray had an elaborate dinosaur-themed bash. A life-sized red Raptor with his mouth wide open was the first thing guests spotted when they walked up. Across from it was the Beignet box food truck wrapped in camouflage. Guests then walked into a smoke-filled dinosaur cave that led to a table filled with party treats that were decorated with dinosaur claws or eggs, and guests could stop to get "Raptor Juice" at a makeshift hut. Multiple DIY craft stations that included a "Jurassic Jewelry" stop, as well as "Dino Domes" were created so that the kids could make their own dinosaur habitats. There was also a ball pit, bounce house and a dig site with helmets, goggles, shovels and more. Reign was dressed perfect for the occasion. He wore a blue beanie, a t-shirt with drip con written on the front, a red and black lumberjack button-up over it, black joggers, Nike socks and Jordan 1 Retro High OG sneakers. A gold chain Cam gifted him with his name written in diamonds shined from his neck.

Holding Beaux's hand, Cam led her to her party venue. Her amusement park birthday bash was even more insane than Reign's. The entrance to the party was comprised of a giant head made to look like her face. When Cam walked inside there was a table that had guidebooks that mapped out all of the attractions. Guests could venture into multiple rooms where various wonders awaited their arrival. The "Frozen" themed room had music from the hit Disney movie playing, a woman dressed as Elsa, an ice sculpture of Olaf, a craft station, a bounce house, and furniture made from ice. The "Trolls" room had rainbow decor and dancers dressed as characters from the movie as well. The largest room, which was dedicated to Beaux, had a giant slide, a ball pit shaped like the letter "B," and dancers on stilts. There was also a section of the party with "Crazy Dumbos" where guests could go on a ride inspired by Disney's "Dumbo." Attendees could also be entertained by a claw machine game, a photo booth, and a tie-dye station. It was literally the craziest shit Cam had ever seen. Beaux had the time of her life dressed in a red, white, and blue logo Fendi jacket, matching t-shirt, shorts, Fendi socks and sneakers. Mimicking Tupac, Cam tied a Fendi scarf around her head.

Last but certainly not least was Cam's sweet baby Sky's tea party themed birthday. The site was transformed into a butterfly paradise with a massive topiary, floral arrangements and moss that looked like something you'd find at Disney World. A playhouse was decorated with blooming flower boxes and delicate butterfly decorations. Pastel colored butterflies surrounded grassy arches over a beautifully decorated seating area. Gray and the party planner set up fairy dust stations with multicolored glitter, a lavender ball pit branded with Sky's name, and a magical swing-set. The wedding worthy table decorations were an explosion of bouquets, butterflies, candles, and flower boxes. No party was complete without themed food. Sky had no shortage of colorful sweets and cookies. There were also sandwiches that matched the tea party aesthetic. The cleverest treat of all were the butterfly-shaped pigs in a blanket. Pink colored drinks matched Sky's pastel nails and pink tulle gown with butterflies all over it. Tea party guests were dressed in pastel-colored outfits, and some wore sparkly wings.

One hundred children, along with their parents, were invited to join the fun along with Cam and Gray's family. When Cam said that no expense should be spared he didn't mean this. He thought Gray would spend a hundred grand max on the party. This extravagant affair had to have cost over a mill.

"Gray, what the hell?" He walked up on her as she talked to Selicia and Tee-Tee.

"What?" She played dumb.

"I should knock yo' fuckin' front tooth out."

"Ooh." Tee-Tee purred. "I love me a roughneck."

"Why?" Gray ignored her over-the-top friend.

"Nigga, you know why. How much money did you spend?"

"One point two mill." She said with ease.

"The fuck!" He screeched. "That's a whole damn house! Do I look like Kylie Jenner to you?"

"That ain't even that much. Quit being a cheapskate. You said do it up, so I did it up big."

"No muthafucka you did it obese! Gimme my fuckin' credit card back!" He reached out his hand.

"Nope. What's yours is mine, remember?" She grinned wickedly.

"Well, I got a hole in my stomach. You want that too?"

"Nigga, please. You always overexaggerating." Selicia said with a yawn. "Gray, the party looks nice. You did a great job. This shit better than Stormi and all the other Kardashians."

"Facts." Stacy agreed.

"You shut your fat ass up!" Cam barked.

"Aww friend!" Stacy bear-hugged him. "You're back. This the first time you told me to shut my fat ass up since you woke up from the coma. I been waiting on this moment."

"Get yo' fat ass off of me!" Cam pushed him away.

"Just like old times." Quan joined the conversation.

"You shut the fuck up too. Where the hell you been?"

"Nigga, I ain't yo' bitch. The fuck." Quan wrinkled his nose.

"I ain't playing, Gray. When we get back to the crib, you giving me my shit."

"Quit complaining." She waved him off. "It's the triplets first big birthday bash. Back in Paris it was just us. They deserve this, Cam. All of our family and friends are here. This will be a birthday they'll never forget."

Cam couldn't argue with that. No matter the expense his kids were happy. The look of joy on their faces made up for the outlandish cost. A million spent wouldn't hurt his pockets. He'd spent that on several cars.

"I can't even front. This shit is lit!" Stacy smacked his lips. He was chowing down on one of Beaux's cake pops. A plate full of other goodies rested in his hand.

"Daddy, can I have a party like this?" His daughter Kyla asked.

"Fuck nah. We going to Chuckie Cheese li'l mama. I can't afford this."

"That don't make no damn sense." Selicia shook her head. "Stop being cheap and give that girl the party she want."

"Right. Daddy, listen to Miss Selicia." Kyla folded her arms and stood back on one leg.

"Miss Selicia gon' fuck around and get her ass kicked if she don't mind her business."

"You ain't gon' do shit. Matter fact, Kyla I'ma make sure your daddy give you a party that's ten times bigger than this."

"Yay!!!!!" She ran off to join Press and King.

"Uh ah! Don't tell her that bullshit! We going to see the big grey mouse!" Stacy yelled after her.

"Gimmie that." Selicia snatched his plate. "I thought you was on a diet?"

"Shiiiiiiiiiit. Who said that?"

"You did. Remember you told God that if He brought Cam back you was gon' start eating healthy."

"You a muthafuckin' lie. I ain't never say no shit like that."

"Yes, you did." Priest joined the conversation. His plan wasn't to stay long. He just swung through to show love and drop off his gifts. Children parties weren't really his thing. Hell, parties in general weren't his idea of fun. Being OCD and being around a bunch of germ-ridden children didn't mix very well.

"Nigga, shut yo' weird ass up. I ain't listening to nobody wit' a nipple ring."

"Nipple rings are sexy." Selicia blushed, biting her lower lip.

"I know that's right." Tee-Tee fanned his self. "I have fantasized about that nipple and that ring being in my mouth several times."

"That's enough." Gray chastised him.

"You know it's the truth. Don't front cause yo' baby daddy standing right here."

"Don't get fucked up." Cam warned, giving her the evil eye.

"Boy hush." She turned her face and grinned. Flashbacks of the night before flashed before her eyes.

"Hold up." Stacy focused on Selicia. "I asked if you wanted me to get a nipple ring and you said no."

"And I meant it. Nigga, your titties is bigger than mine. What are you like a D cup? The piercer wouldn't even be able to give you a barbell, you'll fuck around and a need a pair of hoop earrings or some shit."

The entire crew erupted into a fit of laughter.

"Yo water head ass got jokes, huh? You still keeping that pussy on lock down." He pulled her into him.

"You damn right. Clink! Clink! Nigga." She stepped off to the side so his arm could drop.

"Clink! Clink! My ass. You gon' fuck me."

"Stacy, please. We are just friends."

"Friends fuck." He argued as Noon cut through the crowd and greeted Gray with a hug.

Everyone got quiet. They all were waiting on Cam to blow a gasket. Gray reluctantly hugged him back as Cam watched on. She, too, was expecting him to go off. But to everyone's surprise, Cam kept his cool. There was nothing to be mad about. Noon was a joke to him. How could he possibly be mad or jealous of a man that came to a kids' party dressed in a blue short-sleeve button-up, blue chinos and dress shoes with a fanny pack fastened across his chest.

"Good afternoon everyone." Noon spoke politely.

"Hey." Tee-Tee and Selicia spoke back.

Stacy ignorant ass thought about being cordial, but his silly ass just couldn't hold back. The jone was sitting right there in his throat begging to come out.

"This lame ass nigga gotta baby bag across his chest with no baby." He bugged up laughing.

Unfortunately for Noon, Cam, Gray, Quan, Selicia and Tee-Tee laughed too. Noon's face reddened with anger as he balled up his fist. He was mortified that someone would talk to him that way. It was a must he get Gray away from these barbarians. They were nothing but ghetto hooligans. With her fame and stature, she shouldn't be associated with such trash.

"What you ballin' yo' fist up for? I dare you to say something, pussy!" Stacy jumped at him 'causing him to flinch a little bit.

"I told you to stop wearing that." Gray said, feeling bad for him.

Noon inhaled and exhaled oxygen through his nose he was so tight.

"Aye, yo my man, can you breathe?" Stacy patted his chest. "Nigga gotta a whole portable oxygen tank across his chest."

"It's actually a Fendi fanny pack but you wouldn't know anything about that." Noon defended himself.

"Nah, nigga that's a Fendi faggot pack and it got cheetah print on it. What you keep in there lip-gloss?"

"Nah, that nigga keep tampons in there. Kotex at that." Cam joined into the fun.

"You smell that?" Stacy sniffed the air.

"Yep." Quan nodded.

"Whew." Selicia fanned her nose.

"I don't smell anything?" Noon sniffed his under arm, which smelled of Dove deodorant.

"I smell!" Stacy pretended as if he was about sneeze. "I smell!"

"PUSSY!" The group said in unison then broke out in laughter.

"Real mature guys. Real mature." Noon huffed as steam blew from his ears.

"On some real shit. I expected more outta you Gray." Stacy shook his head. "Fat people gotta stick together and this who you choose?"

"Shut up, Stacy. Leave that man alone." Selicia scolded him.

"What? Everybody was thinking it."

"C'mon, Gray. I wanna go say hi to the kids." Noon took her by the hand and pulled her away from the crowd. Cam watched as she went off with him. He wanted to stop her, but it was their kids' birthday party and for once he didn't want to make a scene. This was their day. Cam would be damned if he or anyone else ruined it. Noon would be out of the picture soon anyway.

DESPITE IT BEING A KIDS' PARTY, AOKI, THE TWINS, PRINCESS AND Li'l Quan were having the time of their lives. They were running around playing just as much as the little kids. When the day was over, Aoki would probably have a stomachache from all the treats she'd devoured. She was having so much fun that she'd completely forgot that Paris was coming. It wasn't until she received a text from him that she remembered.

PARIS: Come outside

All the butterflies at Sky's party entered her belly. Aoki should've known he'd pull a stunt like this. Paris liked playing with fire. Which meant they were a dangerous mix because Aoki was a risk taker. Telling him no should've been her response but being in his presence would be the highlight of her day. Checking her face with her camera phone, she made sure the black beanie on her head was intact. The lump from the day before was still ever present. Thank God the beanie didn't take away from her beauty. It enhanced her look. It paired perfectly with the small gold hoops, gold necklaces, white cut-off t-shirt, black Calvin Klein sports bra, emerald green corduroy jacket, matching skirt and Doc Martin boots. Aoki looked good, damn good. She was sure Paris would think so too.

"I'll be back." She placed her phone in the pocket of her Balenciaga cross-body bag.

"Where you going?" Ryan pried.

"None of yo' business li'l nosy ass girl." Aoki sauntered off before anyone else could question her. It took her a minute to find Paris. There were a million cars parked. When she spotted him, he was leaned against his old school. His hands were tucked in his pocket and one leg was crossed over the other. Dressed in a blue, orange, and white Cleveland Cavaliers Starter jacket, white tee, fitted jeans and Air Max sneakers he resembled a god. An orange beanie was cocked to the right on his head. Designer tinted shades covered his eyes while sparkly diamonds danced around his neck. Aoki's heart thudded. No one had to tell her. She was obsessed with this nigga. It was a damn shame he was so fine. Only his brother got her this riled up. Paris left every nerve ending in her body exposed. His swagger was all the way right. Nicole Wray's *I Can't See* came to mind every time she gazed at his gorgeous face. Damya and her parents be damned. She had to have him. It didn't matter that she was young in age. She wasn't trying to live in a world where he didn't exist.

"Didn't I tell you not to come?" She placed her hand on her invisible hip.

"You should know by now I don't follow the rules." His sleepy brown eyes roamed over her statuesque frame. Paris was in over his head, but it was all right. Aoki was worth the risk. His big cousin would surely have a problem if they started dating. He was a street nigga and she was Cam's precious baby girl. The two of them together was a recipe for disaster but the heart wants what the heart wants. And damn did Paris want her. When he was with Aoki the world around them disappeared. He drowned in the depth of her ocean blue eyes. In a short amount of time she'd had a profound effect on him. Girls in the past didn't care about his wellbeing, but she did. She always encouraged him to do better and be better. If he relaxed his mind and let her all the way in, he was sure they'd have a love that would last a lifetime.

"Yeah, well nigga I ain't trying to die behind you. My pops is crazy."

"I am too." He toyed with a long spirally piece of her hair.

"There's a such thing as crazy and then there's Cam crazy. You ain't that."

"You must think I'm worth it 'cause you came out here to fuck wit' a nigga."

Not only did Aoki's cheeks burn red but her whole face did as well.

"You a'ight." She blushed bashfully. "You know the Homecoming dance is coming up. You going?"

"Nah, gangsters don't dance, we boogie."

"You stupid." Aoki giggled.

"On some real shit. That ain't my thing but how the party going? Go get me a piece of cake."

"No. They haven't cut it yet. And you see how the party's going. They spent about a million dollars on this shit."

"Shit, more than that."

"All I know is they better go dumb for my birthday."

"When is it?"

"Same day as Homecoming. On Halloween."

"I should've known yo' demonic ass was born on the devil's day." He chuckled.

"You got me messed up. I believe in the Lord. You're the sinner."

"Me and God homies. I read the bible all the time." He lied.

"Bye, Paris. I don't believe nothing you say."

"Dead ass. Test me."

"What's your favorite scripture?" She cocked her head to the side, skeptical.

"Psalm 34."

"What is it?"

"Shit if I know." He shrugged his shoulders, amused.

"Yo' ass just thought of somebody jersey number or some shit. Now I gotta look it up." She pulled out her phone.

"What it say?"

"Psalm 34 says I will bless the Lord at all times. His praise will continuously be in my mouth—"

"That's a pause. You gotta pause that." Paris cut her off.

"Nah, you wildin'. He said *praise*, nasty!" She hit him playfully.

"I will bless the Lord at all times." Paris said slowly. "His praise will continuously be in my mouth. Nah son."

"You can't pause the bible bro." Aoki argued, putting her phone back in her purse.

"Nah, fam you gotta pause that. You cannot tell me that scripture don't sound wild."

"I'm not messing wit' you. God ain't gon' strike me down. You better chill out with all that."

"God know my heart. He laughing at that one too."

Giggling at his sick sense of humor, Aoki rubbed her hands together. It was starting to get cold because she wasn't in the heated area. Paris pushed off his car and stood at his full height. Aoki looked up into his eyes and watched helplessly as he invaded her personal space. One by one he took her hands in his and placed them inside his jacket. Aoki balled her hands into a fist afraid to touch him. This wasn't like the time they were alone in the pool. Anybody could be around watching them, so she had to be careful. And Aoki was right. Someone did have their eyes on them, and they were watching her and Paris' every move.

Despite the heaviness in her stomach, it fluttered at the feeling of her body pressed against his. She sunk into the warmth of his arms appreciative of the tender gesture. His touch instantly melted away the coldness she felt seconds before. She'd waited months to be this way with him again, but nothing could've prepared her for this moment. In his embrace she was cocooned better than any butterfly-to-be. Paris gazed back at her. Usually her blue eyes were touched by storm clouds, but when they were intimate, they became softer than he knew a pair of eyes could be. Her eyes were fire in water, if you can imagine such a thing. They were passion on ice. They had a thousand hues of blue and a small touch of hazel radiating in softly swooping arcs.

Before they met, Paris thought moments like this only existed in the movies. But this shit was real. The feel of her body so close to his soothed him in ways he never expected. Paris mind swam with the heady excitement of a new relationship. Why deprive himself? If he let down his guard he could have this feeling all the time.

Aoki bit her lip as his warm hand cupped her cheek. It took all the will power she had not to rub against his palm like a kitten craving attention. Like her eyes, her breathing became softer. The pensive look on her face melted away and her muscles relaxed. There was something about Paris' gaze that she would never find in another boy. It was like their souls made a bridge through eye contact. Slowly, he leaned closer. He tried to control his urges but dear God, he couldn't fight the thoughts that were running through him. Her saccharine scent was flooding his senses now. Unable to hold back, his full lips brushed against hers, softly and delicately, like butterfly wings. Paris kissed her like she wanted to be kissed, like no other boy had ever kissed her before. It was perfect. Seeking closeness, they shared one breath, one sensation, one timeless and passionate moment.

Mesmerized by him, the sweet taste of his tongue, the feel of his strong hands, Aoki's head began to swim. When she was in his arms time collapsed into one tiny speck and exploded at lightning speed. Paris gave her peace. Being with him felt as if her heart was dancing around in her chest and a hole she was never aware of was filled. For the first time since she was a child, Aoki felt light. She was on top of the world but with each flicker of his tongue, oxygen left her lungs. By the time they both came up for air she was dizzy with desire. Running her fingertips across her lips, she stepped back.

"Let that be the last time you kiss me while you belong to somebody else." She walked off and left him standing there in a daze.

~

GRAY, MO, KEMA, HEIDI AND DYLAN SAT AT ONE OF THE DINO DOME tables drinking Raptor juice and talking shit. It had been ages since all the girls got together and had a kiki. Gray loved her friends. They kept her grounded and helped her sort through all her mess.

"You excited about the baby?" Dylan asked Kema.

"Hell yeah. It's my first." She smiled gleefully.

"You want a boy or a girl?"

"A girl. We already have a son. Plus, I'm tired of being the only girl. Quan and Li'l Quan always ganging up on me."

"It's so crazy to hear you call Li'l Quan your son. At one point and time, I couldn't even hear that child's name." Mo admitted.

"Really?" Kema said surprised.

"Girl, yeah. I couldn't stand the sight of his face. I was such a bitch to that baby. I remember when I sat him out on the porch and everything."

"Mo, no you did not."

"Yes, I did. I had just lost my baby, so it wasn't my best moment."

"I get that." Kema nodded her head sympathetically.

"I would've never thought in a million years that I could have one baby, let alone six."

"I don't know how you and Gray do it." Heidi chimed in. "I only have one kid and I'm stressed the fuck out."

"I only have one too and I'm trying desperately to have another one." Dylan confessed.

"I'm so sorry, Dylan. With everything I have going on, I forgot to ask. How is the surrogacy going?" Gray inquired.

"You'll be happy to know that the embryo implantation was a success. We're having a baby!" She cheered.

"Oh my God! Congratulations!" Gray squeezed her tight.

The other ladies congratulated her as well.

"Thanks." Dylan gushed. "I'm so happy."

"Do you know what you're having?" Heidi quizzed.

"Yes. A little girl."

"Oh Lord. Dylan with a little girl. The world ain't ready for that." Gray joked.

"They sure ain't."

"So, Gray." Mo popped her tongue. "How many months are you?"

Kema almost choked on her Rapture juice.

"Gray, you're pregnant?!" Heidi examined her closely.

"Shhhhhhh! Say it louder, why don't you?" She looked around to make sure Cam wasn't anywhere around. He wasn't. The coast was clear.

"OMG. You're pregnant." Heidi whispered with wonder in her eyes.

"Yes, but Cam doesn't know yet."

"Why you ain't tell him?" Mo died to know.

"Well, I told him on his birthday but of course he doesn't remember that. Then he woke up and broke things off with me and I was so hurt that I didn't wanna see him. Now it's just a thing of finding the right time to tell him."

"How far along are you?"

"Three months." Gray winced, placing her shoulders up to her ears.

"Girl, Cam is gonna be pissed."

"I know. I know. I'm gonna tell him soon."

"So, you knew about this?" Heidi questioned Kema with an attitude.

"Yeah."

"Oh, so you bitches keeping secrets now?"

"I wanted to tell you friend. I swear, I did but it was already bad that I told Kema before I told Cam officially."

"I understand." She rubbed the back of Gray's hand.

"Just please guys. Don't say anything." She stressed with urgency.

"We got you, girl. Our lips are sealed." Dylan zipped her mouth shut.

HOURS INTO THE FESTIVITIES, CAM FOUND A QUIET SPACE ALONE TO breathe. At times he still became winded, which he hated. He refused to let his family see him that way, mainly Gray. She'd get all worried and start watching him like a hawk. The last thing he wanted was to be babied. He wouldn't make the triplets' day about him. All afternoon, he'd been ripping and running going from Sky's party to Beaux's and Reign's. Between playing with them and mingling with the guests, he was dog-tired. He knew he shouldn't be pushing his self to such strenuous limits, but he'd lose a lung for his kids. Cam wished he could've snuck off with Gray, but he'd barely spent any time with her all day. They both had been running around like chickens with their heads cut off. Gray, however, was not only in mommy mode but hostess mode. She was such a people pleaser. She always wanted the people around her to feel good. When the party was over he had big plans to give her a night of rest and relaxation that would consist of a glass of wine, a steaming hot bubble bath and a hot oil massage. She deserved that and more.

"You know you done fucked up." Noon came out of nowhere and sat across from him.

The last person Cam wanted to see was his goofy ass. He'd done a great job of avoiding him since earlier that day. Cam knew if he came within ten feet of him again, he'd rip his head off his neck. Noon was a nigga that liked to push buttons. Cam could tell by the mischievous look in his eye that he was up to no good.

"First of all, who the fuck you talking to? Don't get embarrassed in this muthafucka. I been doing good with keeping my cool."

"You know . . . I thought we had an understanding." Noon steepled his hands together.

"We don't have shit."

"Obviously, 'cause I thought I'd made myself clear when I told you to stay away from Gray. But you wanna be hardheaded."

"Aye, yo it's taking a lot out of me not to slit your throat. So, I'd advise you to get out my face, homey." Cam clenched his jaw. He was so mad he thought his head was going to explode.

"I intend to do just that, but before I go back to be with Gray and my future step kids, I thought I'd make you aware that I know what you've been up to."

Cam shot him a stony glare. He was not in the mood for this shit.

"See, while you think you're so slick and untouchable, I've had my eyes on you. I know you've been with Gray this whole weekend." Judging by Cam's blank stare and silence, Noon knew he had him right where he wanted. Noon had a surveillance team on him the entire time. "You just can't follow directions can you? You had one job and you couldn't even do that."

"You know what?" Cam turned in his seat and faced him. "You're different?"

"And what's that supposed to mean, Archibald?" Noon leaned in closer.

"I done met a lot of pussies in my life but you a different type of pussy. I ain't never met a grown man so obsessed with one girl, that he goes out his way to blackmail a muthafucka."

Noon shriveled before him, but Cam kept going. It became crystal clear. He didn't have to fuck him up with his hands. It was evident he did more damage with his words.

"The sad part is you really think you got a chance with her and you don't. Whether I'm with Gray or not she's never gonna love you. Get some therapy, my nigga. Clearly, she only wants one man and we both know that man is me."

Noon seethed with anger. Every time Cam opened his big mouth he became angrier. His hunched form exuded an animosity that was like acid-burning. He and Gray had a life before she came back to St. Louis. He wasn't going to lose her to Cam.

"Gray only has feelings for you 'cause she doesn't know any better. Between you and Gunz, she wouldn't know a good man if he smacked her in the face. I mean, what woman in her right mind would want an ex-army vet, with PTSD, a rap sheet, daddy issues, a dead mother and ties to the mafia? Only a woman with low self-esteem and no guidance but that's where I come in."

Cam's knuckles turned white from squeezing his fist so hard. Every word Noon spewed fueled the fire that burned within him. Every violating phrase was like gasoline to it.

"Gray deserves nothing but the finer things in life. She shouldn't be slumming it with the likes of you. And now that you'll be out of the picture, I can show her what a real man looks like. So, enjoy your last day with your so-called family." Noon went to stroll off but stopped. "You know I didn't see myself being a father of five but . . . I think I'll be good at it. Enjoy the party, Archibald. I'll do my best to keep your memory alive." He patted his shoulder mockingly and left as quickly as he came.

"What that pussy ass nigga want?" Quan wandered over. He'd been looking all over for Cam. It was time to cut the cake. As soon as he walked up tho, he knew something was wrong. Cam's eyes flashed with anger, much like lightning on a pitch-black night.

"No more waiting." He grinded his teeth. "We gotta get rid of that nigga tonight."

"You sure?" Quan knew he still struggled with his health.

There was nothing to think about. This was Cam's family. The only thing he'd ever fought so hard for. He'd die if he lost them. Literally. A bullet, knife or poison wouldn't be needed.

"Certain. I gotta get to him before he gets to Victor."

"Say less. What you wanna do?"

∾

BY THE TIME THE PARTY ENDED THE WARM BRONZE SUN WAS swallowed by the horizon. The bright sunny day was engulfed into darkness. A beautiful darkness. A darkness that welcomed coolness to the atmosphere. It was the perfect night to cuddle up in front of the fireplace with the one you love. Cam prayed Gray would let him stay over after he took care of some necessary business so they could do just that. Together, he and Priest brought all of the triplets presents inside. There were so many that they all couldn't fit into his and Gray's car. While they stacked the gifts up, Gray stripped the sleeping babies out of their clothes. It had been a long day. The whole family was depleted of energy. Gray was not only tired but a little down. They'd sang Happy Birthday twice to the kids, once in English and once in Korean. When they did the Korean version, Gray paid homage to their baby girl that died at birth. She tried not to think of her often because when she did, she became extremely sad. That day, however, it was hard not to. Cam did everything in his power to be there for her.

"Aye, yo let me holla at you for a second." Priest pulled Cam to the side.

"What's up?" He huffed. Cam wasn't in the mood for bad news, but he knew it was coming. Priest barely talked, and when he did, it was only to make him aware of something that would affect him in a big way.

"You might wanna talk to your daughter."

"Which one?" Cam's brows formed into a frown.

"The tall one with the weird name. I saw her hugged up with my li'l brother earlier today."

Vomit rose in Cam's throat. A muscle twitched involuntarily at the corner of his right eye; his mouth formed into a rigid scowl. With arms folded tightly across his broad chest, he tried not to pass out. Cam was aware that some li'l boy was sniffing behind Aoki, but he never thought it would be Paris. That was the last thing he ever expected to hear. Outside of attending the same school, he didn't know how they'd even connected. They weren't even in the same grade. From what he knew they didn't even run in the same circles. Then he remembered she used to be friends with that li'l fast ass girl, Kiara, who dated a young street nigga named Meechi. Meechi and Paris were pot'nahs. Cam hung his head back. It all made sense now.

"What you mean hugged up?" He pinched the bridge of his nose. A headache had started to ensue.

"Just like I said. Hugged up and kissing."

"Where you see this at? I ain't even know that nigga was there."

"Outside in the parking lot."

Cam rolled his head around in a circle. Life was catching up to him and fast. The walls around him were closing in, and for the first time, Cam couldn't figure a way out.

"Aoki!"

"Huh?" She speed walked out of her room. Cam hardly ever called her name with such urgency. When she made it to the living room she found him and Priest standing side-by-side. Instantly, she knew something was wrong. They both had stone expressions on their faces. Aoki's heart pounded inside of her chest. What could she have possibly done? And why was Priest involved? Ever since that day at the hospital, she'd barely acknowledged his presence. She went out of her way to pretend he didn't exist, and it had been working, until that moment. When she was forced to be around him all the old feelings she harbored came rushing back to the surface. Like his brother, he was a stunning force of nature. How had she not put two and two together that they were siblings?

"What the fuck is this I'm hearing from Priest that you was outside kissing Paris?"

Aoki looked from Cam to Priest. He stared back at her with no sign of remorse written on his face.

"Fuckin' snitch," she hissed.

"Is that true?" Cam pressed.

Aoki lost it.

"Why don't you mind your business? Don't you gotta girlfriend? Worry about her funny looking ass. Don't worry about me." She spat with venom at Priest.

"Nah, yo' li'l ass need to remember you're thirteen." Cam reprimanded her. "You ain't got no business putting yo' mouth on no nigga's lips. And that better be the only place you put 'em!"

"Really, Pop? Calm down." Aoki tuned up her face, repulsed.

"No, you calm down. 'Cause if I find out you been sucking dick I'ma shoot you in the fuckin' vagina!"

"What are you yelling for?" Gray raced out the back. She'd kick Cam's ass if he woke up the triplets.

"Your daughter trying to send me back to prison, Gray. Did you know her and Paris are fuckin' around?"

"No." She faced Aoki, horrified. She had no clue any of this was going on. "Aoki, is that true?"

"Yeah . . . tell her. Tell ya' mama." Cam shouted, furiously.

"It was just one kiss." She tried to explain.

"How long has this been going on?" Gray tried to keep her cool. She couldn't afford to faint while pregnant and risk losing another child.

"Not long."

"How fuckin' long is not long?" Cam yelled.

"A few weeks . . . dang. It ain't even that serious. We don't even go together. We're just friends. He." Aoki pointed at Priest. "Over here blowing things out of portion and don't even know the facts. He need to focus on him and his bitch. Instead of focusing on me and mine."

"Whoa! Whoa! You ain't got shit!" Cam made clear.

"And watch your fuckin' mouth!" Gray backed him up. She was five seconds away from having a heart attack.

"I'm sorry but he get on my dang-on nerves."

"How the fuck you mad and you're the one in the wrong?" Cam begged to know.

"But I'm not. We're just friends." Aoki groaned.

"No, y'all are practically cousins."

"We ain't blood." She drew her head back.

"Yo, this child gon' give me a fuckin' aneurism. You betta get her, Gray." Cam massaged his temples, pacing the room.

"That's beside the point, Aoki." She spoke sternly. "You're too young. And how old is he?"

"Sixteen." Priest spoke up.

"Nobody asked you." Aoki snapped.

"Oh, hell nah!" Gray blew her lid.

"Have you lost your damn mind?" Cam looked at her crazy. "First of all, you ain't even supposed to be dating, let alone a sixteen-year-old boy, that's your cousin!"

"We're not related and why can't I date? I'm not a little kid. I'm mature. I know how to handle myself."

"You think you do but you don't sweetheart." Gray replied empathetically.

"You are a fuckin' child—" Cam began.

"Teen!" Aoki corrected him.

"You heard what the fuck I said! You don't pay no bills in this muthafucka! Everything in here is on lease to you! If we put you out today you would walk out this muthafucka naked! So, until you get a place of your own, you are a fuckin' child and you will do as we say!"

"Whatever you and this boy have going on needs to end tonight." Gray demanded.

"But—"

"Ain't no buts." Cam cut her off. "Ain't no negotiation. This shit ain't up for discussion."

Aoki's sapphire eyes welled up with a sadness her young years should not possess. They showed her soul. Cam tried to be immune to her weeping. He was a gangster. Gangsters didn't fold. He'd killed men on the battlefield of war, but Aoki's silent weeping was worse than his squad being gunned down by the enemy.

"Listen." He wrapped his arm around her. Aoki buried her face in his chest. She hated to cry. She really didn't want to in front of Priest of all people. It was embarrassing.

"I'ma keep it a hunnid wit' you. I know you're getting older and you think you know everything, but you don't. You ain't never been no sixteen-year-old boy before but I have. You don't know what type of time he on, but I do and you ain't ready for that shit. Niggas like Paris trying to get in where they fit in and then be on to the next bitch. At sixteen niggas ain't trying to wife up no chick and fall in love. This ain't the shit you watch on the TV. Nigga, this ain't The Hills. This real fuckin' life, baby girl. You may think you're ready for a nigga like him but on my mama you're not. Paris got a lot of shit with him that you're not emotionally mature enough to handle."

What Cam and Gray failed to realize was that Aoki wasn't a little girl anymore. She hadn't been a child in a while. She'd grown up faster than she should. Having Gunz abandon her, learning the truth about her paternity and becoming a second mother to her siblings changed her in unexpected ways. At a tender age she saw the extreme realities of life. The world wasn't made of princesses and rainbows. It was ugly, gritty and painful. Happiness came in spurts and pain often lasted a lifetime. People were fickle and often selfish. She understood all of this. She'd witnessed firsthand the complexities of life and love by watching Cam and Gray. She didn't walk around with rose colored glasses on. She saw things for what they were. Her parents didn't need to coddle her or hold her hand. Aoki was stronger than either of them realized. And yes, she still had a lot to learn. She would be naive to think she knew everything. But Gray and Cam had to trust that they'd raised her to make the right decisions.

"But Pop, you don't understand." She reasoned. "It's different with us. I know he be out here in the streets doing him but around me he doesn't act like that. He respects me because I respect myself. He knows I'm a virgin. He knows I'm not doing anything right now and he still likes me. Matter of fact, sex hasn't even been a topic of conversation between us. We talk about music, what we're gonna be when we grow up and believe it or not, God. Trust me. I'm not as inexperienced as you think. I know what I'm doing."

"You say he respects you, but do you know he be running around wit' LaLa li'l dirty ass niece?"

"Actually, I do. That's why we're only friends. I have too much respect for myself to be any boy's side anything."

"But you was outside kissing him? Aoki shut yo' ass up. You ain't ready." Cam released her from his hold. No matter what he said, he wasn't getting through to her.

"The bottom line is when you turn sixteen we can revisit this conversation. But as of today you are not allowed to date." Gray made herself clear. "You don't need to be worried about no li'l boy. You need to be focused on school and that's it. You understand?"

Aoki wiped the tears from her face and sighed. What was one of the best days of her life had quickly turned into the worst.

"Yes ma'am." She sighed, rolling her eyes.

"Now get ready for bed."

Before she left, Aoki shot Priest an evil glare. If she could spit on him she would have. It was bad enough he didn't want her and now he was ruining her first chance at having a real boyfriend.

"I hate your snitch ass. Don't ever say nothing to me again."

"Take yo' ass to your room! He don't talk to you no way!" Cam barked.

Aoki did as she was told, but little did he know, she had no intention on cutting things off with Paris. Moving forward, they were just going to be more careful at not getting caught. Why would she listen to Cam anyway? He was just like the fuckboys he spoke of. He'd gone back on his word and left her mother for a ho just like Damya. His so-called words of wisdom meant nothing to her.

"Thanks, Priest." Gray said sincerely. If it wasn't for him she and Cam would've been completely in the dark.

"You got it." He nodded.

"I'ma go finish putting the kids to bed."

"I'll be in there in a second." Cam replied. When they were alone he turned to Priest. "Thanks for looking out, cuz. I don't know what I'ma do with these kids."

"Say less. You know I got you. You already know shit hectic between me and P. This the last thing I need either."

"Right."

"But I'ma keep an eye on 'em. You can trust me."

CHAPTER 25

"I'ma lowkey freak you don't know me yet."-Jhene Aiko "Maniac"

Seven whole days had gone by and Gray hadn't heard a word from Noon. It was like he'd disappeared off the face of the earth. His last words to her before he left the party was that he'd be by to pick her up for breakfast the next day. She'd looked forward to the meet up. The plan was for them to go to her favorite breakfast spot called Rooster. They had the best French Toast in town. She and the baby had been craving the sweet syrupy goodness. And yes, Noon was often stuffy but Gray genuinely enjoyed his company. Noon was a pleasant man and he was kind. When she'd needed someone to lean on, he was there. They might not have worked out romantically, but she'd always value the friendship they'd shared.

Over and over she called his phone and text, but she never got one response. Gray was worried sick. It wasn't like Noon to go M.I.A. He made it his business to keep in contact with her, so his sudden vanishing act didn't make any sense. She wanted to reach out to someone to see if he was alright but Gray had never met any of his family so reaching out to them wasn't an option. The notion that he'd gone back to New York early because of a business emergency popped in her mind. Gray thought about calling his office to see if that was the case. It was the only contact information she had on him, but she didn't wanna come off unprofessional. Noon took his career very seriously. She didn't wanna overstep and embarrass him. Unsure of what to do, she made it up in her mind that if she didn't hear from him within the next few days she'd call his job then.

In the meantime, she parked her chrome colored Ashton Martin Valkyrie on the cobblestone driveway of an unfamiliar home. Cam text her an address and told her to meet him there in an hour. His other request was that she dress up. Gray never had a problem throwing on her Sunday's best. She hadn't been able to get dolled up since his birthday. This would be the last time she'd successfully be able to hide her pregnancy without him knowing. In two weeks, she'd be four months pregnant. The bump in her belly had grown significantly over the last few days.

Taking advantage of the cool weather she rocked a chocolate leather beret, Anna Karin Karlsson aviator shades, a blunt cut shoulder length bob, a brown leather high neck long sleeve Zimmermann dress with a pleated skirt and gold Casadei sling back heels. Gold bracelets and rings decorated her wrist and hands. Gray looked and felt like a bag of money as she walked up the stoned steps. Just as she was about to knock, the front door opened. Cam stood on the other side of the threshold taking her breath away. Gray had to consciously stop herself from drooling. She gawked openly as she noted his chiseled jaw, chin, and cheekbones. Cam was gorgeous from the depth of his eyes to the gravelly tenor of his voice. On either side of his straight freckled nose were two warm brown eyes fringed with specks of gold. He wore diamond framed glasses, a sky blue, black and grey fuzzy Ambush sweater, ripped Amiri jeans and charcoal gray Yeezy sneakers. Gray thanked her lucky stars that she was his wife. She'd slit her throat if another woman bared his last name.

"Hi." She spoke softly.

"What you being bashful for? Bring yo' pretty ass in here." Cam took her hand and helped her inside. Gray's mouth dropped wide open. Thousands of pink helium heart-shaped balloons floated from the ceiling. Some had weights attached to the ends so they could stay on the ground. More pink balloons covered the floor. If Cam was trying to make her fall deeper in love with him, he was succeeding. It was the sweetest romantic gesture he'd made in years.

"What's going on? Where are we?" She gazed around the expansive abode.

"Home."

Gray's heart skipped several beats as she turned on her heels and faced him.

"You didn't?" Her blue eyes sparkled with wonder.

"I did. It's time for us to be a family again." He laced his fingers with hers. The palm of Gray's hand began to sweat as soon as they made contact. It didn't take away from the fact that her long lean fingers completed the space left in-between his as he took her on a tour of the mansion.

Gray's lips stretched wide into a gaping grin. The house was stunning. It was the most expensive home on the market in St. Louis before Cam purchased it for 13 million dollars. The exceptionally crafted, serene country estate boasted formal and informal rooms and unsurpassed outdoor entertaining with over 30,000 square feet of living spaces. With nine bedrooms and thirteen bathrooms, there was a whole lot to explore on the property. Gray gasped in awe. Every room they went in was filled with balloons. The 2-story foyer featured inlaid limestone floor, a marble staircase, and a domed ceiling. The great room offered a wood burning fireplace and a 10-foot accordion glass door that folded back and opened to the terrace which had views of the rear of the property. A pool, pond, basketball, and tennis court were added amenities that took the home over the top. What Gray really loved was the spacious kitchen. The architect equipped the area with custom cabinetry, stone counters, and high-end appliances. There was also a home theater and a private guest suite. The last stop on the tour was the secluded main floor master wing. Gray's mouth dropped. Inside there was a gracious sitting room, gas fireplace, wet bar, his/her closets, and an elegant bath. A California king bed sat in the center of the room. Pink balloons were everywhere. Above the bed were silver balloons that spelled out Happy Anniversary. The day was October 25th. They'd officially been married 4 years. The rapper J. Cole stood in the corner of the room with a three-piece band rapping one of Cam's favorite songs titled *She's Mine Pt. 1*. Tears the size of lemons drops filled the brim of Gray's eyes. Cam held her from behind and placed his chin on her shoulder as they listened to the live performance.

"Every time you go to sleep you look like you in Heaven
Plus the head game is stronger than a few Excedrin
You shine just like the patent leather on my new 11's
You read me like a book like I'm the Bible, you the Reverend
And, I wanna tell the truth to you
I wanna talk about my days as a youth to you
Exposing you to all my demons and the reasons I'm this way
I would like to paint a picture, but it'll take more than a day
It would take more than some years to get all over all my fears
Preventing me from letting you see all of me perfectly clear
The same wall that's stopping me
From letting go and shedding tears
From the lack of having father, and the passing of my peers
While I'm too scared to expose myself
It turns out, you know me better than I know myself
Better than I know myself, well how about that?"

J. Cole's thick long locs covered his face as he held the microphone to his lips and bobbed his head to the piano keys. Gray couldn't believe he was only a few feet away and in a home Cam had bought for her no less. Together they sang along to the chorus.

"She gets him, you get me
She hugs him, you kiss me
You tell me, you miss me
And I believe you, I believe you
She gets him, you get me
She hugs him, you kiss me
You tell me, you miss me
And I believe you, I believe you
Catch me, don't you
Catch me, don't you catch me
I've fallen in love for the first time."

When the song was over, Cam and Gray gave him a thunderous applause. J. Cole gave them a slight bow. He and his band then left the room so they could have some alone time. When the door closed, Cam walked in front of Gray and stood before her. Gray wilted under his dreamy gaze. Nervous, he licked his bottom lips and held her by the waist. Cam needed something to anchor him in case he stumbled over his words.

"You know a nigga ain't good with expressing my feelings. In the past whenever I tried to tell you the feelings whirling around in my soul, my throat would tighten, and I'd freeze up. But I'm past all that. It's our anniversary, and I felt it was a must you know how much I love you. Four years ago, I made the biggest mistake of my life when I let you go. I was an angry, selfish nigga that chased after things that looked good, or women who were bad but never truly had a place in my heart. But then I met you. No matter what, even when I fucked up you were there. You stood by my side supporting me. Though I didn't know it at the time, I loved you, you were more than just a best friend to me. I could tell you anything and you never judged me. I thought I had shit figured out, but I didn't. Without my knowing, from the moment I you saw you in Principle Glanville's office real love began to take shape in my heart. I only truly realized it on that rainy New Year's Eve night when you left me. Gray, you were so different from the other women I chased. You cared. You gave a fuck about my well-being. And for that you're the only woman I want. The only woman I'll ever need. You're the only woman I love." He paused to gather his self.

"There has never been anyone like you in my life. And I know I got fucked up ways. I ain't the easiest nigga to get along with or understand but I swear to God one day I'm gonna be good enough for you."

"You already are." Gray replied sincerely.

"I know it's a lot to ask considering everything we've been through, but would you be willing to give me . . . to give us. . . another chance?"

Gray pulled out of his hold and brushed her hand across her face. So many thoughts ran through her mind. She was truly overwhelmed. For the first time she was speechless. She didn't know what to say.

"Don't think. Just say yes." Cam tried to persuade her. It would break his heart if she said no.

"I don't know, Cam. Just a few weeks ago you were with Devin and then there's Noon—"

"Why the fuck are you bringing up another man on our anniversary?" He barked, infuriated. The last name he wanted to hear was Noon's.

"Cause he's my friend." Gray said taken aback by his brash attitude.

"That nigga ain't shit to you but a memory."

"What the hell is that supposed to mean?" She eyed him quizzically.

"Exactly what the fuck I said." He kicked a balloon out of his way and sat on the edge of the bed.

"What did you do, Cameron?" She eased towards him.

"I took care of a potential threat."

"What do you mean took care of? Did you hurt him?"

"If I said yes would it affect us being together again?"

"Depends on what you did." Gray narrowed her stormy blue eyes.

Cam sucked his teeth before responding. His reply might change the entire course of the day, hell their future.

"He's on a permanent vacation." He finally admitted. Gray's eyes nearly popped out of their sockets. He had to be playing a cruel joke on her. Cam couldn't have been that demented to kill Noon.

"What did you do?"

Inhaling air into his lungs, Cam let out a long sigh and thought back on the events of that fatal night.

A fetish is typically referred to as a behavior that someone cannot get sexually aroused without. Noon's kink was bondage. Bondage in the BDSM subculture, is the practice of consensually tying, binding, or restraining a partner for erotic, aesthetic or somatosensory stimulation. A partner may be physically restrained in a variety of ways, including the use of rope, cuffs, bondage tape, or self-adhering bondage. Noon got off on torture bondage. In this form of bondage, the restrained partner is purposefully bound in an uncomfortable or painful position, for example as a punishment in connection of a dominant/submissive sexual play. Almost any form of bondage, when the restrained partner is left tied up long enough, can be used as torture bondage. The tight feel of the rope digging into Noon's skin as he was restrained for hours on end did things for his libido that penetration from a woman would never provide. The orgasms he experienced through traditional sex were satisfying but forced orgasms took him to other dimensions and galaxies.

A person being brought to involuntary orgasm would typically be put in physical restraints to deprive them of the ability to control the onset and intensity of an orgasm. Noon liked receiving forced orgasms through cock and ball torture. The method stretched the boundaries of climaxing. It was an otherworldly experience that he craved on a daily. Left to his own devices he'd feed his freaky fetish every day after work but because of his high-profile career, it was a must he curve his appetite. However, whether he was in New York or St. Louis once a week, he visited his go-to sex dungeon where all of his sexual desires were fulfilled. It wasn't like Gray was nourishing his sexual needs. The last time they'd been intimate was weeks before she left Paris for the wedding. She'd friend zoned him and hadn't looked back since.

Torture bondage and forced orgasms weren't his only fetish tho. Noon had a secret sexual attraction to transgender women. Transgender dominatrix at that. It was something he'd discovered in his early twenties. Now, Noon didn't consider himself gay. Cisgender men like himself who were attracted to transgender women primarily identified as heterosexual and sometimes bisexual, but rarely homosexual. He categorized his lure as a part of his kink. To him, it was just a tool he used to get off. If Gray or the women he dated in the past knew about his preferred method of sexual gratification they'd disagree.

That night after the party nothing was different. Noon told Gray he was heading back to his hotel but really he made a detour to The Ringmaster. It was a discreetly placed sex dungeon located on the outskirts of St. Louis. The front of the business posed as an adult sex store but with a secret password and a payment, customers were escorted to the basement that had been transformed into an illegal sexual wonderland. Stripped naked, Noon hung upside down from the ceiling. All the blood rushed to his head, but he didn't care. The lightheaded feeling added to the experience. Temptress, his favorite trans dominatrix, wrapped a twenty-foot rope around his body, placing his arms behind his back. Using the rope, she bound his elbows, wrists, knees and feet together. There was no way he could get out. The rope dug into his waist and in-between his hairy thighs while his dick hung free. The blindfold covering his eyes blocked his visual of the room. Noon liked not knowing what tools she'd use during playtime.

The stench of stale sweat filled the soundproof room. Beads of perspiration ran into his mouth. Sweat dripped in-between his butt cheeks. Temptress sauntered around him in a circle dressed in a black fringed bang wig, black latex cinched waist top, mini-skirt and thigh-high patent leather boots. Using slight force, she cracked the kendo stick in her manicured hand across his lower half, smacking his dick in the process. The sensation was excruciating but the rush of pain sent chills up Noon's spine. A rush of adrenaline shot through his veins, making him feel euphoria. Temptress took pleasure in seeing him in distress. His body jerked back-and-forth from the sting of the stick. Various welts covered his body from head to toe. The red marks on his well-developed frame were the highlight of their torture play. Seeing that he was near his peak, Temptress cracked the kendo stick against his penis once more. Noon released a loud grunt into the air. One more smack and semen would erupt from his redden bulbous tip.

Then suddenly everything went quiet. The last noise he heard was the sound of Temptress' heels clicking against the tiled floor then fading. Silence gnawed at his insides. Noon wanted to ask what was going on but didn't want to speak out of term. Temptress didn't like to be questioned during playtime. So, he hung there waiting for the next blow to come but nothing came. Silence hung in the air like the delayed moment before a falling vase crashes to the ground. The silence was poisonous in its nothingness. It was eerily unnatural. Noon's Spidey senses started to tingle. Then the door creaked open and the sound of footsteps neared. At first he thought it was Temptress returning but these footsteps weren't dainty and light. Noon listened closely. The soft murmur of this stride was like a threatening whisper. Something wasn't right. His mind wasn't playing tricks on him. Like Beanie Sigel, he could it feel in the air. Some shit was about to pop off.

"Mistress T, is that you?" His voice quivered with uncertainty.

Silence.

Noon hoped he hadn't upset her by speaking out of term.

"Mistress T, do I have your permission to speak?"

"Speak now or forever hold your peace." Cam pulled the blindfold from his eyes.

The life in Noon's eyes faded slowly until his iris merged with the whites of his eyes. Saliva thickened in his mouth while beads of sweat trickled down his ass crack. Adrenaline rushed through him so fast he thought he would vomit. Noon's fingernails dug into the palm of his hands. He could literally feel the oxygen flooding in and out of his lungs. Hesitantly, his brown orbs locked in on Cam. Like an omen of death, he was dressed appropriately in all black. Temptress disap-

peared so he could have a few minutes alone with him. It was funny what people would turn the other cheek to for a few dollars. Noon swallowed the lump in his throat. This couldn't be real. He had to be imagining things. No one knew his secret. He'd done a great job of covering his tracks or so he thought. How had Cam found him? He had a topnotch surveillance team monitoring his every move. Unbeknownst to him but Cam learned who'd been surveilling him and paid them double to get lost. What Noon also didn't know was that the whole time he was watching Cam, Cam was watching him. For two and a half months, Cam tried to dig up dirt on him. His attempts to learn about Noon's past were useless. Nothing could be found. Cam started to think he'd failed at finding his weakness. Little did he know all he had to do was have someone follow him around a bit. Noon was predictable. His schedule didn't change much. He went to work, the gym, a few business dinners, to see Gray and his favorite place of all the sex dungeon.

Seeing that he was caught, Noon wanted to run for safety, but the rope around his body bound him in place. With nowhere to go, reality set in that this would be the way he was going to die. Police would find him butt naked, hanging from the ceiling with his dick out. The realization hit him like a ton of bricks, causing him to wet his self. A stream of urine shot like a water fountain from his bruised erect penis.

"Whoa control yourself, G." Cam jumped out the way so none of it would land on him. "I thought you was harder that. You a tough guy, right? You had a lot of shit to say over these last few months. Where all that rah-rah shit now?" He smirked wickedly.

A tremor of terror overtook Noon. Shamefully, he started to cry. Tears raced from the corners of his eyes and landed in his ears. Unfazed by his cries, Cam looked around and examined the place. There was a huge bed draped in red satin covers with under-the-bed-restraints attached to it, an obedience bench, riding crops, bondage tape, paddles, dildos and more.

"Gray know you into this nasty shit?" He balled up his face. "Nah, she couldn't know. Ain't no way in hell she was gon' be tying yo' big ass up."

"I'm telling you, if you do this you're gonna regret it." Noon whimpered, trying his hardest to break loose.

"I ain't gon' regret shit." Cam made clear.

"Man-to-man, we can talk about this."

"Oh, now you wanna talk." Cam chuckled, flicking his nose.

"I'm serious. I really advise you to rethink whatever it is you're about to do. If you care about Gray, if you value the safety of your family, you won't do this." Noon advised.

"Bitch ass nigga, if you cared about my family you wouldn't have tried to blackmail me on some pussy nigga type shit. Don't try to talk your way outta this now. You started this so I'ma finish it." Cam pulled out a 9-inch spiked Bowie knife. The knife was a masterpiece and one of his favorites. The blade was stainless steel with a drop point and an aggressive razor back on the spine of the blade. There was a stainless guard that protected the users hand and kept it from sliding when gripping the four finger choil handle. He hadn't used it in years but now was a good time to put it to use again.

"Listen man. It ain't gotta be like this." Noon pleaded for his life. *"I'll leave Gray alone. You won't ever have to see me again. I'll disappear. If you reconsider this I swear, I can change your life. I can put you in circles you never dreamed of. You think Victor's on top. I can put you ahead of him."*

"You can't do shit for me but rot in hell." Cam grimaced as he sunk the sharp knife into Noon's lower abdomen. It was the same spot he'd been stabbed in by Pastor Edris. Everything happened so fast that at first Noon didn't know he'd been punctured. All of a sudden a cold wind swept through his body. Then slowly his senses began to weaken. A piercing noise rang in his ears as his vision reduced to a blur. He felt the wound but not the bite of it. Crimson liquid seeped down his torso. The pierced tissue began to throb overpoweringly. Noon felt a great deal of discomfort as blood poured from his body. The pain resembled sharp needles, blossoming from the wound and expanding throughout his insides. Pleased with his handy work, Cam smirked and pulled the blade out of his now deathly white victim.

Noon's cry was a glorious sound of guttural chokes mixed with a distressed roar.

"That shit don't feel good do it?" He teased, loving every second. This was payback for when his pussy ass pressed his finger into his wound, knowing Cam wasn't well enough to defend himself.

Noon was in such agony that snot bubbles popped and oozed from his nose. A gut-wrenching sob tore through his chest. Now he knew what it felt like to feel helpless. He'd taken advantage of Cam when he was in a weakened state. Now the tables were turned on him. Because of the precarious position he was in, he couldn't defend himself. Noon wanted to plead, scream, and shout for mercy but it was of no use. He had no one else to blame. He'd done this to his self. Nowhere near done with him, Cam shot him a deathly glare. It pleased him to know that his face would be the last Noon would see before he met his maker.

"Die slow you freaky muthafucka. I'll do my best to honor your memory." Cam used his words against him.

Gripping the handle, he plunged the knife into Noon's navel. A satisfying squishing noise filled the room as he sank the blade in deeper. Then in one swipe he sliced opened Noon's stomach. The cut went from his navel to in-between his pecks. Noon's liver, spleen, colon, and intestines bulged through the opening. Under the dim lights blood left his arteries in violent jets of red. The heart that could take him ten miles on a treadmill was most efficient at emptying his body of fluid, killing him faster. Noon's skin was no longer golden brown but grey. His upper body became sticky with congealing blood. A sick and twisted grin tugged on the corners of Cam's lips as he admired the piece of art he'd created.

"One down." He wiped the fresh blood off his blade. "Two more to go."

Coming back to reality, he gazed over at Gray. There was a ghostly expression on her face. He wished he could tell her everything that went down but he'd never put her in harm's way by telling her his dirty deeds.

"Before you go off, let me explain. Some shit was going on that I couldn't tell you about."

"Shit like what?" Her heartrate escalated to a dangerous rate.

Cam gave her vivid details of everything that transpired the day Noon visited him at the hospital. Gray let the explosive news sink into her brain.

"Hold up." She stopped and looked at him. "So, you mean to tell me you were never with Devin?"

"That's really what you took away from that?" Cam asked, condescendingly.

"*I mean* . . ." She paced the floor feeling shame. "I knew Noon had some shit with him, but I didn't think that he would go to such diabolical lengths to keep me."

"His bitch ass never had you."

"About that." She winced. "Me and Noon were never back together."

"What you mean y'all were never together?" Cam frowned.

"I let you think that we were."

"Why?"

"Cause you were wit' that retail working dick sucking manager!"

"You feel stupid 'cause I wasn't even wit' her funky ass."

"I know that now." Gray shrugged. It was good thing she hadn't called Noon's job. That would've started a world of problems. "This shit is crazy. I can't believe you went behind Victor's back. What you did could get you killed."

"I know. That's why I had to make your friend disappear."

"Why didn't you tell me what was going on?"

"I needed to give myself time to handle the situation."

"So, you still should've told me. I could've helped you."

"Gray, the only thing you would've done is give me a headache. You know you can't stay calm, in situations. Yo' ass go overboard. You would've went off on that nigga and got all of us killed."

"You over exaggerate. I'm not that bad." She flicked her wrist.

"What's that gay ass shit you be saying? LIES honey." Cam mocked her.

"Whatever. I can't believe you left me in the dark this entire time. You let me cuss you out and hate you."

"That's the small price I had to pay to keep me alive and get my family back."

"This is insane." Gray replied, still shaken.

"So, how you feel about your homeboy?" Cam rolled his eyes to the side.

"I'm not gonna lie. I'm shook up. It's scary to know about that other side of you. I don't like when Killa Cam comes out. But at the end of the day it was either you or him. I'll shed a few tears for Noon but if something would've happened to you I would've died. So, to answer your question, I don't like what you did but I understand. Just please, moving forward promise me we won't keep anymore secrets from each other."

Cam pulled Gray between his legs. She circled her arms around his neck.

"In that case, I still have some more unfinished business that needs to be handled so we can move on with our lives peacefully." He admitted.

Gray understood perfectly well what he was saying. Gunz and LaLa had to be dealt with. Usually, she'd try to talk him out of being violent, but after everything Gunz and LaLa had done to him, death was the only answer. They'd never be able to live a safe and normal life if they were alive. She knew they'd have to heavily repent to God about what was to come. They knew it was wrong to commit murder. It was a sin, but they honestly didn't see another way.

"Do what you gotta do. Just make sure you come home to us every night."

"Say less."

"No. Promise me." She held out her pinky finger.

"I swear." He circled his finger around hers and brought their hands to his mouth. Lovingly, he kissed them both. Finally, he had everything he'd ever wanted. He and Gray were on the same page and together as one. From that day on they would never be apart again. No man, woman or supernatural being would get in-between them. Their love was here to stay.

"So, you really forgot our anniversary 'cause I don't see no gift anywhere. This the same shit you pulled on my birthday." Cam griped.

"I told you I didn't forget your birthday. I had a gift for you then and I have a gift for you now." Gray dug inside her purse and pulled out a medium-sized gold wrapped gift box. "Here."

"This bet not be no fuckin' bomb." Cam placed it up to his ear and shook it.

"Just open it." Gray said, dying of anticipation.

Cam tore the paper from the box and took off the top. Inside was a silver picture frame with a photograph of a sonogram.

"Congratulations. You're gonna be a daddy again." Gray beamed with pride.

"Gray, don't play with me. I'm real fragile as fuck right now." Cam said, apprehensively.

"I'm dead ass."

Cam rubbed her belly. Suddenly, it all dawned on him. The bump at the bottom of her stomach, the mind-blowing way her pussy felt. It was all because she was pregnant.

"How far along are you?" He asked mesmerized by the idea of his baby being in her belly.

"I'll be four months next month."

"Four months?" Cam's head shot up. "When the fuck were you gon' say something, when you were in labor?"

"I told you on your birthday when you were in the coma."

"Nigga, one plus one don't equal three! That's the dumbest shit I've ever heard. You act like I could hear what the fuck you were saying."

"They can in the movies." She retorted.

"You better be glad I love you 'cause sometimes I think you was in the slow class." He pulled her into his comforting arms.

"So, that means you're happy?" Gray pecked his lips.

"Hell yeah. Shit, a nigga finally get to see your husky ass pregnant. Yo, whoever tied your tubes did a shitty job cause I be bustin' right through that muthafucka." He crackled up laughing.

"Facts."

"You know that means the prophecy that old lady told us in Indonesia was true."

"I know. I was thinking about that. Four babies . . . wow." She rubbed the back of his head.

"Yo, hold up. You was fighting that bitch knowing you was carrying my child?" Cam thumped her in the forehead.

"Oww. Don't hit me no more." She massaged the area. "Just like you have unfinished business you need to handle, Devin was my unfinished business. Comprende?"

"Don't be getting smart." He warned.

"No, you watch your mouth. Call me husky again." She dared.

Unexpectedly, a thought crossed Cam's mind.

"Ooooooooooh Gray, you gon' get big." He whispered like a child. "I gotta get you something to eat. You hungry? C'mon lets go to Ponderosa." He leaped off the bed.

"No." She tried to stop him.

"Nigga, you know them wings be fire."

"I'm not hungry."

"Gray, don't lie to me. You've been doing good."

"I mean." She twisted from side-to-side. "That do kinda sound good."

"I knew it. Bring yo' husky ass on. My baby wanna eat." He grabbed her purse and pulled her behind him. "Aye, yo Cole! Let's ride out. We going to Ponderosa!"

CHAPTER 26

"I knew you before she came through."-Megan Rochelle feat Fabolous
"The One You Need"

he bass from the subwoofers coming out of Cam's Cutlass Supreme alerted everyone on the block that he was there. All the ladies inside of Tresses ran to the floor-to-ceiling window to see who had pulled up in the old school classic. LaLa was the only one who didn't move. She stood at her station doing her clients' silk press. She knew exactly who it was. There was only one man in St. Louis who pushed a whip so clean. She hadn't seen Cam since the night of Quan's bachelor party where the brawl broke out. When she got word that he'd waken from his coma, she was elated. After All-Star Weekend, she wanted nothing more than to see him rot in a jail cell. Never did she want him to die. It was truly a miracle that he'd survived everything he'd gone through. LaLa now regretted her part in making his life such a living hell. She should've never taken things that far. She should've compartmentalize her feelings and dealt with them in a healthy manner. The sad part about life was that you can't rewind time. She couldn't take back what she'd done. All she could do was ask God for forgiveness and pray that somehow, someway He would lead Cam back to her. Prayerfully, that day her prayers would be answered.

Looking in the mirror, she examined herself. Everything was on point, as usual. The black wide brim hat that covered her 40-inch weave sat perfectly on top of her head. The black turtleneck, black leather high-waisted skirt with suspenders, polka dot sheer socks and lucite 5-inch heels gave her that 90's sex kitten vibe she was going for. The skirt fit so tight that her butt looked even bigger than it already was. Cam always was a fan of her Coke bottle shape. When they were a couple he'd often fall asleep with his head on one of her butt cheeks. Smacking her plump juicy lips together, she blew herself a kiss. There wasn't a bitch in St. Louis that could fuck with her physically. Li'l mama was the shit and carried herself as such.

Cam pulled up his pants and chirped the alarm on his car. It was a nice enough day that he didn't have to wear a jacket. The green knit cap, matching hoodie with the phrase the family written across the chest, Off-White denim jeans and green, white and black Jordan Retro 1's kept him warm against the cool fall air. He'd just left the barbershop. His face and hair was cut to perfection. All the ladies swooned as he made his way around the streamlined car. Cam's swag was on a hunnid. His tall tatted frame, golden skin, pink sexy lips, and beard made all their nipples hard and panties wet. The iced-out chains draped around his neck only added to his drip. He didn't even have to pull open the door to get inside. One of the ladies ran to open it for him. Cam flashed her his winning smile and thanked the salivating woman for her help.

Standing in the doorway of the shop he partly owned, he looked around. Nothing about the salon had changed in the four years since he'd last been there. If anything, the shop appeared rundown. LaLa still had the same furniture they'd purchased together when the salon opened. The once pristine white walls had pencil, pens, and dye marks on it. The leather seats had rips and stains. The floor had scuffs marks on it that hadn't been buffed out. The place looked a mess, but as always, LaLa looked good. The juxtaposition was a metaphor for her life. On the outside LaLa looked like she had it all together but when you looked closely you'd find her life was a complete and utter shit show.

Cam was pissed. All of the blood, sweat and hard work he put into getting the salon off the ground and being a huge success had gone down the drain. Cam couldn't wait to get her ass out of there so he could have someone else take over and turn things around.

"Long time no see." She poked out her shapely hip.

"Yeah, it's been a minute." Cam continued to take stock of the salon. "Aye, let me holla at you in the back real quick."

"Let me find out you here for a li'l afternoon delight." She placed down her flatirons.

"Never." Cam clarified as they walked to her office.

"To what do I owe the pleasure? I ain't think you fuck wit' me no more." She closed the door and took a seat on the edge of the desk. Sexily, she crossed her thick thighs.

Cam took notice of the succulent piece of butter colored flesh, but LaLa's Instagram model frame did nothing for him. Not to say she wasn't a stunning woman, but she wasn't his wife. She wasn't Gray.

"And why is that?" Cam sat in the chair before her with his legs cocked open. "I ain't got no reason to be mad at you . . . or do I?" He waited for her response.

"I'm just saying." LaLa fished for a response. Her conscious was begging her to come clean but she knew telling the truth would be the difference between life and death. "Ever since you been home you been moving different. You act like I don't even exist."

"I got other priorities that were far more pertinent than getting at you but I'm here now. What's up wit' you? How life been treating you?" He pretended to care.

"I'm good. Kamryn so big now. You know he be asking about you."

"Is that right?" Cam ran his index finger across his lower lip.

LaLa imagined it was her tongue gliding across his mouth instead of his finger. She used to love kissing Cam. She could spend hours sucking on his soft lips.

"You know his no-good daddy barely help me with him. He thinks just cause he pays me child support that's enough. You have no idea how I wish I could go back in time and change what I did. Sleeping with Kingston was the biggest mistake of my life. Me and you had a good thing going and I—"

"Speaking of Kingston." Cam cut her sentence short. He didn't give a fuck about her confessing her regrets. "I'm glad you brought him up. The reason I stopped by is because I have a bit of information I think you should know." Cam dug inside his pocket and pulled out his phone. "Right before Quan's wedding, I spotted ole boy and Tia outside of the community center together."

"Okay . . . they probably were taking Gavin Jr. and Kamryn swimming." LaLa shrugged, dismissively.

"This look like swimming to you?" He placed his phone in front of her face.

LaLa examined the photo of her niece and her son's father kissing. In her mind what she was seeing had to be photoshopped. Cam had to have tampered with the pic. There was no way on God's green earth that either of them would disrespect her in such a humiliating manner.

"Boy bye. That ain't real." She pushed his phone out of the way.

"I figured you'd say that." Cam swiped right and pulled up the video. This time he handed her his phone.

LaLa pursed her lips together. Cam was not going to convince her that something was going on between Tia and Kingston, but she pressed play on the video anyway. What she saw would haunt her in her dreams. *"I'm tired of being a fuckin' secret Kingston! You told me years ago you was gon' tell my auntie about us! Nigga, I'm tired of waiting! Gavin Jr. needs to know who his real father is!"* She heard her niece say. In a subconscious gesture of repugnance her nose wrinkled, and she drew back her head. LaLa's whole world fell apart within seconds. This was the beginning of the end, for her. LaLa was more than angry, she was livid. When she tried to speak her voice faltered into unintelligible croaks. What little color was left in her face drained. There her baby daddy and niece were on a street corner arguing and passionately kissing. Hate stained her soul. It spread swiftly throughout her entire system, shutting down all other emotion. The object of her hatred may not have been present at the moment, but the vicious words and violent actions she wanted to throw at the bitch dominated her spirit. Hatred eroded her heart. There was no more room for love when it came to Tia. Hate had taken over her soul.

"I hate to see you like this, but I thought you should know." Cam acted sympathetic.

"This cannot be happening. How could they do this to me?" Hot tears scorched her cheeks.

As LaLa thought of her niece's betrayal, her upper lip curled and nostrils flared. The once loving and heartfelt memories she and Tia shared throughout the years had morphed into something grotesque.

"I bet you eating this up, huh? You think this my karma don't you?"

"You definitely reap what you sow but I ain't here to kick you while you're down. Despite everything we've been through I wouldn't wish this shit on nobody." Cam lied. He wished nothing but the worst for her. She deserved that and more.

"What kind of nasty bitch fucks her auntie's baby daddy and has a baby by him?" LaLa placed her hand out in disbelief like the emoji.

"Yeah, that shit outta pocket."

"I wonder how long this shit been going on."

"It gotta be a while if that's his baby."

"I can't believe they've been fucking around under my nose this whole entire time. You know how stupid I look?"

"Fuck looking stupid. What you gon do?" Cam instigated.

"I'ma fuck both of 'em up. Do me a favor. Forward that shit to me."

Cam used his burner phone to Airdrop her the proof.

"A'ight, I'm up. I just wanted you to hear it from me. It would've been fucked up if somebody else got a hold of the information and tried to throw it in your face."

"Thanks, Cam." LaLa slipped her hand in his. It was the closest they'd been in years. Damn, she'd really fucked things up. Cam was the only man who'd truly loved her. He showed her a different way at life. He helped make her dream of becoming a salon owner come true. He held her down in ways no other man or even her family had. Now, he was married to someone else and here she was single with a rundown shop and a baby father who'd fucked her niece. She'd royally fucked up everything good in her life.

"You always did have my back." She rubbed her thumb across the back of his hand. "I don't know what I would do without you. Maybe moving forward, we can keep in contact? Maybe have lunch or something?"

Cam wanted to shake his head. Nothing about LaLa had changed. Even during the worst time of her life, she still found a way to be a whore and throw herself at him. Cam removed his hand from hers. All he could think about was the bottle of Purell that was calling his name from the glove compartment of his car.

"We'll see but you stay up. Don't do nothin' crazy that's gon' land you in jail. Trust me, it ain't no fun place to be."

Guilt sat on LaLa's chest. What she'd done she couldn't take back. She could make amends in subtle ways, but an admission of guilt wasn't something she could do. Only at night before bed could she speak her heart to God and plead for His forgiveness. LaLa prayed that one day she would feel removed from her sin, washed clean of it, but the guilt was a stain on her conscious.

"Let me walk you out." She grabbed her purse and keys. "I'm leaving too."

"I'm telling you La, don't go over there acting a fool."

"I'm sorry. I can't promise you that." She replied as they entered the front of the salon.

"Shamari, finish Tyleesha hair and lock up for me. I'm gone for the rest of the day. I got to go drag a bitch."

~

The rage LaLa felt couldn't be categorized as madness. This feeling was not human. It was demented and twisted. It burned bad like fire racing through her veins. As she pounded her already redden fist against the door, all she could concentrate on was her desire to hate. LaLa was so drunk with emotion the acidity of hate that lived in the pit of her belly yearned to be spat out of her mouth in foul, vulgar words. But she wasn't going to speak her peace calmly like a rational adult. She was going to scream her grievances with every ounce of breath that dwelled in her lungs. Thank God Tia and Gunz stayed in a safe house in a deserted area of Saint Louis. The nearest house was a mile down the road.

"Dang, Auntie. You banging on my door like you the police." Tia opened the door oblivious to the danger that lie ahead. What happened next couldn't have lasted longer than half a second, but it felt like hours had gone by. LaLa cocked her arm back as if she were a pitcher for the Saint Louis Cardinals. With tremendous force, she extended her right arm forward, and directed her aim towards Tia's disloyal face. LaLa's fist landed with a bang on her left cheek, sending waves of skin cascading back towards her ears. As her fist connected again it made a loud thwack against her nasal cartilage. Tia stumbled backwards till she hit the hard floor below.

"You thought you was gon' get away it, bitch? You thought I wasn't gon' find out?" LaLa barged inside and towered over her niece's crumpled body. The loud shrills of her voice instantly caught Gunz's attention. Swiftly, he ran out of his mancave to see what the commotion was about. For a second, he had to let it register in his mind what he was witnessing. LaLa stood over Tia pounding her fist into her face. She was beating her ass like she was a bitch off the street.

"Yo, what the fuck is going on? Are you dumb? Get your hands off my girl!" He yanked her off of Tia and threw her to the ground.

"Fuck that bitch!" LaLa hopped back up, still wanting to fight. "Little do you know but she's everybody's girl!"

"Fuck is she talkin' about?" Gunz helped Tia off the floor. LaLa had done a number on her. Tia could barely stand. Without assistance from Gunz, her legs would give out and she'd fall right back down.

"I don't even know!" Tia held her jaw. "She just came in here swinging on me like a crazy lady!"

"Bitch, don't play dumb! I know you been fuckin' Kingston!"

A cluster bomb of panic exploded inside Tia's brain. This couldn't be happening. How had she found out? Had Kingston finally told her the truth? No, he wouldn't have without informing her first or would he? Unexpectedly, her body wracked with raw sobs and she shook like a leaf. Fear consumed every cell in her body, swelling them with terror. With each second that slipped by, she felt the rise of her blood pressure. A cold sweat broke out on her skin. If she could, Tia would lay down and die because there was no way she was coming out of this situation alive.

"Don't listen to her, Gunz! She lying! You know that ain't true! I would never cheat on you! Especially not with your boy! I don't even get down like that!"

"You don't get down like that? Oh, that's your word?" LaLa said amused by her performance. It was far easier for Tia to lose herself in the theatrics of her mind, casting herself as the victim, than to admit even an ounce of truth. Reaching for her purse, she pulled out her phone. "So, bitch this ain't you?"

LaLa pressed play on the video and shoved it in Gunz's face. His brain formulated no thoughts other than to register that he was shocked. At a loss for words, he closed his dry mouth, then looked at his shaking hands before glancing back up to catch Tia's tear-filled eyes. Gunz wanted to spew words of hate but nothing came out. He'd been reduced to a heap of nothing. Every inch of him had gone numb. His mind was well aware of the pain Tia had caused, but when you've just found out the person you were supposed to trust the most, has been carrying on a secret life, your body actually feels the pain too. Until that moment, he didn't have an understanding of betrayal beyond movies, television, and books. Now he understood fully well. Now he knew how Gray felt when she'd learned of his infidelities. Tia had actually gut-punched him with her lies. Was anything about this bitch real? Did she ever love him? Was he a pawn in her game this entire time? He'd lost his mother, grandmother, uncle, and the rest of his fam because of their relationship. He'd left his family for this girl. They were a family. She'd given him the thing he most wanted in life, a son, but now he knew Gavin Jr. wasn't even his.

"You hear her, Gunz? You hear what the fuck she said! That's his fuckin' baby! She lied to all of us! She had all of us fooled!" LaLa trembled with rage.

"Wait a minute! Please, Gunz! I can explain!" Tia tugged on his arm, pleading for dear life. Gunz stood frozen in place like a statue. He still hadn't digested what he'd heard and saw.

"Explain what, bitch? How you been fuckin' my nigga?"

"Your nigga?" Tia came out of character, appalled. "I know for a fact he don't fuck wit' you!"

"What cause he told you so?" LaLa challenged.

Tia stood silent.

"Yo' young ass so fuckin' dumb. Me and Kingston ain't never stop fuckin' around. That's my son's father, bitch. Fuck you thought!"

"He told me he ain't fuck with you no more! He said he only communicate with you about Kamryn!"

"What the fuck that got to do with you being loyal to me? You trifling, bitch!" LaLa mushed her in the head. "You just like your crackhead ass mother! That bitch will suck the skin off a pastor's dick for a rock! She should've aborted you! You ain't shit, bitch! And to think you'd betray me after everything I've done for you! I made sure your hair was done! I made sure you had clothes on your back and shoes on your feet! I personally made sure you grew up not wanting for shit and this how you do me?" LaLa's lips quivered. She was so shaken up.

"Didn't nobody ask you to do none of that! Bitch, I don't need you! Kingston gon' make sure I'm straight regardless!" Tia shot back indignantly.

CHAPTER 26 | 351

"BITCH!" LaLa attacked her like a rabid dog. This time Tia fought back. There in the doorway she and LaLa went heads up. Gunz didn't do anything to stop them. His mind cycled through emotions faster than a kid flipping through cable channels. A mixture of competing emotions fought for dominance. His mind was broken. That quickly, he'd acquired a bout of intense anxiety. Gunz entire world had gone up in smoke. He'd given up everything to be with Tia's lying, trifling ass. He'd fucked over Gray and abandoned his kids for nothing. The war between him and Cam would've never existed if he hadn't stuck his dick in her. His girls were calling another man daddy because of his affair. Never did he think Tia's young ass would be the one to hurt him. Before that day, Gunz thought he was invincible to pain, but he wasn't. It literally felt like he was free-falling from 30,000 feet in the air. Sheer terror raced through him. Subconsciously, he tried to grab for a parachute cord that would save his life. With each second, his body grew closer to the ground. Gunz tried to tell himself that none of this was real but it was. There was no parachute to save him. Like his reality, his body crashed to the ground and shattered into a million pieces. He'd died an emotional death that he'd feel the sting of until he met his demise.

In a robotic state, he pushed LaLa out of the way. Because of her heels she crashed to the floor. The wind was nearly knocked out of her. Gunz grabbed Tia by her shoulders and slammed her into the wall. Her head thudded against the drywall. His fingers curled around her slender neck. Tia couldn't move no matter how much she struggled. This was it. She was gonna die. She knew Gunz would kill her. Gunz tightened his grip around her throat, cutting off her air supply. His meaty fingers felt like a snake being looped around her neck. Desperation to breathe took over. LaLa scrambled to get off the floor to help her. She might've hated Tia's guts, but they were still family and she didn't want to see her go down the stairwell to hell. LaLa tried with all her might to get Gunz off of her but she was no match for his big broad frame. Gunz strength rivaled Hercules when he was mad.

"Gunz, stop! You're gonna kill her!" She begged, pounding her fist into his burly back.

Gunz disregarded her pleas and squeezed tighter. Tia's lungs started to ache as her eyes bulged. Using what little strength she had, she dug her stiletto nails into the skin of his hand. Scratch marks from her scrapes decorated his flesh. While Gunz resented her gouging and cheap red lines, his adrenaline was too high to feel a thing. She could try to pry his hands away all she wanted. He wasn't letting up. Small ragged gasps escaped her throat. Tia's face began to turn a sickening shade of blue as her sight started to close in on her. Oxygen was slowly being ripped and snatched from her lungs, leaving scars of regret on the weak tissue. Every waking minute was pain. Then the edge of her vision went dark. Her surroundings blurred into a new sick reality. She was about to leave the physical realm. Tia's hands fell to her side. Everything became fuzzy; then she saw nothing. Her consciousness floated through an empty space filled with thick static. Throughout the inky space, Tia's heartbeat pounded loudly, alongside fading pleas for help. *God help me*, she begged silently. God must've heard her plea. Out of nowhere, Gavin Jr.'s wails filled the air. Nothing would've got Gunz to let her go but him. His cries was the antidote to get Gunz to snap back to reality.

Abruptly, he let go of her and stepped back. Tia's limp body slid down the wall and to the floor. Holding her throat she gulped for fresh air. God had given her a second chance. Gunz wiped the sweat from his brow 'causing the blood from her scratches to smear across his face. He looked like a monster.

"You got thirty minutes to pack up all your shit and get you and your illegitimate son out my crib. If y'all still here when I get back, you and that li'l muthafucka gon' be 6F." He pulled his car keys from his pocket.

"Gunz, wait! Please!" Tia slid her weak body across the floor, trying to stop him. Gunz kept walking until the frigid October air cooled his skin. Nightfall was in full effect. LaLa grabbed her things as well.

"LaLa, wait! I'm sorry!" Tia reached out for her leg.

"Get the fuck off me, bitch." She kicked her away. "I only saved your life for my nephew. Oops my bad . . . my son's brother." She gave Tia one last look then followed Gunz outside. Her car was parked behind his.

"I thought you was gon' kill her dumb ass." LaLa said, still worked up.

"Fuck her." Gunz grimaced.

"Oh, don't worry. That bitch is dead to me. The question is what we gon' do about Kingston? We can't let that muthafucka get away this." She didn't want Kingston killed but to be taught a lesson. Gunz thought on it before speaking.

"For now, lay low. I'll reach out to you soon with instructions." He jumped inside his whip.

LaLa got inside hers and peeled off. Gunz made it seem like he was leaving too but really he did a lap around the block and doubled back. Cam and Quan sat in the cut watching as he pulled into the driveway and kept the car running. Cam knew that LaLa's anger would lead him right to Gunz's hideout and he was right. While they were in the salon talking, he had Quan place a tracker on her car. For years, he'd been trying to find where this nigga laid his head at. Cam would've never thought that Tia being a sloppy whore would be all he needed to track his location.

Quietly, Gunz slipped back inside the house. Tia hadn't even bothered to lock it. She still lay in a heap of tears on the floor as Gavin Jr. screamed at the top of his lungs from his playpen. When Tia heard the sound of sneakers squeaking across the floor, she looked up and found Gunz. The cold look on his face gave her chills. His hands were tightly closed around the cold surface of a metallic grey colored pistol. He seemed to have no sense of humanity. His heart seemed to be made of stone.

"I fucked up my whole life for you." He pointed the gun at her head.

"Gunz, no! Wait!" She placed her hands up to block his aim.

With no remorse, Gunz pulled the trigger. Two bullets projected out of the barrel and into the front of her cranium. Each bullet wasn't just loud, it cracked into the air and echoed. Instead of a neat reddened hole the bullet wound oozed with dark thick blood. Tia's screaming abruptly ceased. One minute she was alive and well, and the next she was a pile of nothing on the floor. A little squeeze of a finger and she was dead. Less trouble than peeling a potato. Gavin Jr's wails for help tugged at Gunz's heartstrings for a brief second but the hardened part of him forced him not to care. Tia and her son were dead to him. He no longer gave a damn about either one of them. Gunz had the mind to kill him, too, but he'd let the li'l nigga live. Maybe someone would hear his cries and save him. That was the least he could do. Ransacking the house, he grabbed the necessary items he'd need and burnout. He couldn't stay there anymore. This hideout was hot now. He'd have to find another place to lay low at.

Sitting low in the driver seat, Cam text Quan to follow him. They couldn't lose track of this muthafucka now. While Quan tailed Gunz, Cam pulled in front of the house. He'd heard the gunshots. Cam had to see for himself that Gavin Jr. wasn't dead. If Gunz had killed an innocent child that would send Cam over the edge. He'd always had a soft space in his heart for children and dogs. Softly closing the driver side door, he jogged up the walkway and picked the lock.

Tia lay on the floor lifeless. Her lavender weave was stained with dried crimson blood. Her chocolate eyes were wide open, staring at him lifelessly. Her clothes, a hot pink velour cropped hoodie and matching joggers, were blood-stained. Her body was slumped over, half-sitting, half-laying on the cold gray floor. And the smell. The smell was the most disturbing thing he'd ever inhaled. Her bowels had released into the seat of her pants. She was gone but thankfully her son was still alive. A primal scream could be heard from the back of the house. The shriek was the kind of sound that bypassed your rational thinking and went directly to your emotional response. High pitched and raw, it was the sound of a child in agony. Gavin called out for his mother repeatedly. Cam followed the unbearable cry. A single light lit the room. There the little boy was holding onto the side of the playpen. Tears and snot drenched his face. Cam noticed that he was the same size as the triplets. Swiftly, he picked the wailing child up. He hoped that would get him to stop crying but it didn't. His sobs continued on. His cries told the pain and confusion he felt. The poor boy craved the comfort of his mother's soft skin. He needed her scent, the movement of her body. Unfortunately, he'd never get to be close to his mother again. Doing the best he could, Cam bounced the child up and down as he escorted him from the room. He tried to conceal his young fragile eyes from seeing his mom in such a grotesque state, but Cam was unsuccessful. As they crossed over her lifeless body, Gavin Jr. spotted his mother's blood-ridden corpse and reached out for her. All he knew was that this strange man was taking him away from his mother who was hurt. The image of his mom covered in blood would follow him for the rest of his life. He'd never forget that night or the face of the unidentified man who'd done it.

An hour later, Cam pulled up on the block. Because of the late hour the street was deserted, except for a few of his foot soldiers. The car ride had calmed Gavin Jr. down and put him right to sleep. Cam rolled down the driver side window.

"Aye, yo. C'mere." He called out.

Twan, one of his trusted soldiers, held up the front of his jeans and jogged over to the vehicle. Bending down he came eye level to Cam.

"What's up, OG?"

"I need you to do me a favor."

"What you need? I got you."

"This shit stays between us. Go drop li'l man off at Mama Lucy's house. Just sit him on the porch, then call over there and let 'em know he outside. I was never here. You understand?"

"Say less. You can trust me, OG. I'ma take care of it."

CHAPTER 27

"Oh, this is the start of something good. Don't you agree? I haven't felt like this in so many moons."-Gavin DeGraw "Follow Through"

It was the perfect birthday in every sense of the word. From the second Aoki opened her eyes, she was surrounded by love. Gray and Cam surprised her with breakfast in bed and a slew of gifts. After their anniversary they sat the kids down and informed them that they were getting back together. Aoki didn't know what to make of the news at first. Cam and Gray were all over the place. One minute they hated each other and the next they were all lovey dovey. Aoki was tired of all the back-and-forth. She was tired of being stuck in the middle of their drama. It was the role of the parent to be the rock for their child, not the other way around. Children may be anchors, their needs and love keeping their parents focused, but that is where the lines are drawn. When parents relied on their children, damage is caused. It isn't natural for support to be given from a child to an adult. Children should not be weighed down with the worries of the world.

When parents are truly adults, children could enjoy their childhood without worry. Anything other than that was draining but her parents assured her that this time they were in it for the long haul. There would be no more running and tit-for-tat arguing. Cam and Gray assured her they weren't in this marriage for a season but for a lifetime.

The announcement of their reconciliation also came with the news of another baby and a brand-new house. Aoki experienced sensory overload. It was all too much to consume at once. Once she had enough time to digest everything, she allowed herself to be thrilled by the changes that were occurring. Everything that she'd been praying for was coming to fruition. All she'd ever wanted was two parents under one roof who'd love and never abandon her. She didn't even mind that there would be another whining, bad ass baby in the house. She loved her siblings and was happy that, this time, Cam would be around to experience the birth of his child. Aoki wouldn't have to play mama. She'd be able to sit back and live her young teenage life.

She really was about to turn-up now. It was her 14th birthday and her first Homecoming. Life was sweet. Her parents gifted her with the best presents ever; a $2,268 Pioneer DDJSZ2 Professional DJ Controller with a case, a $50,000 vinyl collection that ranged from Al Green to Travis Scott, lifetime Live Nation concert tickets and the biggest gift of them all was a private DJing session that summer with her idol Steve Aoki. Aoki thought she'd be disappointed if she didn't get a million-dollar gathering like the triplets but the gifts she'd received were far better than any party. If that wasn't enough her mom got her the exact Homecoming outfit she wanted. Cam was going to shit a brick and probably try to kill her but risking her life would be worth rocking a $12,000 Elie Saab dress. Aoki was going to shit on every girl at Forsyth Academy. What fourteen-year-old girl got to rock Elie Saab to Homecoming? Grown women couldn't even afford the designer.

It took her nearly four hours to get ready for the dance. Gray hired a glam squad that consisted of hairstylist extraordinaire Mina Gonzalez, her godmother and makeup artist Heidi and Cardi B's nail tech,

Jenny Bui. By the time they were done making her over, Aoki looked like she should be attending the Oscars. She went from fourteen to twenty-one in an instant. Gray thought she looked beautiful. Seeing her baby girl all dolled up brought tears to her eyes. She hoped Cam wouldn't cause a scene when he saw her. Mo, Boss, Kema, Quan, Tee-Tee and Bernard had arrived with their kids so all the teens could take pics before the dance. Everyone was waiting in the living room for them to come down.

"You ready?" Gray asked, excitedly.

"Yeah." Aoki answered breathlessly. After taking one last look in the mirror she picked up her clutch and followed her mom down the hall. Her day had been picture perfect so far. The only thing that would've made it better was if Paris was her date. He'd called that morning to wish her happy birthday. She hoped he'd changed his mind on attending the dance, but he hadn't. Aoki would be going to Homecoming alone. It was a good thing she had her cousins and friends to kick it with. If it wasn't for them, she would've stayed at home.

"Aoki! You look stunning!" Her Auntie Mo gasped, covering her mouth.

Aoki looked down at her dress and smiled. Her long hair was slicked to the back to showcase her flawless face. Heidi had given her a youthful beat that wasn't too grown. Three-tiered drop diamond earrings dangled from her ears. The deep red ruffle one-shoulder, split detail dress, with a bow waist and matching thigh-high boots that graced her tall, slender physique was nothing short of a showstopper. Aoki waited with bated breath for Cam's reaction. The color and style of the ensemble was chosen to pay tribute to him.

"What you think?" She asked timidly.

Cam stood next to his sister, holding his phone speechless. He was experiencing a father's worst nightmare. Aoki looked like a grown ass woman. He wanted to yell, cuss and demand that she go back to her room and change but none of it would change the fact that she was growing up. She couldn't help how she physically looked. Aoki might've not been his biological daughter, but she possessed so many of his traits. None of which eased his spirit at the moment. Much like him, Aoki was so independent and fearless. She was also a hothead who thought she knew everything. Many days Cam's only option was to fall back and offer no resistance. Then there were days like this where Aoki needed a mother's touch. And so, they veered from one to the other, her taking the lead when she could, and being forced to follow when she couldn't. Maybe one day this whole raising a daughter thing would get easier, but Cam doubted it. He still had three other daughters to lead and protect. Each time bits and pieces of his heart would chip away.

Cam walked over to her slowly. Everyone waited for his reaction but that day there would be no show. Cam pulled Aoki close and wrapped his arms around her. His embrace was warm. The world around Aoki melted away as she squeezed him back. If she could, she'd stay in his safe arms forever.

"You look good Li'l Boosie Bad Ass." Cam whispered, choked up.

Aoki smiled a mile wide. Her smile shined like the stars in the sky, with no bright city lights to dim them. It was like the sun opened its eager light to shine down on her.

"You still mad at me?" He kissed the top of her head.

"No. You're my dad. I could never stay mad at you for long."

"Okay, that's enough." Gray sniffled, rubbing her belly. "We gotta take pictures so these kids can get out of here."

Cam and Aoki reluctantly pulled away from each another. As she lined up with the twins and the rest of the kids, the same phone Cam was about to take pictures with rang. It was an unknown number. That could only mean it was one person. Cam stepped out of the room to answer the call.

"Hello?"

"Get the fuck over here now."

Click!

Cam's arm dropped to his side. Nervous energy rushed through him like a tidal wave. Had Noon gotten to Victor before he got to him? If so, his hours left on earth were numbered. After everything he'd gone through this couldn't be how things would end for him. He'd just gotten his wife and kids back. God wouldn't be so cruel, but the devil would.

"Baby, is everything okay?" Gray placed her hand on his shoulder.

"I gotta go see Victor." He gazed deep into her now worried blue eyes.

"Is it about—"

"I think so." Cam replied.

"I thought you took care of that?" She hissed.

"I did but there's still a chance he sent him the pictures."

Gray doubled over in distress. All of sudden, she couldn't breathe.

"C'mon, Gray. Don't do this to me." Cam helped her back up. "I can't worry about this shit and you."

"I'm sorry." She started to cry. "I just can't lose you. I just got you back."

"You won't, Star. I promise."

"You can't promise me that, Cam." She responded wearily.

Cam held her by both of her arms.

"Have I ever made you a promise I couldn't keep?"

"No."

"Well alright." He kissed her forehead then lips, fervently. "Everything will be fine. Get Li'l Boosie Bad Ass off to the dance and I'll be back here in no time." He guaranteed to calm her fears. However, Cam wasn't so sure he'd make it back in one piece or at all.

∽

If you wanted to
We can up and leave here
'Cause I still wanted to
Get inside your mind
I needed someone who
Makes me feel
I'm craving something different

Someone new

MAKIAH'S SPRING 2020 COUTURE ZUHAIR MURAD GOLD ANCIENT Egyptian, hieroglyphic chart embroidery long sleeve crop top, fitted skirt with a back slit and single sole gold ankle strap heels twinkled under the disco ball. Her natural hair was styled into a fro. Red matte lipstick adorned her sumptuous lips. In her own world, she grooved to the mid-tempo beat. When Makiah danced it was as if it were the only way her body knew how to speak. Verbally, she was guarded. Physically, she would shrink and fade into the background no matter where she was. Unlike her sister and cousin, she didn't like to be the center of attention. She was perfectly fine letting them have center stage. But when Emotional Oranges *Motion* came on and she hit the dance floor, her sensuality burst through into the most vibrant picture of a beautiful soul.

Meechi sat at a table alone sipping his spiked drink. Kiara had gone to the restroom to freshen up. He needed the reprieve. She'd been doing the most all day. Between the nonstop calls, text, IG posts, and TikToks, he was over her and the dance. The only reason he'd agreed to come was because he knew if he didn't he'd never hear the last of it. So far, Homecoming had been a snore. The state of the art gymnasium was filled with a bunch of rich kids who didn't appreciate shit they had. Meechi had to hustle for everything he owned, down from a pack of bologna to the shoes on his feet. Nothing in life came easy to him. The only person that seemed to relate to his struggle was Paris. He'd had it just as rough as him. With the way they lived goodness didn't come their way often. They'd seen and done too much fucked up shit to believe they'd get a break in this world.

It wasn't until his earthy brown eyes landed on Makiah Carter that he realized God placed angels on earth. Watching her move to the music filling the gymnasium was the equivalent to winning the lottery. It was a blessing to be in her presence. For the most part he was her only audience. He didn't mind that at all. Meechi was aware that if another nigga ogled her the way he did there would be a problem. A real big problem. Burnt Sienna never looked so beautiful on a girl. There was a deep richness to her dark skin. It was as rich and deep as molasses. With black hair of wool and her head held high, she swayed her hips effortlessly to the beat. Meechi had never crushed on a girl before. Chicks stayed on his dick because of his street status so there was no need to chase but there was something about Makiah Carter that hit him like a ton of bricks. She was special. Like the quote from A Bronx Tale she was one of the great ones. Girls like her only came around once every ten years.

Lost in the music, Makiah rocked back-and-forth. As she turned, she saw him sitting there. Meechi was less skillful at hiding in plain sight then she was. Aliens could spot his ass from outer space. The nigga wore every diamond chain he owned. His gaudy ass was such a coon. Caught staring, Meechi dropped his eyes momentarily before looking back up. With his head tilted to one side, a seductive grin played on his lips. Suddenly, Makiah's black and white world turned to color. The admission of liking someone like him would never cross her lips but she did, and she hated it. Meechi wasn't the kind of guy she went for her. He was crass. He was rude. He was arrogant and a street nigga. He was everything she never wanted in a boy, but he was undeniably handsome. It didn't help that he knew it and was cocky with it. His hazelnut skin, diamond shaped eyes and blonde locs would have any girl willing to risk it all, including Makiah. She thanked her lucky stars when Kiara walked up behind him and kissed his cheek. Her presence quickly reminded her that Meechi had a ho' for a girlfriend and that he had no business eye-fuckin' her anyway. Niggas like him were nothing but trouble and she vowed to stay far-far away.

Aoki was having the time of her life. Everybody went up for her dress. All night long she'd taken pic after pic. She was the bell of the ball. Damya and her stank ass friends did nothing but hate on her all night. For once, Aoki didn't care. She wasn't going to let them ruin her night. She and Blizz slow danced to Ari Lennox *Bound*. He'd gotten better since Kiara's basement party. Dancing with him was cool but he wasn't Paris. She wished it were his arms she was in, but he was nowhere to be found. So, she and Blizz continued to dance and spin. The lights twinkled with every step as Aoki spun in delicate circles, her red dress billowing out. Then just like in all those 90's movies her mom liked to watch the object of her affection appeared.

Kisses like marshmallow melts on my neck
A whimsical warning too sweet to forget
Let's get lost, somewhere in the night
Tell your stories and I'll tell you mine

Aoki blinked several times to make sure she wasn't seeing things. She wasn't hallucinating. Paris was there, live in the flesh. Aoki's feet stopped moving. Her heart thudded against her ribcage. He looked like an African king in his midnight blue velvet tuxedo and bowtie. The tux fit him like a glove. Paris was so fine he could've been a cake topper. Aoki wanted nothing more than to run and kiss him. He'd come for her or was he there for Damya. She'd be crushed if it was the latter.

I'm bound
Bound
Bound
I'm so in love now

Wondering why she'd suddenly halted, Blizz stopped dancing and looked over his shoulder. Everything was going great. He had the prettiest girl at the dance in his arms. All the other guys were jealous. Blizz was the man. For a few minutes he had it all then Paris had to pop up and shit on his entire existence. Within an instant he became chopped liver and Paris became the main course. All Aoki could focus on was him. All her worries were put to rest when he stepped through the crowd and walked in her direction. Damya watched furiously as Paris tapped Blizz on the shoulder.

"Move," he growled.

Nothing else needed to be said. Blizz didn't want to cause a scene.

He'd been embarrassed enough by Paris. The last thing he wanted was more smoke with him. Aoki didn't know what to make of what was going on. He'd vowed never to step foot inside a high school dance.

"I thought you weren't coming."

"I came for you. Gimme your hand."

Aoki nervously did as she was told. Everyone was lowkey watching their every move. The whole school knew that Paris and Damya were a couple. Paris blatantly ignoring her and making a beeline for Aoki was the ultimate sign of disrespect. The line was being drawn in the sand. Damya was no longer the queen bee. There was a new queen in town. Paris slipped a white rose corsage onto Aoki's wrist.

Down

Down

When you're not around

Oh stay here

Stay here

I need you around

"Thank you. It's beautiful." Her heart fluttered.

"Dance with me?" He gazed so intensely she thought he saw her soul.

Aoki hesitated. Everything was happening so fast it felt like she was caught up in a whirlwind.

"I'm not here to bullshit you. I just wanna hold you, look into your eyes, vibe wit' you and you vibe with me." Paris professed his feelings.

"I can do that. I'm just shocked you're here." Aoki tried to steady her breathing. It was like she was living in a dream.

"I told you I was feeling yo' pretty ass." He made her dance with him anyway.

"Yeah but you were with Damya. I've always known how I feel about you. You were the one stuck in limbo. Have you finally made up your mind?"

"That's why I'm here. I want you to be my girl."

"Does Damya know that?"

"She does now."

Staaaaaaaaaaay here!
Staaaaaaaaaaay here!
I need you, oh baby

Paris held her close as the guitar rhythm strummed. His left hand rested firmly on her hip. Aoki securely wrapped her left arm around his back. Her right hand was locked with his. This was perfection at its finest. All that mattered was the beautiful human being before her. The rhythm of their bodies danced slowly with the soul-stirring music. Staring at the beauty before him, Paris breathing became shallow. His heart suddenly felt heavy inside his chest. Becoming this emotionally available scared the shit outta him. He was strong. He'd been doing fine at making it through the world alone. Then came this tall, curly haired girl whose eyes gave way to the stars. She was different from all the girls he'd fucked and discarded without care. With Aoki he couldn't use sex as a crutch. She forced him to open up. So, here he was putting aside his fears and committing himself to being faithful to one girl and one girl only. His past would no longer define him. He'd find a way to let go of all his past traumas. With Aoki by his side, he'd be able to conquer his demons.

Maybe silly dreams can come true
Daily doubting then I found you
Ahhhhhhhhhhhhhhhhhhhhhhhhhhh

With their bodies pressed together and their faces so close, Paris brushed his full lips against hers, just so he could inhale her breath, feel the warmth of her skin, and relish the taste of her lipstick. He didn't give a damn who saw them. Aoki was his.

Tears sprouted in Damya's eyes as she stormed out of the gym. It was bad enough Tia had gone missing. She didn't have the energy to deal with this shit too. She'd never been more humiliated in her life. She swore on her mama that Aoki and Paris would pay for making a fool out of her. Things were just as grim for Blizz. His spirit was crushed. He really liked Aoki, but no matter what he did, he just wasn't the one she wanted. He often wondered what was it about him that wasn't good enough. No, he wasn't the best looking nigga in the world, but he treated her good.

Aoki's face turned a light shade of pink. Caught up in Paris, the dimmed lights, every twirl of their bodies, Ari's soprano voice, the guitar, hand claps and tambourine that made up the crescendo of the song, Aoki locked eyes with his. Her heart began to race. How would she be able to keep her newfound relationship with Paris a secret when she wanted to shout it from the rooftops? It would be nearly impossible for them to stay away from each other now.

Paris dipped her forward and gazed into her eyes. His fingers tightened on her ribs as his left foot came forward. Caught off guard by his fancy footwork, Aoki paused. Toe to toe, he pulled her hips in close to his. Aoki gasped for air. Her slim physique melted into his. Paris leaned down. The bristles of his beard scratched against her soft cheeks. Aoki worked her mouth against his, their tongues battled back-and-forth like wrestlers, each trying to pin the other. There was nothing sweet about this kiss. They ravished one another. With each flick of their tongues their souls merged. From that day on Aoki's universe would begin and end with him. The hole inside her heart was finally filled. She no longer felt alone. Paris completed her and she completed him.

Sometimes I wonder if it's even real
But I could never fake what I feel
Ahhhhhhhhhhhhhhhhhhhhhhhhhhhh

∾

TWO ARMED GUARDS ESCORTED CAM INTO VICTOR'S OFFICE. CAM inhaled deep and exhaled a slow anxious breath as he eased into the distressed leather chair that sat before Victor's desk. This couldn't be the way he'd be taken out. He'd just learned Gunz's whereabouts. He'd had eyes on him since the day he'd killed Tia. Cam was just biding his time before he made his move. There were other people he needed to check off his hit list before he got to Gunz. God wouldn't be cruel enough to let him die before he was able to exact revenge. On top of that, he had Gray and the kids to worry about. His family needed him now more than ever.

Victor sat in all his glory with his hands steepled together. Power radiated from his being. Victor was the real deal. He wasn't someone you wanted to fuck with. The man was ruthless. He didn't give a fuck about much except his family. Anybody else could get it. Dressed in a two-button, Tom Ford blazer, black turtleneck, fitted dress pants and Saint Laurent ankle-wrap boots, he glared at Cam with contempt in his eyes.

"So, you really didn't think I was gon' find out? Didn't I tell you I have eyes and ear everywhere?"

Cam started to sweat bullets. He knew. Victor knew that he'd betrayed him. Aoki's birthday would be the day he went home to glory.

"Look, Jefe, I can explain." He sat up straight.

"Explain what? How fuckin' incompetent you are? How you've been a thorn in my side since the day you were promoted to second in command? Matter of fact, how is it that you just got out of a coma and you're still fuckin' up? Your actions show that you haven't learned anything from your traumatic experience. You're still making the same dumb decisions you were making four years ago. You were more useful to me when you were in jail."

"Come on, man. Now that's rude. I've done a lot for this organization."

"You have. You've put federal attention on us, and you've killed Aubrey Simmons." Victor barked.

Cam paused. Was that the reason he was there?

"What that nigga got to do with anything?"

"Goddamn you so fuckin' stupid. You don't even know what you did, do you?" Victor narrowed his dark eyes.

"Yeah, I got rid of the nigga." Cam replied, confused.

"But do you know who that nigga is?"

"Aubrey Simmons aka Quarter Till or whatever that lame ass nigga name is. He had to go, Jefe. He ain't gon' be missed. He was just a pencil pushing, fanny pack wearing nigga that liked to get tortured by contestants from RuPaul's Drag Race. That nigga ain't even got no family."

"Is that what you think?" Victor scoffed, mockingly.

"Yeah, I did my research."

"No dip shit. You're wrong. He does have a family. A well-known one at that." Victor leaned forward and placed his forearms on the desk.

"Who? 'Cause I couldn't find shit on that nigga."

"That's because Aubrey Simmons isn't his real name. When he turned eighteen he changed his name from Christian François to Aubrey Simmons. Apparently, he didn't want to be associated with his notorious crime family. He wanted to branch out on his own without the stigma of his family's name."

Cam wondered if he needed to clean out his ears. He hadn't heard right. Victor couldn't have said Noon's last name was François. But it all made sense. His connection to the François cartel was how he'd gotten Gray out of jail that night, how he'd gotten photos of him with Valentin in the park and his offer to elevate Cam to a real position of power. Noon's ass had more power than Cam ever expected or thought.

"Yeah, let that marinate, dickhead. You killed Don Valentin François' brother."

"How you figure that?" Cam questioned in disbelief.

"I hate this, nigga. I swear to God I do." Victor massaged his temples, frustrated. "Valentin called me last week saying his brother went missing and was last seen in my city. He asked me to look into it, so I did. And wouldn't you know. I found out that an unidentified black male in his mid-thirties was found gutted at The Ringmaster, the same day Valentin's brother went missing. Valentin came down and identified the body and low and behold it was his brother."

"That don't mean I killed him." Cam maintained.

"You already admitted it you fuckin' idiot!" Victor pounded his fist on the desk. "Plus, the way he was killed had you written all over it. Not to mention he was fuckin' your Japanese wife."

"Korean but that's neither here nor there. Does he know it was me?"

Victor inhaled and exhaled. It was taking everything in him not to lose his shit and shoot Cam in the head.

"No but he has an inkling it was you. He just doesn't have any proof."

It was a good thing Cam had paid Temptress to skip town or he'd really be a dead man.

"Rule number four is also saving your ass."

Cam thought back on the oath he'd sworn to follow. There were seven rules and customs members of the cartel had to adhere to. Rule number four titled "Blood for Blood" stated if a family member is killed by another member, no one can commit murder in revenge unless the boss gives permission.

"Like I said, he doesn't have physical proof that you killed his brother, but your name was brought up. Valentin is a smart man. He's not going to stop until he learns the truth. When he learns what you did, 'cause he will, I will give him permission to seek revenge. I will not protect you."

Cam couldn't do anything but respect that. He'd made his bed. One day he'd have to lie in it.

"Why'd you kill him?" Victor died to know.

"I had my reasons. It was personal." Cam explained. There was no way he was going to tell on his self and admit the truth. Valentin would never reveal the truth either. He'd gone behind another Don's back and provided one of his members a favor without permission. Doing so was not only a sign of disrespect but considered treachery. He'd never be trusted amongst the other commission members again.

"Yeah well, Valentin is going to personally fuck you up if he finds out."

"He won't. So now what?"

"We're done. You're no longer apart of this organization." Victor laid down the gauntlet. He should've killed him for committing such an egregious offense but despite Cam's incompetence, Victor had a soft spot for him and his family. They'd been through enough. He'd let him leave with his life. Relief swept over Cam. This was what he'd wanted since the day he got out of jail. Being a cartel member no longer fit into his lifestyle. He was a family man now.

"That's my punishment? A'ight cool. Are we done here?"

"You really think this shit is a game don't you?"

"Nah. Unless you gon' say something. Is that the real punishment?" Cam prayed to God it wasn't. Getting rid of Gunz was already stressful enough. He didn't know if he had the strength to go toe to toe with a Don of the cartel.

"No, your punishment is that you're gonna have to live the rest of your life looking over your shoulder wondering when this shit storm you've created is gonna catch up to you. Cause please believe it will. That's the thing, shit always come out in the wash. When you're most comfortable and when you least expect it, life has a funny way of turning your whole world upside down. Mark my words, Archibald. You gon' remember this day. You gon' remember this time. Most importantly, you gon' remember this conversation. And when your day of reckoning comes, don't reach out to me. You are no longer associated with the Gonzalez cartel. When Valentin learns the truth, cause one day he will, don't come looking for me. You better have your homeboy's strap up. But not the fat one. His fat ass is slow. And you better hope your wheezing ass can breathe. 'Cause them Creole niggas ain't to be fucked with." Victor forewarned him.

"Neither am I." Cam said down for whatever may come his way.

"You better hope so. 'Cause you're on your own, nigga."

CHAPTER 28

"Somebody gon' die tonight."-50 Cent "I'm Supposed to Die Tonight"

*L*aLa's hands quaked as she stretched out her fingers for the doorknob. With every move she made, she became more and more terrified. What had her life become? After the big blowout with Tia, later that night she and Gunz came up with a brilliant idea on how to payback Kingston. The plan was set in stone. Then things started to get weird. Gavin Jr. suspiciously ended up on Mama Lucy's doorstep alone. Tia was known to be careless and to throw temper tantrums from time-to-time, so when she didn't answer her phone, everyone assumed she was mad because she'd been found out and dipped off alone. With Gunz not policing her every move she'd do some foul shit like that. When LaLa asked Gunz had he seen her, he informed her that he hadn't been back to the house since he left. LaLa didn't even bother calling Kingston because he'd been laying up underneath her, which was all a part of their plan. When she'd told him that Tia had gone missing, he played down his concern, but she knew by the anxious look in his eyes that he was sick with worry.

Three days went by and there was still no word on where Tia was. That's when LaLa started to become concerned. Something was wrong. Tia wouldn't disappear that long without contacting someone. LaLa called the police and had them do a wellness check at the safe house. That's when she received the startling news that Tia's body had been found with a bullet lodged in her brain. When she'd left she was alive. LaLa knew immediately that Gunz had returned to the house and finished the job he'd started before they left.

LaLa knew Gunz had a fucked-up side to him. She just never knew he'd go to such lengths to destroy the ones who'd hurt him. Now she was scared out of her mind. She didn't want anything to do with him. She wanted to be as far away from him as possible. LaLa feared for her life. If Gunz could so easily kill the woman he'd been with the last few years, there was no telling what he'd do to her. She didn't want any parts of him or his scheme against Kingston anymore.

Trickles of sweat slid from her neck down to her spine. Tightly, she gripped the knob and twisted it. LaLa's breath quickened as she pulled open the door. Gunz stood there in all his one-eyed glory dipped in black. At one point in time, she used to think he was fine, but now that she'd seen for herself he was a stone-cold killer, nothing about him was attractive.

"Come in." She ushered him inside.

Gunz walked into her home and looked around. He'd never been to LaLa's crib before. It was nice but in a minute it would be a bloody mess.

"Thanks for coming over." She stood by the door in case she'd have to escape.

"You ready?" He cupped his hands together in front of his crotch and faced her.

"I've been thinking about it, Gunz. I can't do this."

Furious that she was trying to back out last minute, he cracked his neck and glared at her. His penetrating stare sucked the life out of LaLa.

"You can't do what?" He frowned.

"Set up Kingston." She ringed her hands together. "I think we should call the whole thing off."

"Why?" Gunz inched closer.

"Cause I know what you did to Tia." She backed further into the door. "They found her body today."

"And? What the fuck that mean? She deserved that shit."

"So, you're admitting it. You did it?" Her stomach shifted, uneasily.

"You already know what type of time I'm on. She got what was coming to her and now it's Kingston's turn." Gunz towered over her cowering frame.

"Kingston?" She drew her head back. Her whole body was shaking like a leaf. "No, I might hate him for what he did but my son is not growing up without a father. I thought we were just gonna fuck him up or send him to jail like we did Cam."

"Killing him is fucking him up. It's just permanent."

"I ain't down with that, especially since I know you killed my niece." She ducked past him and stood in the middle of the living room. "How could you do that? You said you loved her! How you think that's gonna effect my nephew? He's still your child!"

"Fuck that bitch and that li'l nigga ain't my son." Gunz looked at her like she was dumb. "You act like she ain't ruin my life?"

"No, Gunz, you ruined your life!" LaLa pointed her finger in his direction. "You can't blame this all on Tia! Yeah, she had her faults, but didn't nobody put a gun to your head and tell you to cheat on Gray! You did that shit cause you wanted to!"

Gunz's eyes turned rigid and cold. It was like the demon inside his soul took over his body. The whites of his eyes turned midnight black. How dare LaLa throw that shit up in his face. If he were honest with himself he'd admit she was right but Gunz never took responsibility for his actions. It was Gray's fault their relationship failed. She put her career before him, which caused his eye to wonder. If she would've taken care of him as a woman, he wouldn't have strayed. Within a half a second, he closed the space between them. Glaring into her frightened eyes he spoke with a low, menacing growl.

"And I killed Tia cause I wanted to. So, what the fuck is your point?" He pointed a Maxim 9 pistol with a built-in silencer at her temple. "You wanna die too?"

It took everything in LaLa to hold the piss that wanted to trickle down her thigh. She'd never had a gun pulled on her. Why did she ever get caught up with this crazy ass nigga? Linking up with Gunz had to be the biggest misstep of her life. Fucking around with him would get her killed. Then a thought popped in her head.

"Were you the one that dropped Gavin off at Mama Lucy's house?"

"No." He grimaced, confused by the question.

Internally, LaLa wondered if he didn't do it then who did?

"Look, I just wanna put all of this shit behind me. I wanna get the fuck outta Saint Louis and live my life with my son. Whatever you do to Kingston is on you. I don't want no parts of it. I'm done." She tried to stand her ground, but the shakiness of her voice told that she wasn't as confident as she tried to seem. Gunz analyzed the features of her face. LaLa was pretty in a sexy ass Miss Piggy kind of way. When all of this was over, he might fuck her.

"See." He used the silencer to push her hair away from her face. "That's where you got me fucked up. You're done when I say you're done and you ain't nowhere near finished. You just getting started, sweetheart. So, unless you wanna live to see Li'l Kam grow up, I suggest you get your fuckin' head in the game and call your baby daddy like we discussed. Time is ticking and I got places to be."

A great tremor overtook her. LaLa's body wracked with an onslaught of sobs and tears. She mumbled incoherent things through her hands and choked on her cries as her shoulders bounced up and down.

"Please Gunz, don't make me do this?" She begged and pleaded with everything she had.

Feeling not one ounce of empathy, Gunz curled his finger around the trigger. LaLa literally saw her life flash before her eyes. Sweat drenched down her skin, her eyes throbbed and the sound of her heart thumping against her chest could be heard in her ears. She was about to die. Gunz was about to kill her.

"Okay! Okay! Okay!" She shrilled, quivering.

"Call him." He handed her a burner phone.

"Why I just can't call him from my phone?" She questioned, confused.

"We ain't leaving no paper trail. You gon' be the last person he talk to."

LaLa hesitantly took the phone and released a deep breath. She couldn't believe this was happening. She was about to become an accomplice to murder. How had she gotten here? This was not supposed to be how her life turned out. Shuddering, she dialed Kingston's number. After a few rings he picked up.

"Yo."

"Kingston!" She shrieked.

Kingston took the phone away from his ear and looked at the screen. He didn't recognize the number.

"Who the fuck is this?" He asked.

"LaLa!"

"Oh, what's up? What number you calling me from?"

"Don't worry about that. Tia's dead!"

"What?!" He jumped up. There was no way he'd heard right.

"She's dead! The police just found her body!"

"Where?"

"At her and Gunz's hideout. They said she had a bullet in her head."

"Where the fuck my—" Kingston swiftly cut himself off. He was about to tell on his self. Now wasn't the time to reveal that Gavin Jr. was his son but soon he'd have to tell the truth. "Yo, where you at."

"I'm at home. I need you to get over here now."

"A'ight. I'm on my way." He ended the call.

"He's coming." She spoke in a daze and gave Gunz the phone back.

Gunz didn't respond. He tucked his gun inside the back of his jeans and hid in her room. LaLa sat nervously, tapping her foot against the floor until Kingston got there. Dread owned her and pushed against her like an invisible windstorm, attempting to reverse her steps back to a simpler time. Trepidation had her lungs locked up tight. It felt like no air was getting in or out. The alarming sound of the doorbell sent her over the edge. LaLa anxiously tried to hide how fearful she was. It was damn near impossible. She could control the tremor in her voice over the phone. She could consciously will her body not to be so robotic. She could even make herself smile somewhat, even if it looked pasted on. But the pit stains under her arms were a different story. That was something she couldn't hide. Dread took over her face like rigor mortis. Locking her teeth together, she wiped her sweaty palms on the front of her jeans and rose to her feet. It was game time but oh how LaLa wished she could ride the bench. Putting on her game face, she summoned the courage she'd need to move forward. She couldn't even pull the door all the way open before Kingston barged through and buried his face in the crease of her neck. He was overcome with tears.

"I can't believe she's gone." LaLa cried along with him.

"Do the police know who did it?"

"Not yet."

"I bet you it was Gunz. I told her to leave that nigga alone."

LaLa pulled out of his hold and stared at his distraught face. She'd never seen Kingston so upset.

"You a'ight? You're shaking." He ran his hands up and down her arms.

"When did you talk to Tia about Gunz?" She quizzed.

Kingston quickly realized that he'd said more than he should.

"I mean . . . we ain't talk like that." He shrugged, awkwardly. "Any word on the kid?" He changed the subject. LaLa knew what he was doing. All the signs of his and Tia's tryst were right there in her face. How had she missed them before? For a very brief second she started not to regret what she was about to do.

"That's another thing." She turned her back to him. "Somebody dropped him off at Mama Lucy's house. We don't know who or when. He was just sitting there on the porch. We don't even know how he got there."

"Yo, this shit is wild." He sat in the center of the couch. "How Mama Lucy doing?"

"How you think? She's a wreck, just like me. Tia ain't deserve to die like that." She spoke honestly as a flood of tears gushed down her ashen cheeks. Thinking about what Gunz had done to her and what he was about to do to Kingston was tearing her up inside.

"Yo, stop crying. We gon' find out who did it." He brought her back into his embrace. LaLa held onto him tight, for this would be their last time together.

"I know. I just can't stop crying." She pressed her cheek against his. LaLa started to feel like she was having an out-of-body experience as she placed a soft kiss on his wet cheek. Several smaller kisses followed.

"Yo, what you doing?" He asked, becoming aroused.

LaLa wasn't the type to become intimate for the sake of being intimate. For her to make the first move there had to be a reason. She wanted to fuck. Then he heard her moan, "I just need you to hold me. Take my mind off of this. Make me feel good."

"You trying to do this now?" He groaned, groping her butt.

"Shhhhhhh just kiss me."

Kingston's large hands roamed her curvy body, exploring. LaLa leaned in and softly kissed his dark tender lips. As they kissed, she reached down and unbuttoned his jeans. Stiff as a brick, Kingston helped her push down his pants. Once they were around his ankles, LaLa eased her way down to the floor and rested on her knees. Seductively, she gazed into Kingston's sleepy brown eyes. Lust flowed through his veins as he slid his dick into her wanting mouth. LaLa's eyes burned red as the head of his dick hit her tonsils. A rapid stream of tears dropped from the corners of her eyes as she slurped and sucked his cock. Caught up in the moment, her warm mouth, and wet tongue, Kingston leaned his head back against the couch. Now was the time to strike. A guttural urge to throw up caused her to cough and gag. It wasn't because his dick was too much for her to handle. It was because it sickened her that Gunz was forcing her to do this. Hot tears blinded her eyes then spilt over and flowed down her face like a river escaping a dam. Soft whimpers escaped LaLa's dry lips through the suppressed sound of hiccups. At any second she was going to purge the contents of her stomach. Over and over she tried to think of a way out of this mess, but the only way out was death. She was literally stuck between a rock and a hard place. Kingston was so into her oral education that he didn't even notice the distress she was in. He just thought she was into what she was doing so he kept fucking her mouth. A sobbing mess, LaLa gradually reached her hand under the couch cushion and pulled out the kitchen knife she'd planted there. The blade was sharp enough to cut flesh as if it posed no resistance. Wrapping her clammy hand around the handle, she held it next to her side ready to strike. Once the deed was done, her life would never be the same again. What little inno- cence she had left would be gone. Suckling the tip of his dick, she stroked his veiny cock with her left hand and then used the sharp blade of the knife to slice his dick off with the right. At once, a fountain of red came from the wound.

A scream from deep within forced its way out of Kingston's mouth, as if his terrified soul had unleashed a demon. With the speed of light- ening, he jumped back and started flopping around like a fish out of water. Adrenaline surged through his body. A sharp pain exploded like a bomb inside of him. Every beat of his pulse felt like a hammer banging on the wound. The panic and the pain made his breathing uneven and caused him to sweat. Pain seared through his groin, it burned around his guts better than scolding hot water. Kingston was in more pain than he could've ever imagined possible. A bullet would've been a hail Mary at that point.

LaLa didn't blame him for acting like a bitch. The attack had to be painful. There his flaccid dick was in her manicured hand. Blood dripped, creating a small pool of plasma on the floor next to the knife she'd dropped. Blood gushed with sickening determination from Kingston's mutilated penis. The burgundy gore lashed over the living room, painting the scene of the crime. It was the most ungodly sight she'd ever seen. Nausea clawed at her throat. LaLa tried to swallow down the vomit but it was of no use. With one violent contraction, she lurched forward. The day old contents of her stomach ripped through her esophagus and landed on the couch and his leg. As if on cue, Gunz sauntered from out the back with his pistol in hand.

"Shut the fuck up." He smacked Kingston across the face with his gun. The cracking of his teeth could be heard around the room.

"What is this, amateur night at the Apollo? What the fuck you crying for?" He bopped LaLa in the back of her head. There was no crying when committing murder. Yet, she couldn't stop. Realizing Kingston's severed penis was still in her hand she threw it across the room. It landed by her brand new lavender ottoman. Blood was everywhere. If Gunz didn't kill her, she was going to jail for sure. LaLa wiped puke from her mouth. The acidic residue formed a glossy patch on her shirt sleeve. Her face was white and dripping with vomit, sweat, and tears. The pungent disgusting odor attacked her nostrils, causing her to dry heave. Watching Gunz move around the room with such ease was truly disturbing. It was hard to digest that they were of the same species. He looked the same, walked the same and spoke the same but all of his wiring was skewed. Mama Lucy always said folks were just one or two screws loose from losing their shit. Gunz had lost all his marbles. The nigga was a walking psychopath. He thought he was invincible.

"What the fuck? My dick!" Kingston screamed at the top of his lungs.

It felt like someone was pinching his skin with a metal claw then punctured him with a million needles. His brain tried to deny how much agony he was in, but the pain was endless. After that everything went numb. At any second he was going to black out.

"Your dick is what got you in this trouble in the first place and it's about to be the reason you take your last breath." Gunz admired the ghastly scene in front of him.

"Come on, Gunz! What you doing? I ain't even do shit!" Kingston cried profusely.

"That's the same thing Tia said before she took a bullet to the dome. I always knew you was a snake ass nigga but you the dumbest muthafucka I know. You let pussy fuck up everything around you. You really thought you was gon' get away with fucking my girl and then on top of that have me raise *your* son? You had to know I was gon' find out."

"We was gon' tell you but I ain't know how! I ain't wanna disrespect you man!" He groaned in anguish. He was becoming extremely lightheaded.

"I ain't trying to hear that shit. Nigga, you disrespected me the minute you put your dick in my bitch."

"But I was fuckin' her first so really you disrespected me!" Kingston clarified. Shocked that he'd talk out of term, Gunz lost his shit.

"Pussy!" He whacked him with the barrel of the gun again. The blow was hard enough to give him a concussion. Tired of hearing his mouth, Gunz decided to put Kingston out of his misery once and for all.

"I'll see you in hell muthafucka. Say hello to Tia while you're down there."

The moment played out in slow motion. LaLa and Kingston thought Gunz would finish him with a bullet to his brain but that's not what happened at all. As swift as an alley cat, he snuck up behind Kingston with the kitchen knife in his gloved hand. Taking hold of his head, he pulled it back, so his neck was fully exposed. No trepidation was written on his face as he moved the blade in a smooth motion across his throat slicing through his trachea and esophagus as well as the arteries on both side of Kingston's neck. He then punched forward and down, cutting his vocal cords. Kingston tried taking giant gasping breaths through his severed windpipe but he couldn't because he'd started gargling blood and coughing. Thick gore flowed like a river from his mouth. LaLa was sure she was gonna vomit again. Gripping his neck, Kingston tried to prolong the inevitable, but no matter the pressure he applied, the blood still gushed between his fingers and oozed under his hand. Despite his futile attempts at saving his own life, blood still drained from his rapidly paling flesh. Seconds later, his eyes went still, and he slumped over and died.

Satisfied with the outcome, Gunz tossed the knife down on the couch next to Kingston's deceased body. You would think murder was his favorite pastime, but it wasn't. It was nothing but a necessary chore rather than a pleasure. Every drama filled moment of his life was the fault of someone else's. Never once did he look in the mirror of his own soul and ask what different choices he could've made, not for his own sake, but for the sake of others. In each moment, Gunz made choices for himself. Others be damned. Taking out his phone, he hit up his cleaning crew. They had a body to dispose of and some heavy duty scrubbing and washing.

LaLa couldn't hear her rapid breathing. She felt it. Mortified, she eyed Kingston's corpse. Terror churned in her guts, giving her severe cramps. Fear engulfed her body, making it drastically exhausted. Her jaw dropped in a silent scream of horror. She covered her mouth to muffle her scream. On his way out the door, Gunz paused and said, "If you even think about going to the police, you'll be next."

CAM SAT IN BACK OF THE CROWDED CHURCH. KINGSTON'S FUNERAL service was slower than a country bus, taking just as many detours. Everyone had a memory to share. Kingston's mother, Abigail, must've agreed to every request. Halfway through the service, Cam was ready to leave but despite he and Kingston's beef, it wouldn't have been right if he didn't give him a proper send off. No one deserved to die the way he did. The poor guy couldn't even have an open casket service. His maimed corpse was found stripped naked on the side of the road for everyone to see. The word on the street was that he'd received a buck fifty to the throat and a detached cock. Cam knew Gunz was behind the grisly murder. His men who he paid to keep tabs on him informed him of it. It was clear he was sending a message to Cam that he was alive and well and coming for him next.

Even though they shared a sordid past, Cam hated to see Kingston's life end so tragically. When they were kids, he and Kingston used to be thick as thieves. Now he was gone, and they would never be able to make amends. Cam still struggled with the idea of if he even wanted to. Some things were better left alone but there was still so much that needed to be said between the two men.

Cam was nothing less than overjoyed when the service was over. He was itching to get back home to his pregnant wife and kids. Before he left, he headed to the front of the church to pay his respects. LaLa was a mess. She hooped and hollered throughout the entire eulogy. Her light skin was covered in red blotches from crying so hard. She sat with her son, Gavin Jr. and Damya.

"You a'ight?" He asked, faking concern.

"No. This shit is too much. First my niece and now my baby's father. What in the world did I do to deserve this?"

It took the spirit of Denzel Washington for Cam not to make a face. Pretending to care about her feelings was harder than he anticipated.

"Yeah, it's a lot. I heard about what happened to Tia. That's fucked up."

"We just laid her to rest the other day. Mama Lucy can barely get out of bed. I don't even know how I made it here."

"Y'all going through a lot." Cam shook his head.

"Umm." LaLa lowered her tone and pulled him to the side. Nervously, she looked from side-to-side to make sure no one was watching. "Now isn't the time but after the holidays can we met up?"

Cam furrowed his brows taken aback.

"I don't know about that." He stuffed his hand inside his pocket.

"I know you're married. I get that, but Cam, I really need you." She grabbed his free hand and lowered her voice to a whisper. "There's a lot of shit that's been going on that you need to know about. I can't talk to you about it now but trust me this is some shit you wanna know."

"A'ight." He slipped his hand from hers. "Just hit me."

"Thank you, Cam. You have no idea how much this means to me." LaLa breathed a sigh of relief.

"No problem. Y'all be safe out here." He turned with a sinister sneer on his face. Cam wished he could be on his way, but funeral etiquette demanded he visit the family. Kingston's mother and his father, Cam Sr., were next to the pulpit speaking to the reverend. The rest of the Parthens' clan would be attending the wake together. The sight of his father so close to Abigail ignited a flame of rage inside of Cam. All of the emotions he kept bottled deep inside came flooding to the surface. It had been years since he last saw them together. He hated it then and he hated it now. Swallowing his anger, he remembered why he was there.

"Just wanted to offer my condolences."

Abigail placed her hand over heart, stunned. Cam hadn't spoken a word to her in ages.

"Thank you, Cameron. I really appreciate that." She dabbed her eyes with Cam Sr.'s pocket square.

"I know things have been strained between us over the years but I'm really happy that you could put your personal feelings aside and be supportive. I know wherever Kingston is he's smiling down on us."

"Up or down but whatever." Cam mumbled under his breath. Oblivious to his snarky comment, Abigail continued speaking.

"It would've meant a lot to him to know that you were here. I just wish the two of you could've been closer."

"Yeah, well we can't always get what we want. Can we?"

"C'mon, son." Cam Sr. placed his hand on his shoulder. "You have to let that go. What happened in the past is in the past. Please, let's just leave it there. Kingston is gone now. There's nothing we can do about that. For our family and for Abigail's sake, it's best we leave all of that drama behind us and move on."

Cam shouldn't be surprised that his father would negate his feelings, but he was. It didn't matter how much time had passed. Nothing was going to change the way he felt.

"If only it were that simple, dad. If only it were that simple."

CHAPTER 29

"I got demons huntin' me. I tell death to keep a distance. I think he obsessed with me. I say, "God, that's a woman, "I know she would die for me."-Saba "Life"

$\mathcal{A}$ month and a half had gone by since Aoki and Paris made it official. There wasn't a day that passed where they didn't Facetime or text. At night when her parents thought she was asleep, they'd sneak on the phone and talk until they drifted off. During lunchtime they sat side-by-side, holding hands and stealing kisses. The young couple were glued at the hip. They'd quickly become each other's best friend. Paris and Aoki laughed and talked about everything under the sun. They even had their own secret language and inside jokes. Love was blooming at a rapid rate. That particular day she slept next to him. Aoki lay as still as a brick. She was the perfect person to lay next to. She wasn't a wild sleeper at all. She lay on her side in one place. The only movement that came from her was the slight rise and fall of her chest and the gentle snuffling noises she made as she breathed. She was the personification of an angel. For Paris, having her there in his bed was a dream he never thought would come true. But they'd schemed and plotted to get her there. Aoki told her parents that she'd signed up to feed the homeless with her school that Saturday. The gag was when they dropped her off, she never went inside the building. Paris was there waiting to pick her up. Together, they grabbed some food and headed back to his crib. Priest was out of town for a few days, so the coast was clear. For the first time, they had the opportunity to spend some alone time together.

There they lay on his king-sized mattress that was on the floor. It didn't bother Paris at all that he didn't have a bed frame. He was used to the bare minimum. Having just a mattress on the floor fit his personality to a T. He'd grown up in an environment where he had to fend for himself at a young age. Living in a high-rise apartment was an upgrade. The exposed brick wall, life size photo of a gorgeous heavily melanated woman, black leather chair, marble nightstand and black fur rug were all things he'd only fantasized about acquiring.

Not having much growing up made him a minimalist. He didn't like clutter and mess. Priest was the same, but he went overboard with the shit. His neurotic behavior led him to develop Obsessive Compulsive Disorder. Paris was happy he hadn't picked up the trait. It drove him nuts to see his brother constantly counting his steps, putting items in alphabetical order, and constantly cleaning.

Poetic Justice played softly in the background as he and Aoki lay. The movie was on the infamous part where Regina King's character, Iesha, drunkenly cussed her boyfriend Chicago out for not having any stamina in the bedroom and a little dick. Aoki faced him sound asleep in the fetal position. She'd dozed off halfway through the movie. Soon, he'd have to wake her up and get her back to school. The only problem was, he didn't want her go. He wanted her near him forever. When he was with her he lost track of time. He wanted nothing more than to stay in the world they'd created. Snuggling next to her was the only antidote to get him through this fucked-up world. When she wasn't near, Aoki took the best parts of him with her. When she wasn't around, he wasn't himself anymore. Paris became a broken shell of a young man. All the thoughts and fears he tried to push down with weed, pills and sex came rushing back. When he was with Aoki he didn't need to use those things as a crutch. Her presence alone calmed him. That's how he knew she was the one. No other girl or human being on the planet made him feel that way. Letting go of Damya was a no brainer. She wasn't anywhere near on Aoki's level. What he and Aoki shared transcended their age. Yes, they might've been young, but their connection was stronger than couples who'd been together for 20 years. She even needed him in her sleep. Slowly, her warm hand slipped under his shirt and caressed his abs. Paris pulled her close. In seconds, her body molded into his. Holding her, he shared his body heat as effortlessly as she shared her heart. Being affectionate was foreign to Paris but he could never let another chick get close to him like this. Aoki's whole vibe was different. He'd never known a person to always want the best for the people around them. There was a purity to her, naivety perhaps, but she was the only girl to capture his undivided attention and his heart.

Cuddling alone brought him a peace he'd never known. Paris swore he was gonna do right by her. She deserved nothing but the best of him. His job as her boyfriend was to love her, keep her safe and defend her at all cost. Other than Meechi, she was the closest person to him.

Aoki's body shifted as she stirred in her sleep. Waking from a heavy slumber the loamy fragrance of Paris' cologne floated up her nose causing her to smile. She loved his scent. It was always clean and masculine. Aoki was shocked she'd even fallen asleep. Poetic Justice was one of her all-time favorite films. She practically knew the entire movie line for line. She also wanted to spend every waking moment possible with him. They only had a few more hours together. He must've felt the same way 'cause when her eyes opened they landed on him staring at her. It wasn't in a creepy way tho. They say the eyes are window to the soul and that was true. She could see right through his. Specs of longing, resentment, hurt, and abandonment lay in his brown orbs. She took notice of how every emotion he harbored forged together to form the art of his soul. It all formed a picture she could see and comprehend so well. Being held in his warm embrace wasn't enough. She needed to be closer, so she reached out her hand to touch his pensive face. Aoki quickly realized that something slightly heavy was weighing down her arm. Checking out her left wrist, she noticed there was a gold charm bracelet attached to it. The bracelet hadn't been there before she'd fallen asleep.

"What is this?" She asked. Sparks of excitement danced in her eyes.

"Merry Christmas, Thief."

Paris and Aoki agreed to exchange gifts before the holiday, since they wouldn't be able to do so on the actual day. They'd be at Cam Senior's house amongst family. There would be too many eyes and ears around for them to venture off by themselves. This was the only chance they'd get to be alone. Aoki couldn't take her eyes off the mesmerizing piece of jewelry. Paris damn near passed out waiting for her reaction. He'd never spent bread on a chick before. He never cared enough to. But for Aoki, he was willing to go into his stash and drop a couple of bands. Paris had been saving money for studio time and an apartment of his own. Kiara's mom had agreed to co-sign a crib for him too. The stacks he'd spent on Aoki put him down significantly. He'd have to get out in the streets and hustle hard to recoup his funds. Paris stared at Aoki. Her facial expression showed nothing. He didn't know how she would react. She was a girl that had everything at her fingertips. Would she even appreciate the gift? What if it wasn't expensive enough? He hoped she didn't think it was lame.

"You like it?"

Aoki examined the $1,500 gold charm bracelet. There were only three charms on it; a diamond Eiffel tower that represented his name and her time in Paris, a gold vintage record player that signified her love of music and wanting to be a DJ and a lock and key that represented her having the key to his heart. Each charm was a thousand dollars apiece.

"If you ain't feeling it, I can take it back." He said ready to take it off.

"Paris." Aoki's eyes started to water with tears. Without saying another word, she pressed her lips against his and kissed him with everything she had. Heat rose in her cheeks as her tongue touched his. The growl that slipped through his lips was a sign of love and possession. Paris couldn't get enough of her. Kissing Aoki was like an explosion of the best flavors in the universe all at once mingling together and creating the best taste and sensation he'd ever felt. The kiss lasted an eternity. If Paris didn't end it when he did, things would've escalated to a level she wasn't ready for. Until Aoki gave him the okay he wasn't going to take it there. They were already in too deep. Sex would only complicate things. It would have them ready to commit murder behind each other. Aoki took a deep breath, thankful that he'd stopped when he did. 'Cause she sure as hell didn't have the will power to. Every time they kissed, she became dizzy with lust.

"Judging by that kiss I guess yo' bougie ass liked it."

"Whatever, nigga. You ready for yours?" She grinned, happily.

Paris gazed at her lips. Her smile was the prettiest thing he'd seen in a while. It extended to her eyes and deep into her soul.

"Yeah, I'm ready." He sat up and rested his back against the brick wall. Aoki reached for her black leather Balenciaga backpack and unzipped it. Inside was a white envelope with Paris' name written on it.

"Here." She handed it to him.

Sitting Indian style, she waited impatiently for him to open it. Paris knitted his brows together. The envelope was too light to have money in it. He was thoroughly confused. He had no idea what her gift could be. Perplexed, he unsealed it and found a flight itinerary. Tickets were purchased for him and Meechi to go to Paris for spring break. Aoki wished she could've gone with him, but she was underage and so was

Paris. Meechi was old enough to accompany him on the flight. Paris stared at the piece of paper thunderstruck. This was what being loved felt like. He'd never felt it before in his life. Aoki wrapped her arm around him. Paris rested the side of his face against her shoulder. He was trying his best not to cry as she rubbed the back of his head.

"Remember when you said you'd never been anywhere but the five boroughs of New York and St. Louis?"

"Yeah." He replied choked up.

"What was my response?" She placed a loving kiss on his forehead.

"You said if I was good to you, maybe one day you'd take me to Paris." He tried to keep his composure.

"As you can see. I kept my word."

"You did li'l mama. You did." He wiped a lone tear from his eye. "How you do this?"

"I have money that my parents gave me saved up."

Paris couldn't stop staring at the itinerary. The feelings he had for Aoki grew to brand new heights. This was yet another confirmation that she would be the love of his life. There would never be another girl like her to cross his path. What had he done to deserve someone so good? Paris prayed to God he didn't fuck this up but judging by his past, he would.

"I can't accept this shit, man." He passed the paper back to her and sat up.

"Why not?" Aoki's heart thudded.

"I don't deserve it."

"I don't understand." Her eyes were wide with fear.

"I know you don't. That's the problem. You think you know a nigga, but you don't." He gripped his head.

Aoki rubbed his well-developed back in a circle. How had things gone to shit so fast? She could feel his grief with every stroke of her hand. Paris held his head down. He couldn't even look at her face. His insides drew tight. The emotional pain he had left invisible scars on his soul. Like a cyst, the wound needed to be opened to heal but ever since he was a child, Paris had learned how to hide his pain, how to look normal. What he didn't know was that Aoki understood how a person could turn cold to escape the pain of abandonment, why they let their compassion wilt and die: numbness over feeling, mental anesthesia. Paris had been pushing back against pain for so long, medicating with drugs and bitches but no matter what the agony always came back.

"What is it that I don't know that I should?" Paris' angry eyes told a story of pain untold, and she wished he'd read her every page. If he let her in, Aoki would weather every storm he faced with him, but he had to promise to keep her safe. If he were good to her, she'd be the best for him.

"I fuck wit' you the long way. I want what we have to last but I don't know if it can." He dropped his head back.

"Why you say that?"

"Life don't mean shit to a nigga that ain't never had shit. Since the day I was born, my mama told me I wasn't gon' be shit, just like my daddy. I don't even know that nigga. She hate that muthafucka, so when she look at me I know she sees hate." He paused. It was a battle for him to reveal his demons. Aoki looked on somberly waiting for him to continue on. It took a minute, but Paris finally found the words to speak.

"I had to get it out the mud. My mama ain't give a fuck about me. She so bitter and fucked-up in the head. Priest got outta dodge as soon as he turned eighteen. He was tired of us going from house to house and her going from nigga to nigga and dick to dick. You know how many "uncles" I had coming up? Too many to fuckin' count. It was a revolving door of muthafuckas in and out the crib. That bitch was so worried about who she was fuckin' that she ain't give a fuck about my wellbeing. Without Priest around I had to take the brunt of her shit. She'd beat my ass if I breathed wrong. And I don't mean a spanking with her hand or a belt. I mean punches to the face, to my chest. I got beat with extension cords, broomsticks, wire hangers, shoes or whatever else she could get her hands on. I ain't have nobody to save me. I had to save my muthafuckin' self."

Paris' emotional distress poured from deep down within. It physically hurt Aoki to hear what he'd gone through.

"Shit was hard for me too." She confessed. "My biological father raped my mother and she killed him. That's how I was born. I was a product of rape. I came out of fear, violence, and misplaced trust. Maybe that's why I'm so rebellious. I don't wanna be held down by nothing. If that ain't bad enough, my parents didn't even tell me. I had to find out on my own."

"How old were you when you found out?"

"Ten. I felt like I couldn't trust nobody, not even my own mama. My whole life the people closest to me had been lying to me. It was like I ain't have nobody. Then the lousy ass nigga that raised me said fuck me and my sister for some bitch half his age. He straight got a new family and said fuck us. Once again, I was abandoned and alone. I mean, don't get me wrong, I had my mother, but she was so caught up in her shit with Cam that I don't even think she realized how bad that shit impacted me. It wasn't until we dipped off to Paris that me and her got our stuff together and I was able to forgive her. I still have my moments where I feel like I don't belong but when I'm with you the pain lessens. I feel complete, like I belong to someone." She pressed her body against his. "Let me belong to you."

Paris wanted to ease her worries, but he'd promised to keep it real with her. He couldn't just sell her a dream.

"You don't even know the reason why I'm here."

"Tell me." She practically begged.

Paris couldn't believe he was about to tell her his deepest darkest secret. It was the thing that had defined him for months. The shame of what happened followed him everywhere he went. Paris heart raced so fast he thought he'd vomit. He could taste the saliva in his mouth thickening to a sour paste.

"My mama . . . she umm. . ." He twiddled nervously with his

fingers. "She put me out after I told her the nigga she messing with tried to violate me."

"Violate you how?" Aoki pulled away, shuddering.

Paris wished he'd never opened his big mouth. He hadn't even told the full story and she was already looking at him differently.

"No." Aoki reached for his arm. "I'm not judging you. I'm just scared of what you're about to say." She assured.

Relieved that she hadn't switched up on him, Paris started to relax.

"My ole bird was gone to work so it was just me and her nigga at the crib. I'm in my room taking a nap. So, I guess this nigga thought he could try me. I'm knocked out. I'm thinking I'm having a wet dream or some shit, but the shit was feeling so realistic. I opened my eyes Aoki and I see this faggot muthafucka on the side of my bed, on his knees sucking my off. He was sucking my dick while I was sleep." His voice croaked. Paris could barely breath. A rush of heat washed over his body. It was like he was experiencing the incident all over again.

"Can you believe that?" Tears flooded his eyes. His nose turned red. "I tried to kill that nigga. I swear to God, I did." He pounded his fist into his hand.

"We was bangin' for what felt like hours. I ain't gon' front. That bitch ass nigga got the best of me, but I ain't back down. When my mama got home, I told her what happened, and that bitch told me I was lying." He said in disbelief. "She called me a fuckin' liar. She said I just wanted to ruin her life like I did everything else and told me to get out. She chose him over me. Her own son. Her own flesh and blood. I ain't have no place to go. I ain't want nobody to know what happened so I slept in my car until my face healed then I called my brother and asked could I come stay with him." Paris cried as if he was being gutted from the inside out. Torturous pain flowed out of every pore on his body. Since the incident, he'd tried his best to put the whole matter behind him but every day he woke it was there. Waking up to his mother's boyfriend, giving him head conjured thoughts and emotions he was too young to be experiencing or worrying about. Because he was aroused when it happened, Paris started to question his manhood. His mother's boyfriend even accused him of enjoying it because he was hard, which further confused him. Paris then decided to go above and beyond to prove to himself he wasn't gay by having sex with as many girls as possible. The whole experience had seriously mind-fucked him. Not having anyone to talk to about the sexual trauma only made matters worse. Because of his uneasiness with men, Paris only had one male friend and gravitated toward guys who were super-masculine to further prove he wasn't soft.

As a young man, a black man at that, it wasn't accepted to be emotional about sexual assault. He had to put on a strong face and not seem bothered. Imprisoned by shame, it was much better to suffer in silence than make the world aware of his victimization. Because African-American boys are in an environment that applauds 'macho-ism,' they feel powerless when they are violated, and they feel as though they have failed themselves by allowing something like this to happen. Yet, even in the supposed confines of a family environment, where a child should be protected, boys are still at risk. Poverty and broken families exacerbate the problem.

Aoki digested what he said as mournful tears fell from her distraught eyes. Suddenly, it all hit her at once. At first she didn't trip off when he made fun of Blizz and constantly picked on him. Now she understood why. Paris used Blizz as a punching bag because it made him feel in control and powerful. She'd read somewhere that people who were victims of sexual abuse often become predators themselves. Paris wasn't a sexual predator, but he was a bully and much like sexual predators he used physical strength, threats, and intimidation to place fear in his victims. Paris' confession made her see him in a brand new light. She got why he was so closed off and angry. She would be, too, if someone had taken her innocence. Gazing at his handsome face, she wished she could absorb all his pain. If she could she'd take it all away. No one as beautiful and special as him should ever have to carry around so much discomfort. The areas in his life that his mother and father had failed to nourish and protect she vowed to heal. She'd fix the broken pieces of his heart just like he was fixing hers.

"I tried to bury the shit. I tried to move on, but it stays here." He jabbed his forehead with his finger. "It's like a scar I can't get rid of. That nigga violated me in the worst way."

"Nah, call it what it is. You were molested."

This time Paris jerked away from her. There wasn't any misunderstanding tho. He was heated and offended. Wiping his face, he glared at her with contempt.

"I wasn't no fuckin' molested! That nigga didn't fuck me! It ain't even get that far! I fought back! I ain't no fuckin' pussy!"

"But he still touched you in an inappropriate way. That shit ain't cool." She tried to make him understand. "That man molested you. He touched you without your consent. He forced himself on you and engaged in a sexual act against your will. For that, he needs to pay. Have you told anybody besides your mother?"

"Fuck nah."

"So, Priest don't even know?"

"No and you ain't gon' tell 'em. This shit stays between me and you." He gave her a warning glare.

"Of course. I wouldn't dare betray your trust, but I do think you need to talk to somebody. Therapy helped me a lot. I think it would do wonders for you."

"You trying to say I'm crazy?" He snarled, curling his upper lip.

"You don't have to be crazy to go to therapy. I went."

"Exactly." He mocked, with a chuckle.

"Nigga, I ain't crazy." Aoki rolled her neck.

"That's debatable."

"No, for real." She tugged on his arm. "Stop making a joke out of this. This shit is serious."

"I know it is. Look, I'll think about it but I ain't making you no promises. Niggas just don't be out here talking about they feelings and shit. It's a lot that I'm even doing it with you. I ain't never told nobody this shit. Not even Meech."

"But why? You should at least tell Priest."

"What's the point? My own mama didn't even believe me. You

always talkin' about I need to take life more seriously, but nobody ever taught me how. My own mama don't give a fuck about my life. My daddy sure in the fuck don't. Priest basically said fuck me when he dipped. I ain't have time to worry about school and grades. I had to get out here and hustle to survive. Why you think I joined a gang? I did it for fuckin' protection. Since I was eleven I've been on my own. I ain't never have nobody around to defend me so the Rollin' 30 Crips became the closest thing I had to family. So, fuck tellin' Priest. I ain't need that nigga then. I don't need that nigga now. Fuck him and fuck her. As long as I got you I'm straight." He took her hand in his.

Aoki took it back.

"Well, if you wanna keep me you gon' have to make some changes. I really like you, and I want nothing but the best for you. Being a street nigga ain't where it's at. You got a world of potential. Like I told you that night at the pool, you can be the biggest rap star in the world. Hell, I could be your DJ." She pinched his cheek.

"Chill." He laughed.

"Real talk. You can't be a megastar if you don't know the business. I can't be with no dummy. Just use school as your steppingstone to know the business. Trust me, you'll thank me later."

"I don't know, man." Paris shrugged, unsure.

Aoki placed her index under his chin and made him face her.

"Ambition neutered by self-doubt is a recipe for disaster."

In that instant Paris fell madly in love with her.

"Do you trust me enough to leave the streets and try something different?"

Paris always believed that trust should come before love, but that wasn't always the case. Love and trust can arrive at the same time. When love is given in this way, immediate, no explanations, the trust arrives too. Maybe that's why people warn to tread lightly or call it stupid. Love is love, always a gift from God up above. The love that brewed for Aoki wasn't physical, that shit rested in the depth of his soul. So even though trust is the base to all human relationships, it doesn't always come first. It can come as part of a package deal.

Paris wasn't sure he'd be able to give Aoki everything she was asking for. He'd spent his whole life not giving a fuck about anything. For as far back as he could remember, he'd been walking this world alone, doing shit his way so compromising and changing his ways would be a feat. Could he walk in his purpose? Would he be able to exercise his demons? How could he wash away the stigma of being sexually violated by another man? Would his heart heal from never having a mother's love? How would he learn how to be a man, a husband and a father when the man that was supposed to teach him was absent?

Laying on his back, Paris pulled Aoki on top of him. He could feel her muscles tense, but to calm her he soothingly massaged her back. Their bodies fit together perfectly. Her legs that he loved so much were almost as long as his. Her full coily hair hung forward drowning her face. Paris brushed her curls over her shoulder so he could take in the essence of her. Being with her felt unreal. Was she even human? Aoki was overwhelming beautiful. Sometimes, being with her was too much to handle. To him she was too good to be true. The shoe would eventually drop. Nothing good in his life lasted forever. He was a street kid, a hustler and if need be a killer. Aoki had no business being with him. Deep down he knew he should let her go but Paris was a selfish nigga. In her presence he felt showered with love and in her eyes shone a gentleness that told him at last, he was home.

"Yeah, I trust you." He answered truthfully.

Aoki's heart settled but her body was still tense. She'd never been this intimate with a guy before. Was this the moment he'd take it there? She hoped not 'cause she wasn't ready. She was already overwhelmed with how much she cared for him. Knowing that he trusted himself with her only deepened their connection. She never wanted another girl to be close to him like this. To feel his heartbeat against her chest, his minty breath on her lips, his callous hand rubbing her back was heaven sent. She'd die if a day came where he wasn't hers. They'd built an emotional bond that couldn't be duplicated. And yes, she was only fourteen. Her feelings for him shouldn't be this deep but they were. In

Aoki's heart of hearts, she knew Paris was her soulmate, the boy whose last name she'd eventually bear. God had created her with him in mind.

"A'ight act like it then." Aoki gave him a quick peck on the lips. "Cause if you wanna be mediocre you can go and be with special ed, Damya, and her each-one-teach-one education."

"I'm good. I ain't going nowhere. Well . . . except to Paris." He grinned, boyishly.

CHAPTER 30

"Sometimes I feel like a motherless child. A long way from home."-
Odette "Sometimes I Feel Like A Motherless Child"

*T*he world was silent. It was always that way on Christmas. Gray missed those Christmas mornings where the streets were filled with snow. Because of global warming, winters became hotter each year. That day the sun rose ordering the stars to take their nightly rest. As nightfall surrendered, every color of the sky changed from charcoal to a vibrant shade of blue. Gray pondered if humans even deserved such a divine gift. Propped up on a king-sized pillow, she ran her fingers through Cam's soft tendrils. The side of his face rested on her bare five month old belly. This was their morning routine, silence and cuddling. He'd pushed her black silk negligee up over her stomach and lay his head there. Her round honey colored stomach was the shape of a half moon. The linea nigra also known as the dark pregnancy line traced the center of her belly. Cam couldn't stop running his finger up and down it. He was fascinated by the entire process. He'd signed up for a daily app that told him new facts about the baby. Right now, he or she was about seven inches long and approximately the size of a large banana. The baby also weighed a whole entire 1 lb.

Cam wanted to feel as close to the baby as possible. There wasn't one second of this pregnancy he was going to miss. Seeing Gray's body change, hearing the baby's heartbeat and witnessing the ultrasound were all gifts from Jehovah. Each morning before they rose and at night when they rested for bed, he'd kiss and talk to their little one. Each time, Gray would squirm. His beard and diamond chains tickled her stomach, but she wouldn't dare ask him to move. She'd prayed for moments like this. Her husband was her best friend, her lover, her protector, her security blanket, and her nightly wet dream. He was so fucking fine. Everything about Cam was sexy from his smooth facial hair, to the hundreds of tattoos that covered his back and carved out muscular arms. She prayed their baby looked like him. Not only was he handsome as hell but loving.

That morning, Gray woke from her slumber feeling queasy. She thought a few sips of ginger ale would calm her stomach, but it didn't. Cuddling with Cam was the medicine she needed. Being close to him felt like a little touch of heaven. Gray wished she could extend the night just so she could stay closer to him longer. Having him hold her and the baby brought a sense of peace she'd never known. Soon the kids would rush into their bedroom and order them to get up so they could open presents. This was the calm before the storm. She was going to relish every peaceful second.

Until then, she'd enjoy her man, their new home and the stillness that surrounded her. It had been a few weeks since they'd settled into the mega mansion Cam had copped for their family. This was the most at home Gray had ever felt. There were still a few rooms that needed to be furnished but they'd gotten most of the house done. This was their forever home. The house they'd raise their six children in and grow old together. She and Cam's life was finally on track, things were finally good. They'd weathered the tornado that had been their existence. Life could only go up from there.

"*Hellooo.*" Cam sang into her belly. "*It's daaaaaaaddy. I looove you, looove you, looove you, loove you, looove you.*"

"Are you really singing Dangerously in Love to my baby?"

"Our baby and hell yeah. I don't fuck wit' Beyoncé like that but that song slap. How's it going in there, buddy? Did you eat your vegetables? Are you sleeping? Is it warm in there? Do you need a blanket? It's time to wake up and make mommy's life a living hell."

"No, please don't." Gray begged.

"I can't wait for you to get here. Gimmie five." Cam raised his hand like the baby would actually slap it back.

"You know it might be a girl."

"Nah, this my li'l soldier in there." He kissed her stomach. "Ain't that right li'l man? Kick mommy and tell her you're a boy." Cam waited for some kind of movement but got none. "Really buddy? You gon' do your old man like that? I thought we was homies. Me and Reigny can't wait to play basketball with you, watch the game and build go-carts. Daddy's gonna be your best friend. I'ma show you how to ride a bike, how to get on girls and how to break down a brick."

Gray didn't hesitate to smack him upside the head.

"Have you lost your damn mind?"

"I'm just playing." Cam cracked up laughing.

"Have you been to your auto shops lately?" She asked.

"Yeah, I went by there and the liquor stores a few times. Quan made sure everything stayed up and running. I'm thinking about opening up a few new locations since I'm technically retired."

"I think that's a great idea."

"For right now, I'ma chill with you and the fam but eventually I'ma have to figure out what I'ma do with myself."

"Take your time, babe. You've been through so much mentally and health wise. There's no need to rush. It's not like you're struggling financially or are you?" She paused.

"Nah, Quan handled my businesses, properties, stocks and investments while I was down. I went in worth 50 mill and came out worth 82."

"Damn we rich-rich."

"Oh, now it's we." Cam grinned.

"Yeah, boo. What's yours is mine and what's mine is mine." Gray joked.

"You ain't shit."

"Listen." She resumed, stroking his hair. "I've been thinking about baby names."

"Oh Lord." Cam groaned, caressing her belly.

"Hush." Gray giggled.

"Don't piss me off, Gray. If it's a girl it bet not be nothing stupid like Hail, Sleet or Snow."

"Do you really think I'd name our child after the weather?"

"You just did. The fuck. You named our kids rainbow sky. Why wouldn't I think that?" Cam teased.

"I love the triplets' names." Gray poked out her bottom lip.

"I ain't gon' front. You did your thing. Their names are fly as fuck."

"Okay, for a boy, what about the name Hugo?"

"Hugo, as in Hugo Boss?"

"Yeah."

"How about *Hugo* over there and pick out another damn name." Cam pointed to the corner for her to have several seats.

"I hate you." She playfully hit him.

"Seriously, if we're gonna name my son after a designer, I think we should do one that isn't sold at Macy's."

"You know what? Oh my God." Gray covered her mouth and laughed. She didn't wanna wake the kids up. "Okay, what about Otis?"

"Otis? Are you conscious? Nigga, this ain't 1932. I ain't naming my son that ugly ass shit. I was thinking about Radrick?"

"Ain't that the dude from Game of Thrones?"

"Nah but I feel like if I name my kid after Gucci Mane, good things could come from that."

"That's that nigga's real name?" Gray said, surprised.

"Yeah."

"Sorry to that man but I hate his name."

"Damn." Cam said, disappointed. He was really pulling for that one.

"I like the name Winnie too."

"Yo, why you keep coming up wit' all these old ass names?" Cam raised his head and looked at her.

"What you traumatized, Archibald?" She arched her brow.

"Yo, don't get fucked up, but on some real shit, hell yeah. I'm tired of y'all niggas calling me that."

"It's your name. Get over it."

"Nigga, I know you ain't talkin'. You're named after a color. A depressing ass color at that. Your mama jinxed the shit outta you. No wonder you done been through so much bullshit. You was doomed from birth."

"Shut up. My name is the shit." Gray clapped back.

"Yeah, sad as shit."

"Whatever, Winnie is not an old name."

"Shit. I got a great aunt named Winnie. Aunt Windell, that's what we call her."

The baby must've agreed that the name was trash because he or she kicked the shit out of Gray.

"Oww." She cupped her stomach.

"See. Even the baby ain't wit' that bullshit." Cam rubbed the spot where the baby had roundhouse kicked her dumb ass.

"Mommy! Daddy!" The triplets raced into their master suite. "It's Christmas! It's Christmas!" They jumped up and down with glee.

"What time is it?" Aoki stumbled into the room wiping eye buggers from her tear ducts.

"Early as shit." Cam snatched the comforter from off his long body. "Where Pretty Girl?"

"Right here, Appa." She stepped past Aoki. Unlike the other kids, Press had already brushed her teeth and washed her face. She was always anal about her hygiene.

"Merry Christmas." He kissed her cheek. One by one Cam wished each of his children Merry Christmas and gave them a sweet kiss.

"C'mon, Pop." Aoki took him by the hand. "Bring yo' slow ass on. I gotta Bottega Venetta bag downstairs with my name on it."

"I'ma beat yo' ass. How you know?"

"Santa Claus told me." She winked her eye at Gray.

"Yo ass can't hold water. You getting a spanking later."

"Promise." She smirked, being flirtatious.

"Don't start nothing you can't finish." He warned. "Daddy like that freaky shit."

"Eww. Children are present." Press swallowed down her disgust.

"Y'all go downstairs with daddy. I'll be there in a second." Gray slowly eased out of bed. Being five months pregnant had slowed her down.

"You need my help, baby?" Cam asked before leaving.

"No, I'm fine. I gotta tinkle." She assured, making her way to the master bath. When she approached the his-and-hers sinks, two Post-it Notes that were stuck to the mirror caught her attention. They weren't there before she'd gone to bed. Cam must've put them there after she'd dozed off. On the yellow, squared notes he wrote:

Gray,
I will never let you go. . .
I will put your love on a pedestal. . .
I will always miss you when I'm gone. . .
I will always come back home. . .
I will always ask for forgiveness, as well as forgive. . .
I will always put you and our family first. . .
I will always support our family in any way possible. . .
I will never dishonor you. . .
I will always love you.
-Cam

Gray no longer needed to pee. She race-walked out of the room to get to Cam. There was a time when she couldn't even get him to admit he loved her. Look how far they'd come. Gray couldn't get downstairs to him fast enough. Her heart ached for him. When she finally made it to the first floor, she was in for the shock of her life. The entire space was filled to the brim with yellow flowers. There had to be over 10,000. A pathway was cleared that led to a yellow rose heart shaped archway where Cam and their smiling children stood awaiting her arrival. It was then that Gray knew they were in on the surprise. Aoki was recording her reaction with her phone.

Gray took in the decor. Beyond and around the arch were rows and rows of blooming sunflowers that nearly consumed the foyer and living space. Cam chose the color yellow not only for the Coldplay song *Yellow* that was playing but because the color yellow represented hope, happiness, positivity, optimism, honor, joy, and loyalty. Hanging from the ceiling via yellow strings were pictures of her and Cam as well as the kids. Each photo told the story of their love. Gray studied the pics. There were pics of their courthouse wedding, the kids birth photos, pics from her and Cam's birthday parties and more. The attention to detail was astonishing. Gray couldn't believe he'd done all of this while she was asleep. Gray was living out every girl's fantasy. Finally, she was getting her happily ever after you. This was what true happiness felt like. Tears tickled her cheeks as she took in the ambiance and made her way down the aisle to her man.

Cam's chin trembled as she neared. He'd envisioned this moment since he watched her walk down the aisle at Quan's wedding. After a near death experience it was finally coming true. By the time Gray stood before him, he was overcome with emotion. The first time he'd proposed there was no emotion behind it. It was just a question he'd posed to keep her. This proposal had so much more meaning. He and Gray were one. When he found her, there was no need to search for anything else. Gray was everything he needed and more. Without her he'd lose his best friend, his heartbeat, his smile, his laugh, his soul. Tenderly, he took her shaky hand in his and gazed deep into her eyes. He needed her to feel every word he was about to say.

"From the day we met, you walked into my life like you always lived there, like my heart was a home built for you. I tried like a muthafucka to fight that shit too. What I learned is that we found each other in this crazy fucked up world because we belong together. We belong in each other's arms. See Gray, we're connected by more than love, commitment, our children or by fate itself. You're my laughter. The reason people ask me why I'm smiling when I don't even realize it. You're my love story. I write you into everything I do, everything I see, everything I touch and everything I dream. You're the words that fill my pages."

Gray couldn't keep her composure if she tried. Tears strolled down her cheeks at lightning speed and landed on her chest. In the four years she'd known Cam, he'd never been more romantic.

"I know you may feel sometimes we get lost in all the drama that surrounds us but know that I have never lost track of what you mean to me. In this new season of our relationship, I wanna be your partner, your provider, and your protector. I wanna show our six kids how a woman is supposed to be loved 'cause there was a time I didn't love you right. I wanna give them an example of how a man takes care of the household and his wife. But most of all I wanna love you properly and be that example for them. You're my match. I have never been saner than when I'm lost in the beautiful insanity of our love. There's my heart and there's you. A nigga don't even know if there's a difference. I'ma lucky man, Star. I couldn't imagine living this life without you. You're my entire world. I'm yours and you're mine. I love you beyond measure. Do you love me?"

"Yes." Gray sobbed like a baby.

"Prove it." Cam eased down onto one knee and presented her with a 6 carat heart-shaped diamond with pavé diamonds going down the side. The sparkler cost close to a half a million dollars. Gray's eyes started to hurt the ring was so blinding.

"Gray Rose Parthens, will you marry me . . . again?"

Unlike his first marriage proposal, Gray had nothing to contemplate. The answer was a no brainer.

"I wanna spend the rest of this life and my next with you. So . . . to answer your question, yes, I will marry you. I'll marry you fifty million times."

Elated, Cam slipped the Harry Winston diamond onto her somewhat puffy fingers then rose to his feet, kissed her deeply and swung her around. He and Gray embraced with extreme intensity. Neither wanted to let go, so they didn't. Their arms clasped around each other as warm tears flowed down their cheeks. The kids clapped and cheered then buried them in one big giant hug. It was by far the best Christmas for the loving couple. Never in a million years did Gray expect to wake up to a marriage proposal. She didn't realize how much she yearned for Cam to propose again until he'd done it. They'd done everything so out of order the first time around. This time they both were going to make the conscious effort to go about loving each other right.

By mid-morning, every gift in the sitting room had been opened. Wrapping paper was thrown about everywhere. The little kids had fallen back to sleep. Neither Cam nor Gray mind. They needed the nap. That afternoon they'd be heading to Cam Senior's house for Christmas dinner. It wasn't something either of them looked forward to, but it was necessary they show their faces. The holidays were the only time Cam came around. After nearly dying, he made the decision to work on his familial relationships. At least once a week he spoke to Curtis and Cal. Their brotherhood had grown leaps and bounds. He and Mo would always be straight. They'd been close since they were kids. Mo wasn't just his sister; she was his heart.

Cozy on the couch, he and Gray sat snuggled next to each other, basking in the glow of their love, their engagement, and their family. Hours had gone by and Cam was still blown away by Gray's gift to him. She'd purchased him his very own island. The stunning piece of land called Bonefish Cay cost her a cool seven million dollars. The unique 13-acre island was located in the Abaco Islands in the Bahamas. Over the past seven years the formerly deserted island was turned into a first-class getaway with white sand beaches. Five buildings totaling 15,000 square feet were constructed of the finest materials imported from Europe and the United States. Two luxury owner's suites and six additional suites could accommodate up to 16 people. The entire complex was hurricane-proof. The perfect getaway in the Bahamas was also fully air-conditioned, and Bone Fish Cay generated its own electricity and had its own desalination plant. All communication services (telephone, fax, and internet) were provided. A newly and very solidly built jetty and several boats were also included with the island.

For New Year's, she'd booked a private plane for them along with Quan and Kema. They were all heading to Bonefish Cay so they could have the honeymoon neither of them got to have. Cam thought nothing could top that. Then Aoki shocked the hell out of him with a gift of her own that he wasn't at all expecting. Timidly, she approached him and handed him a box which was somewhat large in size. Cam tore the wrapping paper off.

"Before you look inside, there's something I need to tell you."

Cam placed the gift on his lap and gave her his undivided attention. Gray rubbed his arm soothingly. She could tell he was anxious to find out what was going on. Press watched on too. She too was clueless. Aoki cleared her throat.

"A few days ago, me and ma went in front of a judge."

Cam looked at Gray puzzled, then gazed back at Aoki.

"Don't worry, Pop. I'm not in any kind of trouble. I went in front a judge for my last name to be changed to Parthens."

Cam instantly shot up straight.

"You did? Are you serious?" He looked back-and-forth between her and Gray. A look of sheer excitement was written on his face.

"It's official." Gray confirmed. "Open the box."

Cam pulled the top off and found several pieces of paperwork inside. The first one was a petition to the court that the judge had approved. Cam's throat tightened. It was hard for him to breathe.

"Y'all trying to kill a nigga."

"There's more. Read the letter inside that I wrote you." Aoki twisted from side-to-side like a little girl.

Cam rubbed his eyes to clear the tears that were clouding his vision. He was a fucking mess and he hadn't even read the first sentence yet.

"I Aoki Lee Parthens, on this day, December 25th, ask that you become my dad forever."

Cam's eyes grew to the size of planet Earth. Sniffling, he wiped his nose.

"From the moment you came into my life, you showed me what it's like to have a father who loves you unconditionally. You've been there for me when I talked back, when I tried to push you away, when I got busted for shoplifting and even when you went to jail. No matter what came our way, you never stopped caring for me. You discipline me when I need it and love on me when I need it most. Thank you for teaching me what real love is and what it's like to have a loving, caring father. Some people might say you're not my real dad, but I know that isn't true. We've had our ups and downs, sometimes it's hard to bend but you've always been there when I needed you and that's what matters the most in the end. You've been patient, kind and funny as hell over the years. You've never treated me any different than your biological children. And though we're not tied by blood, the love and trust you've given me is a precious gift; that's what counts as a real dad to me. So, will you please make me the happiest girl in the world and adopt me?"

Cam's head shot up. He never knew Aoki felt this way. He thought she was fine with things the way they were. He wanted to adopt the girls and make him being their father official, but it was never a subject they'd broached. Without even thinking he stood up and said, "Of course. Adoption or no adoption you'll always be my daughter."

Wrapping her in his arms, he hugged her with all his might and cried what felt like a million tears. Aoki cried too. For the first time in her life she felt complete. All of the missing pieces of the puzzle that made up her life were now connected and in place. She was on top of the world. She had it all, a fantastic mother, a supportive dad, great siblings, and a boy that cared for her as much as she cared for him. Life was perfect. Nothing could bring her down.

Press sat on the floor watching her sister and Appa share a precious moment. On the outside she smiled like she was happy, like there was no part of her that sorrow lived. She displayed no mannerisms that showed damage of any kind but on the inside she was dying. Her big sister was perfection right down to her core. Aoki was the pretty one, the confident one, the fearless one, the bell of the ball and she? Well, Press was the mousy bookworm sitting in the corner that everyone overlooked.

She'd sell her soul just to be Aoki for one millisecond, to walk in her shoes instead of her own. If that was considered jealousy so be it. She didn't care. How fair was it to be born so ordinary and for her sister to have everything including Cam. Everyone in their family would bear his last name but her. Once more she was the odd man out. She wanted to be a Parthens too. It was apparent that Gunz was never going to be the father he once was. He'd practically left her for dead. He hadn't called her once since they'd been back. Cam was the only stable male force in her life. It wasn't fair that everyone got permanent pieces of him but her.

GRAY CHECKED HERSELF OUT IN THE MIRROR. CONSIDERING SHE'D gained twelve pounds she looked good. Mina had given her a sickening middle part sew-in. Thirty-two inches of Raw Indian straight weave reached down to her waist. The hairstyle went perfect with the smoky cat-eye, Lily Ghalichi lashes and Fenty Beauty mattemoiselle red lipstick. Her outfit wasn't too shabby either. Baby bump and all she rocked the hell out of a white high-neck, sheer puff sleeve top. Under it she wore a white lace camisole. A black belt with a pearl buckle and gold cross chain belt accentuated her curvy hips. The black fitted pants on her shapely legs and the patent leather, decollette pointed-toe Christian Louboutin heels had her ass sitting up right. For a mother of six mama was serving face, body, and major sex appeal.

Cam walked up behind her smoking a blunt dressed in his Christmas best. He looked good as fuck. The black knit cap on his head, Cartier frames, gold chains, neon green, red, white, and black Iceberg sweater, black fitted joggers and Maison Margiela sneakers that matched his shirt had Gray's nipples hardening on sight. Cam's dick print was on full display, causing her mouth to water. Somebody needed to lock his big dick ass up. That muthafucka was hanging lovely like Captain Hook. Visions of her dropping down on his meaty python played in her head. He'd had her legs spread wide open the night before but Gray always craved more.

Taking a toke from the blunt, Cam inhaled the smoke deep into his lungs while eye-fuckin' the shit outta Gray. His wife was the baddest woman on the planet.

"*Woooork it!*" He eyed her round ass.

Gray dropped her shoulders and frowned at him through the mirror. Cam played entirely too much but she couldn't help but feel her cheeks rise into a shit eating grin.

"You betta work, girl! Are you a haunted house 'cause I'ma scream when I'm in you!"

Gray gasped, appalled.

"Get away from me smoking." She narrowed her eyes at him. Cam put the blunt out and came closer. Cocking her head to the side, Gray ran her tongue across the inside of her cheek. Cam stood behind her and pressed his hard dick in-between her butt cheeks.

"Is your name winter 'cause you'll be coming soon?"

"Nigga, really? Bye Cam."

"Are you an elevator? 'Cause I'll go up and down on you." Cam continued to throw out corny pick-up lines.

"I'ma smack you."

"Real talk. You look good as shit, bae. Can I say yass bitch?"

"Absolutely no—"

"Yasssssss bitch!" He cut her off and snapped his fingers in the air.

Gray paused and shot him a stern look.

"You know you like that shit." He placed a trail of tender kisses up her neck.

"If you don't get out my face." She laughed. "For real babe, do I look good? I feel fat." Gray puckered her red painted lips.

"Gray, don't ask me no shit like that. Let's not go there. It's Christmas morning. I ain't gon' let you steal my joy. We was doing good."

"I'm just saying." She whined like a child.

"You husky, bae. Get over it."

Gray's jaw dropped.

"But you fine as fuck tho." He squeezed her tight. "Work them bundles, girl. Get in formation. Twirl on yo' haters. Ain't that how Kema and Tee-Tee say it?"

Gray almost choked from laughter.

"You are a whole fool, but I love you." She circled her arms around his neck.

"I'ma fool for your fine ass. You gon' sit on my face when we get home? I wanna eat you for dessert." He massaged her booty.

"I'm already mentally there."

It was a little after 3:00 p.m. when Cam pulled his Range Rover onto his father's street. He cruised down the block with one hand whipping the steering wheel. Yo Gotti's *Trapped* bumped from his speakers. The music had Cam's windows shaking. Paris, King, Zaire, Deoni, Khadeen and Curtis' children were out front playing football in the street.

"Uncle Cam!" King ran down the road.

Cam rolled down the driver side window.

"Get out the way boy before I hit you."

King stepped onto the sidewalk next to Paris. Press was happy King couldn't see her ogling him from the backseat. The tinted windows shielded him from seeing her salivate over him. Press' heart swooned every time she came in contact with King. His hair looked like it had gotten longer in the week and a half they'd been out on winter break. King was incredibly handsome. He was also one of the few friends she had. She wished he liked her like she liked him but having him as her best friend meant more to her than anything.

"Y'all ate already?" Cam asked him.

"Nah, Unc, we was waiting on you."

"Priest in there?"

"Yeah." Paris answered, tossing the ball into the air.

"A'ight."

Cam parked the car in front of the house. *Trapped* still played as he and the fam got out. Mo pushed open the screen door and glared at him. Cam Sr. lived in a quiet neighborhood where everyone that lived on his block was sixty and up. Cam knew damn well their father and the neighbors would have a fit over his loud ass rap music.

"She gon' cuss me out." He grinned amused by her death glare. "What?"

"Don't what me, nigga! You know exactly why I'm looking at you!" She snapped on ten.

"I'ma cut the music down! Take yo' ugly ass in the house!" Cam stood with the driver side door open. "Y'all go on inside. I'll be in there in a minute."

As the kids got out, King tried not to stare too hard at Press. He and Sanya were boyfriend and girlfriend but the underlining feelings he had for Press were still very much alive. Every day at school, and during family functions, it became harder and harder to hide the way he felt. Press was the truth. Even with her glasses, braces and small weight gain, he still found her to be one of the prettiest girls in their grade. Maybe one day they'd become more. King couldn't honestly see himself with anyone but her when he got older.

The wintery sun shined down on Aoki as she hopped out of the back of the truck and situated her skirt. Her mane of hair was pulled into a messy ponytail. Coral pink gloss emphasized her full lips. The dusty pink turtleneck, black and white houndstooth button up, skirt, black over-the-knee-boots, and white Balenciaga tote bag had her giving Serena van der Woodsen tease. The only thing missing from her ensemble was the charm bracelet Paris had given her. She wished she could've worn it, but Cam and Gray would've questioned where she'd gotten the expensive piece of jewelry from and didn't nobody have time for that.

Much thought was put into her look tho. She hoped Paris appreciated the effort. The last time she'd seen him in person was the day she'd snuck over his house. Aoki had nothing to worry about. Paris ceased tossing of the ball and eyed her. He loved the way she looked from her head down to her feet. Aoki could make a brown paper bag look good. The feeling was mutual cause Aoki couldn't take her eyes off the blue knit hat, matching hoodie, iced out chain, ripped jeans and UNC Jordan Retro 3's he donned. Their connection was so strong that even Cam peeped their staring contest.

"P!" He shouted his name which caused Aoki to jump. Paris cut his eyes at him.

"What?"

"Go tell Priest to come hit this gas real quick."

"The fuck I look like? Go tell that nigga yourself." He tossed the rock to King and went inside the house. Aoki swallowed down the lump in her throat. She'd never witnessed anyone talk crazy to Cam and live to talk about it. The rest of the day was sure to be a shit show.

Cam slammed the door shut. Paris hot-head ass was only going to get so many passes with him before he put his foot on his neck. One by one they all entered Cam Senior's house, leaving the front door unlocked. The whole family was there except for Aunt Vickie. She was supposed to come but decided to rest in bed instead. Cam made a mental note to go visit her after the holiday. Entering the house, Cam looked around. Everything was exactly how he remembered it. The family portrait of him, Cam Sr. and his siblings all dressed in white still sat on the mantel above the fireplace. Photos of all the grandchildren except his lined the wall. Cam lowkey felt some kind of way. Yeah, he'd just learned of the triplets, but Cam Sr. hadn't made one attempt to spend time with them or Aoki and Press.

"Archie!" Curtis extended his arms for his baby bro.

"Don't start that shit." Cam sucked his teeth but gave him a hug anyway.

"You looking good there boy." Curtis patted his back.

"It's good to see you on your feet." Elizabeth hugged him too.

Cal used his well-developed arms to push the wheel of his chair over to his brother.

"If you don't get yo' ass up." Cam quipped. "Rolling around in a wheelchair you don't need is mad disrespectful. Especially, coming from a man who couldn't use his legs at one point."

"You know my sciatica been acting up." Cal retorted.

"I thought you had mesothelioma?" Mo placed her hand on her hip.

"I do. What about that don't you understand?"

"Mesothelioma ain't got shit to do with your legs, you fuckin' hypochondriac. Ain't nothin' wrong with you. Yo' ass need to get up and get a job."

"I'm on disability. I don't need no damn job. Plus, I just got diagnosed with Down Syndrome, Gout and they think I'm going blind in one eye."

"I ain't never seen a lazier nigga in my life." Mo curled her upper lip.

"I will bite you in your left titty." Cal warned.

"You ain't gon' touch her titty. That titty is mine." Boss pinched the side of Mo's breast.

"TIIIIIITTIES! Titty's-titty's-titty's-titty's-titty's! I . . . love . . . titties!" Beaux pumped her fist in the air.

"It won't be long till she's at Magic City swinging from a pole." Kerry quipped, sitting in front of the television with his legs crossed. He thought he was the shit in his Brioni wool-blend suit and $2,000 Berluti dress shoes.

Cam took a deep breath. He'd promised his self that he wouldn't engage in Kerry's negativity. He wasn't worth the trouble of raising his blood pressure. He was willing to give him a pass for not visiting him in the hospital. It wasn't like they were close, and Kerry hadn't shown him any kind of compassion in years. There was no need to expect anything more from him. Plus, Cam knew once he got riled up it would take Jesus coming down from heaven to stop him from going in. Stressing Gray out and scaring the kids would only add stress to his life, not Kerry's. He and Gray were reengaged, and he was officially adopting Aoki. He refused to let his goofy ass brother ruin his glorious day. The thing about Cam and Gray was that when one of them was chill, the other one was on go. Gray played about a lot of stuff, but it was never her kids.

"Fuck you say?" She charged towards Kerry.

Cam swiftly caught her by the arm and held her back.

"Nah, babe. Let me go. Why would he say some sick shit like that about his niece?" She fought to break loose.

"Chill, ma. You're pregnant." Aoki blocked her mother's path.

"Oh Lord. Another Bebe's Kid." Kerry groaned with a slight chuckle.

"Fuck you call my kids, pussy!" Cam whipped past Gray to get at his brother.

"You bet not lay a hand on him!" Cam Senior's loud voice boomed.

The entire Parthens' clan froze. When Cam Sr. spoke, everyone listened.

"I will not have this foolishness in my house. Your mother didn't raise y'all to act like this."

Cam Jr. rolled his eyes. The nerve of him to bring up his mother. Grace was off limits, especially considering his betrayal of her trust and their marriage. Gray too felt some kind of way. She couldn't stand Cam's father.

"She would not want this. So, in memory of your mother please put your grievances to the side. It's Christmas. We're all here together. . . alive and well." He stressed. "Be thankful for that and stop all of this senseless bickering and arguing." He gave his children a stern glare.

"Now c'mon and eat. Your sister been slaving over the stove all morning." He shuffled back into the kitchen.

"This shit ain't over." Cam growled, lowly.

"This shit ain't over." Kerry mocked him. "Be careful little brother. I would hate to see you behind bars for the birth of another child."

Cam's chest heaved up and down. He tried to maintain his cool, but it was damn near impossible. All he wanted to do was rip Kerry's head off his shoulders. Noticing his kids, his nieces, and nephews eyes on him was the only thing that stopped him from doing so.

"C'mon y'all." Mo ushered everyone into the dining room to their assigned seats.

When the coast was clear, Gray grabbed Cam by his shoulders and placed her forehead against his. Closing her eyes, she said, "The light of God surrounds me. The love of God enfolds me. The power of God protects me. The presence of God watches over me. Wherever I am God is."

Cam took in her energy and nodded his head. This was why he loved his wife. She was truly a blessing. She kept his head on straight. She tamed the beast inside of him.

"We're not gonna let him affect us. Today is our day. You hear me?"

"I just wanna know why he hates me so much." Cam allowed a broken piece of his heart to show. He could only be this vulnerable with her. For years, he'd put on a mask and pretended not to care about his older brother's disdain. Deep down the shit tore him up. There was a time they were thick as thieves. He used to idolize Kerry. Growing up all he wanted was his acknowledgment and approval. No matter what he did, Kerry always responded with resistance and hate.

"His ill will has nothing to do with you and everything to do with him. Don't put that burden on your shoulders. You've done nothing wrong." Gray rubbed his cheek with her thumb. "We're gonna get through this together. Let's go in there, eat and enjoy the people that care about us. Anything else is irrelevant. This is only a few hours of our lives. These people don't define us."

"What would I do without you?" Cam softly kissed her lips.

"Thank God you'll never have to find out." She kissed him back. "Two hours. That's the longest we'll stay." She laced her fingers with his.

~

CHRISTMAS WAS THE MOST WONDERFUL TIME OF YEAR, FILLED WITH cheer and joy. It was a day where you were surrounded by love and cared for by the people in your life who cared the most about you. The Parthens' family sat in the formal dining room laughing and eating a feast fit for a king. Mo had gone all out. She'd made macaroni and cheese, collard greens with smoke turkey, sweet potatoes, black eyed peas, fried okra, ham, turkey, pot roast, cornbread, pies, cakes and more. Because of their large family, members were seated at two long wooden tables. When Aoki tried to sit next to Paris, Cam made her get her hot ass up and sit next to him. She pouted the entire time, but he didn't give a fuck. The further they were from each other the better. What Cam didn't know was that Aoki wasn't only upset she'd been pulled away from Paris but that she'd be sitting next to Priest and his bitch Britten. Being next to them was the last place she wanted to be. Bearing witness to Britten drooling and fawning all over him made her lose her appetite. It was disgusting. Aoki hoped she didn't look that thirsty when she was all up on Paris.

It was bad enough she was so far away, yet so near. She hated being in the same room and not being able to talk to him. Paris looked so bored and lonely. Aoki was all the way off tho. Paris was anything but bored. He'd never had a holiday like this before. Usually, he'd be somewhere alone eating a frozen dinner or takeout. His mother didn't put much effort into the holidays. Being around his family and eating such a delicious meal under the roof of an immaculate farmhouse was some shit he'd only seen on TV. Shit like this didn't happen to niggas like him. This was some ole Fresh Prince of Bel Air type shit. Yeah, his older cousins bickered, and he and Priest barely said a word to each

other but underneath all the murk was love. Paris made a mental check-
list that one day he and Aoki would have a home like that one and
family dinners too.

"So, Gray, how far along are you?" Elizabeth asked, stuffing a
piece of turkey in her mouth.

"Five months." She smiled, happily as Cam rubbed her stomach.
His hand had been there throughout dinner.

"Oh my God. You look good, girl. I would've never been able to
get away with wearing something like that. When I was five months I
already looked like a whale."

"Facts." Mo agreed. The shade went completely over Elizabeth's
Caucasian head.

"That means the baby is due in April?"

"Yep. We're having an Aries baby."

"Do you know what you're having?"

"A boy." Cam replied.

"Nothing's been confirmed." Gray rolled her eyes. "We wanna be
surprised."

"Daddy." Sky patted Cam's arm. "How does God come here if . . .
if . . . if we can't see him?"

"Huh, baby girl?"

"Why can we not see God?" She looked over each of her shoulders
for him.

"You just can't baby girl but he's in here." He pointed to her
heart. Sky peaked inside the collar of her shirt to see if God was
there.

"He's always in your heart." Beaux rocked her head from side-to-
side.

When she didn't see him, Sky looked back at her dad, further
confused.

"Why can I not see him, daddy? I wanna go inside of dit."

"Cause your heart is inside of your chest." Cam tried to explain.

"Oh nooooooo." Sky dropped her head back and whined. "I'm
gonna be an old grandma."

"Where that come from?" Cam picked her up and placed her onto his lap.

"When you get older, you're gonna be a grandma like Mrs. Claus." She rubbed her nose with her shirt.

"What's wrong with that?"

"I don't wanna be a grandma. I just wanna be a kid." She rested her head against his pecks and cried.

"Everybody gets old love."

"I don't wanna get old." Sky wiped her face with the hem of her pretty pink dress.

"You don't wanna be a big girl like Aoki and Press?" Cam rocked her back-and-forth.

"I just wanna be a big sister, that's all."

"I like being a grandma, daddy." Reign snickered.

"You gon' be a grandpa buddy." Cam corrected him.

"Nah, you was right the first time." Kerry mumbled under his breath. He should've been thanking his lucky stars that Cam hadn't heard him 'cause he would've surely killed him.

"Ooh mama. Is this you?" Ryan ran over with a pic of Mo when she was a teen. Mo took the picture and looked at it. It was a picture of her sitting on the hood of a drop-top convertible during Freaknik.

"Yeah, that's me. Ya' mama was the shit back then."

"Let me find out you was having a hot girl summer." Ryan joked.

"She was but now she having a fat girl fall." Cal cackled.

"Fuck you Wheelchair Jimmy." Mo hissed.

"Dad-dad." Sky patted his chest. "Look at me. I don't wanna be old and wrinkly like him." She pointed at Cam Sr.

"Oh no she didn't." Mo stifled a laugh.

"Oh yes she did girlfriend." Elizabeth put on her best black girl voice.

Mo side-eyed the fuck outta her.

"Calm down, Becky with the good hair."

"Sissy, chill. You're gonna be squishy. It's gonna be fun." Beaux tried to soothe her sister.

"But I don't wanna be squishy." Sky cried even harder.

"Sky, everything's going to be fine. It'll be a long time before you become old and squishy." Gray assured, rubbing her tiny golden leg.

"So, Cam." Cam Sr. placed down his fork. "How have you been feeling? I haven't spoken to you much since you left the hospital."

"I'm good." He held his baby girl close. "I finished rehab a few months ago."

"That's good, son. I'm happy to hear that."

"You know for a minute we thought we'd be having Christmas without you." Curtis said, somberly. "It was real touch and go there, bruh."

"It sure was but look at God. You're home." Mo gushed with tears in her eyes.

"Can we please change the subject?" Kerry sighed, pushing his plate away. "Why are we glorifying street life? You all act like he was an upstanding citizen or an innocent bystander. He was stabbed because he's a part of a gang, the cartel, he's a drug dealer, a murderer, the list goes on. And to think you were mommy and daddy's favorite. I bet she's somewhere turning over in her grave right now." He picked at his teeth with a toothpick like he wasn't at the table.

Cam stared at him. His glare held so much intensity that it tightened Kerry's chest.

"No, the only thing that's gon' be turning over is this table if you don't shut the fuck up. I been letting you slide all day, but you've exceeded your limit." Cam warned with a deathly sneer.

"Spell exceed. I'll wait."

"D-E-A-D. Now keep fucking with me."

"See, dad. He's nothing but a thug. A near death experience hasn't changed him at all. No one at this table should feel sorry for him. He brought all of this onto himself. When he gets stabbed or shot again, none of you should waste your time running to the hospital. I sure as hell won't."

Fed up with Kerry and his shit, Cam handed Sky over to Gray.

"Baby, don't engage."

Cam disregarded her warning. Placing his elbows on the table he steepled his hands together and stared at his brother. What he was about to say was long overdue.

"You so jealous of me. You've been jealous of me since the day I was born. But what I wanna know is why?"

Kerry sat silent. It was so quiet you could hear a pin drop.

"Is it because I look better than you? Cause I'm smarter than you? I always got better grades than you, I'm more athletic than you, and I had more bitches than you."

"Like that's something to be proud of."

"It's not but you know what is?" Cam cocked his head to the side. "The pennies you make at that nut-ass investment banking firm don't even touch my millions. Is that why you're so mad? Cause even with your college education, your Ivy League friends and Fortune 500 company, you still don't compare to me?"

Kerry sat up straight. The pain soaring through his chest burned hot. Cam had literally shot him in the heart with his words.

"You mean the millions you made killing the African American community?"

"Nah, I don't do that no more. I got fired." Cam released a snarky laugh.

"That's enough boys." Cam Sr. tried to interject.

"Nah, Pop. Let's stay on topic. Your son is obsessed with me. He wishes he were me. Maybe it's because I got a sexy ass wife that's not only beautiful but intelligent as shit. I got five dope ass kids and another baby on the way. I have multiple businesses. We just copped a 13 million dollar estate. Meanwhile, you go home every night and beat your dick to your yearly Porn Hub membership."

"How the hell do you know about that?" Kerry pounded his fist onto the table. "Do you have someone cyber stalking me?"

"Ughn, Kerry. You nasty." Mo scooted her seat away from his.

"If you think I wanna be anything like you, you're sadly mistaken. You're a pathetic excuse for a man." Kerry started to foam at the mouth he was so angry. "I don't know why mommy and daddy invested so much time into you. You're nothing but a waste of sperm. Mommy and Daddy treated you like you were a goddamn prince. They coddled you. Every time I turned around, it was Cam this, Cam that. Dad put his all into you and look how you turned out. So, tell me Dad, was all that father and son time worth it? Were all those days you spent one and one time with Cam worth your other son feelings like he was fuckin' invisible?"

A lightbulb went off in Cam's head. Everything became crystal clear. The bitterness consuming every inch of Kerry's body, the demon that burned away all logic and reason was because he was jealous of the so-called relationship Cam had with their father growing up. An onslaught of tears crawled up his throat. Kerry had wasted his entire life harboring this jealousy of him for no reason. Little did he know but Cam would've traded places with him in a heartbeat. Their father didn't spend time with him out of love. It was to cover his own ass. He used Cam, his youngest son as a tool to cheat on their mother with—"

"WHERE IS HE?!" Aunt Hope came barreling through the door like a mad woman. Her natural red hair blew in the wind behind her. Hope was a pint-sized woman with big breasts, a slim waist, round hips and a whole lotta ass. Chaka Khan could've been her sister. Cam retreated inside of himself. His brain shut down. His hands became clammy and a sheen of sweat sprouted on his forehead. Shocked by her presence, his eyes grew wide like someone had scared him. Trapped in his own psychosis, a living nightmare for one, he examined his mother's twin sister. He hadn't laid eyes on her since he'd confronted her and his father about their seedy affair at Grace's repast. Seeing his Aunt Hope was like seeing the ghost of his mother. They looked so much alike it was scary. This was the last thing Cam needed. He literally felt his heartrate slowing. This was it. This would be how he died.

Cam Sr. sat glued to his seat, unable to speak. His sordid past was right there in his face. Since Grace's funeral, he'd been able to pretend like what he'd done hadn't happened but now with Hope only a few feet away there was no way of denying the mess he'd made.

"What did you do to him?" She gripped Priest by the collar of his shirt.

"Auntie, what you doing?" Mo asked flabbergasted by her disheveled appearance.

"This ain't got nothing to do with you, Mo Money. This between me and my no-good ass son. Answer me muthafucka! Did you hurt 'em?"

"I don't know what you talkin' about." Priest responded with so much nonchalance it made Hope's skin boil.

"So, help me God if you laid one finger on him. I'll kill you my damn self." She hissed.

"Aunt Hope!" Cal said shocked by her venomous words.

"Let him go! What the fuck you even doing here?" Paris pulled his mother off Priest.

"You shut the fuck up!" She reared her hand back and smacked piss from his mouth. The whole family gasped, horrified by her erratic behavior. The slap hurt but sadly it wasn't anything Paris wasn't used to. Smacking him was mild compared to all the other abusive shit she'd done to him. Aoki shot up ready to fight. Paris shook his head slightly. It was his way of telling her not to react.

"It's your fault Earl done gon' missing! Haven't you ruined enough?"

"How is it my fault?" Paris screwed up his face, perplexed.

Finally coming to his senses, Cam Sr. lifted from his chair. Tenderly, he placed his shaky hand on her shoulder and soothingly said, "Hope, calm down. Tell me what's going on?"

"This li'l weird muthafucka killed him! I know he did it!" She shrugged his hand away.

"Killed who?"

"Nigga, is you hard of hearing? Earl . . . my man! He killed 'em and I know it's because of this lying muthafucka!" She mushed Paris in the forehead. "He never touched you! You just don't want me to be happy! I already let this one ruin my life!" She eyed Cam up and down with disgust. "I ain't gon' let you do it too!"

Thinking hard, Paris looked down at his feet. Why did his mother think that Priest had killed Earl because of what he'd done to him? None of it made sense. He hadn't told his brother shit. But it was apparent by Priest's choice of words that he'd murked their mother's boyfriend. Paris knew his brother like a book. He hadn't flat-out denied it, so he'd done it, which meant someone had told Priest his secret. The only person who knew was . . . fuming, his eyes turned black as he glared over his shoulder at Aoki.

"You told him?"

Aoki's life flashed before her eyes. Her whole body turned into a puddle of nothing. Unexpectantly, she began to cry. It wasn't because she'd betrayed him but because her loyalty to him was in question. All signs of betrayal were pointed her way, but she was innocent.

"No, I would never do that to you," she swore.

"Whatever he told you, he lying!" Hope said to Priest.

"I ain't tell him nothin' and why the fuck would I lie about some shit like that?" Paris barked. "You ain't believe it 'cause you so fuckin' scared to be by yourself! You go from one nigga to the next!"

"I did what the fuck I had to do! Neither one of y'all daddy was around to help me. I worked my fingers to the bone to take care of you and your brother. I never got a thank you or a pat on the back. You ever stop to think I get tired of being alone? I was gon' get my little piece of happiness anyway I could. It sholl wasn't gon' come from raising two snot-nose boys that just take and take and take!" She pounded her fist against his chest. "You should be happy that I sacrificed my body and my heart to keep a roof over our head. It's kids out here that had it worse than you. So, if you think you gon' get an apology out of me, you got another muthafuckin' thang coming."

Hope's hateful words shouldn't have hurt Paris, but they did. He couldn't turn down his emotions and temper them the way his brother did. Priest let the shit bounce off him like he was Superman. Nothing fazed him. Maybe that made Paris soft for giving a shit that their mother hated their existence. Every word she spewed added a new scar to his invisible list of wounds. He would've rather she took a knife to his skull than treat him so cold.

The pain Cam harbored ate away at his stomach. Nausea took over too. Cam swore he was going to pass out. Gripping the edge of the table for support, he breathed in and out slowly. Cam prided his self on pushing his pain down and continuing on with life as if nothing were wrong but that wasn't possible. Every disturbing emotion from his life since the age of nine flooded his body at once. The feelings owned his thoughts and dictated his actions. The pain dominated every area of his brain. It was the kind of pain that burned, as if some invisible flame was held against his skin. Lies, betrayal, death, they all were there.

"On my mama." He seethed with anger. "One of y'all get her the fuck outta here before I lose my shit."

"Cam, no. We trying to figure out what's going on." Mo exclaimed, frightened by her aunt's behavior.

"NO! GET HER THE FUCK OUT!" Cam pushed the dishes and food in front of him off the table. Plates, forks, and glasses went crashing to the floor as Mo, Boss, Elizabeth and Curtis jumped out of the way.

"I don't want this scandalous ass bitch nowhere near me! Trust me. If you knew what I knew you'd feel the same!" He directed his wrath towards his father.

"Cam, stop." Cam Sr. pleaded with his eyes.

"No, you stop! This all your fuckin' fault! You started this shit! You're the one that betrayed mommy!"

"Can somebody please tell me what's going on?" Mo clutched her stomach. An avalanche of hot tears poured from her worried eyes. She could feel it in the air. Some shit that was about to destroy her life was about to be revealed.

"I ain't going nowhere until he tells me where Earl is! Answer me! Did you kill him?" Aunt Hope questioned a stoic Priest.

"Like I said." He turned his back to her and resumed eating his meal. "I don't know what the fuck you talkin' about. But if he's missing, I'm pretty sure he got what he deserved."

Nothing else needed to be said. Priest's last words were all she needed to hear. He'd done it. He'd killed Earl. Hope sank to her knees. The pain that flowed from her was as palpable as the air she breathed. Her loose shoulders shook. She was so hysterical she couldn't even lift her hands to wipe away her tears.

"*I hate you.*" She cried what felt like a million tears. "Y'all just wanna see me unhappy. I can't never have nothing good. Grace got everything I ever wanted. She got the house, she got the man, she got the money. And what I get? Two spoiled bitches for sons and a man that chose my sister over me!"

"Hope, stop. Don't go there." Cam Sr. warned.

"Why not?" Cam jumped in. "Somebody need to say it!"

"Say what?" Mo screeched at the top of her lungs.

Cam shot his father a look of revulsion.

"Tell her, dad. Tell your precious Mo he's our fuckin' brother!"

To be continued in "Mine". . .

ABOUT THE AUTHOR

Keisha Ervin is a mother of one and the critically acclaimed, best-selling author of over 20 novels. After years as a successful author she decided to venture out and create the popular YouTube channel: Color Me Pynk. With over 32,000 subscribers and 8 million views Keisha has proven she is a force to be reckon with.

For news on Keisha's upcoming work, to buy books and merch keep in touch by following her on any of the social media accounts listed below.

INSTAGRAM >> @keishaervin
    https://www.instagram.com/keishaervin/?hl=en
    SNAPCHAT >> kyrese99
    TWITTER >> www.twitter.com/keishaervin
    FACEBOOK >> www.facebook.com/keisha.ervin
    Please, subscribe to my YouTube channel, to watch all my hilarious reviews on your favorite reality shows and drama series!!! YOUTUBE >> https://www.youtube.com/colormepynk

OTHER TITLES BY KEISHA ERVIN

Made in the USA
Middletown, DE
14 July 2020